THE JOURNEY

KEITHA SMITH

Other books by Keitha Smith

Maybury Place

The Tender Conflict

The Bell Curve

Non-fiction work :

Mothering Heights
by Keitha Smith & Susan Brereton

PUBLISHED BY JUDSON PRESS

THE JOURNEY

The Journey

To all those who
are part of my journey,
with much love.

CHAPTER ONE

Robyn had just switched on the television to start watching her favorite program when Will came exploding into the room in his usual frantic manner. Something in him seemed to find it impossible to do anything at a reasonable pace. His hair stuck out every which way and his clothes looked like he'd slept in them. He had a damp tea towel slung over one shoulder. His boyish face wore an expression of deep concern. He sighed dramatically and transferred the limp towel from one shoulder to the other.

"She's in there packing," he said.

Robyn shrugged. "She is going on holiday tomorrow. It's perfectly customary to pack before you go away."

"I know that," Will said heavily. "The point is, should she be going at all? On her own? It's completely crazy. You know how, how...well, how vulnerable she is."

It was Robyn's turn to sigh. "Maybe it will be good for her. Maybe getting away and standing on her own two feet for a change is exactly what she needs. Did you consider that?"

"But she's hopeless with meeting strangers. You know how long it takes her to befriend anyone new."

Robyn could feel herself getting exasperated. The ads before the program had commenced.

"The problem with you," she said, "is that you've got super-hero syndrome."

"Super-hero syndrome? What on earth's that?"

"Ever since we first met Lindsey - when you saved her from that very embarrassing and less-mentioned-the-better situation - you've taken it upon yourself to be her very own super-hero. You've spent so long looking after her, making sure she's all right, it's a wonder you haven't started wearing your underwear on the outside of your trousers."

Will's face colored with outrage. "I have not."

"Have. Look Will, it's time to face facts. Either admit that you're in love with her - and then spend the rest of your life running after her and making sure she's okay - or take off the cape and let her get on with it. Lindsey's a big girl. She's twenty-seven years old, for crying out loud. If you can't let her go off on holiday for two weeks without panicking then something is very much out of kilter."

Will fell silent. Robyn could feel her gaze being pulled to the television. She hated missing the first part of a show. It could make the rest of the episode very confusing. It felt like missing out on a really big secret and knowing all the time that you were the only one not in on it.

"I'm not in love with her," Will said quietly.

Robyn's eyes swiveled from the screen. "No?"

Will shook his head. "It's not a crime to be concerned for a fellow flatmate, is it?"

Robyn made an expansive gesture. "As long as that's all it is, then no. But don't kid yourself, Will, and don't waste your life on a dream either. Now, if you don't mind, I've got some serious watching to do here. And if I'm not mistaken you still haven't finished the dishes."

Saturday mornings in the flat were ordinarily very restful. No one got up early unless they had some place to be. The three flatmates would often have a leisurely brunch together if someone had remembered to go shopping. Other times they would stroll down the road to the nearest cafe and take their time eating, drinking coffee and watching the world go by. Since the owner plainly had a crush on Robyn they could sit for as long as they liked without any pressure to free the table up for other paying customers.

This Saturday had proved to be no different. Lindsey wasn't flying out until three in the afternoon, and being a domestic flight, she only had to be at the airport about three quarters of an hour beforehand. After lunch they returned to the flat. Robyn had to depart straight away for a family get-together at her sister's house.

"It'll be about as much fun as having my legs waxed," she said, "only without the silky feeling of satisfaction afterward. The day I start craving the sort of life my sister has, kids and dogs and smeared walls and constant cries of hunger, you have permission to shoot me."

Lindsey laughed. "I'll miss you."

Robyn gave her a quick hug. "Likewise. I would say send us a postcard, but the chances are you'll be home before it would arrive. Do have a great time, though."

"Thanks," Lindsey said with a nervous little grimace. "I'm sure it will be very sedate. Lots of retirees."

Robyn rolled her eyes. "Sounds fantastic. Walking and wall-to-wall support hose." Her expression softened. "Sorry I can't come with you to the airport."

"That's okay. Will's taking me."

Robyn's gaze moved to Will who lurked in the background. "Yes, good old Will," she said. To Will she added with an arch expression, "Don't forget what I said, Underwear Boy."

"What?" Lindsey asked.

"Nothing," Robyn replied. She gave Lindsey another quick hug. "See you in two weeks."

Twenty minutes later Will and Lindsey were in the car and on their way to the airport. Will drove as erratically as he did everything else. Strangely, this didn't bother Lindsey very much. She knew, had always known, that she was safe with Will.

"Now, you're sure you've got your tickets?" Will asked. "And whatever else you might need? I don't suppose you need your passport for a flight to Wellington."

"No," Lindsey said. "I've got my e-ticket and photo i.d."

"And you know where to go when you get there?"

"Hmm. The group is meeting up at a hotel for the night. I just have to get from the airport into the centre of the city. That shouldn't be too difficult, especially since I'm not in any great hurry. If worst comes to worst I can always take a taxi."

Will sighed lavishly. "Tell me again," he said. "Give me the run-down on the complete holiday."

"You're worse than my father," Lindsey laughed but then sobered. "No, I take that back. You're much, much better than my father. You just don't need to worry about me so diligently."

"Indulge me," Will said.

"All right, although it would have been more sensible to have photo-copied the itinerary. I'm not sure why I didn't think of it. Like I said, today everyone makes their way to Wellington from wherever they live and we stay overnight in an hotel. Then tomorrow we head for... for... I can't remember, some little town. We then have another overnight stay there before setting off on the walk proper the following day."

"And?"

"For the rest of the time we move about a lot, gradually northward. Almost every day we walk from one house to another, mostly through wine country. It should be very peaceful. There's the odd day where we stay two nights in one place but that's usually so we can climb a nearby mountain or just have a bit of a rest. If the weather is fine, it should be glorious."

"I suppose you've picked a good time to go," Will conceded. "February weather is generally very settled. Plus you have the added advantage of the fact that school kids are back in their classrooms after the summer holidays. You said something about staying in houses?"

"Most of the accommodation is in people's homes, some big old country properties, some new. A lot of the accommodation is based at wineries and most of it sounds pretty luxurious. They're probably hoping we'll buy lots of their most recent vintage on our way."

"You couldn't lug wine on a walk."

Lindsey smiled. "We don't have to lug anything. The tour guide, or whatever he's called, travels from place to place with us in a mini bus while we walk. He takes our luggage and we just have to carry a daypack with lunch and whatever. I can't imagine anyone is going to be roughing it."

"And meals?"

"All provided, except three evenings I think. That's part of the attrac-tion. It's really for people with a passion for good food and fine wine, with a bit of exercise and sightseeing thrown in for good measure. You walk during the day, no more than twenty kilometers at one stretch, get to see the sights and sample vineyard life, then in the evening eat gourmet food and try the local brew. It's a sybarite's dream."

Will jerked the car across two lanes of traffic to turn off for the airport. "That hardly sounds like you. Sybaritic, I mean."

"No, I am more of a stay-at-home-ite, than a sybarite. But this trip sounds just the thing I need. It will hopefully give me plenty of opportunity to sketch and study the natural environment. You know that's the main rea-son I'm going. Besides, it all sounds very sedate. And although I will admit to being a bit nervous about meeting the others and looking like a complete fool because I know next to nothing about good food or wine, I'm hoping most of the group will be tolerant of me, if not friendly. I know you're worried because, well, I'm not always the most confident person, but I have to do this Will. I have to. I've got to start getting my life together before it passes me by."

The airport heaved with people milling about as they often do in airports, endlessly waiting. If they weren't waiting to check in, they were waiting for boarding time, or to say good-bye to someone else doing the traveling that day, or for someone about to arrive, or for their bags to come mysteriously off the carousel. People chose all sorts of ways to fill in that time, idly thumbing books they had little intention of purchasing in the bookshop, visiting restrooms, having cups of tea then visiting the restrooms again, pacing up and down, standing about talking to one another while their eyes nervously darted about. Some just slumped on a collection of the world's most uncomfortable chairs, waiting for time to pass.

Lindsey had come into the airport by herself. She'd had to be very firm with Will, uncharacteristically so, but she wanted to start as she meant to go on, by herself, not endlessly relying on other people to help her make her way in the world. Will had looked crestfallen but Lindsey stood firm. In the end he'd no option but to acquiesce. Now, faced with all these people milling about, Lindsey wondered what on earth she had been thinking. It would have been so much more comforting to have someone with her. She felt as though she might be the only person in the entire airport complex not to have someone there to wish her well, someone to help her feel less overwhelmed and isolated.

The problem, Lindsey decided, lay in the need for somewhere to be, to just be able to sit, or stand, and to not feel as though she was sticking out like a sore thumb. Checking in with her e-ticket had been so painless that half an hour still remained before the flight departure time. In the end the lesser evil seemed to be to go straight to the gate and wait patiently there.

Lindsey made her way through the security checkpoint, then up the escalators to the gate. Enormous tinted windows overlooked the tarmac. Down below she could see a flurry of strangely silent activity going on as planes were loaded and unloaded. She stopped to look out, feeling all of a sudden overwhelmed with what she'd chosen to do. She swallowed hard. She must have been crazy to think she could manage this trip on her own. At the very least she should have asked a friend to come with her. Someone like Will, reassuring and reliable.

Maybe, Lindsey thought, squeezing her eyes shut, it wasn't too late to back out now. Sure, she'd lose her money, but worse tragedies could and did happen. When she thought about it, worse tragedies could still happen, especially if she went ahead with this foolhardy idea. She opened her eyes again and looked down at the activity going on around her plane. Would her bag have been loaded on by now? What sort of rigors would she have to go through if she asked for it to be unloaded?

The temptation to rest her forehead against the cool panes of glass took Lindsey's breath away. It made her realize she needed to pull herself together. Nothing could be gained by panicking unnecessarily. Besides, she needed to do this, for herself, for her future. Instead, she turned to the bank of chairs by the gate which were already starting to fill up, and made herself choose one as close to the little security desk - and as far away from the exit - as possible.

Lindsey thought about taking something out of her carry-on bag to read but knew she wouldn't be able to concentrate. The book would only be an added distraction when it came to getting on board. She knew that looking at the faces of the other travelers would be a mistake so focused her energy on studying her fingers in her lap, rubbing the pad of one thumb over the nail of the other, then lacing her fingers together and unlacing them again.

When Lindsey did look up it seemed as though every person on the flight had now congregated in that little waiting area. All seats were taken. Latecomers stood around the perimeter of the room, obscuring the view of the tarmac. Two airline officials had appeared and positioned themselves at the security desk. One laughed over something the other said then spoke rapidly into a walkie-talkie. They looked completely at ease, the business of flying no harder for them than catching a bus.

The intercom ding-donged, and a message to begin boarding the plane got relayed. Passengers started scooping up belongings and gathering up coats and jackets. One woman picked up a small boy who had started to whimper. Another mother had to forcibly separate her two boys who were arguing over the ownership rights of a toy car. Life suddenly seemed extraordinary and comfortingly ordinary at the same moment.

Lindsey fought her natural inclination to hang back and let everyone else go first. She had no desire to draw attention to herself or get in anyone's way. This time though, she forced herself to join the queue, neither the first nor the last, to hand over her boarding pass, then take the strange walk down the jetway where the sounds of the airport and the smell of aviation fuel assailed the senses after the cocooned atmosphere of the terminal.

"Welcome aboard," the flight attendant said, her smile radiant and her face full of confidence behind multiple layers of make up. She looked down at Lindsey's boarding pass. "Down this way, on your left of the aircraft."

Lindsey gave a weak smile, muttered her thanks then shuffled after the person in front of her. She scanned the bulkhead for row fourteen. When she located her seat she found she'd been allocated the middle of three, surely the worst spot to be in. The other two seats were already occupied. A bulldog of a man in a smart suit on the aisle stood up awkwardly to let her pass. By this time both Lindsey's voice and her courage had completely deserted her. She darted into her seat as fast as she could manage. Like an automaton, she stowed her bag beneath the seat in front of her, buckled herself, then leaned back and closed her eyes, keeping them shut until the purser called for everyone's attention to watch the safety demonstration.

"They hardly fill you with confidence," said a voice on Lindsey's right, as the demonstration came to a finish.

Lindsey turned to see who had spoken. In her haste to be as little trouble to the bulldog she hadn't so much as glanced at the woman who sat by the window. Looking now, she saw a lady of indeterminate age, perhaps in her late fifties. She had, Lindsey thought, one of the most elegant faces she had ever seen outside of a picture theatre, like an aged Audrey Hepburn, immaculate, sophisticated and pretty much everything Lindsey was not.

"Sorry?" Lindsey managed.

"The safety demonstrations. They don't exactly fill you with confidence, do they? First they herd everyone inside like sheep. Then they shut the doors and begin telling everyone what can go wrong, with the icing on the cake being the fact that in event of an emergency you need to put your head between your legs and kiss your derriere good-bye. Hardly awe-inspiring. Still, everyone says it's safer to travel by air than by car, so what can you do?"

"I'm not sure," Lindsey said, amazed at such confidence from a stranger.

"I only mention it because you look a little nervous," the woman continued. "Of flying, perhaps?"

Lindsey shook her head. "Not about flying," she said. "Not especially of flying." Then, emboldened by this woman's confidence and curiosity she added, "I'm sort of more nervous about, well, life, I suppose."

"Oh? Hmm. I can imagine that must be a bit difficult. So are you going anywhere special then? No, don't answer that. I'm dreadfully nosey. It's just that I can't help speculate what would get you out of your comfort zone and into this elongated cigar case, that's all."

Lindsey couldn't help smiling. "No, that's okay. I'm pretty amazed about it right now myself. To be honest I almost changed my mind at the last moment. I'm off on a walking holiday, actually. Two weeks through wine country. Quite a departure for me, to say the least."

"No! Not, by any chance, with De Vine Tours?"

Lindsey sent the woman a searching look. "How did you know?"

"Well, you aren't going to believe this, but that's exactly where I'm going. De Vine's two-week walking tour through wine country, with luxury hosted accommodation and gourmet food. Meeting today at the Stansfield Hotel, departing tomorrow after breakfast for all points north."

Shaking her head with the very predicted disbelief the woman had anticipated, Lindsey said, "Yes, yes, one and the same. Are you really going on the tour?"

"Certainly am. I think this calls for introductions at once. What an amazing stroke of luck, to have met you in transit like this. I'm Eleanor Atkinson. And you are?"

"Lindsey McIntyre."

An extremely relieved Lindsey McIntyre, who could not believe her good fortune to have met so friendly a person before the tour had even begun. "Very pleased to meet you," she added, not being able to recall the last time she had said that to someone and truly meant it.

"Well, Lindsey McIntyre, I couldn't agree more."

The short flight from Auckland to Wellington was over before Lindsey knew it. Eleanor kept up a steady and undemanding stream of conversation, mostly revolving around the flight and the upcoming trip. She produced the De Vine brochure from her bag and she and Lindsey spent a lot of the time perusing it in more detail. Eleanor confessed to not being a fine details person, that she had signed up on the tour on a bit of a whim and hadn't bothered to read a lot of the information she'd been sent. By contrast, Lindsey valued detail as a coping strategy for how she managed her life. Since she had read every single word of the De Vine literature, Lindsey could point out a lot of the interesting features she'd already gleaned. This seemed to satisfy Eleanor's curiosity without taxing her with the minutiae.

In Wellington they agreed to travel in to the Stansfield Hotel together since it made sense to do so. Eleanor suggested they be done with it and share the cost of a taxi.

"Haven't been to Wellington in a lifetime," Eleanor said breezily as they headed out of the terminal pushing a luggage trolley between them. "I suppose it's changed like all big cities in that time. Just look at Auckland. Every time I go away and come back the place is unrecognizable, especially if I go anywhere outside my immediate stomping ground."

"You don't live in Auckland?"

"Well, yes. And no. I usually spend a good half of the year out of the country. I'm not really a big fan of winter, pretty much anywhere in the world. I've probably only had one winter in the past five years. My son and my sister both live in London - not together of course - so I usually spend some time with each of them every year and then I just see. See what happens. Last year I got offered a villa in Tuscany for two months. I had a fabulous time mixing with the natives and trying out the local wine. One particular family had many questions about New Zealand wine. I felt sadly undereducated so thought I'd better do something about that. Look, here's a taxi. Let's beat that old couple dithering over there."

Eleanor maneuvered their trolley with the skill of a rally driver. She gave pleasant and slightly imperious instructions to the turbaned driver about stowing their bags in the trunk. Lindsey slid into the taxi with a sigh of relief. Although she knew she wasn't exactly standing on her own two feet she felt inspired to be with someone who had such a zest for life and who made things look easy.

"The Stansfield, please driver," Eleanor directed as the man climbed in behind the steering wheel. "You know where that is, I assume."

The man nodded. Somehow, with his turban perched on top of his head it seemed to set off a full body motion.

As they drew away from the curb Eleanor asked, "Have you been to Wellington before?"

"Never," Lindsey admitted. "My family weren't big on travel during my childhood. I'm generally more of a home body."

Eleanor nodded as though she understood completely. Lindsey found it rather refreshing to be with someone who didn't press her for more details the second they'd met. Lindsey had never been very good with questions.

"Well, we aren't here long," Eleanor said. "Take a good look now, while you get the chance."

Lindsey did just that, taking in the streets and the houses and the hills and the way the three seemed to come together like a finished jigsaw puzzle.

"We should go through the tunnel under Mount Victoria, I think," Eleanor commented, "although I'll be blowed if any of this looks familiar."

By this point the taxi driver had started to have a series of rapid dialogues with someone on the other end of the two-way radio. The conversation, carried out entirely in another language, sounded about as confusing as the driver's body language suggested. Neither woman had the slightest idea what had provoked such a stream of urgent communication. But their suspicions began to grow, especially when the driver took the opportunity to consult a road map when they stopped at a red traffic light. Eleanor rolled her eyes and pointed out the right window.

"That's Mount Victoria," she said. "Mount Victoria, home of the famed tunnel I spoke of. Wherever we are, it's seems highly unlikely it will involve any tunnels unless we have to resort to digging our way to the centre of Wellington."

Lindsey's face registered her concern but Eleanor remained unruffled. "My good man," she said to the driver, giving Lindsey an amused look as she relished her imperious role, "is there a problem?"

"No problem, no problem," the man said, as though he regularly took his passengers on wild-goose-chases and thought nothing of it.

"We seem a little off the beaten track," Eleanor remarked.

"Traffic," the man replied.

Eleanor leaned against the back seat. "Yes, well," she said to Lindsey in lowered tones, "I'm not so sure about that. If he's thinking of charging us over the odds, I'll show him some traffic."

Lindsey couldn't think what to say. She knew that if she had been on her own she would have started seriously panicking about this point.

At the next intersection, the driver took a right into a much more main looking road and there before them they could finally see the towers of downtown Wellington. The rest of the journey passed without incident. When they arrived at the Stansfield Hotel, Eleanor supervised the unloading of their bags then took the man out of Lindsey's earshot and did some rapid talking of her own. The man seemed to visibly pale. He did a lot of nodding. Eleanor then handed him some money.

"Not to worry," Eleanor said to Lindsey as she went to ask how much she owed. "We can settle up later. Let's go in, shall we?"

At the check-in desk, Eleanor again took charge. She gave the woman behind the smooth counter her name explained that she and Lindsey were both there to join the De Vine Tour.

"Of course, madam," the immaculate receptionist said. "I'll page Mr. Hutton for you while we go through the check-in formalities. He's the tour leader. I know he's around here somewhere. I saw him not long ago."

A few minutes later a man appeared behind them.

"Well, hello," he said. "Welcome. Found your way here all right?"

Eleanor smiled at the tall thin man, who looked as though he might be around forty. "We very nearly ended up in Timbuktu on our way here from the airport, but otherwise we've arrived unscathed."

The man grinned and the years seemed to dissolve off his face. "Very good. I'm Dennis Hutton, by the way, owner and operator of De Vine Tours. And you are?"

"Eleanor Atkinson, and this is Lindsey McIntyre. We had the great fortune to meet on the plane on the way down."

"You did? What a coincidence. Still, they say it's a small world and to prove it here you are. Nice to meet you both. Hopefully we'll be in for a great two weeks. The long-range weather forecasts are looking very promising. The majority of the country you'll be walking through is very pleasant indeed. Once you've checked in feel free to make yourselves at home, then for those that are interested we'll congregate in the bar just through there, about seven-ish, and have a meal together. Of course the program doesn't officially start until tomorrow but in the past I've found that most people are more than happy to meet each other right off the bat. I can also answer any questions you have. Does that suit you?"

"Of course," Eleanor said before Lindsey had a chance to say that she thought she might just have dinner in her room.

"Great," Dennis beamed. "In the meantime, if you have any questions or problems, just give me a call. I can be contacted at any time via reception. You'll be all right finding your rooms?"

"Naturally," said Eleanor.

And with that, Dennis departed without Lindsey having uttered so much as a word.

The hotel room was surprisingly spacious. It had a little lounge and kitchenette together with a separate bedroom and bathroom. A television stood in the corner, but Lindsey had not the least intention of watching that. At the window end of the lounge a ranch slider window opened out onto a small terrace. After dumping her bag in the bedroom Lindsey let herself out onto the terrace to take in the view.

From one angle lay a distant view of the harbor, dotted with an array of pleasure craft. Down below a steady stream of traffic threaded along the street, periodically stopped by the phases of the traffic lights. The sound echoed upward. It felt to Lindsey like looking at life through a microscope, removed but interested nonetheless. The late afternoon sun caused long shadows to stretch out over the surrounding buildings and city. Although sunset would still be quite some time away, there seemed little doubt that the day ebbed toward its end.

Lindsey felt at a bit of a loose end as she always did when alone and unoccupied. She had never been particularly good at just relaxing. There seemed little point in unpacking since tomorrow morning they would be off again. Her senses felt so scrambled from the trip, from meeting Eleanor, from the reality of being somewhere completely new and different, that she found it hard to put a coherent thought together.

One concern persisted above all others. She did feel a tiny thread of guilt in having met Eleanor then so quickly and gratefully relied on her to smooth the way. Lindsey's intention in taking this trip was to branch out and learn to be more courageous, to stand on her own two feet. So far her only crowning achievement in that department lay in managing to get on the plane without backing out at the eleventh hour. Ever since then she had glided along very much in Eleanor's slipstream.

Still, Rome wasn't built in a day. Looking out over this unfamiliar city would have to be a good enough start for one day. There lay ahead two full weeks in which anything could happen. And although such a thought would ordinarily make Lindsey exceptionally nervous, she recognized within herself the seeds of anticipation and expectation. Now that she had come this far she couldn't wait to see what would happen next.

In the end Lindsey did not have to wait particularly long to find out what would happen next. Eleanor knocked on the door right on cue at seven o'clock.

"Well then," she said warmly, "how's your room?"

"Come in," Lindsey invited.

"I will. Oh, yes, your room is almost identical to mine. Same layout, just different finishing touches. Not too shabby at all."

"No."

"You're ready?"

"As I'll ever be," Lindsey replied.

"Oh dear," Eleanor said, giving Lindsey a penetrating look, "you really weren't exaggerating about being nervous of life, were you?"

Lindsey shook her head. "Bit hopeless," she muttered.

"No," said Eleanor, "not hopeless. Just a little sad and unfortunate. Mind you, at least you're here. That indicates some stoutness running through your veins, and more than a little hope I'd say. Let's get going before you have a chance to change your mind."

Lindsey picked up her handbag and room key. Eleanor had a rich chocolate brown skirt on, with a chic white blouse that emphasized, but did not over emphasize, her generous chest. She'd finished the outfit off with cute little shoes that would not be out of place in the salons of Europe. Her make-up was immaculate. Lindsey, on the other hand, wore a floral top and the most basic white skirt. She'd worked her long auburn hair into a plait. She felt as though she might be underdressed to go to the store let alone to meet a bunch of strangers in a nice hotel. She fumbled the key card as she went to lock the door. She felt tempted to take this as a sign that she should stay in but could feel Eleanor's assessing gaze boring holes in her back.

"Need some help?" Eleanor asked.

"No, I've got it."

"I'll press the button for the lift."

Lindsey fumbled some more. Every time she tested the door handle it swung easily open. The lift bell pinged to announce its imminent arrival.

"Lift's here," Eleanor called.

At last Lindsey seemed to secure the door. She made a little dash down the corridor to catch the lift with Eleanor. The lift glided silently downwards and the doors slid smoothly open to reveal the bustling foyer. Most of the chairs dotted around the foyer were occupied. Several people awaited attention at the check-in desk.

They went to turn right toward the bar when Eleanor glimpsed Dennis off to their left. He saw them and smiled and waved. He excused himself from the two men he stood with to come over to speak with them.

"So ladies, all refreshed?"

"Very much so," Eleanor said.

"Everything all right with your rooms?" Dennis asked.

"Fine," Eleanor told him. "No problems."

"Great. Look, I've just got to finish dealing with this little situation and then I'll be right in. One or two of the others on the trip have already gone through. Look out for an older couple. They're called Mr. and Mrs. Jones. He's wearing a rather loud Hawaiian shirt. Shouldn't be difficult to spot."

Eleanor and Lindsey both managed something between a grin and a grimace.

"Right you are," said Eleanor. "See you shortly."

Once they were out of earshot Eleanor said, "Did you see those two men with Dennis? I can't imagine what the 'little situation' that he's dealing with is, but it didn't look so little to me. One of them looked thunderous. The other looked as though he'd been struck by lightning. All sort of shocked. Do you think they're part of our group?"

"I don't know. Could be. How many tours do you think Dennis is running at once?"

"Only one, I'd say. Our one. How old do you suppose those young men would be?"

"Early thirties? A bit older than me at a guess."

"Which is how old?"

"Twenty-seven."

"Spring chicken. Wait til you get to my age. I'll not be seeing your side of sixty again and that's a fact. Well, let's go and find this Mr. Jones and his loud Hawaiian shirt, shall we?"

Lindsey followed in Eleanor's wake across the remainder of the immaculate foyer and through double glass doors into a bar area, which in turn led through to a restaurant. They paused momentarily on the threshold but it took neither woman long to spot the infamous shirt. The stocky man who wore it sat at a table with another man and a woman - presumably Mrs. Jones - who wore the sort of hairstyle that suggested she'd changed it very little in the past three decades.

Approaching the table, Eleanor asked, "Mr. and Mrs. Jones?"

"That'll be us," said Mr. Jones, his accent unmistakably east London. His periwinkle blue eyes smiled. "I would say the ones and only, but that would hardly be true with a name like Jones, would it? Dime a dozen. Are you more tour victims?"

Eleanor laughed. "Yes, lambs to the slaughter, both of us. I'm Eleanor, and this is Lindsey. Lindsey and I had the great fortune of meeting on the way here."

"Did you now?" said Mr. Jones. "Well, I'm Eddie and this here's Vi. No need to stand on ceremony. After all, we're going to be seeing an awful lot of each other over the next two weeks. And this here is...blimey," Eddie said to the tall, thin man who sat beside him, " I know you only told me your name ten minutes ago, but it was in one ear and out the other."

Vi Jones made a tiny guffaw. "Been like that his entire life," she told Lindsey and Eleanor in the same accent as her husband. "I was quite surprised he remembered me enough to get married even though I'd know him a good year or two beforehand. It's been all down hill since then I'm afraid. Don't, whatever you do, ask him to pop down to the corner shop and get him to buy you something. Chances are he'd never remember what you'd sent him for by the time he got there."

Eddie patted her knee affectionately. "Broke the mold when they made me, and no lie. Still, we're here and happy. You can't ask for too much more than that."

"No indeed," said Eleanor, clearly highly amused by these new acquaintances.

Eddie suddenly remembered the other man. "Right then, let's be having you. Who are you again?"

The man looked highly embarrassed to find himself the centre of attention. Lindsey felt for him. He reminded her of a Swiss army knife with his elongated body and arms and legs that seemed to stick out like implements that could retract at any moment. She supposed his height and the barrel-shaped bar seating combined to make looking comfortable impossible.

"I'm Cedric Olliver," he said, "but likewise, call me Cedric."

"Good-o," said Eddie. "I'll remember that this time."

Vi's expression said no one should count on this.

"Pull up a pew then, ladies," Eddie suggested. "Take the weight off. I know we won't start walking tomorrow but we may as well enjoy sitting while it lasts."

"You sound as though the idea of walking is not particularly attractive," Eleanor said.

Eddie laughed. "I can't say it's my absolute favorite thing. But I like a good holiday and I like a good drop of wine, so this tour sounded just the ticket. Not too energetic, and at the end of the day you get to enjoy good nosh and a nice drop of plonk to wash it down. Besides, there's nothing actually wrong with my pins that a bit of willpower won't overcome. Plus the missus has always wanted to see this bit of the country, haven't you Vi?"

Vi nodded. "Something romantic about wine country, I've always thought. And since the idea of a holiday in the south of France is a bit beyond us these days, this seemed ideal."

"I assume you live here now?" Eleanor asked. "You never went to France when you lived in England?"

"Not bloody likely," Eddie said. "Too many blinking frogs."

"You're not a fan of the French?" Eleanor asked.

"I think the term you're looking for is Francophobe," Cedric supplied. "Phobia of all things French."

Eddie laughed again. "That's it, that's me. Just call me Frankie from now on."

Eleanor smiled. "So where are you from then, Frankie?"

Eddie nudged Vi. "We've got a funny one here," he said to her. "Have to watch this one." To Eleanor he said, "London, originally, but we've been out here a good fifteen years now, haven't we?"

"More like twenty," Vi said. "We settled in Christchurch when we moved out. Eddie was in the scrap metal business and had a contact there, so that's where we ended up and that's where we've stayed."

"Christchurch," Eleanor said. "What a terrible time you've had with the earthquakes."

Vi's face fell. Eddie said, "It's been a bit rough and no mistake. Even now it seems hard to believe that such a lovely city could have been so devastated."

"I couldn't even begin to imagine it," Eleanor said. "How badly were you affected by the big February quake?"

"Luckier than some and not as lucky as others," Eddie said. "We were home when the quake struck and knew instantly that it was a massive one. Six point three on the Richter scale. Knocked both of us clear off our pins, toppled our chimney and our television, smashed a lot of our household goods and caused a couple of big cracks in the walls. But we were lucky that day, as I say. Many died but we didn't even get hurt. And we didn't get plagued with liquefaction. Ghastly stuff, bubbling up from the aquifer below the city. Bloody shame."

"It was so awful," Eleanor said. "I think the whole country felt so sorry and so helpless in the face of such devastation and suffering. I think we all still feel sorry. Trying to say so makes one feel inadequate. You all deserve medals in my book."

Eddie patted the front of his loud shirt. "That sounds good," he said with a grin. "I've definitely got the chest to pin it on."

Eleanor smiled in return but did not look entirely convinced by Eddie's bravado.

"And how do things stand now?" she asked.

Eddie waved a hand. "We soldier on," he said. "Life's mostly returned to normal. Our house has finally been repaired. Many people are optimistic and keen to see a new Christchurch rise like the phoenix from the ashes. It's going to take a while, though. Decades, even."

"What about you?" Vi interjected. "Where are you originally from?"

Eleanor grinned. "Well, like yourselves I'm an import. I grew up in Hampshire. And although I have a house in Auckland I like to think of myself as a citizen of the world. I spent some of last year in Italy and will probably go away again later this year, although I'm not sure where. I've had an invitation to spend some time in Moscow but I'm not so sure. The Iron Curtain may have fallen but I very much fear the iron bedstead and the iron bathroom remain."

"Moscow has more dollar billionaires than any city in the world," Cedric informed them. "More even than New York."

"That a fact?" Eddie said. "Knowledgeable fellow."

Cedric blushed and looked apologetic. "I think they might have broken the mold when they made me as well. Unlike yourself, I seem to have a wonderful memory for everything."

Eddie looked a touch envious. "That must come in handy. Where are you from, then?"

"Hamilton," Cedric replied.

Eddie's eyebrows shot up. "Hamilton? What do you find to do in Hamilton?"

Cedric's blush deepened. "I work for the Department of Internal Affairs," he murmured.

Eddie's eyebrows pushed even harder against gravity. "Blimey. Here's another one to watch then, Vi."

Vi appeared unmoved. Instead she regarded Lindsey, seemingly the first of the group to realize she had yet to have uttered a word.

"What about you dear?" Vi asked. "Where are you from?"

"Auckland," Lindsey said.

"Not a citizen of the world, then?" Eddie asked with interest.

Lindsey gave a little smile that she felt sure looked fifty percent grimace. "I'm afraid not."

"That doesn't sound like a true Aucklander speaking," Eddie teased. "Aren't you all supposed to be full of yourselves and know everything?"

Lindsey gave a small shrug. She felt embarrassed by the direction the conversation had headed. She did not want to be quite as open with this group as she had been earlier with Eleanor about her sense of caution in life. She had no problem with being self-important.

"Being full of yourself and knowing everything is not a trait particular to Auckland compared with some places in the world," Eleanor said quickly. "In some European countries you can be thrown out for not being opinionated. They'd eat the average Aucklander for breakfast."

"Here we are then," said a voice behind Lindsey. She turned to see Dennis approaching. "Getting acquainted are we? All introduced?"

Eddie grinned. "We've made a bit of progress."

"Great. This is us for tonight, I'm afraid. Two of our other tour members have arrived but have their own plans tonight. The last member of the group won't join us until tomorrow morning. She lives here in Wellington and there seemed little point in her coming to stay at the hotel for the sake of one night. So if you're all happy, let's all go to dinner and get acquainted some more, shall we?"

CHAPTER TWO

A knock on Lindsey's door heralded Eleanor's arrival the following morning.

"How did you sleep?" she asked, coming in the room looking cool and crisp.

"Surprisingly well," Lindsey told her, trying not to feel like the dowdy country cousin. "Comfy bed. You?"

"It took me a while to drop off but that's nothing surprising. I'm often awake until well past midnight anyway. And after meeting our new acquaintances I found myself with plenty to think about. Still, on the whole everyone so far seems nice, don't you think?"

"Yes, very pleasant."

"Very safe you mean," Eleanor said knowingly. "Now as to the other three, that remains to be seen, doesn't it? If those two young men we saw with Dennis were in fact part of our group they certainly didn't distinguish themselves as being either accommodating or amiable."

"Maybe they'd had a bad day," Lindsey suggested. "Like encountering our taxi driver multiplied by ten."

"That would definitely be enough to put anyone in a bad mood," Eleanor said. "Are you ready to go down to breakfast?"

"Yes," Lindsey said.

She felt considerably more relaxed this morning. In fact she hovered on the verge of feeling quite proud of herself. Here she was, in Wellington, without Robyn and without Will. She'd made a new friend in Eleanor, had overcome the hurdle of meeting some new people, and had started to feel quite optimistic about the coming two weeks.

The hotel restaurant where they had dined last night had been transformed overnight. Tables had been spread out along the length of one wall then covered in cereals, fruit, croissants, toast, jams, milk, yoghurt and juices. On an adjacent table hot drinks had been laid out. The smell of fresh coffee permeated the air.

Eddie, Vi and Cedric were already seated together and had chosen a table big enough to accommodate Eleanor and Lindsey as well. Lindsey noted that Eddie had exchanged one loud tropical print for another. In the light of day his face seemed considerably more florid than it had the night before. Vi appeared to be wearing a dress made from some old tablecloth fabric, and Cedric had assumed the David Attenborough about-to-go-on-safari look. He only lacked the pith helmet.

As Eleanor and Lindsey approached the table, Eleanor caught Lindsey's eye and indicated she should look toward the back of the room. There the two young men sat quietly together.

"That's them, isn't it?" Eleanor asked. "The men from last night?"

"I think so," Lindsey said. "One of them has his back to us so it is a bit difficult to tell."

"If it is them and they are part of our group, I have to say that they aren't looking any more cheerful than they did last night. Or at least the one we can see doesn't."

"Maybe there was something wrong with their room. Maybe they had water pouring down their walls or the toilet was blocked. I heard one of the receptionists telling someone they were fully booked. In which case there'd be nowhere to shift to."

Eleanor scrutinized Lindsey. "You make up excuses for other people remarkably rapidly," she observed. Then her expression softened. "Maybe they've just had a big argument over something. Or maybe things are not to their liking. Anyway, here are the others. Morning people."

"Good morning to you two ladies," Eddie said. "Got yourself some breakfast? We wondered if you'd decided to give it a miss."

"We've got plenty of time until we have to meet at ten o'clock, haven't we?" Eleanor asked, putting down her plate and looking at her elegant gold watch. "It doesn't take that long to eat breakfast."

"It does if you want to have seconds or thirds," Vi said elbowing Eddie.

Eddie appeared unrepentant. "A man needs to stoke up," he said. "A person should never assume they know where the next meal is coming from."

Vi patted Eddie's stomach. With his relatively short stature and stocky build he wasn't ever going to be a lean man.

"Much more stoking and people are going to start asking you when the baby is due," Vi joked.

"Did you know that the average human body contains enough fat to make about seven bars of soap?" Cedric asked Lindsey, who had sat down in the empty chair beside him.

"No, I didn't," she replied.

"I think in Eddie's case, twelve bars would be more like it," Vi laughed.

Eddie looked wounded but his face soon wrinkled with amusement. "You only live once," he said. "No point at my age in trying to deny the inevitable. May as well enjoy myself while the going's good. Oi, oi, here comes Dennis, and who's that he's got with him?"

All eyes at the table were drawn to the doorway where they saw Dennis walking in with a young woman of similar age to Lindsey. She had the appearance of someone who had been buffed and polished like some sort of precious stone. Right from the top of her blonde head down to her immaculate, coordinated shoes, strode a woman who evidently spent a lot of her time and effort on personal presentation. She wore an outfit that was a cross between shorts and tee shirt and a suit. She could easily have been mistaken for a cruise director on a luxury liner.

Dennis and the mystery lady were deep in conversation so that when they reached the table Dennis almost needed to recover himself, as if surprised that he'd ended up in front of them. Lindsey felt sure they were about to be introduced to either a member of his team or one of the hotel staff, and was a little taken aback when Dennis spoke.

"Morning everyone," he beamed. "Everything in order, I trust? Good breakfast? No problem with your rooms? Great. Welcome to day one of our tour. May I introduce one of your fellow traveling companions? Everyone, this is Bianca Caton. Bianca, let me introduce everyone to you. First names all right? Good. Then meet Eddie and Vi, Cedric, Lindsey, and last of all Eleanor."

Eleanor, Lindsey, Cedric and Vi smiled politely. Eddie grinned as though he'd just discovered he'd won lotto and gave a funny little wave. Bianca moved her mouth into a little pout. Lindsey could only presume she intended this as a smile, but it held little warmth. Still, faced with a similar situation Lindsey knew smiling warmly would be beyond her as well. In fact, she'd be downright terrified.

Bianca Caton seemed anything but terrified. With the assessing look she gave them it seemed clear that the only thing that pleased her was herself. Unlike Eddie, she had the air of someone who had lost a winning lotto ticket and found a dud instead.

"Welcome to the clan," Eddie said, quite undeterred by the frosty Miss Caton. "We should be in for a few laughs I should say."

"Let's hope so," Dennis said when Bianca failed to say a thing. "Now just to bring you all up to speed, everything is going according to plan. As it says in your itinerary, please meet in the lobby at ten o'clock. Bring all your belongings with you because we won't be coming back. At this point we'll get the mini bus loaded up with your luggage and hopefully be on the road by ten thirty.

"As you know our ultimate destination today is Brookfield. There we'll have another overnight stay before starting the walking part of the holiday." Dennis looked at his watch. "It's probably about two and a half hours' drive to Brookfield, so the plan is to stop and have some lunch along the way. There are one or two very nice eateries as we go so we'll see what takes our fancy, shall we?"

Lindsey thought the chances of finding something to match the tastes of everyone assembled were relatively slim. And of course no one yet knew anything about the other passengers.

As though reading her mind, Eddie said, "I thought there were eight of us on the tour. With all of us here, that only makes six."

Lindsey watched Eleanor glance over into the corner. She followed her gaze and to her surprise the young men were gone.

Dennis cleared this throat then gave a grin. "Yes Eddie, there are eight of you altogether, nine if you count myself. The other two passengers will be meeting us in the lobby. They've had their own arrangements for the overnight stay in Wellington."

Eddie made a small assessing gesture with this mouth. From his expression it seemed clear he considered the latecomers weren't really getting into the spirit of things.

"He probably wants to eye up the competition," Eleanor said when they were in the lift going back to their rooms after breakfast. "He strikes me as the sort of man who looks as though he doesn't give a damn about anything other than Vi and having a good time. But underneath it all I bet he has a fundamental need to run the show. Not knowing who the last two travelers are probably puts a serious dent in his ability to be the man of the party."

"What about Cedric?" Lindsey asked. "He's a man, isn't he?"

"Not," Eleanor said, "the sort of man to bring your masculinity into doubt though, is he? Still, we'll soon find out. I'll go and finish packing, then we can both go and see together."

On the dot of ten Lindsey and Eleanor emerged from the lift and into the bustling foyer. There seemed to be plenty of people checking out. A number of groups stood huddled together, exchanging that sort of desultory conversation that takes place in an interim situation. People discussed the weather and the breakfast and tried to think up amusing things to say to keep their companions from falling into the sort of stupefaction that often harries those in a lull.

Over by the enormous glass windows that fronted the Stansfield, Lindsey spied Cedric and Bianca standing together. Cedric held a jacket that he kept nervously transferring from one arm to the other. As Lindsey and Eleanor approached it seemed clear that Cedric had been trying unsuccessfully to engage Bianca in conversation. She, on the other hand, kept glancing to the left, then to the right, as though either watching a tennis match or waiting for the number eight bus.

When she caught sight of Lindsey and Eleanor coming near, Bianca gave the first hint of a true smile, even if provoked by the immense relief of not having to wait on her own with Cedric. Lindsey had to swallow an uncharacteristic smirk.

"Here we are," Eleanor said heartily. "All dressed and pressed. Well rested and well fed."

"I know it helps," said Cedric, "all that sleeping and eating, but the truth is that you can actually survive without either for quite some time. In fact you can live longer without eating than sleeping. They say that most people can go about eight weeks without food but only about ten days without sleep."

Eleanor sent him an arch expression. "Is that right? I certainly hope that such a regime is not standard practice on a De Vine Tour. You might be able to survive, as you say, but it's hardly what I'd call living. It certainly contains none of the ingredients of a good holiday."

"Damn right," said Bianca. "In fact I've already got serious doubts that this trip will have any of the elements of a good holiday, even with good food and good sleep."

Lindsey paled. This hardly seemed the attitude to have as they embarked on the trip. Even her own reluctance seemed preferable to outright hostility.

Eleanor clearly agreed. "Come now," she said. "Let's not put the cart before the horse."

Bianca tossed her head. "Hardly the analogy to fill a person with confidence, if you don't mind me saying."

"All right? All right?" came Eddie's voice across the foyer. He walked toward them carrying the strangest suitcase Lindsey had ever seen. It looked as though it had been purchased in the 70's or 80's, was large, thin, battered and lacked wheels. Vi trailed in Eddie's wake, oblivious to any glances he got from fellow hotel guests as they took in the sight of his loud shirt, impossibly knobbly knees and strange luggage. "You haven't gone without us, then?"

"There's little chance of that," Eleanor replied. "Dennis seems far too organized to leave anyone behind."

"Shame," Lindsey heard Bianca mutter.

"Wanted to be down here five minutes ago but had a small denture crisis," Eddie confided. "Bloody choppers. Can't live with them, can't live without them."

"I've been telling him all his life to look after his fangs," Vi told them, "but he'd no more listen to me than fly to the moon."

Eddie shuddered. "No, that's one place you wouldn't catch me: space. Too bloody cold. Give me sunshine on terra firma any day. Where's Dennis?"

Cedric pointed through the windows to where they could see a compact mini bus pull up under the imposing covered entrance to the hotel. They watched him climb out of the driver's door and come in through the main entrance door. Catching sight of them he gave them his trademark grin.

"All here are we?" he said.

"Yer, except those other two," Eddie said.

"No," Dennis said, "they're right here."

Lindsey turned toward the direction of Dennis's gaze. Sure enough the two young men, one with jet-black hair, the other sandy, emerged from the lift. They walked toward the group almost in slow motion, watching and being watched, looking uncomfortable and unhappy and completely out of place.

One person, however, did rally at the arrival of these two good-looking young men. Lindsey heard Bianca say distinctly in her ear, "All right. Now things are looking up."

Dennis collected their room keys then directed the group to congregate outside on the sidewalk in front of the hotel. While he went to finalize their check-out, the eight new acquaintances maneuvered their bags through the main door. A sharp breeze blew around the corner of the building taking the warmth out of the air. It was the sort of wind that cast litter adrift and had a nearby oak tree dancing.

When Dennis reappeared Cedric offered to help him stow the luggage in the compartment on the side of the bus. The excess bags were to go in a little trailer the likes of which Lindsey had seen airport shuttle services use. Everyone else stood in separate groups, as though suddenly shy about the idea of getting into a confined space with one another. Eddie made a big deal about stowing his own bag safely. Vi watched him with exasperation. Bianca had made herself known to the young men but neither seemed to be paying her much attention. After a minute one of the young men, the one with sandy hair, seemed to remember himself and went to help Cedric and Dennis.

Eleanor and Lindsey stood to one side.

"No sense in getting in the way," Eleanor said.

"No," Lindsey agreed.

"Feels quite exciting, doesn't it, launching off into the wild blue yonder?"

"Mostly," Lindsey agreed. "Perhaps six parts excitement and four parts sheer terror?"

"You'll be fine," Eleanor said in the breezy way Lindsey was becoming quite accustomed to. "Just think of all the good things that could come out of this journey."

"There's quite a few good things that can come from staying home," Lindsey said. "Believe me, I know."

Eleanor gave her a sharp look. "Now, now." She fell silent for a few moments then reflectively said, "Interesting, don't you think, what you can tell about a person by their bag?"

"I thought you were supposed to be able to tell a lot about people by their shoes."

"Shoes. Hmm. Maybe. But shoes are so commonplace. Most of us purchase them fairly regularly, especially these days when everything is made in China and nothing lasts like it used to. A bag is something different. Those you buy rarely unless you're an American socialite and have to have a different one for every outfit your dog wears. You have to think more about a bag. Functionality, design, fashion. Look at what I mean. Look at Eddie and Vi's bag. That bag's probably close to thirty years old and has been booted around from pillar to post. It's a bag with history. Look at the size. You could fit a kitchen sink in there as long as it was thin. Lots of storage, easy access, durable fabric. Not flashy. Solid, I'd say, a bit like Eddie and Vi themselves.

"And madam there. Look at her matching luggage with, of course, one more bag than the literature said we were allowed to bring. Immaculate, chic, designed to impress. Whether it's practical is another thing. No compartments. When you stand it upright everything probably crushes on top of the things below. But in the scheme of things, it's luggage that gets noticed, especially in that bright pink."

"What about my bag?" Lindsey asked.

Eleanor looked down at Lindsey's bag. It was brown, solid, dependable.

"Borrowed at a guess," she said. "That doesn't count."

This took Lindsey by surprise. "How did you know?"

Eleanor tapped the side of her nose. "It wasn't difficult."

"Really?"

"What? From the stay-at-home kid? It makes sense that you wouldn't own one yourself. Besides, I think if you gave yourself a chance, you've got style Lindsey McIntyre. Whose is it, by the way? The bag?"

"My flatmate's. Will's."

"And is he like this bag?"

Lindsey thought of Will, and of how good he had been to her, how solid and dependable. She looked at the bag again then couldn't help laughing. "Yes," she said, "I think he very much might be."

When it came time to board the bus a small scramble ensued as everyone tried to get to sit with the person they wanted to be with, in the place they wanted to be in. Eddie, an old campaigner, whisked Vi in front of him like some sort of dance move. He propelled her up the stairs and into the front two seats in spectacular fashion. Bianca seemed torn between supremacy and the desire to stay as close to the young men as she could. She hung back, waiting to see what they would do, while they hung back even further. Cedric showed his chivalrous side by letting Eleanor and Lindsey get on after Eddie and Vi.

When Lindsey entered the bus she saw more clearly the layout of the seating. Along the driver's side were four double seats with an aisle running along the passenger side that led to a seat wide enough to accommodate three along the back. Taking into account the empty chair beside the driver this allowed seating for twelve, thirteen including Dennis. Plenty of room for them all, especially since they would spend very little time in the mini bus after today.

Lindsey followed Eleanor into the seats behind Eddie and Vi. Cedric fell in behind them. Lindsey watched Bianca's face as she entered the bus and attempted to choose whether to sit behind Cedric or slip into the back seat in the hope that the young men would join her. If they didn't, though, she would risk being left in the back seat by herself. Lindsey could not imagine her willingly sitting beside Cedric. Sure enough, she opted for the seat behind Cedric, leaving the back seat for the men.

As they came onto the bus the man with the sandy hair gave a small smile at everyone, an almost apologetic smile, while his companion remained stony faced. Lindsey gave a brief smile in return then looked quickly away. Eleanor raised her eyebrows in speculation but said nothing.

Once they were all seated, Dennis's cheerful face appeared at the doorway.

"Right," he said, "I think we've got everything safely stowed and I've battened the hatches, so to speak. Everyone got everything? No need for last minute dashes to the bathroom? Fabulous. Now, just before we set off there's one last set of introductions. Of course I should have thought to do this while everyone stood conveniently on the sidewalk, but you can't win them all I suppose. Everyone, meet Simon Ellery and Andrew Powell."

At the sound of the name Andrew, the more friendly of the two gave a little wave, so Lindsey presumed he must be the latter. His friend grimaced, pained by the focused attention of the others. For the benefit of Simon and Andrew, Dennis rattled off everyone's names, then gave a shrug as if to indicate that he'd done his best. The rest relied on the eight of them to set the tone between them.

Dennis climbed into the driver's seat and they pulled out of the Stansfield entrance way and into the main road. Sunday morning traffic was light. Unlike Lindsey's previous trip through the streets of Wellington, Dennis negotiated the roads faultlessly, driving well and knowing precisely where to go. After wending his way through the central city streets, Dennis turned the bus onto the motorway, where they followed the main state highway route north. This eventually led to the turn off onto State Highway Two in a northeasterly direction.

Slowly the scene outside the windows changed from city skyscrapers to suburban sprawl. Eventually the sea of houses diminished to odd dwellings here and there. Instead of the land being cultivated by snug urban homes, it was farmed and put to the sort of use one associates with rural life.

Everyone on the bus had fallen silent. As they had crawled out of Wellington, leaving behind the cozy hills dotted with homes, Lindsey had been aware of Bianca trying to make conversation with Simon and Andrew. Whether she had been rebuffed by monosyllabic replies or whether she had tired of swiveling around in an attempt to talk, Lindsey did not know, but all conversation from the rear of the bus had ceased. Eddie and Vi sat in the way many couples of long association do, companionably, and in silence. She and Eleanor, though of recent acquaintance, sat in much the same way, occasionally exchanging a glance and a smile.

Lindsey felt herself bordering on contentment, a feeling she usually only associated with being at home and relaxed. Sunshine streamed down and the prospect of being out in the countryside over the next couple of weeks gave her a pleasant sense of anticipation. Eleanor proved to be a rare find, being so undemanding to be with. Eleanor had not pressed her with questions, interrogating her like something out of the Spanish Inquisition. She seemed content to let their burgeoning friendship develop in the moment without being weighed down by the past.

Dennis appeared to be equally friendly and outgoing, a bit like a faithful hound determined to do his best. Eddie and Vi were a little like an ongoing comedy double act, while Cedric seemed harmless enough in an eccentric sort of way. Admittedly, Bianca had come across as being rather overpowering, but if she did befriend the young men – who thus far seemed more than content to keep to their own company - they might well not need to interact with her – or them – too much anyway.

All in all, the beginning to this trip had far exceeded Lindsey's expectations. Her courage had been somewhat bolstered by the presence of Eleanor, but right at this moment Lindsey felt almost proud of herself. She had finally taken the plunge to branch out, and it had begun with such success.

As the miles flashed by and the landscape changed, Lindsey began to absorb more of the natural beauty around her. Their route took them along the Hutt Valley to the base of the Rimutaka Range, and from there they began a winding ascent that had the mini bus weaving along like a switchback railway. They reached the summit of the Range after half an hour of careful driving by Dennis then began to descend down the other side. The countryside that lay before them was less dramatic than one might find in the South Island, lacking the towering presence of the Southern Alps. Instead it had that steady, predictable North Island scenery of rolling hills, flanked here on the western side by the Tararua Range, lying like a large lizard warming itself in the February sunshine.

The land seemed to be a veritable fruit bowl, with apple orchards, olive groves and the odd vineyard dotted amongst farms with grazing sheep and cattle. Now and then Lindsey caught sight of features as diverse as fields of lavender or stands of native bush. The rich and fertile area appeared sparsely populated and had a rustic, untouched feel about it, as though giving a glimpse into the New Zealand of yesteryear. Occasionally the road would rise giving a distant glimpse of the brilliant sea rising up to meet the rugged coastline.

They drove for half an hour more before Dennis pulled over into the car park of an olive orchard whose owners had branched out from the fundamental business of tending their groves to take advantage of the passing traffic. As Lindsey emerged from the bus she saw that they'd stopped before a pleasant building plastered in rich cream tones that looked as though it might have been transported straight from Tuscany - or at least Lindsey's idea of Tuscany. She saw Eleanor's eyes narrow critically at this sight then give a little shrug of indifference.

The owners had established a cafe and a shop selling numerous products containing the fruit of the olive. Dennis beseeched them to look around and make themselves at home.

"Thought we might stop here," he said airily, "perhaps for about an hour or so. That way you can have a look around, stretch your legs a bit and have a bite of lunch before we meander on. This will probably be your first and last stop at an olive orchard so make the most of it, we won't be back this way."

Eleanor looked meaningfully at Lindsey. "We'd better do as we're told then, hadn't we?"

Lindsey smiled. "I guess we better had."

"Fancy going into their shop or shall we wait until after lunch?"

"After, I suppose."

"Not hungry already?" Eleanor asked.

"Not especially. Wow, can you feel the heat from the sun?"

Eleanor lifted her face to bask in the warmth. "Gorgeous. Do you suppose stretching our legs might include allowing us to take a little walk amongst the trees before lunch?"

"Not sure," Lindsey replied. "Perhaps Dennis will know."

Dennis did indeed know. He replied that they were more than welcome to wander around the olive groves as long as no one went too far. He didn't relish the prospect of losing any tour members on the first day.

By this stage the rest of the group had dispersed. Simon, Andrew and a dogged looking Bianca had headed straight for the cafe while Eddie and Vi were nosing around the gift shop. Cedric had found one of the staff to talk to and had begun grilling them about aspects of olive growing. The expression on his face rivaled the earnestness of Bianca's.

Eleanor and Lindsey followed a path that ran around the side of the main building and crossed a grassy area dotted with picnic tables. Someone with green fingers had evidently attempted to establish a garden here. There were signs of new retaining walls and recent planting. Toward the far side of the lawn the path petered out before a small gate which Eleanor opened to allow them access to the olive groves.

The leafy boughs swayed in the light breeze that ghosted almost indiscernibly beneath the rows of carefully spaced trees. The smell of sun-drenched grass filled the air. With every step the sounds of the road and the restaurant faded away.

"These trees are all fairly young," Eleanor observed, breaking the silence.

"I suppose they would be," Lindsey said. "After all, the olive growing industry would probably be in its infancy in this neck of the woods."

"Indeed," said Eleanor. "You should see some of the groves in Italy. Some of the trees appear ancient, with gnarled boughs and wide trunks."

"How old do you think they grow?"

"I'm not sure. I have more experience with eating olives than with growing them, truth be told. Maybe I'll have to go on an olive trip one day, to add to my knowledge. I had it in mind that olive trees can have a lifespan of thousands of years. Someone once told me that some of the olive trees on the Mount of Olives in Jerusalem have been there since Jesus' time, but I don't know whether that's true or not."

"Thousands of years? That's incredible. Do you suppose they still bear fruit?"

"I don't know that either," Eleanor said. She stopped by one of the trees and ran her hand down its smooth bark. "Have you ever wanted to grow things?" she asked.

Lindsey tilted her head. "Like olives, you mean?"

"Perhaps. Or other fruit or vegetables. Even farming."

"I can't say that I've ever thought about it. I would imagine that relying on crops or agriculture for your income must take a certain amount of audacity, especially these days when the climate is so unreliable."

Eleanor considered this. "That's true. I think perhaps you have to have the right combination of courage and forbearance. Still, the rewards must be tremendous if everything goes to plan."

"Monetarily?"

"Not necessarily. I suppose I mean the satisfaction from the process. From seeing something you've nurtured come to fruition."

Lindsey nodded. "You didn't feel that about being a parent?"

Eleanor laughed. "Oh no. Parenting is far too random for that sort of satisfaction. Growing things is a lot more predictable, give or take the weather, as you say. Take this olive tree here. Presumably it does not have a mind of its own, to petulantly decide to produce fruit or not, as the case may be. It has no free will. It cannot just get up and leave if it so desires, nor grow beyond its intended purpose. Children, on the other hand, are far more arbitrary. All the positive nurturing in the world can disappear overnight in the face of a child's freedom of choice and stubbornness of mind. And ultimately, the aim of the game is to raise them to independence. They're never supposed to stay with you."

"Was your son like that when he was growing up?" Lindsey asked as they walked on.

Eleanor laughed again. Her eyes sparkled as she recalled the past. "Sebastian? Yes and no. He's was a great kid in many respects, intelligent, humorous, fairly even-tempered. There were things about him that were a little bit too much like his father for his own good, and odd personality traits that made me want to throw my hands up in horror. But he's turned out fine in the end. At times I think he could do with a bit more adventure in his life, but it's not my place to say so any more, not when he's settled and a grown man of forty.

"I wasn't only thinking of him, though. In my younger days, a former life you might say, I was a school teacher. I taught mostly nine and ten year olds. If you ever want to know anything about arbitrary, that's where you should start. I've seen children with perfectly good brains wasting them away because some alternative seemed more attractive."

"You must have had that basic desire to nurture within you from the start, though?"

"Perhaps. I suppose you naively feel as though you could make a difference by being a teacher. I suppose I did once feel idealistic." Eleanor threw Lindsey a sharp glance. "You're not a teacher, are you?"

Lindsey shook her head. "I don't think I could be a teacher in a million years although I do like children. I'd probably be useless at trying to maintain discipline and I'd want to take all the sad cases home with me."

"I can imagine that. So what do you do?"

"Art."

"Ah. I can imagine that as well. What sort of art?"

"Predominantly illustration these days, although I have trained as a graphic designer and can turn my hand to other things."

"Illustration? I wouldn't imagine that would be particularly lucrative."

"Not especially. I do some commissioned work, as well as my current focus, and also have a group of clients, mostly graphic design businesses, who will ask me to do work for them when they have too much work on. It's one of those sorts of industries where workflow is very difficult to predict. I suppose you would say that I get by."

"And your current focus?"

Lindsey could feel herself coloring. She might have known that Eleanor was too sharp to have missed that comment. "Children's books," Lindsey muttered.

"Illustrating children's books?" Eleanor pressed.

"Well, and writing them too."

"Ha. How fabulous. Have you already got some published?"

Lindsey nodded imperceptibly. "Two."

"Two? Oh well done, Lindsey. They're picture books, I take it. What are they called?"

"One is called *'Gilbert's Outing'*. The other's called *'Charlie's Neighbors'*," Lindsey told her bashfully.

"Marvelous. And the third? I presume there is to be a third?"

Lindsey colored even further. "I'm hopefully going to write a story about some little creatures who live under grape vines. That's sort of the reason I've come on the trip. It's a form of field research. I'm hoping to learn a little about viticulture and have the opportunity to make some preliminary sketches along the way."

"How utterly delightful," Eleanor said.

"You won't mention this to the others will you?" Lindsey asked hastily.

"Whyever not?" Eleanor asked.

"I don't know. I suppose I just want to keep things low key. Maybe I'll lose some spontaneity or inspiration if I feel as though people are watching and interested. Not you, of course," Lindsey added, lest Eleanor feel she was included with the others. "Can you see what I mean?"

Eleanor looked at Lindsey with a clarity Lindsey had barely seen before. "Of course," she said. "You can rely on me. Speaking of the others, I think it's time we started heading back."

In the end it was after two o'clock before the party set off in the bus bound for Brookfield. The main reason for the delay had been that Dennis's worst fears were realized, and on the very first day. One of the party had disappeared, seemingly without a trace. As it turned out Cedric had become fascinated about olive growing and production to the point where he had wandered off and ended up over a ridge at an outbuilding used for pressing olives. He had become so engrossed in watching proceedings that he had quite lost track of time.

Lindsey had felt for Dennis who, before discovering Cedric's where-abouts, had to not only mount a search party but also placate the rest of the group. Some were less than impressed to be delayed by more than an hour in a place with limited attractions. Eleanor, Lindsey and Vi had found themselves a place to sit in the shade of a tree. Eddie sat with his head in the shade but basked his white legs in the sun. This provoked Vi to joke that Eddie's legs were so white they shouldn't be allowed out in public without some sort of health warning. Meanwhile Simon, Andrew and Bianca didn't seem to know what to do with themselves. Lindsey could not help but notice that Bianca's expression grew more petulant with every incremental ten minutes that passed. Simon looked pained to the point of explosion.

When Cedric had finally been located and recovered he appeared back at the bus looking sheepish and apologetic. Dennis tried to reassure him that there wasn't any harm done even though this seemed far from certain at such an early point in the proceedings. Eddie slapped him on the back and said that they'd have to keep him on a shorter leash in future. No one else made much comment at all. Everyone just wanted to get on the road and make some progress.

They reached Brookfield a little after three o'clock. Lindsey had not really known what to expect of Brookfield and when she finally did see it there seemed little about it to immediately recommend it to outsiders. It was a practical town that served the surrounding agricultural community: a place to shop for groceries, post mail, buy wool or string or pegs, to get a spare part for your tractor. The shops were strung out along a main road divided down the middle by a wide grassed median strip dotted here and there with reluctant trees, a memorial to the district's war dead, drooping beds of flowers crying out for water, and punctuated every hundred meters or so with pedestrian crossings.

As Dennis drove them down the main street Lindsey caught sight of a farm store, two dairies, a couple of takeaway bars, a shoe shop and a stationery shop. One single bank clung tenuously on, no doubt resisting closure like so many other rural branches. Window displays were lackluster. The wool shop's display looked like it hadn't been changed since 1972. Here and there were signs of industry, as though the townsfolk had not given up all together, perhaps with the expectation that prosperous times were not far away. Some business fronts looked freshly painted. One particularly optimistic owner had erected hanging baskets cascading with flowers in front of their establishment.

Dennis pulled off the main road and into a side street of residential homes. On the corner stood an old wooden church advertising their campaign to fundraise for a new roof. Someone ambitious had painted a sign with a thermometer to indicate the ultimate target needed to re-roof, and progress by degrees from the bulbous ball at the bottom. Lindsey noted with a moment of sadness that the mercury had a perilously long way to climb before restoration work could begin. A few properties down from this lay their destination for the night, the Golden Sands Motel.

The mini bus came to a halt in the motel forecourt. Everyone sat looking out of the window at their home for the night. Although Dennis had already hopped out and opened the passenger door no one seemed inclined to move in a hurry in spite of having been cooped up for a further hour. They watched his figure stride in his long legged way across the car park and in through the door labeled "Office", wondering if this could possibly be the right place, and hoping against hope that it wasn't.

"Blimey," Lindsey heard Eddie say. "This is a bit of a comedown from the Stansfield."

Eleanor leant forward. "I suppose we shouldn't entirely judge a book by its cover," she said, surveying the tired brick complex with miniscule looking rooms. Each had tiny windows covered with ageing net curtains. "But I'd say blimey just about sums it up perfectly."

Eddie swiveled around as best he could. "When do you suppose they last painted or decorated?"

Eleanor shrugged. "Nineteen fifty seven?"

Vi giggled. "Perhaps it should be renamed the Tarnished Sands instead."

Eddie laughed. "Bit of a potty name anyway, if you ask me. We must be miles from the coastline let alone any sort of beach."

"They could mean the golden sands of time," Lindsey suggested.

Eddie's substantial eyebrows shot upward. "Yeah, the sort of time that passes incredibly slowly. Sort of like it did in school days when I sat trying not to die of boredom and hanging out for the end of day bell."

"Look lively," Vi said. "Here comes Dennis."

Dennis lollopped back across the forecourt and stuck his head in the passenger door with his broad smile firmly in place. Lindsey wondered whether he imagined that being upbeat would prove to be contagious, that if he faked enthusiasm well enough they would all fall for it. She suspected he might be up against a difficult crowd here if that was the case.

"Well folks, we've arrived. I've checked you all in and have your room keys here. Perhaps if we unload the luggage I could dole them out to you one at a time?"

"I'll help," Cedric said from behind Lindsey, doubtless keen to redeem himself in whatever way he could.

"Good on ye, Cedric," Eddie said approvingly, at the same time making it very clear he had no intention of helping whatsoever apart from handling his own bag.

After this they all filed out of the bus and stood uncomfortably in the forecourt awaiting bags and keys while Dennis, Cedric and Andrew manhandled the luggage once again. Bianca, Lindsey noted, stood to one side with Simon.

"This place looks like some sort of antipodean Auschwitz," Bianca said scathingly.

Simon remained aloof and said nothing in spite of giving the impression of heartily agreeing with her sentiment. He stepped forward to take a bag off Andrew then withdrew hastily, as though fearing some sort of invisible contamination. Lindsey knew her own quiet disposition and social ineptness made her anything but the life and soul of the party, but Simon appeared to have developed disdain to a fine art. He seemed about as likely to socialize as an antelope in a pride of lions.

Once the bags were all unloaded Dennis handed out the room keys. Lindsey, Eleanor, Cedric and Bianca all had rooms to themselves, while Eddie and Vi, and Simon and Andrew, had a room together. Andrew said something briefly to Dennis, but Lindsey did not catch the words. Dennis shook his head with a negative reply, causing Simon and Andrew to exchange glances of exasperation.

Dennis seemed unperturbed.

"Right then, folks," he said, "take your time settling in. You've got a free night tonight to spend as you will. There are a couple of eateries in the town. Get some sleep and then we'll start rounding up at nine thirty in the morning. Be ready with your walking shoes on and your daypack filled only with those items you want to carry. As you know, I'll be taking the extraneous baggage in the bus with me. We'll have a bit of a briefing then try to have you off on your big adventure before ten. Let me know if there are any problems but otherwise, have a good evening."

He gave them all a quick salute, like a contented ship's captain heading off to his ready room, leaving them all to shuffle off toward their accommodation with barely a murmur between them.

When evening came Eleanor, Lindsey, Eddie and Vi met as arranged in the forecourt of the motel at seven o'clock in order to go forth and enjoy the nightlife of Brookfield.

"Ready to subdue the natives?" Eddie called out as he and Vi appeared out of their motel unit.

"When faced with the spectacle of his shirt the natives will probably concede to anything," Eleanor said to Lindsey out the side of her mouth. She called, "Ready as we'll ever be."

"I can't imagine where he gets them all from," Eleanor added as they waited while Eddie, then Vi, had trouble locking their room door. "He must have combed the globe for the world's worst shirts because surely one store alone could not be responsible for such atrocities."

Lindsey had to smother a laugh as the Joneses approached.

"Bloody door," Eddie said with feeling. "How's your room?"

"An eclectic mix of horror seventies decor and white painted brick boredom. You?"

"Ha. Much the same," Vi said. "Candlewick bedspread circa nineteen fifty four, and a television set from not long after. Eddie's most put out because it only gets one channel and not his favorite one at that. How about you, Lindsey?"

"All of the above together with a lovely perfume of mold killer in the bathroom."

"Course," Eddie exclaimed. "That's what that smell is. I kept saying to Vi it reminded me of something. Eau de Mould. Where's Cedric?"

"Is he coming too?" Eleanor asked.

"He asked us what we were doing for dinner and I said he could join us. No sense in keeping him in the dog box forever, although if he doesn't turn up in a minute I could start changing my mind about that."

"Go and knock on his door," Vi urged. "I feel starving already."

While they waited for Cedric, Lindsey put her hands into the pockets of the jacket she had donned over her thin summer dress and her hand hit some paper. She drew it out to find she held a twenty-dollar bill.

Vi saw her surprised expression and said, "Half your luck. I never find money in my clothes. How long has that been there?"

Lindsey thought then remembered. Robyn had given it to her one evening on a rare occasion when Robyn and Will had persuaded Lindsey to go to a barbecue at the house of one of their former fellow students. Robyn had been going to drive them all home but at the eleventh hour had met someone who, Robyn said, had wanted to talk about sports.

"But you hate sports," Will had stated.

"Where could the harm be in a little hockey?" Robyn had replied.

"Hockey? You double hate hockey," Will said.

"Not tonsil hockey," had come the knowing retort, at which point she had given Lindsey twenty dollars so that she and Will could get a taxi home, with strict instructions not to wait up. Lindsey and Will had set off to try to find a taxi but had so little success they ended up walking the entire way home.

"Since before Christmas," Lindsey said to Vi, shoving the money back in her pocket and trying not to feel overwhelmed with nostalgia for her flatmates.

"Here's Cedric now," Eleanor said, watching as he emerged from the motel office clutching a wad of promotional brochures for local activities while Eddie continued his fruitless banging on Cedric's room door.

"Come on," Vi hollered to Eddie. "Here he is."

"All present and accounted for?" Cedric asked breezily, as though completely unaware that he had yet again been responsible for a delay in proceedings.

Eddie muttered something beneath his breath and they set off down the road, past the church on the corner and into the main street of Brookfield.

The streetlights were already on even though darkness was still some way off. The amber glow gave the town the sort of fake tan a sunbed user acquires after one too many tanning sessions. The group quickly discovered the main street largely deserted apart from one or two hardy souls hanging around outside a takeaway bar. Here the aroma of cooking fat wafted through the air in an overpowering wave.

"Hmm," said Eddie appreciatively.

Vi elbowed him in his ample gut. "Not on your life, hot shot," she said to him. "You know what the doctor said. No fried food."

Eddie pouted. "Bloody conspiracy."

They continued walking down the street but every shop - including eateries - appeared to be firmly closed.

"It is Sunday," Cedric said, as though that explained everything. "Maybe the takeaways will be our only hope."

"Surely not," Eleanor said.

Eddie looked positively gleeful at the prospect.

At that moment a new model car pulled up beside the curb. A neatly dressed man in his late fifties slid from behind the wheel with a bundle of letters in his hand, bound for the nearby post box.

"Ah," Eleanor said, "this looks like a local. Let's ask him to recommend us somewhere. Excuse me," she said to him, "would you take pity on a poor group of out-of-towners and point us in the direction of somewhere to have dinner?"

The man turned his still handsome face toward Eleanor who, as usual, looked like something out of a Vogue magazine for the older person. He smiled.

"Oh, poor bereft out-of-towners, is it? Washed up on the foreign shores of Brookfield?"

"Just for the night," Eleanor replied, and told him briefly about the tour.

"Most interesting. And so you were hoping to fortify your souls with a hearty meal before setting off into the wilds of the countryside tomorrow were you? In Brookfield? On a Sunday night? You certainly know how to have an adventure, that's for sure."

"So there's nowhere open?" Eleanor asked, looking a little crestfallen.

"Almost nowhere. The only place apart from the takeaway you just passed, and the one further down the street, is the little dining room at the pub. That's another two minutes' walk in the direction you're headed. The food is pretty simple - steak, chicken, salad and fries, perhaps a baked potato if it's a red letter day - but it's nice enough and the lady who runs the establishment is very friendly. That'll be your best bet."

"Thank you," Eleanor said. "Most appreciated."

The man gave a little bow and a warm smile. "Always a pleasure to help a damsel in distress," he said before turning on his heel and heading back to his car. He drove away swiftly with the briefest of waves and a matinee idol smile.

"I'm starting to like Brookfield," Eleanor said, looking thoroughly charmed.

"Yes, well, it isn't every day you get called a damsel, that's for sure," Vi said, sending a glance of exasperation at Eddie.

"What?" Eddie said indignantly. "You haven't seen the other side of damsel since before that bedspread in our motel unit was made. Flash Harry. Come on. I want my dinner."

They found the pub just where Flash Harry had described it would be. The car park was quite full and in the main bar a noisy crowd jostled one another jovially. The group hovered in the doorway. If the crowd had fallen silent and stared at them all like some strangers appearing through the swing doors of a bar in a western movie, Lindsey wouldn't have been at all surprised. No one, however, appeared to have noticed their arrival until a lady with a large smile and even larger chest approached them to save the day.

"Meals, is it?" she asked knowingly. "Come right this way."

The five of them got settled. Looking around, there wasn't a sign of Simon, Andrew or Bianca, which made Vi speculate where they would be eating tonight. The buxom hostess supplied them with menus and took an order for drinks, then left them to it. The small dining room was plain in the extreme and very warm so Lindsey took her jacket off and put it over the back of her chair.

"Here we are then," Eleanor said as they got settled.

"Although quite where here is could be another question entirely," Eddie said.

"Brookfield's not to your liking?" Eleanor asked.

"Don't tell me you meant what you said about liking the place?"

"As a staging post for the rest of our holiday it's neither here nor there. It's a convenient place to stop for the night. All right, I admit that the Golden Sands does leave a bit to be desired and this establishment is a bit of a comedown from the meal we had at the Stansfield last night, but it has some rustic charm about it, wouldn't you say?"

"I'd say more rust than rustic, more farm than charm, but I suppose you're right. It is only for one night," Eddie conceded.

"I for one thought the day was very interesting," Cedric said.

As he finished speaking everyone stared at him as though daring him to mention one single thing about olives. Cedric went to reply but got interrupted by the arrival of a burly young man whose neck and head showed no definition between one and other. He appeared at their table, precariously balancing a tray of drinks. He wore a bored expression, as though the presence of these five strangers in his territory could not possibly add to his life anything worth knowing. He looked as though he had to resist the temptation to bang the drinks onto the table in silent protest at their intrusion. Instead he settled on grouping the drinks altogether in the centre of the table rather than ask which drink belonged to each person.

The young man turned on his heel and strode away. As he did so Eddie caught sight of something on the floor. He reached down to pick it up.

"Twenty dollars!" he said. "Fancy that. Half my luck."

Vi frowned. "I've seen that twenty before. Isn't that yours, Lindsey?"

Lindsey gave a little shrug then felt into the pocket of her jacket. The money had gone.

"Yes, it is mine," she said. "It must have fallen out when I took my jacket off."

"Hand it over, Ed," said Vi.

Eddie reached across the table. "I like a woman who knows how to throw her money around," he said with a wink as he handed the money back.

Lindsey colored. "Technically the money isn't even mine," she mumbled.

Eleanor laughed. "And I like a woman who knows how to throw someone else's money around," she said, ably taking the attention off Lindsey as everyone laughed.

They sorted out the drinks and Eleanor said, "Perhaps we should have a little toast before setting out on our adventure? Something to send us on our way on this voyage of discovery?"

"Good idea," said Vi.

"My ex-wife went on a voyage of discovery once," said Cedric, his expression wistful. "Actually I suppose it was more of a trip than a voyage, or then again, maybe sojourn might be a better description. Well, in reality I suppose it was more like a day excursion on a bus somewhere."

Everyone stared incredulously at Cedric. He seemed to have quite a talent for making statements that stopped people in their tracks. Lindsey didn't envy him that.

"Doesn't sound much like a journey to me," said Eddie. "What did she discover?"

"Oh," Cedric said loftily, "just that she was a manipulative, self-centered egomaniac and she liked it that way. Ironically, it took me years to find out about her."

Eleanor coughed. "Yes, well, I had been thinking of something more along the lines of a toast to the journey. May it be no less than you expect, and no more than you deserve."

The group raised their glasses and brought them together as one in the middle of the table, saying, "To the journey."

CHAPTER THREE

Breakfast got delivered to the motel room door at eight o'clock. The tray held a couple of miniature packets of uninteresting cereals that majored in bran and had scant acquaintance with anything as exotic as even a sultana. A small jug of milk, a pot of sweetened yoghurt and a slightly bruised banana fought for space with an ageing toast rack containing four triangles of toast. The toast had been cooked some time earlier and had since taken on a strange consistency of sponge rubber. The Golden Sands also seemed to have a great fondness for things in packets: jams, butter, Vegemite, as well as all the packets of tea, coffee, sugar and ultra high treated milk that sat permanently in a plastic box beside the in-room kettle.

A pale, silent girl with the stringiest hair Lindsey had seen in quite some time, delivered the tray without flexing so much as a single facial muscle. At the last minute she shoved a copy of the morning newspaper on top of the lot. After seeing the breakfast selection it occurred to Lindsey that the most nutritious item might in fact be the newspaper itself, or failing that the cardboard cereal packets. After making herself a cup of tea she settled on trying some of the toast thus giving her jaw quite an unexpected workout.

As instructed she presented herself to the mini bus at nine-thirty. Vi and Cedric already loitered. Vi had dressed in a voluminous pair of shorts and baggy tee shirt. Cedric wore another David Attenborough number, ready for safari. Vi stood guard over her luggage while Cedric had buttonholed Dennis. They were in the middle of an intense conversation whereby Cedric seemed to be doing most of the talking.

"Morning, love," Vi said cheerily.

"Hi," Lindsey replied. "All ready?"

"Ready as I'll ever be. The proof of the pudding will be in how things go today. Who knows whether the old pins have still got some life left in them?"

"I hope you'll be okay," Lindsey said with some concern.

Vi waved a dismissive hand. "Course. Don't tell anyone, but me and Eddie have been practicing. I've been making him take daily walks for a month now. Mind you, Christchurch is as flat as a pancake and there's always been the reward of a cream cake at the end for Eddie. But the point is, we're not quite as unfit as we appear."

Lindsey smiled. "Good. What's become of Eddie this morning?"

Vi grimaced. "Let's just say he's working off his breakfast. Between you and me it's a lot safer out here in the fresh air."

Eleanor opened her room door and waved across at them.

"Here we are, D-Day," Eleanor said as she joined them in the forecourt. "Sleep well, everyone?"

"I did," Vi said. "Must have been that plain food last night. No chance of indigestion after a meal like that."

"Indeed not," Eleanor agreed, "although perhaps the same can't quite be said for breakfast. If anyone didn't eat their toast the motel owners could always sell it off as boat ballast."

Lindsey and Vi laughed.

"What's the big joke?" Eddie said, appearing at Vi's side. He wore yet another contender for the World's Most Obnoxious Shirt Award. His legs had also taken on a fluorescent pink sheen, perhaps from sitting in the sun yesterday while the search party looked for Cedric.

"You," Vi said, elbowing him in his amply covered ribs.

"Not again," Eddie said, quite unruffled. "What's happening?"

"Nothing yet," Eleanor said. "Oh, here come Simon and Andrew."

The young men emerged from the motel unit and brought their luggage over to the side of the mini bus. As usual they kept a discreet distance from the rest of the party. Lindsey couldn't help feeling as though the pair of them had got in the wrong vehicle yesterday. They looked more suited for the ride heading to shoot pictures for a glossy menswear magazine. Both were dressed in shorts and polo shirts with sturdy footwear and sensible daypacks. Everything was immaculate, as though never worn before. They both had an affluent man-about-town sort of look incongruous with the wilds of Brookfield. Lindsey found them frankly intimidating. One thing they wore had not changed however. Simon's expression continued to be removed, almost hovering on the brink of unfriendliness. Andrew's guarded look spelled out a sense of caution. The more they kept themselves to themselves the better, she thought.

No sooner had Simon and Andrew appeared than Bianca emerged from her room and made a beeline for them. Lindsey suspected she'd been watching out of the window until she'd deemed it safe to emerge without fear of contagion. At the same time Dennis suddenly realized that everyone had assembled and managed to extract himself from Cedric's company.

"Morning all," he called, as jovial as ever. "Gather around, gather around. That's the way. Now before we set off I want to run through a few things so that we're all reading off the same page and know what's what. After all, we don't want anyone getting lost, do we?"

Numerous pairs of eyes swiveled in Cedric's direction but he appeared not to notice.

"Too right," said Eddie.

"Very good," Dennis continued. "Now, first things first. Who amongst you has a cell phone?"

Simon, Andrew, Bianca, Eleanor and Lindsey put up their hands.

"Fully charged?"

Everyone nodded except Eleanor.

"I plugged mine in to charge up overnight. Nothing happened. The socket must have been faulty. It's dead as a dodo."

"Right. For those of you without a phone I have some that I'll issue to you so that, should worst come to worst, you'll have a way of contacting me and we can sort out whatever you need. Perhaps Eddie and Vi, you could share? Cedric is already sorted but I'll come to that in a moment. That just leaves Eleanor."

"I don't really need one," Eleanor said. "I'll probably just stick with Lindsey. Well, if that's all right with you, Lindsey?"

"Of course," Lindsey said, intensely relieved. She'd been wondering how she would ask Eleanor if they could walk together without being too pushy or presumptive.

"Well, if you're sure," Dennis said. "For the others, I'll give you some operating instructions and a bit of a demonstration shortly. Next, I want to hand out the details for today."

Dennis reached into the front passenger seat and extracted a set of laminated sheets which he passed out to everyone.

"Each walking day I will give you a new one of these. They're laminated so that you'll not have difficulty should it rain. Nothing worse than having a soggy bit of paper as all that stands between you and getting lost. On the top of the page you'll see I've noted down my cell phone number and also that of a first aid person. We've never needed to use the first aid person in the past but in case something untoward were to happen on the walk you can call and the nominated person will come to your assistance."

"It's like being back on the plane again," Eleanor whispered to Lindsey. "Why does everyone feel the compulsion to tell you all the things that can go wrong before you've even started?"

"In this instance Cedric has volunteered to carry the first aid kit," Dennis continued, choosing not to acknowledge Eleanor's furtive whispering, "and he will aim to walk somewhere in the middle of the field. Should you require help, dial that number and that will connect with the phone I've issued Cedric - unless the emergency is dire - and he'll come to wherever you are."

"What's cell phone coverage like out here?" Andrew asked.

"Generally very good. Admittedly there are some black spots. If you can make your way to slightly higher ground you should be able to get service. Hopefully you won't need to worry anyway, but there's a lot of sense in being prepared for any eventuality. So, if you look down the page further you'll see a map of where you'll be walking today together with route information and points of interest. On the reverse side are some more detailed written instructions that will help if you can't find the right path, and failing that you can call me. Now, does anyone know the first rule of the bush?"

Cedric stuck up his hand as though they were at school but Dennis did not appear to notice.

"Never go in it unless you really have to?" Bianca suggested in heavily sarcastic tones.

Dennis gave a short laugh. "Yes, very droll. Anyone else?"

Cedric strained his arm up higher without response.

"Take something warm to wear?" Vi asked.

"Good, yes, take something warm to wear. Hopefully you all read the literature I sent you before the tour and have in your daypack a jersey and a light rain jacket. We're not expecting to have trouble with either cold or wet, but you never know. As you're all New Zealand residents you'll know no one can guarantee the weather. Conversely, I hope you all have heeded my warning about the dangers of overexposure in the sun and have liberally plastered yourselves with a broad-spectrum sunscreen. Broad brim hats are also highly recommended. Especially you, Lindsey, I would have thought, with that fair skin and red hair of yours. Back to the first rule of the bush, though. There is one other thing. Cedric, perhaps you know?"

Cedric lowered his arm with an expression of relief. "If you get lost, stay where you are. Don't wander off or try to find your own way out."

"Yes, correct. Quite correct. Now we are not going to be venturing into any bush whatsoever over the next two weeks. We'll be in open country dotted with farms and houses, but nevertheless the same rule applies. If you really get lost, can't get the cell phone to work, lose your instructions or can't make head or tail of them - and you can't see any inhabited landmarks to head for - stay put and someone will come and find you. Understand? Under absolutely no circumstances should you try to find your own way if you are really confused. Got that?"

Everyone murmured assent.

"Furthermore, we all need to show respect for the land we are traveling across. Some of the route runs along quiet backcountry lanes but the majority of the walking will be over private land that we have secured permission to cross. As such it is vitally important that all land and property is treated with utmost respect. Most days you will be given a packed lunch to carry with you. Please do not leave any rubbish behind. Also, most properties are fenced. If you come to a gate and it's closed, you will need to open the gate to get through, but it is imperative you secure the gate behind you. Needless to say, none of us want to be responsible for freeing a stampede of cows, however inadvertently. Any questions about that?"

"Should we climb over the gates instead?" Eddie asked.

"If you think I'm doing any climbing you can forget it," Vi said. "And besides, have you looked in the mirror lately? I can't see you doing any climbing either, tubby."

"No, no," Dennis said briskly. "All the gates should be secured but otherwise unlocked. Just open the gate and shut it behind you. Now, there was something else. What was it? Oh, yes, that's right. When walking along any roadways, however quiet they appear to be, please walk on the right hand side of the road so that you're facing oncoming traffic. That's just basic common sense. Also, one last thing. If you do have any specific health requirements, anything you think I should know about, medicines you are taking, or allergies that might be relevant, please let me know before we set off. All information will be treated in strictest confidence. All right?"

Everyone nodded. Lindsey found herself increasingly daunted by the possibility of all that could go wrong.

"Fantastic. On a lighter note, today's destination is a place called Christian House, which is about ten kilometers as the crow flies from the drop off point on a road that runs east of Brookfield. Christian House is a charming homestead set on a vineyard. As you'll see from the information sheet, it's owned by a couple called Stuart and Allyson Green. They'll be expecting you toward the middle of the afternoon and are preparing what I hope will be a sumptuous feast for you all this evening. Now are there any questions?"

"Do we have to stay together?" Bianca asked.

"By all means, if you want to stay together that would be great," Dennis replied, deliberately misunderstanding the thrust of her question, "however in the past we have found that individuals have their own pace. It may not be realistic to stay together all of the time. I'm sure that, after a few days, the group will take on a rhythm of its own. Anything else?"

The group waited speculatively for someone to speak but when everyone remained silent Dennis beamed at them all in his trademark way and said,

"Right then, without further ado, let's get going."

It took twenty minutes to reach the drop off point, with just one stop at a bakery in Brookfield to pick up the packed lunches that Dennis had ordered. Eleanor expressed relief that their lunch for the day was not being provided by the Golden Sands, an establishment to which none of them would ever willingly return. Dennis then headed the bus north and drove for about ten minutes before turning off at a signpost that indicated the start of Churchman Road. This road immediately narrowed. The ribbon of tarseal that stretched before them lacked a centre white line. It had dense grass verges running along either side, suggesting the presence of ditches. As the bus was wider than a car Lindsey could not quite imagine what would happen if they met oncoming traffic. Dennis seemed unconcerned and only altered his speed when the road began to twist and turn as it threaded out eastward toward the coast.

Once again very little conversation passed within the confines of the bus. Everyone seemed content to nurse their own thoughts, keeping them firmly to themselves. Once or twice Lindsey thought she heard Bianca turn and say something to Simon and Andrew but if they replied Lindsey did not hear. She noticed that Vi had become obsessed with her daypack which she picked up, delved into, then put down again only to repeat the whole process again a few moments later. Lindsey herself could get quite fidgety when especially nervous but for her the hard part appeared to be over for now. The thought of a day out in the countryside with Eleanor for company seemed a welcomed prospect.

After a further ten minutes of winding this way and that, up and over a few modest hills, the road straightened again, running through a stretch of flat farmland dotted with grazing cattle. At the far end of this the bus crossed over a one-lane bridge, rose up over another hill and dropped down on the other side. They slowed beside a tidy house on the left hand side of the road. The entrance to the property was marked by a set of gates and a wide entranceway into which Dennis maneuvered the mini bus. He brought the vehicle to a stop, climbed out of the driver's door and came around to open the passenger door.

"This is it folks," he said, sticking his head through the doorway. "All out who's getting out."

Everyone filed out of the bus and waited on the gravel driveway. Dennis caught sight of a woman coming from the house and went over to talk to her. The woman greeted Dennis like an old friend, eager to talk. The group stood out of earshot but it seemed clear from the amount of gesticulating that there might be one or two last announcements before they set off. Meanwhile everybody shuffled uneasily. They weren't sure whether to wait - like athletes poised for the starter's gun - or to forge ahead and get going.

"Right then," said Dennis, returning to the group, "everyone happy? No last minute questions? Doreen, she's the farmer's wife, says that you shouldn't encounter any foreseeable problems while you're on their land. Your route today will take you across about five kilometers of their property. She said the low rainfall of late had made the ground firm and dry. They've got the majority of their stock over more toward the main road so you shouldn't encounter too much wildlife of an agricultural nature. So if you're all fine, you walk straight down here like it shows on your map, then veer right at the first gate. Bon voyage, and see you at Christian House."

Eleanor smiled at Lindsey.

"Here we go then," she said. "Ready when you are."

"All ready," Lindsey replied.

They all started walking as one group. Simon and Andrew led the way, followed closely by Bianca who had to work hard to keep up with their longer strides. Cedric kept casting glances at them all, evidently taking Dennis's words about staying in the middle of the pack quite literally. Lindsey and Eleanor followed with Eddie and Vi at the rear. Vi kept stopping every few feet to adjust the shoulder straps of her daypack. With the added weight of lunch these seemed to be sitting in the wrong place.

The sky stretched overhead, a palette of blue, intense right above, fading to the palest baby blue toward the horizon. Small groups of clouds trailed across the sky. They reminded Lindsey somehow of dawdling school children doing their best to pass by without the slightest bit of haste. Before them lay a grassy paddock at the end of which lay the familiar sight of the sort of wire fence with which rural New Zealand is embroidered. Beyond this lay a pine forest to the left. To the right, where they were headed, rolling pastureland appeared to stretch on without end. In spite of the recent lack of rain the hills were still dappled in shades of green that subtly altered as the terrain rose and fell. It seemed clear that if the dry spell continued the grass would soon dry to an earthy brown.

By the time Lindsey and Eleanor reached the gate at the far end of the pasture the group had strung out considerably. It would not be long before the front group disappeared from sight altogether. Cedric's head had become a swivel. His gaze went forward and back as he struggled to fulfill his duty as first aid officer. Eddie and Vi had dropped back some way. Vi appeared to have conquered her bag problems and had taken on the appearance of a dogged packhorse. Eddie puffed away by her side, his face hued with a sweaty tinge. Vi had assured Lindsey and Eleanor that they were happy to take the walk that their own pace, and that neither woman should be too concerned for the well-being of the indomitable Mr. and Mrs. Jones.

"Smell that," Eleanor said at length. "Good, hearty farmland."

Lindsey nodded. "I can't get over how peaceful it is."

"You will let me know if you want to stop and sketch at any time, won't you?" Eleanor said. "I don't mind in the slightest. After all, we're in no great hurry."

"No, that's fine. You're very kind to mention it."

"Not at all. I'm delighted to have your company and am happy to fit in with you, especially given the fact that you've come with a purpose."

"Right at the moment it doesn't feel as though it matters much. In fact I can't imagine wanting to do anything at all for a day or two. I thought I'd just take everything in at this stage and simply see."

"Do you know what you're looking for?"

"More or less. I've already worked quite a bit on my story outline so need to find some drawing inspiration to fit in with that. It'll probably be one of those 'know it when you see it' sort of things."

Eleanor nodded. "Don't hesitate to shout out at any time."

"Thanks. I appreciate that, and your company. Likewise, do let me know if there's anything special you'd like to do. It would be great if we could stick together."

"I couldn't agree more. Somehow - and this is no reflection on your fine company - I do not relish the alternative prospect of being paired up with either Cedric or Bianca. Wouldn't you agree?"

Lindsey grimaced. "They both seem such intense people in their different ways. I feel certain Bianca and I won't have much in common. I do feel for Cedric, though."

"Really?"

"He reminds me of me, in a way. He's socially awkward, but you can tell that underneath it all he wants to fit in. I just think he doesn't know how."

"You could have something there. I must say it came as something of a surprise to hear that he'd been married, although perhaps slightly less of a surprise to find that it hadn't lasted. He strikes me as the sort of man who would still be living with his mother, unable to free himself from the comforts of home and wanting nothing more than to live a neat, tidy existence with no demands. He certainly didn't have anything favorable to say about his ex-wife."

"I don't suppose many people do."

"That's true, but not always. I think sometimes people come to the realization that the person they married wasn't the person they thought they were. Or the reasons for being together simply aren't there any more. That can make parting a lot less unpleasant. Like many things in life, your outlook can be largely governed by your expectations. I know that was certainly the case in my marriage."

Lindsey wasn't quite sure what to say. She did not want to pry, but in the end asked, "You're divorced?"

"Oh, yes. Donovan and I divorced twenty years ago."

"And you parted amicably?"

"Absolutely. He came from a very affluent background, you see, so we had no need to argue about money. Sebastian was twenty when our divorce got finalized, and already off at University. There were few of the ties that bind."

"You must have married quite young."

"Indeed. I was twenty-three, and Donovan almost twenty-six. Our families had known each other forever in a distant sort of way. He was dashing and handsome and everything a girl could want, including financially secure.

He entranced me. And of course at that age I thought I knew everything. In those days the pinnacle of a girl's ambition lay in securing herself a husband, settling down and producing offspring. And while that does sound remarkably pleasant in a Jane Austen sort of way, reality proved a little different."

"In what way?"

"Like I said before, it all has a lot to do with expectations. I expected our marriage to be a partnership, to enjoy spending time together and raising our children together. I expected we would enjoy a good social life and be as solid and secure as our parents before us. Donovan, on the other hand, expected he would be able to please himself, make arbitrary decisions and carry on a bachelor lifestyle. I found trying to reconcile those two approaches to the same marriage most exhausting and, ultimately, a fruitless waste of time. So you see, when it came down to it our parting was amicable. In the end we both gained what we wanted: our freedom."

"You speak of it so calmly. I'm sure it must have been painful at the time."

Eleanor shrugged indifferently. "Not really. The thing with Donovan is that he's a mirage. I thought, I *assumed*, that there was more to him that met the eye. I thought he was young and carefree. In fact this jocundity just masked his shallowness. He still is shallow, truth be told. He's become, by all accounts, an ageing Lothario, the sort of man that sends shivers down your spine and makes decent men lock their daughters up at his approach. No substance to him. Actually, I suspect our Miss Caton is much the same sort of person. All glitz and glamour on the outside, as deep as a puddle on the inside."

Eleanor and Lindsey came to the end of yet another long paddock bordered by the now familiar sight of wire fencing. Here a stile had been installed. The wooden steps latticed through the wire, with a large wooden pole in the middle, anchoring everything together and providing a sort of handrail. Lindsey went over the stile then waited as Eleanor did the same.

Eleanor jumped back onto solid ground and gave a little grimace.

"Stiles were definitely not invented for grandmothers," she said. "I hope Eddie and Vi manage that all right. Vi's legs aren't very long and you heard what she said about climbing."

"Do you think we should wait for them?" Lindsey asked.

They both looked back across the ground they had just covered. Eddie and Vi were nowhere in sight.

"No. Let's press on. They said not to worry about them. We should take them at their word. They've got the cell phone if anything is amiss. And don't forget we could always dispatch Cedric to look for them if needs be."

"They seem such a nice couple," Lindsey remarked.

Eleanor gave a short laugh. "Yes, indeed. What you'd call salt of the earth. I wouldn't mind betting though, that Eddie gave Vi a run for her money in his younger days. Now, where do we head for next?"

Lindsey extracted the laminated instruction sheet from her daypack. "According to this map, I think we're here. See the little symbol of the stile. From here we're supposed to climb this ridge and drop down on the other side where there should be a little stream."

The first hill of the walk lay before them. It challenged them to come forth and demonstrate what they were made of. The contours of the land looked as though a giant piece of green velvet had been thrown over carelessly piled objects. Lindsey and Eleanor spent some minutes consulting the map and, in the absence of any defined trail, they considered the best way to tackle the ridge.

"No sign of anyone before us, is there?" Lindsey asked.

"None at all. I guess we can only assume they've already dropped down on the other side. It's a wonder Cedric hasn't positioned himself at the top to watch out for us stragglers."

"True. Are you ready?"

"Yes," Eleanor said, stoic in the face of their first real challenge "ready when you are."

The ascent wasn't as difficult as it looked. The hillside proved to be threaded with tracks made by farm animals. One track flowed naturally to another and within ten minutes they had reached the top. The view before them was worth the climb, revealing more of the same rolling countryside before them, with a larger hill, perhaps a small mountain, now prominently visible on their left toward the far horizon. A distant view of a thin sliver of azure sea could be seen on their right.

Eleanor and Lindsey stopped for a drink and to consult the map again. As indicated, they could see a babbling brook flowing gently between the ridge on which they stood and the next ridge across. Their intended path took them down into the valley and then led them back up again across this second ridge.

Lindsey turned around and gazed back down across the flat farmland they had just crossed.

"Look," she said. "Isn't that Eddie and Vi?"

"Where?"

"About half way along that last paddock before the stile. See?"

"Oh, yes. I'm not sure how I could have missed them. You can clearly see Eddie's loud shirt from here. In fact I wouldn't be surprised if you could see that shirt from space."

Lindsey laughed. "At least we know they're okay," she said.

"Too true. They seem like they're making steady progress, albeit a bit slower than the rest of us."

"I wonder how far ahead the others are."

Eleanor looked at her watch. "I can't say I feel overly concerned about any of them. Maybe we could stop at the bottom of the hill and have lunch by the stream. I don't know about you but I'm beginning to feel a bit peckish."

"Good idea," Lindsey agreed. "That might give Eddie and Vi a chance to catch up a bit."

After stowing away the map and drink bottles they began their descent into the valley, finding it much tougher going downhill than up. Lindsey took much greater care where she put her feet. Although the stock tracks were still helpful, they had a habit of coming to an abrupt end and leaving no clear way forward to proceed at all. At one point both Eleanor and Lindsey lost their footing on the tussocky grass that seemed to lend itself to helping the unsuspecting tramper on their downward path, whether they wanted the help or not.

At the bottom they found a spot under a tree and sat down to eat their lunch. Eleanor eyed the sandwiches and cake she extracted from the lunch bag dubiously.

"Oh dear," she said. "I certainly hope this is not Dennis's idea of gourmet food. I know that having this sort of thing bouncing around in your pack does nothing for it in terms of presentation but to be honest I'm not sure we would have been that impressed anyway."

Lindsey's sandwich hung limply in her hand. "I know what you mean. Perhaps we'll need to stock up on some muesli bars and fruit if this sort of thing continues. What's in yours?"

"Egg, by the looks. Yours?"

"Same. Too bad if you don't like egg."

"Eat the cake," Eleanor suggested. "At least that might give you a bit of a sugar rush to get you up that next hill."

In the end there seemed little choice but for Eleanor and Lindsey to try to make the best of their lunch. They swapped best and worst food stories. Eleanor, with her years of overseas living, had many tales to tell. They were glad of the shade of the tree. The ridge on either side provided shelter from any sort of breeze and the summer sun beat energetically down upon them. Occasionally the sound of a skylark could be heard, or the drone of a bee. Otherwise they were quite isolated from the world in as pleasant and peaceful a spot as you could hope to find.

As they talked Eleanor and Lindsey both kept a lookout for Eddie and Vi. Finally, after about twenty minutes, the figures of Eddie and Vi appeared at the top of the ridge. Eleanor and Lindsey waved vigorously and eventually Eddie and Vi spotted them and waved in return. It look another fifteen minutes for the pair to make their way precariously down the side of the hill to join them at the bottom. They both threw themselves down onto the ground with gusto, looking thoroughly exhausted.

"Bloody mountain," Eddie said disparagingly. "Who put that there?"

Eleanor smiled indulgently at him. "You made it, though, didn't you?"

"Too bloody right. You don't think I'd let a thing like that conquer me?"

"Good on you. You all right, Vi?"

"I will be, once I catch me breath. I thought coming down would be the easy bit."

"It was hard," Lindsey said to her. "I nearly slipped."

"We both did," Eleanor confessed.

"Had your lunch then?" Vi asked.

"Such as it was," said Eleanor.

"Eddie ate his ages ago."

Eddie's expression was indignant. "I was starving."

"You can have my egg sandwich," Lindsey offered.

"Could I? Are you sure?"

"Of course."

"What did you eat?"

"My cake and the banana from breakfast. Something made me stow it away at the last minute. Probably the fact that I was raised to never waste anything."

"More than most young folks these days," Eddie said. "How far do you think we have to go?"

Lindsey picked up the map she'd been perusing earlier.

"As far as I can see we have to go up and over this second ridge, then drop down and cross the last of the farmland until we reach this road shown here. We follow the road for a couple of kilometers then go cross-country through another farm for about a kilometer. That should bring us out at the back of the vineyard. I'd say we're about half way right here."

"I suppose some of those youngsters are there already. Probably keen to cadge for free samples of wine and outstay their welcome before the rest of us arrive."

"We were thinking of heading off soon," Eleanor said. "Do you want us to wait for you?"

"Certainly not," Vi said with fervor. "We'll be right as rain once we've had a bit of nosh and a rest. No hurry, is there, if we're already half way?"

Eleanor and Lindsey exchanged glances. In spite of her bravado Vi looked far from fresh.

"You're sure?"

"Course. Now get going, you two. We'll see you there."

At the top of the second ridge Eleanor and Lindsey paused once again to take in the view. The climb had been steeper than that of the first ridge but once they had found a rhythm, the climb to the top didn't seem so bad. The sense of achievement at having made it was compounded by the land-scape that lay before them. Rather than being confronted with the sight of yet more rolling hills both Eleanor and Lindsey were surprised to find that the land tapered off in a gentle slope from the top of the ridge, converging somewhere in the hinterland into flat ground which stretched for miles in an easterly direction.

The land had been put to good use. From their vantage point the two women could see the end of the farm they had been crossing, bordered just as the map said by a snake of black road. Beyond this lay the sight of more farmland. In the distance lay their destination, bordered by swathes of neat, orderly rows of grape vines. Lindsey pointed out what she assumed to be the roofline of Christian House, set in the middle of the vineyard. Eleanor smiled happily at the sight and hoped for better things than they'd experienced at the Golden Sands.

Before they set off toward the road, Eleanor and Lindsey turned around and looked back over the way they had come. They were struck by the contrast of the view looking north against the landscape of the south. It was almost as if they were crossing the border from one country to another, swapping farming for agriculture of an entirely different kind. They waved in case Eddie and Vi were looking but got no response. Vi appeared to be packing up and making preparations for their departure.

Half way down the slope, on their way toward the road lay a small grove of native trees. As they neared they were surprised to find Bianca sitting there with one shoe and sock off, massaging one of her toes. Her expression was far from pleased.

"I wondered when you would get here," she said huffily. "I've been waiting for ages."

Eleanor raised a sculpted brow. "I hadn't realized we would be so sought after. Had a small problem with your foot?"

"Bloody blister. It's giving me hell."

"Have you called Cedric? I must say I'm surprised not to find him here. He strikes me as the type to take his responsibilities very seriously."

"I told him to get lost. I'm not having that ridiculous buffoon touch me," Bianca snapped. "Do you think I'm entirely mad?"

Eleanor's expression suggested that, given half a chance, she would very much like to tell Bianca exactly what she did think of her.

"You don't have a plaster with you?" Lindsey asked.

Bianca turned her attention to Lindsey, giving her the sort of assessing glance that made Lindsey feel as though she ought to have asked for permission to speak.

"No. Surely that's perfectly obvious."

"I've got some," Lindsey told her taking her daypack off to fish them out.

"What happened to Simon and Andrew?" Eleanor asked. "I thought you were walking with them?"

Bianca tossed her head petulantly. "Those two are just the icing on the cake as far as this trip is concerned," she said, her tone vehement. "Bloody poxy tour. What have we had to endure so far? Cramped mini bus trip, the world's most boring stop at that olive dump - made worse still by that idiot disappearing up his own arse - a night in the most hideous flea-infested motel this side of the equator; vomitous food. And then, to top it all off, as though the rest of it hadn't been bad enough, it appears as though the only two interesting and single young men on the tour are as gay as a picnic basket."

"Really?" Eleanor asked. "You think Simon and Andrew are a couple?"

"Of course. Either that or they're so up themselves it's not funny. If their noses were any higher in the air they'd be breathing ozone. Both of them have got the conversational skills of cattle. They certainly made it abundantly clear that they want to be by themselves. What else can one assume, short of outright asking them?"

A small stunned silence ensued. Eleanor looked thoughtful. The silence stretched on so long that Lindsey felt compelled to break it by lamely saying, "Here are the plasters."

Bianca took them wordlessly.

"I'm surprised a girl like you would opt for a trip like this," Eleanor observed at length.

Bianca paused in mid plaster application. "Opt? Yes, well, there wasn't a lot of 'opt' about it. I'm a travel agent. My boss, Austin, is a friend of Dennis's. *He* was supposed to come on this dung-ridden trip himself, to review it so he could recommend it to clients and help Dennis out. From what I can gather, De Vine Tours isn't exactly attracting the numbers or sort of client base Dennis had hoped for. Then, at the eleventh hour Austin's mother-in-law - who by the way he can't stand the sight of - got diagnosed with the big C. He had to pull out so he can be around to comfort his sniveling wife who doesn't know her arse from her elbow at the best of times."

"I see," Eleanor said. "So this is what, some sort of junket, for you?"

Bianca nodded. "With the emphasis on junk."

"What a shame," Eleanor said cryptically, her tone suggesting to Lindsey that the shame wasn't so much for Bianca but for everyone else having to put up with her.

Bianca ignored this comment. She focused instead upon putting her sock and shoe back on. She stood up and walked around experimentally.

"That feels better," she said. She bent to pick up her daypack. "Well, come on. Let's not waste time if there's wine to be drunk."

And with that she turned on her heel and strode away. Eleanor rolled her eyes and Lindsey grimaced but in the end there seemed little option but to follow her lead and head off together toward Christian House.

The three women had no trouble finding the driveway to the Christian House vineyard even though it appeared to be the back entrance to the property. As such it wasn't very well signposted. They entered the vineyard by way of a gravel service road that wove its way amongst the uniformly neat rows of grape vines that had been laid out with mathematical precision.

Lindsey could feel her excitement grow as she entered the property. Contrary to what she had told Eleanor earlier she found herself wanting to stop and investigate the vines more closely there and then. However, with the presence of Bianca to take into consideration, Lindsey baulked at the idea of stopping to slake her curiosity. The idea of having to explain herself to Bianca was more than Lindsey could stomach.

The service road took a meandering path westward before taking a sharp right at the brow of a small rise to higher ground upon which the homestead had been constructed. As soon as they turned this corner the house came finally into full view, surprising Lindsey with both its size and grandeur. The house was double storied with a high, pitched grey iron roof. It was built from unstained cedar that had weathered to a charcoal grey. The windows had wood surrounds, painted a smart white and the panes were checkered with latticed timber. To one side an addition had been tacked on, constructed from ochre bricks, out of which a chimney majestically rose.

At the turn, the service road divided into two. The left fork headed toward some outbuildings where the hub of wine production took place. The right fork lead toward the house. As they neared, the road swept into a crescent providing car parking, including space for De Vine's mini bus, which had arrived safely before them. From this point the road gave way to a path that meandered through immaculately manicured gardens toward a grand arched entranceway framed by pots containing topiaried buxus.

No sooner had they planted their feet on the welcome mat than one of doors flew open to reveal Dennis standing there grinning. A woman hovered behind him.

"You made it," he said like a proud father.

"We did," Eleanor said, swinging her daypack off her back. "Relatively unscathed."

"Great." He looked beyond them. "No Mr. and Mrs. Jones?"

"They're coming. They didn't want to overdo it by rushing. Last we saw they were on their way down the slope at the end of the farm, heading for the road. I'd imagine they'll be another half an hour to an hour," Eleanor said. Her gaze went to the woman in the background. "That should give you enough time to start brewing up the tea."

The woman smiled and stepped forward. "Welcome to Christian House. I'm Allyson Green. I'm sure you'd all like some refreshment after your first day of walking. Tea? Coffee? Wine?"

"Wine," Bianca said hastily. To Dennis she asked, "Have the others arrived?"

"Simon and Andrew arrived about three quarters of an hour ago, Cedric about fifteen minutes after that."

"And where are they?"

"Cedric is in the lounge clinging onto his cell phone in case any of you calls for assistance. Simon and Andrew have gone to their room I think. Getting settled I suppose."

Bianca sent a knowing look Lindsey and Eleanor's way as if to say, "I told you so."

There was a lull in conversation during which Dennis made proper introductions. They decided that all the women would like to be shown to their rooms first, freshen up then meet in the lounge for refreshments at a quarter past four.

Lindsey's room, like both Eleanor and Bianca's, was on the top storey of the house. It had a high, gabled ceiling, beautifully lit by the natural light coming in through the landscape window. It had been tastefully decorated in the same warm honey tones that spread throughout the house. Here and there this warm background color was lifted further by splashes of red cushions, or by intensely colored drapes. The main emphasis seemed to be on uncluttered luxury and sophistication, obliterating even the faintest memory of the Golden Sands in one fell swoop.

Lindsey gratefully freshened up and unpacked her daypack. She then spent some time looking at the artwork on the wall and at the small stack of house and garden magazines from the coffee table by the window. After having had such an enjoyable day - perhaps aside from the final leg of the walk with Bianca - Lindsey was finding herself more and more expectant about what the rest of the walk might hold. If Christian House was anything to go by it would be a real treat just to be allowed into homes such as this one and see what people had done with them. And then she would need to find time to look at the vineyard and get further inspiration for her book. Just looking out of the window at the sight of all those lovely rows of vines had her imagination buzzing in all directions.

At four o'clock she made her own way down to the lounge. She felt emboldened by the sense of comfort and wellbeing that the house, and the tour, had engendered within her. She took the main staircase down to the entrance foyer. An imposing set of double doors led into the spacious lounge in the opposite direction to the accommodation wing. The room was cavernous, the wooden vaulted ceiling two storeys tall, with the same warm light flooding in from high windows and from French doors that opened up into the ornamental garden. Enormous bookcases dominated each end of the room, crammed with books that must have taken a lifetime to collect, and with antique figurines and collectables.

Cedric entered the room and came over to stand by Lindsey as she looked at the shelves.

"How was your walk?" she asked.

"Very tricky," Cedric replied. "Those young men powered ahead and I didn't know whether to try to keep up with them or not. Then, when I decided to drop back, I discovered that young lady with her blister problem. She sent me packing even though I'm suppose to render assistance to the sick and infirm."

"Oh dear," Lindsey said. "How trying. Still, I guess you can only offer to help. If someone doesn't want that help there seems little you can do about it."

"I'm hoping Dennis will have a word with everyone," Cedric confided. "Just spell out a little more to everyone what my role is."

"Of course," Lindsey said, drifting off to look at some of the ornaments on the bookcase. There were a couple of figurines of waterfowl and one of a man lighting an old fashioned lamp. She carefully picked up a slender piece made out of some green material that Lindsey wasn't familiar with. It had the body of a woman and the head of a lion.

"I think they call that an amulet," Cedric said, coming up behind her. "It's made from a substance know as faience."

"It's so beautiful," Lindsey said. "And it looks so old. It's like something Cleopatra might have owned."

"Did you know that sometimes, when she was performing her royal duties, Cleopatra wore a fake beard?"

Lindsey looked at him. "Really?"

"I read it once," Cedric told her, as though that settled that.

Fortunately, Lindsey got saved from thinking up an appropriate reply by the arrival of Eleanor. In her wake came Eddie and then Vi, who was having a detailed conversation about footbaths with a sympathetic looking Allyson. She in turn came bearing a tray of coffee and cups. Lindsey couldn't help smiling to herself, amazed to discover how quickly she had come to make new friends of these people, and how pleased she was to see them. It had been a long while since she had put herself outside of her comfort zone. But right now, at this moment, she felt extremely glad she had.

CHAPTER FOUR

"Do your shoes feel tighter today?" Vi asked Eleanor as the majority of the group set off the next morning down the main and much more impressive driveway of Christian House, bound for unknown territory. Overhead the sky was a faint eggshell blue, the same color as Vi's accursed shoes. The air echoed to the sound of gravel crunching beneath their feet.

"You know, I think you might be right," Eleanor replied. "Maybe our feet have swollen after yesterday's exertion. Or maybe we've all put on weight after that gorgeous dinner last night. It might've gone straight to our feet. Have you developed any blisters?"

Vi rolled her eyes as she adjusted her backpack for the tenth time in two minutes. She carried it like a dead weight. It might have been a sack of bricks, although she supposed that in some ways she had no one to blame about that but herself. Traveling with anything less than the kitchen sink made her very nervous. A person could never have too many "just in case" items, even if you ended up feeling like a Nepalese Sherpa as a result.

"I've got one blister the size of a pancake," she admitted. "Just awful. I've got four plasters on it."

"No wonder your shoes feel tight," Eleanor remarked.

"Haven't you got any?"

"Not a one. I've got these great shoes that I bought in Italy. They're real leather, softer than a baby's behind. I'm sure that must help."

Vi looked at Eleanor's shoes with envy. They seemed to be made of the sort of stuff proper gloves were made of, like kid. She glanced sadly down at her K Mart trainers and allowed herself a small sigh. Sometimes life with Eddie had its down sides, especially where synthetics were concerned. Still, he made her laugh. That's why she'd been attracted to him in the first place. There hadn't been a lot of laughing in her family home when she'd been growing up. There'd been three girls and two boys growing up in a two-bed-room house, a tyrant for a mother and a father with what today would be called "anger management issues".

People had said to her, what do you want to get mixed up with that Eddie Jones for, are you out of your mind, his family are nothing but trouble. That sort of thing. Vi's mum in particular had been most opposed. But Vi hadn't cared about that then, not even about what her mother had said. She still didn't care now. Through all their married life - all forty eight and a half years - Vi had never regretted her decision to marry Eddie even if living with him was like living with someone who forgot to grow up entirely. Sort of like having another child, she thought to herself, as she watched the back of his blue shirt emblazoned with logos of Maui as he walked ahead of her talking to that Cedric fellow.

"Do you have children, Eleanor?"

"I do. Well, not children, a child, and not that any more either. Sebastian just turned forty. He could hardly be classed as a dependent by any stretch of the imagination."

"Just one boy? That's just like Eddie and me. Fancy that."

"What's his name?"

"Jack. Jack Jones."

"Where does he live?" Eleanor asked.

"London. Out Ilford way. What about your boy?"

"London also. Chiswick, I think it's classed as. It sort of borders about four suburbs."

"Funny old place, London. Sometimes I miss it real bad. Other days I think I must need my head read just to've thought like that. Still, there's something about the place you were born and brought up, don't you think?"

"There can be. Perhaps men feel it more, especially English men with their strong sporting loyalties."

"What? Like football?"

"I was thinking of cricket. But when you mention it football is far more obvious. The amount of time and energy spent on sports is astounding."

"I know what you mean," Vi said. "Eddie could live at the South Pole itself and he'd still want to know whether Arsenal won over the weekend. Governments could come and go, royalty could be toppled and Eddie wouldn't really give two hoots. But if he misses out on the scores you'd think the world had come to an end. You should have seen the fuss when Jack announced he was going to be a West Ham supporter. As far as Eddie's concerned it's still the most incomprehensible, illogical decision of Jack's entire life."

"Men," Eleanor said, shaking her head. "They're like another species entirely, aren't they?"

Vi nodded. "You're not still married, I take it?"

"Long divorced. Every so often I meet someone who I think I could settle down with into my old age. But by the time you get as old as we are there's generally too much baggage to warrant the trouble and effort."

"Any grandchildren?"

"Just the one. He's called Edward. He's five and already thinks he knows everything. I absolutely adore him. You?"

"Two girls. Polly and Ruby. Polly is nineteen and training to be a beautician which, from what we hear, she'll be great at. Every photo we've ever had of her shows her plastered in feather boas or with more hair decorations than your average chemist shop sells or with great gobs of lipstick. Bit too fond of leopard skin print. Gor blimey, to think of it.

"Ruby is sixteen and wants to be an opera singer. Everyone in a four mile radius around Ilford thinks this is hilarious but more power to her I say, if she can make it. Course we haven't seen the girls for eight years, since we last went back, so she could sound like a strangled cat. But I hope she makes it. It'd make a nice change to see someone in the family make good."

"What does your Jack do then?" Eleanor asked.

Vi glanced toward the horizon. They had reached the end of the main driveway and turned right onto the roadway. They headed toward the coast so that the range of hills lying to the west were behind them, crouched like a sleepy dragon.

"He's a bit of a jack of all trades, if you'll pardon the pun," Vi told her. "He's always having brilliant ideas."

Eleanor's eyebrows arched with comprehension. "Quite the entrepreneur?"

"Yes, quite. What does your son do?"

"He's a barrister."

"Oh," Vi said. She paused. "How far are we walking today? Did Dennis say?"

Eleanor shrugged. It was the sort of effortless gesture that only women like Eleanor seemed capable of. It made Vi feel distinctly dumpy.

"I tuned out a bit," Eleanor said apologetically. "I'm sort of relying on Lindsey to take notes for us. Perhaps it says on the map."

"I'll ask Eddie." Vi sped up. "Eddie, Eddie, where's that blooming map

Dennis gave us?"

"What d'you want it for?" Eddie asked over his shoulder.

"I want to know how long today's walk is."

"Blimey, don't tell me you've had enough already?"

"Course not. Does it say how far on the map?"

"Dunno," Eddie said, passing her the laminated sheet. "Take a look for yourself."

Vi peered at the map but it seemed impossible to decipher, especially while walking.

Eddie said to Cedric, "I suppose you're a dab hand at map reading."

"I did a cartography course once," Cedric told him. "Most interesting."

"Perhaps you can help the missus out with how far today's walk is, then."

"Certainly." He adjusted is own map so Vi could follow. "See here. That's where we are now, just leaving Christian House Vineyard. And over here, toward the west, is where we are heading. See that little series of concentric circles? That denotes Te Rongopai Peak."

"Oh," Vi said in a small voice.

"If you look up at the landscape, you can clearly see Te Rongopai Peak there in the middle distance. Redpath Lodge - our next stop - is at the foot of that peak."

Vi looked dismayed. "But that looks miles away! And if we are heading west, why are we walking east at the moment?"

"Because this road feeds down to another road which takes a far more north westerly direction than if we went west from here. This road that we're on runs south west to north east, so if we had turned left at the bottom of the driveway instead of right we'd be going back the way we came, not forward."

Vi shook her head. "But how long?" she pressed.

"That depends on the speed at which you walk and the amount of time you stop for breaks on the way."

"Gordon Bennett man," Eddie said. "Give the woman a break. Can't you generalize?"

Cedric shrugged indifferently. He studied the map some more. "I'd say, by the scale at the bottom that we've probably got about twenty kilometers to travel today, some on the road, but the majority across farmland. Which, if the topography on this map is right, as is my own observation of the lay of the land, should be fairly easy walking. No hills like yesterday."

"There we go, Vi," Eddie said encouragingly to his wife. "Just twenty little kilometers between you and the next slap-up feed. And we're staying at

Redpath Lodge two nights so you'll be able to rest up on the day in between. Not only that, as Cedric says, we're walking across a lot of flat farmland. Nice, safe, solid pasture. We'll be there in no time."

Cedric dropped back a pace to fall in line with Lindsey. Almost as an aside he said to Lindsey, "I suppose now would be the wrong time to tell Mrs. Jones that farmland can be far from safe. It's a known fact that you are far more likely to be attacked by a cow than by a shark."

Lindsey grimaced. "It's probably something best kept to yourself," she said.

"Yes, I suppose so. Most elderly women seem to be naturally squeamish. Take my mother for example. She's a strong, proud Presbyterian woman but show her a spider and she becomes hysterical. I've tried to explain to her about how incredible spiders are, how useful they are for cleansing the air of unwanted flying insects, how they are amazingly creative. Did you know, for instance, that no two spider's webs are the same?"

"I didn't."

"It's true. But does Mother appreciate this? No. Instead she shrieks and wails and demands that I drop whatever I'm doing and come and rid the house of the spider straight away."

"Isn't that a little inconvenient?"

Cedric dropped his voice again. "Truth be told I do live with my mother," he said. "Since my father died it seemed only sensible to live under one roof what with both of us being on our own. Why pay two lots of rates and phone and power when we could pay one?"

"Sorry to hear about your father," Lindsey said.

Cedric waved a hand. "It's all water under the bridge now. He passed away sixteen years ago."

Lindsey glanced at his profile. It had begun to occur to her as she regarded Cedric's thin, almost pinched face and his fine boyish hair that stuck up at the back, that a person's inability to be truly independent could take many surprising forms. Perhaps she wasn't so different from a lot of people after all.

"Yes," Cedric said, resuming his former train of thought, "I always find it quite astounding what people assume to be safe. For instance many people are apprehensive about flying yet in terms of transportation it's one of the safest ways of traveling. In reality, more people world-wide are killed annually by donkeys than die in air crashes."

"That's bollocks," said Bianca, stepping forward a pace to join in the conversation.

"No," Cedric said, "it's perfectly true."

"World-wide perhaps," Bianca said scathingly, "in somewhere like Guatemala or Zambia or Azerbaijan, but not in New Zealand. How many people do you think are killed annually by donkeys in cities like Auckland, Wellington or Christchurch?"

"Admittedly not very many," Cedric conceded.

"Try none. That would be more accurate."

"But doesn't Cedric have a point about the flying as well?" Lindsey said, feeling a sudden brave need to stick up for him.

Bianca looked at her as though she was crazy, but then gave a shrug. "I suppose in one way. As a travel agent I can assure you that I have never lost a client yet, not from any sort of overseas misadventure, let alone a plane crash, and definitely no donkey injuries in sight."

Cedric looked unperturbed. Lindsey felt Bianca pull her on the arm so that the two of them stepped to the back of the group, away from Cedric's listening ears.

"That guy's a fruit loop," she said. "You want to watch him."

"He's all right," Lindsey said. "He certainly knows some interesting things."

Bianca rolled her eyes. "You need to redefine your idea of interesting. Seriously. Now, what I want to know is, where are Simon and Andrew?"

Lindsey had no idea. In fact she hadn't seen them since yesterday. Neither of them had come to the dinner last night, nor breakfast this morning. Neither had appeared at the rendezvous time for departure this morning. Dennis had been so businesslike about giving them their marching orders for the day that no one had dared ask about their whereabouts.

"Do you think they've called it quits?" Bianca asked. "Maybe they've decided the walk is not for them and Dennis has had to take them somewhere so they can get back to civilization. God knows, I can see why. If I didn't have to be here I'd make tracks as well. This party is about as lively as something growing in the refrigerator. There might be life present, but it's old, moldy and very, very cold."

Lindsey sighed. "I really couldn't tell you what's become of them," she said, "but to be honest I can't think of anywhere right now that I would rather be."

Except, Lindsey thought, away from Bianca Caton.

Unlike the previous day, the group - minus the missing duo of Simon and Andrew - stayed together for the morning. Everyone seemed strangely reluctant to make a break from the others, perhaps, Lindsey thought, for fear that they would be stuck with someone on their own. Bianca had made it clear she did not want to be on her own with Cedric. Lindsey did not want to be without Eleanor and Eleanor did not want to be on her own with Bianca. Eddie and Vi did not want to be without each other. Cedric simply did not want to be on his own at all and in consequence seemed happy to talk to anyone about anything.

They paused for about ten minutes to have a drink and a bit of a breather at the point where their path left the road to once again cross farmland. As soon as Eleanor made a move to pack up - maybe with the futile hope of being able to take Lindsey with her and make a run for it - everyone else hastily began stowing possessions and zipping bag zippers.

It was a perfect day for walking. As the morning had lengthened the sun shone more intensely. A zephyr blew in from the northeast to take the edge off the heat, bringing with it a delicious and tantalizing hint of the sea. On the odd occasion that conversation petered out between the various group members the air was redolent with the sound of birds. At times, when they passed by thickets of bush or near strings of fencing, they were serenaded by chirping cicadas. The fragrance of grass and the distant smell of gorse filled the air. They experienced the occasional whiff of odors that reminded them about the realities of farm life and animal husbandry.

At midday, when Eddie started looking lavishly at his watch every two minutes and Vi started fidgeting again with the weight of her pack, Eleanor took pity on them and suggested a lunch stop for all those that were interested. Everyone agreed with alacrity. They'd reached the top of a gentle slope on the crest of which stood a copse of native trees that masked the fact that the land fell away more sharply on the other side. After pausing to look at the view they all found somewhere to sit in the lee of these trees overlooking the rocky outcrop.

From their vantage point, Te Rongopai suddenly loomed larger. Cedric pointed out that they could see in the distance yet more uniform rows of vineyards snaking down some sloping terrain toward the foot of the peak.

Cedric also said he was certain he could make out the outline of a building which he presumed to be the homestead of the Redpath Lodge Vineyard to which they were headed. Predictably, no one else could make out a thing.

As lunch concluded, Eleanor once again set the pace by beginning to pack up. This caused another flurry of activity, especially from Vi who had unpacked almost the entire contents of her bag in the course of the half hour stop. She'd confessed to Lindsey that she felt sorely tempted to take her offending shoe off and take a look at how things were progressing with her blister but was very much afraid of not being able to get her shoe back on as a result. Lindsey had seen her delve into her own little first aid kit four times. She'd even consulted Cedric with all the solemnity of a doctor's appointment for his advice as First Aid Treatment Officer, as he had dubbed himself.

When everyone had readied themselves to set off Eleanor suddenly discovered her own shoe problem, a very perplexing event considering the reliability and comfort of her Italian shoes. She thought, upon consideration, that she might have been unfortunate enough to have taken on board a foreign body and would perhaps need to remove her shoes.

"No, don't wait," she said to everybody as they watched and waited for both diagnosis and treatment. "I don't want to hold you all up. Just carry on and Lindsey and I will catch you up shortly."

Lindsey breathed a sigh of relief at her invitation to remain behind. She watched as the others all hesitated, uncertain whether to heed Eleanor's advice and continue or to make an issue out of it and stay. In the end Eddie gave a shrug and said his farewells, which prompted everyone else except Lindsey to follow in his wake.

Eleanor and Lindsey watched them go. When the group had made their way across the outcrop to where the land fell away less sharply Lindsey turned her attention to Eleanor's shoe. Eleanor bent over and fiddled with the lace, then glanced up at Lindsey and said,

"Are they gone yet?"

Lindsey looked over her shoulder. "They're practically at the bottom of the incline. Why? Do you want me to call them back? Do you need Cedric?"

"The FATO?" Eleanor asked incredulously.

"What?"

"FATO. F.A. T. O, or First Aid Treatment Officer as Cedric likes to call himself."

Lindsey regarded Eleanor's face trying to work out if she was joking or not.

"Relax," Eleanor said to her, continuing to play with her shoelace, "I neither need nor want the FATO. In fact I neither need nor want any of them altogether."

"Do you want some help getting the shoe off?" Lindsey asked.

Eleanor laughed. "Whatever for? There's nothing wrong with either my shoes or my feet."

"But you said..."

"I said what I said because I thought it was high time you and I had a break from the rest of them," Eleanor said, straightening up and giving away all pretence of a problem, "especially that Bianca with her pseudo-sophistication and self-aggrandizing."

"So the shoe problem was a ruse?"

Eleanor grinned. "Completely and utterly. What do you think? Was I convincing?"

Lindsey smiled back. "Very. I fell for it entirely."

"Good. That should buy us some time to let a bit of ground stretch between us and them. I don't mind Eddie and Vi really, but walking together like that had begun to get on my nerves. I came to enjoy the peace and tranquility of the countryside and to learn more about New Zealand wine. I didn't come to hear how Bianca's beauty therapist said she had the most naturally clear skin of any client she'd ever treated. Nor did I need to hear that her daddy still gives her a clothing allowance even though she's working because less senior travel agents - she couldn't bring herself to say the word junior - were grossly undervalued when it came to remuneration."

Lindsey felt relieved to hear of Eleanor's antipathy, not because she liked the thought of any people not getting on, but because a part of her had been afraid that Eleanor, herself a very elegant and sophisticated woman, might find Bianca's worldly and confident approach more to her taste.

"She hates Cedric," Lindsey observed.

"She would. Admittedly Cedric does go on a bit but there's no need to take such a dislike to the poor man."

"I suppose it must be difficult for her, what with having no choice to be here," Lindsey said.

Eleanor scoffed. "Difficult? I can't say I'd mind a job where the boss sends me off on a two week holiday all expenses paid, would you?"

"I suppose not."

"She should be grateful if you ask me. Mind you, I think that boss of hers needs his head read, emergency or no emergency. He's supposed to be doing his friend a favor by trying out the tour with a view to promoting it to his clients, isn't he? So either Bianca is a good actress at work and doesn't show her true colors - which I personally find very hard to believe - or he's not a very good friend to Dennis. If Bianca carries on moaning the way she's been doing, it would have been more of a kindness to have pulled out from the trip altogether rather than send an over-critical egomaniac who doesn't know which side her bread's buttered."

"Perhaps it's not so much the tour as the tour party who have let her down," Lindsey suggested.

Eleanor stood up and laughed. "Well, I'll give you this much, if there's any possible redeemable reason that Bianca could be excused for her behavior, you'll think of it."

Lindsey looked apologetic. "Sorry," she said. "Force of habit."

Eleanor appeared to be about to reply when something over Lindsey's shoulder caught her attention.

"Well, well," she said.

Lindsey turned and almost started when she saw Simon and Andrew crest the brow of the hill.

"Goodness," Lindsey said, moving to stand slightly behind Eleanor.

The two men saw Eleanor and Lindsey at the same moment. Lindsey saw an expression flick across Simon's face, as though he had quickly closed the shutters on himself lest they see more than they were entitled. Andrew appeared more open and gave a faint smile and a small wave.

There seemed little way of avoiding each other. It reminded Lindsey of characters in a Georgian novel trying to evade the making of a new acquaintance but knowing that, in the end, good manners would dictate over personal preference.

"Hello," Eleanor said as they drew near. "We wondered where you'd got to."

Andrew smiled, more warmly this time, and looked from one of them to the other. "We were a bit late starting out today. We were both interested in learning more about the vineyard. We asked Dennis if someone could spare us a bit of time to show us around before we left."

"Oh," said Lindsey before she'd even realized she had spoken.

Andrew looked at her quizzically. "Would you have been interested?"

"Oh yes," she confessed shyly, "but I suppose there'll be other opportunities along the way. I hadn't thought of asking especially."

He smiled kindly at her, his glance softly assessing. "We'll let you know next time, then." He glanced around. "You're on your own? Lindsey, isn't it? And Elaine?"

"Eleanor," she corrected.

"Right. Sorry. I'm Andrew and this is Simon. Still, I suppose you already know that. It's probably just me who's a bit hopeless with names."

Eleanor seemed on the verge of saying something cutting about not knowing their names because of keeping to themselves but she appeared to think better of it.

"Great day for a walk," she said. "How are you enjoying the tour so far?"

Simon and Andrew exchanged glances. "Let's just say that some things have not turned out quite as expected but that we are making the most of it anyway."

"I see," Eleanor said.

"And the others?" Andrew asked with a degree of haste. "Have you seen them?"

"We all set out together," Eleanor replied, "and only recently stopped for lunch. The others left about ten or fifteen minutes ago. We stayed behind to fix up a bit of a shoe problem and are about to get under way again."

"Nice vantage point for a lunch, don't you think, Simon?"

Simon gave a momentary glance at his friend which suggested he'd rather be boiled in oil than spend any effort on passing the time of day with an old lady and her timid companion, and that he couldn't really give a toss about the view. For one awful moment Lindsey thought he might actually give voice to such sentiments but in the end he gave a nonchalant shrug and said, "Here's good as anywhere, I guess."

Both men took off their daypacks as Lindsey and Eleanor donned theirs once more.

"See you at Redpath Lodge," Eleanor said. "Enjoy your lunch."

"Do you think we'll be disappointed by Redpath Lodge after enjoying Christian House so much?" Lindsey asked as they drew near to the property. About twenty minutes beforehand she and Eleanor had joined the main road after walking at a leisurely pace across the remainder of the farm they'd been crossing. Once or twice they stopped to examine various plants. Some grew in craggy uncultivated corners, which often bore flowers with the sort of wild, ethereal beauty you never saw in town gardens.

The road wound its way along the base of Te Rongopai between fields planted out in neat rows of vines. All burgeoned with clusters of dark purple fruit which, from a distance, looked the color of ebony. They were headed toward the main service road which coiled itself like a snake up the low reaches of the peak and which would take them to Redpath Lodge. To date they had neither seen the advanced party nor been caught up by the pair behind them.

"I suppose that all rather depends on what you expect," Eleanor replied. "I've discovered in life that a good deal of things can be ruined by unrealistic expectations, including events, people, houses, trips - and as I alluded to yesterday - even marriage."

"How so?"

"I find that anticipation often makes people imagine things that ultimately prove to be untrue. Take meeting a person for the very first time, someone you know quite a bit about but for some reason have never met before. Like a cousin or a pen pal, or these days perhaps someone you've met in some awful chat room. Beforehand, before the meeting, you'll spend time thinking about what the person will actually be like.

"Will he be as tall, dark and handsome as he says he is? Will he or she be an interesting conversationalist? What will we talk about? You'll picture yourself having mock conversations with this unseen person, based on assumption and expectation. Before you know it you've developed a whole catalogue of expectations. Of course, when the actual meeting takes place, if expectations have been too high, disappointment will be enormous. He'll turn out to be lanky rather than tall in the broad sense. Her voice might say all the right things but who was to know that she'd sound like a bandsaw? Who could have anticipated that annoying habit she has of trying to finish your sentences for you before you've stopped speaking after years of swapping letters where turn-taking is a necessary part of correspondence? See?"

Lindsey thought about this. "So is it imagination or expectation that's at fault?" Lindsey asked.

"A-ha," Eleanor said, "I see I've got a real thinker here on my hands. Great. You've surprised me. You see how wonderful lack of expectation is?"

Lindsey made a face. "It wouldn't matter much anyway," she said. "I'm rather used to not living up to the expectations of the others."

"Nonsense," Eleanor said dismissively. "That just says more about the person with the expectations than it does about you. Look at Bianca. She's hating this trip because of unrealistic expectations. The trip isn't at fault, she is. Even Andrew said the trip hadn't gone the way they expected and are they having a good time? Probably not. Perhaps they're disappointed because they expected others on the trip to be of their persuasion. I don't know. However I will say that I think Andrew seems to be managing his disappointment a lot better than Simon. Did you see his face? You have to wonder whether that man has cracked a smile in the last decade."

"I thought he looked tortured," Lindsey said. "He might just as easily be wrestling with a terrible fate or predicament without the slightest idea of what to do about it."

"Maybe he wants to break up with Andrew and doesn't know how to tell him," Eleanor suggested. "Maybe this trip is a last ditch effort to see if they can make things work between them."

Lindsey shrugged. "You didn't answer my question about imagination and expectation."

"No, quite right. That's a tricky one. When I think about it, I'd say imagination can be part of forming expectations, but not always. Take your original comment about Redpath Lodge. You wondered if you'd like it as much as Christian House. This involves comparison, taste and judgment rather than imagination. What you saw and appreciated about Christian House will be used as a measuring rod once you see the reality of Redpath Lodge. Christian House has set a standard or an expectation by which all other accommodation en route - perhaps with the exception of the Golden Sands - will be measured. No imagination required whatsoever.

"At other times, though, imagination does play a part. Take Andrew for example. I suppose it came as rather a surprise to find him so friendly. I imagined him to be quite different to how he came across. I had no point of comparison because I know full well that everyone is different. But based on the little I did know of him I expected something else."

"Like what?" Lindsey asked.

Eleanor waved her hand speculatively. "More reserve? Less interest in us? Less interest in wine making? More camp behavior? Perhaps all of these, and more besides. I certainly wouldn't have picked him as being gay if he'd been on his own. It's the old adage of never judging a book by its cover. Although in some cases, such as Miss Bianca, a picture can paint a thousand words. Oh, here's the road we need to take now, nicely signposted."

"According to this map, there's only one road anyway."

"I will admit odds like that shorten the chances of getting lost dramatically. Onward and upward then."

This road rose sharply at first then began to snake along the lower slopes of the peak. These shallow inclines had been extensively cultivated with vines, no inch left unutilized. Lindsey noticed that here, on the higher ground, the grapes that hung in perilously heavy bunches were green and not the dark purple they had seen earlier. She wondered if perhaps there was a difference in the suitability of the soils or whether the different variety merely indicated taste and range of production.

There seemed little sign of a homestead until Eleanor and Lindsey rounded a bend in the road. There before them lay Redpath Lodge, set below the road line on a surprisingly flat stretch of ground. Beneath the house and gardens the terrain fell away more sharply, subsiding into yet more neatly manicured rows of grapes. From a distance the house hardly seemed large enough to contain their tour party. As they neared it became apparent that the main house masked a series of outbuildings, one of which appeared to be a guest wing. Adjacent to the main lodge sat another smaller building set back behind the gardens that bordered an inviting aquamarine swimming pool.

The homestead had a grey long run roof that lay atop walls made of some sort of thick chalky looking stone that Lindsey had never seen before. As they descended the short driveway Eleanor and Lindsey came quickly to a cobbled pathway flanked by immaculate gardens that led around the side of the house. As they turned the corner the front entranceway came into view, canopied by a sharply pitched roof supported by massive wooden beams that had surely been recycled and saved from some previous occupation.

The front door sat ajar. Had Lindsey arrived by herself she would've hovered uncertainly on the threshold, not knowing whether to knock or ring a bell. Eleanor had no such qualms and led the way into the magnificent foyer.

"Hello?" she called.

Moments later a dark haired lady, perhaps mid-fortish, came out of a side room, a small white dog running at her heels, sniffing the air experimentally. She had a broad, open face that smacked of the sort of practicality required to run a vineyard with one hand and host accommodation with the other. She wore an apron covered in brilliant red poppies over her clothes and she came drying her hands on one corner of it.

"Hello," she said heartily. "Welcome to Redpath Lodge, ladies. I'm Pamela Gressingham." She wiped her hand some more then proffered it for them to shake. "Sorry," she said apologetically. "Occupational hazard. Don't want to cover you in tonight's dinner."

"Not to worry. I'm Eleanor Atkinson."

Pamela turned her sharp gaze onto Lindsey who muttered her name and gave her best attempt at a warm smile.

"Come through into the lounge. How was the walk?"

"Lovely. It's a beautiful stretch of countryside here," Eleanor said.

"Quite right," Pamela agreed, "although I find I have to make myself take time out to enjoy it. Otherwise it becomes rather like wallpaper. Life is often so busy that scenery - one of the very things that attracted us here in the first place - does start to assume quite a low priority. As you can see by the view from the lounge, the outlook is quite spectacular."

Lindsey turned to look out of the picture windows to find that from this angle the house appeared to be higher up the side of the peak than she had realized. The countryside stretched out before them glimmering in the afternoon sun. They could now see, ever so distantly, the sea on the horizon.

"Marvelous," Lindsey whispered, feeling sure she could never get tired of such an outlook, nor relegate it to the category of wallpaper.

"Have the others arrived?" Eleanor asked.

"A little while ago. I think by chance that Dennis drove past the point where you left Dyer's Farm to come out onto the road. They all hitched a ride with him the rest of the way."

Eleanor feigned outrage. "What cheats!"

Pamela smiled. "None of them seemed too concerned. The older woman, Vi I think she said, has been having trouble with her feet. I've given her a foot spa to ease the discomfort. Her husband said his legs had started to feel a bit like jelly and went off to have a lie down. Dennis has taken the other chap off with him to get more gas for the mini bus down the road a stretch. If you're looking for anyone, the only one around is the young woman. You'll find her out by the pool area. I'll take you out there as your accommodation is that way."

She led the way toward the far end of the room and out a set of bifold doors that opened out to the pool. There, as described, was Bianca. Rather than being in the water she had positioned herself on one of the loungers beside the pool donned in what must surely have been the most miniscule bikini in recorded history. She'd tied her blonde hair up with some sort of silky scarf and sported a pair of trendy sunglasses. She looked very much at home and very much like a Hollywood starlet. Eleanor simply rolled her eyes.

"Your rooms are side by side," Pamela said. "Dennis has already put your luggage in there ready and waiting for you. Make yourselves at home, especially as you're going to be here for two nights. The other young lady is

in the room next to this one, and Cedric the room after that. Dennis and
Mr. and Mrs. Jones are in the main house. The young men are in what we
usually call the honeymoon house, which is that small cottage adjacent to
the swimming pool.

"You'll meet my husband at dinner - he's called Keith - and if your luck
holds you'll completely miss the dubious honor of meeting our odious fifteen
year old son Alec, who will hopefully call me in half an hour to say he's staying the night at a friend's house. Just so you know where everyone is if you
need someone. I'll put out some afternoon tea in the lounge in about half an
hour but do give me a shout if you need something before that. You'll find
me in the kitchen working wonders with lamb, tomatoes and aubergine for
tonight's dinner."

With that she waved a cheery hand and disappeared.

Dennis explained to everybody - except Simon and Andrew who, although they had arrived, were predictably not expected to join the group
for afternoon tea - that the following free day would be theirs to do with as
they pleased but that the view from the top of the peak would be well worth
the investment in energy to get there. It was, he assured them, far from an
arduous climb. And with all day to make the ascent there would be no time
pressures for those that chose to make the journey. In fact, he went on to add,
the whole rationale behind having a two-night stop at Redpath Lodge was to
facilitate just such an excursion.

Lindsey and Eleanor stood at the back of the group where Eleanor had
been admiring the Gressinghams' array of collectables. She'd been quite tak-
en with a figurine of mother and child and with a pair of Japanese ladies
carved from ivory. Eleanor felt sure the pair would fetch a nice price if ever
be put up for sale.

"Are you keen on the climb?" Eleanor asked her.

"I'd like to see the view," Lindsey said.

"That settles it. We'll do the climb tomorrow. It shouldn't take all
day in case you wanted to have your turn at lazing around the pool like
Miss Caton."

Lindsey made a face. "I rather thought I might start on sketching some
of the vineyard if any time remained."

"Good for you," Eleanor said. "It's time you broke the ice. Which suddenly gives me an idea. Hold those thoughts. I need to speak with Pamela."

Eleanor darted off toward the kitchen and returned a few minutes later with a grin on her face.

"I just can't face the prospect of being stuck once again with all and sundry," Eleanor said, "so I've asked Pamela if she would mind packing us a little al fresco breakfast. Then you and I can set off for yonder summit as early as we please and avoid the madding crowd. I suppose if we were really keen we'd make the effort to be up there to see the sun rise. On the other hand I don't relish the idea of thrashing about on an unfamiliar hillside in the half dark, nor the idea of starting out too early on our day off, do you?"

"Oh no," Lindsey said.

"But you are keen?"

"Yes," Lindsey replied. "Very."

They met as agreed at eight o'clock when they could be fairly sure of not putting Pamela out too much, and to have the best chance of leaving before too many people surfaced and wanted to come along as well. Pamela greeted them with the same hale and hearty smile she'd given them yesterday when they'd arrived. She gave them a rough idea as to the easiest path of ascent and assured them at the same time that you really couldn't go too far wrong.

The morning was perfect. The temperature had already risen enough to make jumpers or jackets quite redundant. The air felt as fresh and as clear as they could want for such an event. They set off with a good deal of anticipation, retracing their steps up the driveway and along the road until they came to a cutting beneath a small plantation of pines, just as Pamela had described. This cutting led to a path that zigzagged from one side of the peak to the other, slowly climbing higher by degrees. The narrowness of the track meant that Eleanor and Lindsey had to walk in single file. They could see evidence of animal usage but today none were in sight. They kept up a steady pace, exchanging very little in conversation.

For most of the time the summit seemed out of view making it difficult to discern how much further they had to walk. They stopped periodically to look down and measure their progress, get their bearings and catch their breath. After an hour of concerted effort they finally reached the top.

The view was spectacular and worth every bit of energy it had taken them to get there. From this vantage point it seemed as though the land might be absolutely flat. All the contours of the ground had disappeared from their perspective. They could see in an entire three hundred and sixty degree arc. Although the clarity of the landscape became hazier the further away they looked, nevertheless the surrounding scenery stood out clearly, although in miniature. They could see the Lodge far below, dwarfed by the land in which it sat. They could see the vineyard spread out all around it and beyond that a patchwork of farms and agriculture interspersed with clumps of trees and dotted with houses.

To the west Eleanor and Lindsey were surprised to see that the land fell precipitously away down toward a creek that ran between the peak and another smaller range of hills that seemed to stretch away without end. A smattering of dirty white sheep could be seen in the far distance, proving that the land, though remote, provided rich pastureland for those livestock hardy enough to reach it.

Eleanor and Lindsey found the peak more exposed than the ground below and were pleased they had heeded Pamela's advice to take something warm to wear. It had seemed such a ridiculous notion. They found a spot by a congregation of large boulders. Eleanor observed that they reminded her of some of the circles of standing stones erected by druids in wilder parts of England. There they sat to enjoy their breakfast.

After they had eaten, Lindsey got out her sketchbook and tried to smother her feeling of embarrassment at the idea of drawing in front of Eleanor. As a general rule she preferred to make drawings with some detail, close-ups of flowers or insects, things she could pore over and bring to life. Landscapes, she found, were much more difficult. But here with such grandeur laid out before her, she wanted to try to capture the feeling she had of being just a speck in an awesome landscape.

At first Eleanor sat back in silence and closed her eyes, enjoying the warmth of the sun on her face. She paid no attention to Lindsey's work but after about twenty minutes she roused herself and came over to see what Lindsey had accomplished in that time.

"Oh," she exclaimed, "how lifelike. It could be a black and white photograph."

Lindsey grimaced. "It's not very good. I find the perspective required for landscape quite difficult."

Eleanor sat back. "It's better than ninety nine out of a hundred could do, whatever you say."

Lindsey turned her head to smile at Eleanor. "I'm sure you've seen some much finer talent in your travels."

"Finer? That's an interesting word to use. Anyway, how can a person compare art with art? It's all so subjective. What runs to the taste of one person could be entirely appalling to the next. Half the time a person's genius isn't even recognized until they're dead. I bet you've made more money out of your art than someone like Van Gogh ever made in his career. Look how much his works fetch now."

Lindsey made a face. "I think you overestimate my talent. Painters such as Van Gogh were doing something new, changing the face of art as it was known. I'd have difficulty changing a light bulb let alone art styles."

"Nonsense. Besides, like so many things in our world today, conventions are gone where art is concerned. Drawing something actually recognizable may one day become a dying art."

They fell silent. At length Eleanor said, "I find myself quite intrigued with you Lindsey McIntyre. How is it that a young woman of such extraordinary talent should be here on a trip like this all alone?"

"I told you," Lindsey said, not taking her eyes from the page before her, "I've ostensibly come to do research."

"Yes," Eleanor pressed, "but on your own?"

"You've come on your own," Lindsey pointed out.

Eleanor laughed. "Too true. But I'm good at being by myself, good at traveling alone and very practiced at being able to make new friends wherever I go. You, on the other hand, like safety and security. I would have thought you'd need a lot more than an excuse of research to get you out of your comfort zone."

Lindsey sighed and set down her work. She let her gaze drift off to the horizon.

"I suppose," she said, "that I'm a bit tired of being so dependent."

"Dependent? On whom?"

"Primarily my flatmates. On Robyn and on Will. Over the past few years they've become like my family. I've come to depend on them in ways I never could with my own family. But lately, with a lot of broad hints from Robyn, I've realized that in some ways I've become a burden to them. To Robyn, because I think sometimes she'd like to go and do other things, move somewhere else, have a change of scene. Yet her feelings for me hold her back."

"Feelings?"

"Probably sympathy. Hopefully not pity."

"And are you in need of sympathy?"

Lindsey held her breath. "Maybe that's the trouble. Maybe I've got used to sympathy as a way of life."

Eleanor shook her head. "What about your other flatmate? The famous Will, who's like the bag he lent you?"

"With Will things are much more complicated. In many ways he saved me. I will always be grateful to him for what he's done for me, grateful to both of them. But I sometimes wonder if he wants more from me, if he perhaps might be in love with me."

"And you don't feel the same way about him?"

Lindsey shook her head. "I love him, of course, as a friend. As for anything more, well, I wonder sometimes if I'm even capable of that sort of love."

"Funny," Eleanor said. "You appear to me to have an enormous capacity to love, borne out if nothing else by your desire to see the good in others, to make excuses for them."

"I don't know. That's not the same. That's more like a love of peace and a desire for people to not feel awkward about things that may not be their fault."

"Fault. Another interesting word. I dislike that word intensely. Admitting personal responsibility is one thing. Laying blame is quite another. In general most people use the word far more to lay blame than they do to own up to something."

"Yes," Lindsey agreed in a small voice.

"And would I be wrong in assuming that you have vast personal experience of this word in a negative context from when you were growing up?"

Lindsey felt her throat tighten. She nodded wordlessly.

"Your mother or your father, or both?"

"Both," Lindsey whispered.

Eleanor put a comforting hand on Lindsey's shoulder. "I'm sorry," she said simply. "Sorry to pry, sorry to be overwhelmed with even more questions, sorry to know that you've had to endure a difficult childhood."

"It's okay," Lindsey said. "Strangely, I don't mind."

"Perhaps we could talk more of this?" Eleanor asked.

Lindsey nodded.

"But not now, I think," Eleanor said. "If I'm not mistaken, here come the others."

CHAPTER FIVE

"I suppose there's a good chance the others will feel a bit put out that we came up here on our own without telling anyone what we were doing," Eleanor said as Dennis appeared over the brow of the hill, followed closely by Cedric.

Lindsey grimaced. "I hope not," she said, taking the opportunity to stow away her sketchbook before the group arrived in earnest and started asking questions.

"At any rate we could hardly be accused of making a habit of it - unlike some members of our group."

"Hmm," Lindsey said, "although unless I'm very much mistaken that looks an awful lot like Simon and Andrew coming into view behind Eddie, Vi and Bianca."

"Well, I'll be. Miracles never cease to amaze," Eleanor said as Dennis drew near. "Hello," she said to him. "Pull up some grass. You look done in."

Dennis flopped onto the grass with a great sigh. "Thank goodness," he said, wiping his forehead with the back of his hand. "That's quite some climb."

"I fear you need to spend less time mini bus driving and more on Shanks's Pony. My good man, I do believe you are unfit. Even Eddie and Vi look fresher than you."

Vi flopped down beside Lindsey. "I'm not so sure about that," she said. "I feel like my legs are all at sea."

Eddie joined Vi. He threw his stocky frame onto the grass in the same manner as an elephant might put itself on the ground.

"Blimey," he puffed, "I thought you said that walk was easy, Dennis."

"I may have to rewrite my tourist banter," Dennis confessed. "Either that or the hill has grown since I last made an attempt on the summit."

"You two ladies look as fresh as daisies," Eddie said to Eleanor and Lindsey. "But then I suppose you've had a while to recover what with sneaking off early like that."

Eleanor laughed. "Lindsey might be as fresh as a daisy being young and unencumbered by the ravages of old age. I see myself as being altogether too exotic a flower for such a description."

"Ha," said Eddie. "Too bloomin' right."

As they talked Lindsey watched the progress of the others. Cedric, none the worse for wear, prowled around the summit, taking in the lie of the land. Simon, Andrew and Bianca had also removed themselves some distance and were admiring the view. Bianca appeared to be trying very hard to provoke some sort of response out of either of them but for the most part her comments and observations seemed to fall on deaf ears.

"We were wondering where you two had got to," Vi said. "We're used to certain parties not turning up for meals but when you both didn't appear for breakfast I started to get a bit worried."

"Sorry about that," Eleanor said, sounding anything but. "Bit of a spur of the moment thing really. Up early, nice day, tempting hill. All a bit too much to resist really. And since no one else had surfaced Pamela kindly allowed us to take our breakfast with us. We set off without thinking past the moment."

Lindsey saw Eleanor's glance go toward Dennis, daring him to contradict her and expose their deliberate forward planning.

"Not to worry," Eddie said. "I prefer my sleep-in and my breakfast on a flat surface where I can butter my toast without worrying about half of it ending up on my trousers."

"Anyway, we're here now," Dennis said quickly, "and that's all that matters. And hopefully you'll all agree it was worth the effort."

Cedric came sauntering over, dressed in his usual safari uniform. Today he'd donned a khaki hat that wouldn't have looked out of place on some brigadier general in the armed forces.

"Do you know what the river is called? The one you can see over the far side?" Cedric asked Dennis.

"Not sure," Dennis replied. "I vaguely think it's called something like Lewis Creek but don't quote me on that."

Lindsey felt sure such a nebulous answer would do little to satisfy Cedric's insatiable need for detail. His desire to ask more questions got thwarted by a sudden gust of wind that removed him of his hat and sent him chasing as it rolled further and further back down the hill. Meanwhile, Simon, Andrew and Bianca had moved over to look at the westerly view. Lindsey could see Bianca had started to lose her enthusiasm for scenery.

Vi began to unpack the makings of morning tea to which Dennis added a thermos and tower of plastic mugs.

"Ah, good, a brew," Eddie said heartily. "Who's got the flaming tea bags?"

"Cedric, I think," Dennis said. "You might have to wait for him to come back from his wild goose chase so he can unearth them from his bag."

At that moment Cedric reappeared over the brow of the hill, hat clamped in his hand.

"Goodness," he said, "thought I might never see that again. I just caught it before it went over a bit of a bluff."

"Be careful, won't you?" Dennis said. "We've already lost you once. We don't want to do that again."

Cedric shrugged. "I would have just let it go. After all, it's only a hat. Not important in the scheme of things. Not as important as it might once have been. Did you know that in England in seventeen eighty-four there was a tax on men's hats? They had to have a stamp duty in the lining and if you were caught without it, you'd be fined. And, if you got caught with a forged stamp, you could be put to death."

"Like being caught these days without your proper car license and registration," Eddie said with a laugh, "although perhaps without the death bit."

"Just as well they never thought to introduce a similar tax for women," Eleanor grinned, "although I could imagine having to search a woman's brassiere for the correct stamp might have proved a popular job if they did."

Most of the group stayed on the summit until eleven thirty, enjoyed morning tea and generally relaxed in the summer sunshine. Simon and Andrew departed at eleven o'clock, apparently not finding anything worthy of sticking around. They had not deigned to get involved in the general chit-chat that passed amongst the others. Bianca had long given up attempts at witty and interesting dialogue. She'd since amused herself by making snide remarks every time Cedric passed comment on anything.

Andrew had a word with Dennis off to one side, yet another furtive chat involving lots of nodding on Dennis's side. Lindsey observed that Dennis's face betrayed little emotion during these conversations. He seemed neither concerned nor annoyed at the two men's deliberate isolation. Andrew, however, often looked very grave. He did not appear to be complaining, but his expression indicated things were not going at all well.

While Andrew talked, Lindsey also noticed that Simon held himself aloof. He stood as close to the edge of the cliff as possible without actually plummeting off. He'd fixed his gaze on the horizon and had his face turned as far from the group as he could. It occurred to Lindsey that perhaps he suffered from painful shyness. Yet the way he held himself and the way he dressed seemed to smack of confidence rather than social caution. She found him an enigma.

They took the descent at a slow pace. They had no need to rush and no desire to twist ankles or go flying. Lunch wasn't scheduled until twelve forty five and even at a slow pace the downward journey would not take anything near as long. The group stuck to the same stock tracks that Eleanor and Lindsey had taken on their way up so was forced to walk in single file and exchange only the briefest fragments of conversation. The wind had risen and literally snatched words right out of their mouths, with sentences whipped away before the hearer could make sense of them.

Dennis spoke most often, usually turning around to ask if everyone fared well or if anyone needed to stop to catch their breath. Everyone was fine. Eleanor whispered to Lindsey, when they paused to go down a particularly steep part of the track, that the only person who really wanted a break was Dennis himself.

They reached Redpath Lodge at twenty past twelve. Eddie declared himself ready to take his shoes off and freshen up. With that the group dispersed.

Cedric was the first person to make his way into the lounge as instructed, to await lunch. He'd always been a punctual person and sometimes found it baffling that people could be so entirely late for appointments and meetings, and generally be so unabashed about it as well. Lateness appeared to be a way of life for some people, but not for Cedric. He had never been particularly astute when it came to social matters. While some people treated the conventions of society with an astounding degree of lightness, such rules were one of the few things that made Cedric's life in this sense workable. What had happened on that first day - with him getting sidetracked at the olive orchard - had been an exceptionally rare occurrence for Cedric. He continued to find the whole incident entirely mortifying.

Why other people did not feel the need for conformity he did not know. These days the whole world seemed full of non-conformists who positively reveled in freedom from convention. Those two young men for instance, Simon and Andrew. Cedric couldn't understand how they continued to be so bad mannered as to reject the company of everyone at every meal and every event aside from this morning's walk. Did they not worry about offending the feelings of others? Did they consider themselves in some way superior to the rest of them? Even worse, did they not even consider the others at all?

Cedric had tried to engage the dark headed one, Simon he thought it was, in conversation on the top of Te Rongopai Peak this very morning. He'd got nothing more than monosyllabic replies for his efforts. Cedric thought he might be interested to know - when Simon had given a cough - that coughing releases an explosive charge of air that moves at speeds up to one hundred kilometers an hour. But Simon had just looked at him, without any words whatsoever, so that Cedric felt like he was being held like a piece of meat on a skewer, an object only for scorn or consumption. It had been an eerie sensation to be thus regarded. Cedric had been relieved beyond measure when Andrew had turned from talking to Bianca to draw Simon's attention away.

Which reminded him of the other difficult person on the trip: Bianca. In Cedric's view she was of the very worst sort of female, the type that delighted in making men like Cedric feel as worthless as last week's washing up water that someone had neglected to throw away. He knew there wasn't any way to please such a person, nothing he could possibly think to say or do that would make himself rise in her estimation. Cedric did not really mind the thought that Bianca would never be a friend but he did wish that she might think more *of* him so that she might say less *about* him.

As a general rule Cedric had discovered early on in life that most people found it only too easy to spot the faults of others while being seemingly oblivious to their own shortcomings. Cedric had often wondered whether his mother had not been the worst offender in this respect. If not her, then definitely his former wife, Anne. It seemed a shame that people could spend more time criticizing than they did looking for the good in people, especially in a case like this, after such a short acquaintance. He supposed he should be used to it by now, at the ripe old age of forty-eight. But he wasn't, and knew he never would be.

Cedric had often wondered whether he'd have made a good parent. Perhaps he could've put his energies into protecting a child from the sorts of harmful things that had blighted his own life. Or maybe he would have been a complete failure, finding himself as incapable of defending a small person as he did himself. He presumed that it would not have been so difficult when the child was indeed small - with such open minds and hearts - but he suspected his own heart would have quailed at the prospect of an older child. A child such as the one here, the son of Pamela and Keith Gressingham.

Cedric had seen the boy being dropped off from a car at nine o'clock this morning. Eddie and Vi had been finishing breakfast. Bianca had flounced into the breakfast room and taken off with coffee some time ago. Dennis had gone in search of Simon and Andrew to tell them about the summit walk. Eleanor and Lindsey were conspicuous only by their absence. So Cedric had been exploring the front garden by the driveway to fill in time. He had been slightly screened by a row of head-high pittosporums and had thus been unseen by the lad as he exploded out of the car that pulled up. The appearance of someone with peroxide blond hair glued into a mohawk of spikes, wearing nothing but gothic black and a frightening array of body piercings, would have shocked Cedric had Keith not intimated over dinner the previous evening that all was not well with the boy. What could a parent to do with such an alien creature, Cedric wondered? If even bold, sensible people such as Pamela and Keith could not tame their own offspring, what chance would Cedric have had?

Cedric looked at a couple of figurines of some Oriental ladies. He then put his hand out onto a delicate figurine of a woman accompanied by a small boy. The beautiful piece seemed so evocative of all that was good and pleasing of parenting. No, when all was said and done Cedric knew he should be relieved that such a task had not fallen to him. He knew in his heart of hearts he would not have been equal to it.

Pamela, while clearing up the lunch remnants, found herself having similar sentiments. She wondered how it could be that any sane person would willingly choose parenting as an option. It had proved to be a minefield of endless demands and relentless ages and stages, each of which seemed to bring with it something more pernicious than the age and stage before it. Most people struggled to keep up commitments like gym memberships or sticking with their New Year's resolutions more than seven hours after the stroke of midnight. Yet those very same people - she and Keith included - launched themselves headlong into parenthood as though it was easy as pie.

Looking back through the telescope of time Pamela felt hard pressed to imagine any two people more idealistic than she and Keith had been. Neither of them had had much exposure to babies before Alec arrived. And although rose-colored glasses had no doubt put a rather contented glow on proceedings, neither of them had done very much to really consider if parenthood was for them. In fact Pamela distinctly remembered friends of theirs, people they had long since lost touch with, complaining about the woes of small children. She'd been singularly unimpressed with such an attitude.

"You'd think they'd be grateful to have such a gorgeous pair," she had said to Keith, high on the fumes emitting from her fast-whirring biological clock. "All that grizzling and groaning about the demands of parenthood, the horrors and the deprivations."

"I know. I'd say that if they applied a little more discipline and put more effort into curbing some of that youthful enthusiasm they might enjoy the experience more," Keith had heartily agreed.

"Never was a truer word said," Pamela replied. "I would never allow a child of mine to behave that way. And to get so cross about something as trivial as dropping a drink. You could see it was an accident. No, if you ask me those two are just a couple of killjoys and that's all there is to it."

Oh how naive they had been. Naive to think that they would be any better parents than anyone else who had gone before them. Those who had discovered the intractable will of a two year old, the caprice of three, the independence of four, the aloofness of five and the grossness of six - not to mention every other age into eternity. Naive to think that all the thrills and spills of a child would be handled with serenity and calm, that voices would never be raised, tempers never frayed, patience never eroded.

Now Alec had arrived at fifteen and proceeded to mooch about like an extra from a Bela Legosi movie. His body - that Pamela had nurtured and fussed over for years - had been positively harpooned with piercings, his hair rigid with adhesive, his expression equally super-glued into an unpleasant sneer. His friends were similarly attired, their taste in clothes and music and language so entirely designed to provoke and offend that no one in their right mind could understand the attraction of such choices. And just which parent on earth was equipped to deal with that? Certainly no person Pamela knew.

But then she and Keith's enthusiasm for parenthood had been paralleled in their desire to grow grapes and make wine. Accordingly they'd launched themselves into their new profession with huge idealism, limited knowledge and a dismissive attitude toward critics and detractors alike. There again they had discovered some of the pitfalls of viticulture the hard way. Who knew the relentless power of the mealy bug or the phylloxera? Or that powdery mildew would be so determined? Or that the soil in some places on their land would require such intensive nutrient replenishment? Who knew that some years the yield would be too great and others too small? Or that marketing and diplomacy and accountancy were almost as valuable as the ability to withstand the vagaries of both the weather and people's tastes?

Pamela certainly wouldn't have foreseen that extra income - such as they were receiving from having groups like that of De Vine Tours - would come in handy in lean times. And she'd never have predicted the need to whip up lunches of breads stuffed with hummus, sun-dried tomatoes and rare roast beef, or summer noodle salads or shortbread shaped like vine leaves. It had never occurred to her that one day someone else, namely that most unappreciative and undeserving young woman called Bianca, might be sitting beside her pool, on her favorite lounger, in her courtyard while she, Pamela Joy Gressingham, cleaned up sodding lunch dishes with one hand while busily planning the next eating extravaganza with the other.

No, out with idealism and in with realism, she decided. She was well and truly past the age of pretence. The trouble, though, lay in Pamela's nostalgic feelings for idealism. She'd become altogether heartily sick of realism with all its endless reminders of imperfection. Too much more realism and Pamela would have to tell Keith that she was resigning. End of story.

"I see you've made yourself comfortable," Eleanor said to Bianca as she came into the pool area.

Bianca looked up sharply. She had not heard Eleanor coming and felt caught out, as though discovered doing something wrong. Bianca heard something elusive in the tone Eleanor used with her. It implied, yet did not voice, criticism. So far Bianca had not heard Eleanor use that particular tone with any of the other people on the tour, not even that idiot Cedric, although even she must surely recognize the man to be an absolute imbecile.

"I'm perfectly entitled to sit by the pool," Bianca said, unable to stop herself from sounding defensive. "After all, we have got a free afternoon."

"I'd have thought you would have work to do," Eleanor said. "Some report to write, some facts and figures to jot down for when you give your boss a debrief on the trip. After all, from what you said, I assumed you were to all intents and purposes actually working."

Bianca felt herself gritting her teeth. More implied criticism. Bianca only wished she could think up something stinging to say - some vindictive little retort - but Eleanor appeared above all that sort of thing. The woman, for her age, was gorgeous. She evidently had money and style by the truckload and was smart and savvy too. There wasn't anywhere to go with someone like that. And she had the truth of it. Bianca was being paid to be there, like it or not as the case had turned out to be. Everybody else had forked over hard-earned cash for the dubious honor of being here.

Bianca decided to strategically change the subject. "Where have you come from?"

"I went for a quick stroll with Lindsey after lunch then popped in to see if Pamela wanted a hand with the dishes."

Great, Bianca thought. Bloody Mother Theresa to boot, not to mention more implied criticism because Bianca hadn't thought to do the same herself. As if she would.

"Haven't they got an industrial strength dishwasher?" Bianca asked. "Surely they must."

Eleanor's expression was less than impressed. "Of course they have," she replied, "but there's no harm in asking. Besides, Pamela and I had a very nice little chat about family and the like."

"Where's your offsider?"

"Lindsey? Oh, I'm not sure. We're catching up later, at afternoon tea."

"I'm surprised she can move without you," Bianca said. "I'm not sure I've ever met anyone so mousey and inconsequential."

Eleanor's face darkened. Bianca realized she had probably gone too far and held her breath waiting for a tirade of abuse. Yet moments later Eleanor's expression changed from anger to condescension. "Well, you know what they say, Bianca," Eleanor replied. "You truly can never judge a book by its cover."

And with that Eleanor turned on her heel and walked away.

Eddie felt strangely restless after lunch while Vi declared herself to be utterly done in. She wanted nothing more than to alternately lie on the bed then soak her feet for the rest of the afternoon. Eddie wondered if he might be ailing for something since ordinarily the thought of a couple of hours sprawled out on the bed for a bit of a kip was a recipe for success in his book. Maybe, Eddie thought, all the exercise and fresh air he'd been getting had done something to him. Having had a glimpse at the concept of fitness, his body had reacted with a desire to do even more, rather than the less it had been determinedly used to.

Eddie decided not to get too carried away. He felt the need to circumvent any idea his body might have that would ultimately need curbing once he and Vi got back onto home territory. This ruled out going too far afield. But Eddie thought he might just have a snoop around the outbuildings further down the hill from the main house and see what he could see. He followed the driveway down to where the ground leveled off. The first building he came to was used for vehicle storage. A quad bike sat next to an idle tractor. Around the walls of the building the Gressinghams had stowed an enormous array of paraphernalia: netting, raincoats, an old scarecrow propped up in one corner, tools, some sort of triangular things that looked like bird houses, a couple of old oak wine barrels.

Next door lay the main building. From the outside it looked like a garage, only with a very high ceiling. The enormous doors of the building were pulled across to reveal a sea of stainless steel, virtually from floor to ceiling. Eddie didn't need to be a scrap metal dealer to know that serious money had funded the equipment, the vats and pipes and other machinery. The place looked clean enough for a surgeon to operate. It was completely devoid of workers and as such had a cold, echoing feeling about it.

Suddenly a door on the right opened, taking Eddie by surprise. Keith Gressingham emerged from what appeared to be the winery office. He likewise seemed momentarily surprised to see Eddie hovering uncertainly, but he soon recovered himself and came over.

"Just having a bit of a nosey round," Eddie said by way of explanation. "Never been up close and personal with the business end of wine making before," he added with a laugh. "I'm much more familiar with the other end of the operation, if you know what I mean."

Keith laughed. He was a big man, even by Eddie's standards. He had a slightly weather-beaten face, perhaps from spending too much of his life out of doors. In spite of his outward pleasantness and obvious success it struck Eddie that Keith was a man who had paid for that success with something from within him, something fundamental that had now gone and would probably never return.

"Yes, I've had my fair share of experience with that end of the proceedings myself," Keith said. "It's either a perk or an occupational hazard. I've haven't quite decided which yet."

"Definitely a perk I would have said," Eddie replied.

"Ah," said Keith, "easy to say when you aren't constantly assessing what you've produced, wondering if it's going to quite be good enough. Now Eddie - it is Eddie, isn't it? - you somehow don't strike me as a wine person. How long have you been interested in wine?"

Eddie guffawed. "Yep, it's fair to say I'm more of a recent convert to wine. I suppose in the past I've been something of a lager lout but it seems to go straight to my stomach these days so it was suggested I make the move to the fruit of the vine. Wasn't too keen at all, truth be known, but if I'm going to do anything at all I like to do it properly. No half measures for Eddie Jones. In for a penny in for a pound."

"Of course," Keith said. "Do you fancy a tour?"

"What? Around this shed?"

Keith nodded.

"That'd be great," Eddie said.

"You'd better come this way then," Keith said. "I'm sorry that you won't be able to see the wine making process in progress but we're still a few weeks off harvesting. If you were to come back then this place would be humming."

"I suppose that wouldn't be a good time for you and your missus to be having guests, though," Eddie said, trailing after Keith with his long strides.

"Quite right," the big man said. "It's all hands on deck in harvest time. Any houseguests would either be expected to pitch in or be left to their own devices. And between you and me I would not like to see the look on Pamela's face if I suggested having people to stay over harvest time."

Eddie smirked. "She'd give you a run for your money, I expect," he said.

Keith raised his eyebrows. "Somewhat. Let's start over here, shall we? Now did you know that red wine and white wine are made in slightly different ways?"

"No. I suppose I just assumed you used different grapes."

"Certainly. Anyway, with white winemaking the grapes are either picked by hand or they're picked via a mechanical harvester. If picked mechanically the grapes are put into this machine to be crushed and the stalks separated."

"It looks a bit like a giant dishwasher," Eddie commented.

"Ha. Yes, it's actually called a Crusher de-stemmer. The crushed grapes then go into this separation tank where they macerate for a few hours."

"Macerate?"

"Soften up by soaking, I suppose."

"A bit like brewing tea?"

"Perhaps. After that the macerated grapes are put into a fermentation vat here. See this stainless steel tank here? Meanwhile, handpicked grapes are pressed then put into barrels for fermentation."

"Do you do much hand picking? Eddie asked.

"A bit. The end product is usually destined to be much more delicately flavored, and therefore more highly sought after."

"You mean more expensive."

"Ultimately. From my point of view I find making wines from hand-picked grapes far more satisfying in the long term. It calls for creativity, perhaps even artistry. Anyway, next the wine goes over here to this storage and blending unit, then to these refrigeration tanks which is very necessary to avoid crystallization. From there it's on to the filtration unit to get rid of residual sugars and yeast. Basically anything that might otherwise cause further fermentation once bottled, which is the next step over here."

"Blimey. It's quite a business. What about red wine?"

"Much the same, just a different order. We put the grapes into the crush de-stemmer, then to the fermentation vat with their skins, then to the bag press to separate wine from skins, then into oak barrels. Later we filtrate the wine, but less vigorously than with the whites, then bottle. As simple as that."

Eddie raised his eyebrows. "I bet it's not as straightforward as it sounds."

Keith laughed. "You've got that right. I could talk for hours about temperature control, pumping techniques, fermentation options, carbon dioxide blankets, tasting, testing, acid reduction, blending, filtering, maturing, the science of oak barrels, the works. There's a huge amount to know and learn about viticulture before you even get the raw materials to make the wine. I've learnt so much over the last few years. To be honest I've got to the point where I've decided I'll never know all there is to know and understand about this business."

"Bit like the scrap metal business," Eddie said, casting an adoring eye over all that stainless steel. "You wouldn't think hunks of old metal would be that complicated, but you have to know what compounds are in what, know what's worth a few bob and what's not, even know a bit about metallurgy itself. Sometimes you have to be able to tell at a glance what's what without giving the game away too much, if you know what I mean, and know where you can flog stuff on once you've purchased it. It's a varied and ever changing market, that's for sure."

"But you're retired now?"

Eddie smiled. "Mostly," he said. "Let's just say I keep my eye out wherever I go just in case I see something that takes my fancy that might make me a quick dollar or two. No harm in keeping an eye, is there?"

Keith laughed. "No harm at all," he said.

Lindsey had waited for the heat of the day to ease before heading out from the house toward the vineyard itself. It had given her a chance to rearrange her suitcase within which her clothes had seemed to take on a life of their own, evidently preferring entwined communion to orderly separation. Eleanor, she knew, was taking advantage of the afternoon off to write a letter or two to some friends overseas, in case they had the chance to post anything as the journey continued. She would then have a short siesta, followed by afternoon tea at four-fifteen. Lindsey asked Eleanor to make her excuses if she didn't make it back. Now, at three forty-five, she very much doubted she would.

Lindsey had taken out her sketchbook, double-checked she had sufficient sharpened pencils then slipped out of her room. She avoided the pool area in case Bianca - or any of the others - might waylay her or ask questions as to where she was going. She then headed down the slope toward the vines.

As soon as she dropped down onto lower ground the heat of the day intensified. She left behind the cooling breeze on the heights to walk through the sheltered air amongst the vines. Glancing back up at the house, Lindsey realized she needed to put a bit of distance between herself and the homestead. She walked her way right through one section, across the neatly mown grass access way that divided one plot from another until she found a spot almost at the far end of the second section. There she found a place that seemed just right to her, where the grape vines grew richly. The verdant leaves cast a canopy over the grapes that hung deliciously in their semi-ripeness, plump and firm and exactly as they ought to be.

Lindsey settled herself in a position out of the full sun yet not so much in shadow as to make accurate drawing impossible. For a while she just sat, looking, thinking, breathing, listening. She felt her heart rate slow. As she relaxed she heard beyond the rhythm of her own breath the sounds of countryside: birds singing, the odd cicada chirping, distant noises of machinery. It was the time of day when bees droned drowsily on the afternoon breeze, when animals were still and restful. In a setting such as this a person could almost believe that all was right in the world. And, if you looked hard enough, a person might indeed see a magical folk who lived in the boughs of the vine, with their own lives and loves and challenges.

Caught up in the moment of her imagination Lindsey began to draw, her pencil moving on the paper as if by its own volition. She had no need of an eraser. Her eye translated for her hand, her glance going from branch to paper, branch to paper, a line here, a shade there, until slowly the sketch of the bough began to take shape.

At times Lindsey closed her eyes so that she could picture words, characters and illustration all coming together into one. It was at just such a time that a new and unfamiliar noise came to her attention so that her eyes snapped open just in time to see Andrew come into her view at the far end of the row of vines. He saw her at precisely the same moment. Both were momentarily taken aback to see one another. Lindsey left hand flew to still her heart that had started pounding wildly.

"Oh," Andrew said, "sorry to startle you. If I had had the least idea you were there I wouldn't have given you such a fright."

Lindsey gave a shy smile. "I didn't expect anyone to be out here so far from the main house."

Andrew grinned. "Neither did I," he confided.

For a few moments they were silent. Lindsey found she could not think of anything intelligent to say, but she didn't seem to be able to drag her gaze away. Andrew's expression was unreadable. Lindsey could only imagine he struggled to find anything at all to say to someone as indistinct as herself. She thought he would likely move on but surprised her by coming nearer.

"What's that you're up to?" he asked, surprising her even further by dropping down onto the grass in the shade beside her.

Lindsey resisted the urge to cover her work like a schoolgirl. "Oh, I..."

"May I see?"

Lindsey looked at him, his face so near she could see the lighter flecks in his very blue eyes. She found herself nodding and passed the drawing pad across to him. He took it from her wordlessly and began studying her drawing with great concentration, then flicked to the previous pages to look at some of her earlier work, including the landscapes she'd drawn that morning.

At length he looked up at her. "These are amazing," he said. "Incredible.

What are you? Some sort of famous artist?"

Lindsey gave a little laugh. "Hardly that. I write and illustrate children's books."

"Children's books? What's your full name?"

"Lindsey McIntyre."

He made a rueful expression. "Sorry. I'm not really up on the latest things in children's literature. I don't know anything much past *Spot* and *Thomas the Tank Engine*. Even then I couldn't tell you who wrote either for a million dollars."

"Don't be sorry. I'm certainly not a household name."

"No, but I bet you will be with talent like this. This is work for a new book?"

Lindsey nodded. "It's the main purpose of my trip, I guess you could say."

Andrew looked up. "I wondered," he said, then added, "Have you always been able to draw like this?"

"Pretty much. I did go to art school but I learned more about other mediums there than I did about illustration."

"Yet I get the sense you don't go out of your way to publicize your talents?"

Lindsey gave a small laugh and looked away. "Oh no. Most certainly not."

Andrew's gaze went back to her drawings. Lindsey felt grateful he did not press her further. Perhaps it was written all over her face that she did not know how to talk to strangers about the weather let alone something as intensely personal as her drawing abilities. And yet oddly, as with Eleanor, Lindsey found she did not mind sharing of herself with this man. She did not know why this was since Andrew's good looks alone were enough to intimidate her. In Lindsey's world this usually led to an overwhelming desire to try to escape such company, if by some miracle she had found herself in it in the first place. It was very curious, and she could only conclude related in some way to his proclivities.

"What do you do for a living?" she asked.

"Nothing, compared to this," Andrew answered.

Lindsey's eyes went to his to see whether he was teasing her or not but he didn't seem to be.

"I'm sure that can't be true," she said.

"It is. I'm a business analyst. It's a job all about order and problem solving and logic. There isn't a scrap of creativity anywhere."

"Do you think order and creativity are mutually exclusive?" Lindsey asked.

Andrew's expression was knowing. "Let me ask you this, are you orderly?"

Lindsey thought of the knot of clothes she had unwound earlier. "Not always." Then as an afterthought, when she considered that her life was largely lived by a routine that protected her from just such conversations and from the outside world she said, "Yet in some ways quite a bit."

Andrew's eyes narrowed slightly. Lindsey could see him trying to make sense of her comments but she wasn't about to be drawn into a conversation about the whys and wherefores of how she lived her life. Instead she said, "I have a friend I met at art school, my flatmate actually, who is amazingly talented and who runs her life in the most structured, orderly and detailed way. There's nothing to say you can't be both."

Andrew smiled and handed Lindsey back her folio. "Well, I can testify to being strictly in the camp of the non artistic, especially compared to this. It's a beautiful gift."

Lindsey's eyes dropped to her work and felt unable to speak. She thought that might very well be the nicest thing anyone had ever said to her. Her eyes went back to his and she managed the smallest of smiles.

"And what does Simon do?" Lindsey asked, feeling desperate to deflect the conversation away from her.

"Simon? He's a market analyst. Works for some share-broking firm where serious money changes hands. Also distinctly non-creative."

"Oh. And have the two of you been together long?"

"I met Simon through playing tennis so I suppose we've known each other about twelve or thirteen years. I suppose as his best friend I should know that sort of thing, shouldn't I? Hold on, did you just ask me how long I'd known Simon or how long we'd been together?"

"Together," Lindsey said softly with a growing feeling of unease.

"Together together do you mean? As in partners together? As in gay together?"

Lindsey nodded and could feel herself cringing. She waited for the outburst of anger that Andrew's face suggested. Then, to her surprise and relief, he threw his head back and howled with laughter.

"You think I'm gay?" he said.

"I...I...someone said they thought you and Simon were together."

"What? Everyone thinks we're gay?"

"You're not?"

"No!"

"Eleanor didn't think you were. But the two of you spend so much time together, alone together. People assumed there must be more to it."

Andrew looked at Lindsey in astonishment, then with growing realization. "God. Well, I suppose that's what it would look like to the outside. The separate accommodation, eating alone together, avoiding everyone's company. I just never thought anyone would mistake either Simon or me as being anything other than the red-blooded heterosexuals we are."

Lindsey blinked a few times and could not believe she'd found herself in the middle of such a conversation. This trip seemed to be doing things to her.

"Then?"

"There is a reasonable explanation, believe me," Andrew said with firmness. "You see I'm not supposed to be on this trip at all, but Simon is. He's supposed to be on this trip as part of his honeymoon, hence the separate meals and accommodation. It was all pre-booked. And Saturday, the Saturday that the trip started on, Simon was supposed to be marrying Arabella, with yours truly as best man. So we show up at the church, not too worse for wear on account of the night before. Three hundred guests show up at the church and pack the place to the rafters. Yet one very significant person failed to show up, namely the bride herself.

"Instead, Arabella sent her father to tell Simon that she'd had a change of heart, that she couldn't go through with it. And there's poor Simon standing in front of practically every person he's ever known, dressed up to the nines, facing the fact that the wedding he had so looked forward to would not be taking place. As you can imagine he was - and is - completely devastated."

Lindsey tried to imagine and failed. Even the very idea of standing up in front of three hundred people to get married would be enough of an embarrassment for her. With everyone looking and making judgments, but to then be left standing there - the bride not coming, having to turn around and tell everyone to go home - this lay beyond the level of worst mortification Lindsey could picture.

"Oh, poor Simon," she said. "No wonder he looks so sad."

Andrew made a sound of disgust. "Truly, I've never seen anyone so dejected in my entire life. Nor anyone so humiliated. I always did have an inkling that Arabella could be a bit cold, but to leave the guy standing at the altar like that was heartless."

"You're angry," Lindsey said.

"For Simon, yes. No one deserves to be treated like that, especially with the wedding date having been set for nine months. That's plenty of time to get cold feet and back out. Plenty of time to realize you may be making a mistake. Even if she'd cancelled the day before it would have been better than just leaving the poor guy standing there. And of course he then had to cope with all the comments and the sympathy, the complaints about presents and new dresses having been bought specially that could not be returned, his mother's blind panic about what would become of all the food at the reception and what a waste of the beautiful ice sculptures that had been ordered. Every comment was like an arrow."

"So what happened?"

"I had to get him out of there, anywhere. Away, so that he could have time, clear his head, regroup. After all, Arabella made most of the sodding wedding arrangements. And since she'd done the jilting it wasn't up to Simon or his family to make amends or cancellations, was it? As it happened I'd arranged to have some time off work after the wedding as I've accumulated quite a lot of leave and the powers that be have been at me to use some up. I didn't have any fixed ideas of what I'd do.

"So I suggested to Simon he stick with the original plan, go on the trip anyway, but with me instead of Arabella. After all, the tour was already booked and paid for, plus it had been Simon's idea anyway. So we came, but I must say that when I suggested it I never imagined we'd have to share a room wherever we went. Or that Simon would be so distraught that other company was out of the question. Or that every fellow traveler would think I was gay."

Lindsey couldn't help but smile. "You truly are a best man," she said.

Andrew shook his head. "You've got no idea," he said.

CHAPTER SIX

Lindsey made her way to the dining room of Redpath Lodge at the scheduled time of seven o'clock. Pre-dinner drinks, she knew, had started a while ago but Lindsey had found herself feeling quite contemplative on her return from the vineyard. She wasn't in any hurry to break whatever spell had come over her. She'd lingered a while over her sketches and found herself uncharacteristically pleased with what she'd produced. Of course the sketches themselves were a long way from the finished product and would need to be matched with the perfect words to tell the story. But she supposed that if writing and illustrating a story could be compared to a body then at least she had some good bone structure to work with.

Darkness had not yet descended yet the voices of her fellow traveling companions drifted toward her like night had already fallen. She could hear the sound of Vi talking, of Eddie laughing, the murmur of conversation as the group moved from the lounge into the dining room which had been laid out earlier by Pamela to her usual standard of perfection.

Lindsey let herself in through one of the lounge doors and tacked herself on to the edge of the group. Almost as though she had sensed Lindsey's arrival, Eleanor turned and beckoned for Lindsey to hurry up and join her so they could sit together.

"Where have you been?" Eleanor hissed as she maneuvered them into a pair of free seats at the far end of the table, with Lindsey at the head.

Lindsey smiled apologetically, feeling nonetheless secretly pleased to be so in demand. "Sorry," she whispered. "Sometimes drawing makes me a bit day dreamy."

Eleanor gave her an assessing look then smiled. "I suppose I can forgive you," she said, "even though I got stuck talking to Bianca who basically buttonholed me so that she didn't have to talk with anyone else. I don't know if I've said this to you before but that girl truly is as shallow as a puddle."

The puddle looked at that precise moment as though she might be about to pass out. Vi had come around the far side of the table to sit beside Lindsey, Eddie beside her, while Cedric had plopped himself down on the other side of Eleanor. This meant Bianca had the unenviable decision of whether to sit at the end of the table beside Cedric, or on the opposite side with Eddie. Lindsey could see her making a herculean struggle out of it, but at the last moment the arrival of Dennis saved her.

"Well, well, everyone," he beamed. "Good day, I hope? Nice and rested for getting under way again tomorrow?"

Vi groaned. "My poor feet," she muttered.

"Nothing too serious, I hope," Dennis said with concern.

"No, no," Vi replied hastily. "I've suffered worse. There's a bit of life in the old girl yet."

"Great," Dennis said, his glance lingering on Vi as if trying to assess whether she meant what she said or not. "Now, I'm not sure about the seating arrangements for tonight. Eddie, Vi, how would you feel if I split you two up and popped Bianca in the middle of you both. Would that be all right?"

Eddie looked at Vi. "I suppose I could manage without the old girl just this once," he conceded, getting to his feet and moving up a chair.

Bianca slipped into the chair at Dennis's bidding, looking as though she'd jumped out of the frying pan and into the fire.

"Good-o," said Dennis. "Now we have plenty of room for our other guest. Ah, here he is now."

All eyes moved to the doorway. Lindsey saw Andrew hovering on the threshold, his expression uncertain as though indicating he might have made a bad decision. With a good deal of irony Lindsey noted Bianca's surprise at Andrew's appearance. She was clearly miffed that Dennis had thwarted any opportunity she might have had to sit beside him. While he may not have been exactly warm toward her so far he was at least young and attractive. Conversation with him would probably not include references to corn plasters and rheumatism, which made it infinitely more desirable than one with Eddie or Vi.

As for Andrew himself, his glance went from one person to another until he saw Lindsey. At this point he gave the merest hint of a smile.

Dennis claimed his attention. "Come and sit here," he said, "at the head of the table. I'll sit on the other side from Eddie and beside Cedric. There, now we're all settled."

Lindsey found the fact that Andrew would be joining them quite intriguing. Maybe, in light of their conversation, he'd decided to come out of the closet - as it were - although perhaps not in the way the others might be expecting. It was curious too that Dennis should join them for dinner since up until now he had mostly just got them organized then disappeared to wherever it was he went when not on duty. Lindsey wondered whether Andrew had persuaded Dennis to join the group to help break the ice. With Eddie around neither Dennis nor Andrew should have had such concerns.

"This is a turn-up for the books," Eddie said, his eyes round like saucers as he watched Andrew take a seat. "Something funny come over you? Had enough of your sidekick?"

Andrew glanced quickly at Lindsey then back to Eddie. He opened his mouth to reply when Dennis intervened.

"These last couple of days haven't been ideal circumstances for either Andrew or Simon, actually Eddie. Simon went through rather an ordeal before he started this tour and Andrew has been trying to see him through things as best he can. Poor old Simon needs all the support and understanding we can muster, even though you don't known him too well yet."

Andrew sighed and with all eyes trained on him he briefly recounted the story Lindsey had heard earlier that afternoon. Not having to listen closely to the tale as it unfolded provided Lindsey with the opportunity to study the faces of the other travelers. Vi listened intently. By the time she learnt that Simon had been left quite literally in the lurch at the church her face had become quite the picture of outrage.

"What a cowardly thing for the bride to do," she said. "No wonder the poor man hasn't wanted to socialize. I expect he's still in shock."

"You could say that," Andrew replied, "although I think the initial shock is beginning to be replaced by anger and embarrassment. In any case, it seemed an appropriate time to leave him on his own tonight."

"Been on suicide watch, have you?" Eddie asked, his expression shrewd.

Andrew gave a short laugh, devoid of humor. "Nothing like that. We've only been sharing rooms because there's been no other accommodation available wherever we've been. After all, this was supposed to be Simon's honeymoon, for which very few newly married couples ever request separate rooms."

Eddie guffawed. "No need for him to be embarrassed on our account," he said. "You tell him to keep his chin up."

"I suppose at least he didn't end up marrying the wrong person," Cedric said, as though still getting over the fact that he himself had done just that. "Marrying the wrong person is infinitely worse than not marrying at all."

"I suppose that's true," said Vi, "but the girl could've had the decency to make her mind up about a thing like that at least twenty four hours earlier. Surely the seeds of doubt had been there. I can't think of anything much more humiliating than to be hung out to dry like that. I can tell you something for nothing," she added, leaning around Bianca to look at Eddie, "if old twinkle toes here hadn't turned up on our wedding day I would have skinned him alive."

Eddie feigned shock. "As if I would have passed up the opportunity to marry you, my love," he said.

Bianca, sitting between them, looked confused. "You're not gay?" she asked.

Andrew laughed, all signs of the outrage Lindsey had seen earlier gone. "Not even for one moment."

Eleanor turned to look at Lindsey, her archly raised eyebrow suggesting that Bianca would need serious watching after such a liberating revelation. There were laughs all round from the rest of the group at this comment even though everyone - perhaps with the exception of Dennis - had been more or less convinced Simon and Andrew were together.

At this point Pamela and Keith came through the dining room doors, Pamela carrying two huge platters, one with roasted vegetables, the other heaped with a leafy green salad, while Keith deftly carried several bottles of their very own wine to augment the meal.

"I'll just pop these down here and you can pass them around amongst yourselves when I bring the main course," Pamela said. "Meanwhile, Keith will do the honors with the wine. We are having chicken. More precisely roast chicken with asparagus, bacon and cashews with a lemon infused olive oil dressing. The traditionalists amongst you will probably favor a white, but there's no standing on ceremony here. If you want red, you go ahead and have it."

Pamela disappeared, turning on her heel with a flourish.

"I don't know where that woman gets her energy from," Eleanor said to Lindsey as Keith began taking wine requests, starting with Vi.

"Me either," Lindsey replied.

"How did things go today out in the vineyard?" Eleanor asked.

The memory of the afternoon made Lindsey look directly down the table. She found Andrew watching her. She sent him a shy smile that she hoped he would find encouraging. Certainly she was amazed by his bravery. But then she supposed that from his point of view any amount of awkwardness would be tolerable in comparison with everyone thinking he was something he was not.

In the same instant she found herself surprised to be the focus of his attention. She could only imagine that he must be wondering precisely what she'd said to Eleanor about him. In an instant she made up her mind to say nothing of their encounter.

Turning her attention to Eleanor she said, "Very well. The lighting was just perfect, the size and form of both grape and vine exactly what I'd hoped for. And to be honest it was wonderful just to have some peace and quiet for a while. Oh, not that I mean to imply I don't appreciate your company," Lindsey said hastily, realizing that may not have come out quite the way she intended.

Eleanor laughed. "No need to say anything. I found my own afternoon equally tranquil if not perhaps quite as productive. Would you be willing to let me see what you have done so far?"

Lindsey blinked. She knew it would be churlish to say no, especially when Andrew had already seen her work. "I'd love to show you," she said, "although to be honest you'd be better off waiting for the finished product."

At this juncture Pamela returned for the third time with the last of the plates, just as Keith came to ask Eleanor and Lindsey what they would have to drink. Lindsey chose a sauvignon blanc, while Eleanor cheekily asked if she could try both the merlot and the cabernet sauvignon.

"That way," she said with a twinkle in her eye, "I can give you my decided opinion on both and tell you which goes best with this superb looking meal."

As Pamela and Keith departed, the platters of vegetables and salad were duly handed around. For a while there was a lull in the flow of conversation as people began making headway with their meal.

"This olive oil dressing on the chicken is just divine," said Eleanor.

"How appropriate," said Dennis. "Di-vine, just as the tour name suggests."

Eddie laughed. "Good one, Dennis."

"No, I mean it," Eleanor continued. "Can anyone else taste that hint of lemon in it? A slight tart flavor on the tongue?"

"Did you know that lemons actually contain more sugar than strawberries?" Cedric asked no one in particular.

Bianca rolled her eyes.

"Is that a fact?" said Dennis.

"Yes, it is rather intriguing since, as Eleanor remarked, it does taste sour on your tongue rather than sweet," Cedric said. "And that's something else you may not know: the fact that everyone's tongue is different, just like everyone's fingerprints."

"Don't tell me you're going to suggest that the international policing community do away with fingerprinting in favor of tongue printing?" Bianca asked scornfully.

"Could be fun if they had flavored ink pads to lick," Vi said with a laugh. "Now, madam, would that be cola flavor for you today, or perhaps the raspberry ripple?"

Everyone laughed except Cedric. "I wouldn't advocate that," he said a little frostily. "For one thing it would hardly be hygienic. I was only reading the other day that during a kiss they think that as many as two hundred and seventy eight colonies of bacteria are exchanged. No, no, the health risks would simply be too enormous."

"Well, if that statistic isn't a passion killer I don't know what is," Eleanor said with a degree of feeling. "If they started publicizing that in high schools the need for contraception could disappear entirely. No one would ever want to go near each other."

This comment provoked more laughter but Cedric wasn't finished. "Did you know that the Egyptians were the first known race to use contraception, perhaps as early as two thousand years before Christ? Believe it or not, they used crocodile dung."

Bianca looked as though she was going to be sick. "Bloody hell, Cedric, can't you keep your thoughts to yourself for five minutes? Some of us are trying to eat here."

Silence descended over the table as though someone had thrown a sheet over the party and they could no longer talk. It was difficult to say whether people were more astounded at Cedric's never-ending trivia or by Bianca's complete lack of sensitivity. Lindsey thought Eleanor looked on the verge of giving Bianca a piece of her mind. In the end, as usual, Dennis stepped in and ably saved the day by changing the subject. He began to talk about what lay in store for them the following day.

After dinner Pamela and Keith reappeared to announce that coffee would be served in the lounge if everyone cared to make their way through from the dining room. As they got up from the table Eleanor patted her non-existent stomach and said, "It's a wonder I can stand. That meal was truly delicious and also deceptively filling."

Lindsey smiled. "You can walk it off tomorrow," she said.

"Yes, tomorrow. It's funny, but having been here for longer than we've been anywhere else I suddenly have an overwhelming desire not to leave at all. Do you suppose Pamela and Keith would notice if I didn't leave?"

Lindsey glanced toward the doorway. Cedric, the last of the group other than themselves to make a move, disappeared from sight as he headed for the lounge. Moments after his departure Pamela came gliding in on her usual wave of energy.

"Here she is," Lindsey said. "You can ask her yourself."

"Ask me what?" Pamela said with a broad smile.

"I was just saying to Lindsey that I wondered whether you'd notice if I stayed behind tomorrow when everyone else leaves," Eleanor said.

Pamela laughed as she began stacking the remaining dishes together. "I suspect we might notice sooner or later. I fear the combination of my frightful son and the upcoming harvest might have you regretting such a decision sooner rather than later. Besides, you've some great scenery ahead of you and some other lovely properties to visit. Wait until you see Needham Park House. It's gorgeous. I can't imagine you'd want to miss out on that."

Eleanor looked at Lindsey. "I don't think I've ever been rebuffed quite so nicely in all my life," she said. "And anyway, I couldn't very well abandon you now, could I?"

"Please don't," Lindsey said with a shiver.

Eleanor shook her head. "You'd be fine. I know you would. Now, Pamela, let us help you clear the table."

"Oh no," Pamela said vehemently. "You're our guests. You haven't paid to come and work. That's my job."

"Nonsense. I doubt neither Lindsey nor myself is squeamish when it comes to the realities of preparing a sumptuous meal. Then you'll be able to come and join the rest of us that much faster."

As if daring Pamela to stop her, Eleanor started gathering up wine glasses, threading their delicate stems between her fingers like an expert. Lindsey followed suit by gathering up a number of beautiful bowls in which dessert had been served.

"I should be very cross," Pamela said with mock severity.

Eleanor said, "That honey ice cream you served with dessert was absolute heaven. I would never have thought of such a thing. Did you make it yourself?"

"I'm not that much of a wonder woman," Pamela said with a self-deprecating laugh, "although it is home made. There are some people who live about five kilometers from here who run a business producing honey and assorted bee products. The wife, who is a close friend of mine, makes this ice cream herself. I gather it's a big seller."

"No wonder. Quite delightful. I think that has to be one of the most special things about travel, the chance to try new things and be completely bowled over by them. Most people never try new things in the course of their humdrum existences."

Pamela smiled and waved a hand at the sea of dishes in the kitchen. "There isn't a lot of novelty in the humdrum, that's for sure. But I suppose most of us like the familiar for the majority of the time. If it was new, new, new all the time we'd be worn out with the excitement of it all."

"True," said Eleanor, "very true. I suppose one of the keys to life is trying to find that balance. You have to figure out how to keep things fresh and yet live within the strictures of daily routines and financial realities. I guess I've been pretty fortunate to have had the time and wherewithal to more than occasionally expand my horizons."

"Fortunate indeed," said Pamela, twirling a brush in a sink full of dirty dishes like some sort of virtuoso. "Keith and I have thought several times about having some sort of overseas adventure but getting away from here is a bit more challenging than either of us expected. Then there's our horrid son to think about. The prospect of taking him with us then watching him scowl his way through ten capital cities in Europe is more than I could stand. As for the idea of leaving him behind, well, forget it. I don't really even trust him when he's in his bed asleep at night, let alone picturing him without supervision."

"He's at a tricky age," Eleanor agreed. "Young adults crave freedom then have completely no idea how to manage themselves once they get it. My Sebastian was reasonably sensible in comparison with some of my friends' children but to be honest there were days when I wondered what he'd done with the brains he was born with."

"What about you, Lindsey? Done much traveling?"

Lindsey fixed her eyes on the platter she was drying. "I'm a bit of a novice."

"Really?" said Pamela. "What? Lack of opportunity or lack of desire?"

Lindsey smiled shyly. "A little of both, I expect."

"Good on you then for breaking out of the mold," Pamela said with her trademark hearty enthusiasm. "And if that's the case, that's enough dishes duty for both of you. You must make the most of your holiday while the going is good. Eleanor, I command you to take her away."

Eleanor sent Pamela a look of mock servility. "As you wish," she said with a twinkle in her eye.

When Eleanor and Lindsey rejoined the group they found Cedric, Eddie and Vi clustered on one side of the lounge sitting in a little huddle. Bianca and Andrew stood off to one side. Lindsey immediately saw the way Bianca held herself, leaning in toward Andrew as though trying to claim his attention with every atom she possessed. As Eleanor and Lindsey joined their usual group on an adjacent two-seater Lindsey found herself thinking about the conversation she'd had with Andrew that afternoon. She thought how nice it had been, how unexpected. Yet in spite of her being less reserved than usual, she'd still been her typical shy, timid self. Never in a million years could Lindsey imagine herself standing that close to someone she'd so recently met. Or in Bianca's case had so recently realized was on the menu.

Eleanor quickly became embroiled in a conversation about sleeping. Eddie and Vi catalogued their search for the perfect bed. Eleanor described some of the more unusual places she had slept, including a Mongolian nomad's yurt. Lindsey heard Cedric tell everyone that he had read that, in the course of an average lifetime, a person, while sleeping, eats around seventy assorted insects and ten spiders. Lindsey wondered momentarily if Vi might vomit. He then said that the average person is about quarter of an inch taller at night, to which Eddie suggested with a wicked grin that everyone was the same size lying down, if you caught his drift.

While listening to this friendly banter Lindsey realized she could quite equally hear everything Bianca and Andrew were saying if she really listened. Although eavesdropping wasn't one of her usual pursuits, the temptation proved too much.

"You're from Auckland, I gather?" Bianca asked.

"You aren't going to make disparaging remarks are you?" Andrew replied.

"What? About all Aucklanders not knowing anything about New Zealand because the only reason they ever go out is for a latte?"

"Precisely."

"Wouldn't dream of it. I live in Wellington and we have to endure our own set of jokes about how windy the place is and how full of public servants it is. Living in the capital city should have more prestige than it actually does. Pity we don't live closer together. We could catch up once this godforsaken trip is over."

"You're not enjoying yourself?"

Bianca made a scoffing sound. "What? With this bunch of rejects?"

"It's not Club Med, I will admit," Andrew replied, "but everyone seems quite friendly on the whole."

"That, my dear Andrew," Bianca said heavily, "is because you haven't spent five minutes in one stretch with any of them. You should be grateful that your nursemaid duties have shielded you from the worst of it."

Andrew fell silent. Lindsey could not see his face to be able to read his expression. Was his silence motivated by assent or reproach? Lindsey wondered. Or perhaps Bianca's mention of Simon caused the conversation to halt.

Bianca said, "I suppose the opportunity to view homes like this is a rare one even if we have to drag our sorry butts from one to the other."

"This is a very nice home," Andrew replied. "Million dollar view."

"Million dollar *property*," Bianca corrected. "Asset-wise the Gressinghams must be worth a bob or two. Not sure about their taste though."

Lindsey glanced across to see Bianca disdainfully pick up and turn around in her hand one of the ivory figurines Eleanor had admired the day before. Bianca deposited it back on the shelf like an offensive object.

"I suppose it's just as well we all aren't the same," Andrew said, as if to defend the choices of his hosts without actually chastising Bianca outright. "It would be a pretty boring world otherwise."

"From where I stand it can be a pretty boring world even with all those differences," Bianca said.

"But you must surely get to see a bit more of that world than the average person. I thought travel agents were always being sent off to the four corners of the world so they could see and recommend exotic overseas destinations to their clients."

Bianca laughed shortly. "That might be true in theory. But in my experience the boss always takes the best of those trips. And what they don't tell you about the four corners of the world is that no one seems to be responsible for sweeping or cleaning out those four corners. Some overseas resorts can be plush in the extreme but set one foot outside of the hotel compound and it's like finding yourself in the middle of a refuse dump."

"You're not fond of squalor?"

Bianca wrinkled her nose. "Who is?"

"No one, I suppose. I've always had a bit of a hankering to see somewhere a bit uncivilized though. I wouldn't mind seeing somewhere like India. Northern Indian scenery is supposed to be spectacular "

"Never been myself. Let me know if you ever think of going. I can't say I'd want to go with you but I'd be happy to organize your arrangements. These days, with modern technology, the fact that we don't live in the same city is no barrier to me sorting out your overseas travel."

At that point Pamela and Keith reappeared. Keith balanced a tray laden with cups, a teapot and two plungers filled with coffee so dark you could practically see the caffeine leaching out. Pamela followed with a cheese board and a plate of small cakes that oozed cream out of the side. A veritable insomniacs' nightmare.

Their arrival brought the cessation of conversation on both sides of the room, conversations in which Lindsey had managed not to utter a single word. For a moment or two Lindsey felt blindingly alone and experienced a homesickness so strong she felt suffocated. She thought of Robyn, who at this time of night was probably glued to the television, and of Will. He'd probably be sitting with Robyn asking questions about programs he wasn't the slightest bit interested in. Tomorrow, Thursday, they would fight over who would make dinner since Lindsey usually cooked then and she wouldn't be there.

This made Lindsey realized how important it was to be with people that mattered, with people who showed equal concern for you as you did for them. She heard Andrew be offered and refuse coffee. He thought he'd been gone more than long enough and should get back to Simon. Simon was someone that mattered to him. Lindsey's trouble was that in the grand scheme of things she did not matter to many people at all. A gulf seemed to open up between herself and the rest of the world. She could feel herself becoming anxious at the thought that she did not know how to be someone that people cared about, in fact had never been that sort of person. She was like Pamela's view, little more than wallpaper. She could never be confident or brash like Bianca.

But then, just as Lindsey wondered how she could escape, Eleanor turned to look at her and suddenly everything didn't seem quite so bad any more.

The following morning saw the group assembled and ready for walking by nine thirty. Neither Simon nor Andrew had appeared for breakfast. Bianca only graced them with her presence for two minutes while she came in to get her usual coffee before disappearing back to her room. Some of the group felt a bit lethargic after having stayed up late the previous evening. The mood had changed with the arrival of Keith and Pamela, then of Dennis. Pamela had carried them all on a wave of conversation that hadn't ended until after midnight. Consequently, talk around the breakfast table centered on how tired everyone felt and how little Eddie - and more particularly Vi - felt like walking that day.

They gathered at the front of the house on the gravel driveway with their bags. Eddie was quick to stash his in the back of the mini bus, into its usual place. He then stepped back and watched Cedric help Dennis pack everything else away in the trailer, an exercise that seemed to become harder to complete with every stop they made. Cedric explained that everyone had ceased taking such great care with packing their bags so that the bags themselves took up a larger volume of space even if the contents were exactly the same. Dennis reminded Cedric that this hardly mattered since the passenger area of the mini bus itself sat empty anyway. They could utilize this space however they pleased.

Simon and Andrew were the last to appear. Bianca, who had held herself aloof from the group while Cedric gave his lecture about their newfound slovenly packing skills, let out an audible sigh of relief. Cedric crossed the parking bay and relieved Simon and Andrew of their bags, stowing them in the back of the mini bus as instructed by Dennis. This brief exchange meant that Bianca had to wait momentarily until both sets of eyes were on her, at which point Lindsey observed her begin to preen like a silky cat.

Whether Andrew became aware of watchful eyes Lindsey did not know, but when Bianca finally drew breath he glanced Lindsey's way and gave her a warm, almost secretive smile. Lindsey was inclined to feel embarrassed that Andrew had caught her looking but his conspiratorial grin dissolved any reserve or unease that she felt. Bianca then reclaimed his attention and the moment evaporated. On such little acquaintance Lindsey found Andrew's expression as he regarded Bianca to be quite unreadable. It would be interesting, she thought, to know exactly what he made of Bianca. But then again, perhaps she would rather not know.

Dennis called everyone to attention.

"Right-o folks. Here we are again, another day, another walk. I'm sure you'll agree it's a beautiful day for being out and about in the gorgeous countryside. The forecast indicates the temperatures will climb as the day wears on so don't forget, plenty of sunblock, plenty of water and keep your hats on.

"We're off today to Price Cottage, about a sixteen kilometer walk from here, tracking in a north easterly direction for those of you perhaps inclined to want to navigate by the sun. For the rest of you, Cedric has volunteered to hand around the laminated sheets for today's walk. Thanks, Cedric. If you look at the map you'll see that the route we follow retraces your steps just a little, down this road, doubling back along the main road for about two kilometers, then left at the junction for, oh, six kilometers or so. At this point you will come to another fork in the road with the left fork headed toward Waiata Junction and the right toward Mills Point. It should be clearly sign-posted unless vandals have been at work or the sign has had a fight with a semitrailer. You need to take the right fork, just as it shows on the map and head toward Mills Point.

"With a bit of luck you should be at this fork in the road around lunch time. There's a small collection of houses there. And although the one and only shop shut around nineteen eighty four some public toilets still remain in a small park which might be an ideal spot to stop and have some lunch. From there you follow the road down about another three kilometers, past Rook Ridge vineyard, until you get to a sign indicating the start of a walking track. At this point you'll need to follow the path and the prompts on your laminated sheet which will lead you across country the rest of the way to Price Cottage."

"Is it hilly?" Vi asked.

"Hilly? Not especially. In particular the road is quite marvelously flat with long straight stretches. The walk across country should be fairly easy."

"So when they say 'ridge' as in Rook Ridge, they don't actually mean it?" Vi pressed.

Dennis laughed. "It's just a fancy sounding brand name as far as I'm aware."

Pamela, who had appeared with the lunches and come to stand behind Eleanor and Lindsey some time during Dennis's speech, said in hushed tones, "Typical of Rook Ridge. They're always trying to sound as though they're better than they are."

"Down with Rook Ridge, then," Eleanor whispered back.

"Any other questions?" Dennis asked.

Everyone looked around at one another. Only Cedric moved. He whispered something in Dennis's ear.

"Right folks. Cedric has reminded me to remind you that he has the first aid kit and is reachable via cell phone if required. Which reminds me of something else again. Tonight we must make sure we get all the phones I issued charged up before we set off for the next leg of the walk. Hopefully everyone still has enough battery capacity to last them through the day since the phones haven't needed to be pressed into service just yet. Unless you've all been making illicit phone calls to South America that is."

Dennis laughed at his own joke and Eddie guffawed loudly.

"I know some very interesting people to have illicit calls with in South America," Eleanor told Lindsey and Pamela with an arch expression. "Pity I didn't agree to get one of those phones when Dennis offered."

Cedric whispered again.

"Oh yes," said Dennis. "The other important safety reminder is just common sense really. Since you will be spending a good deal of the day walking along the roadway do be careful of cars. Walk on the same side of the road as oncoming cars and be vigilant should crossing the road become necessary. I'd be surprised if you see much traffic but better safe than sorry.

"So if there's nothing else, the only task left is for you to collect your lunches from Pamela and for me to say, Pamela, on behalf of everyone, thank you for a marvelous stay."

"You're welcome," Pamela beamed as the group clapped with appreciation.

Eleanor and Lindsey held back and collected their lunches last. Eleanor hugged Pamela warmly then Pamela hugged Lindsey, keen not to leave her out.

"It's been wonderful meeting you," Eleanor enthused. "I did mean it when I said I could stay longer, you know."

Pamela laughed. "You'd be most welcome back, either of you. Anyone who helps in the kitchen is always a great addition as far as I'm concerned. We don't ordinarily take one-off bookings, just groups for the odd day here and there, but for either of you we'd make an exception. You know where to find us."

As the group went to depart, Eddie and Vi went over to introduce themselves to Simon. Lindsey heard Eddie commiserating with Simon over his most unfortunate luck, expressing his opinion that Simon was better off shot of someone as flighty as his erstwhile fiancée. Vi wore a fierce expression and reiterated her sentiment that it was the worst thing she had ever heard. As they all turned to walk off up the slope onto the road Eddie slapped Simon heartily on the back a few times, welcoming him officially into their party. With such a gesture he indicated that any ill feeling or distance between them caused by Simon's reticence should be a thing of the past. Simon looked uncomfortable but perhaps just a little relieved to have broken the ice. He managed a word of thanks.

For Lindsey it seemed strange to find herself feeling so nostalgic about leaving somewhere after such a short stay. As they walked up the driveway and onto the road she took one last wistful look back. She thought it most unlikely that she would ever return - and somehow she doubted Eleanor with her jet-set life would ever make it back either - but to know that if you did there would be such a warm welcome was something of a new sensation.

Dennis puttered slowly up the driveway behind them in the mini bus and waved cheerily as he edged past them before driving off at speed toward Price Cottage. They all continued along the road as a group until they reached the main road. Then the group started to fan out. Eddie and Vi had predictably dropped behind. Bianca walked as fast as her legs could carry her, welded as she was to Andrew and Simon. Perhaps sensing new vistas of opportunity upon which to educate and delight, Cedric had also decided to keep pace with the two men. He had buttonholed Andrew and, from a distance at least, appeared to have engaged Andrew in deep conversation. Eleanor could only wonder what pearls of wisdom Cedric now imparted to his newfound friend but on balance it was Simon she felt sorrier for out of the two of them.

"I certainly hope that young madam is not giving that poor man the wrong impression of us all," Eleanor said, her expression formidable.

Lindsey thought this seemed quite an uncharacteristic statement from someone who appeared freer than most from care of other people's opinions. When she said as much Eleanor said,

"True enough. I'm not too bothered by what she says about me, although God knows it won't be anything charitable. She's probably making up stories as we speak about how much cosmetic surgery I've had and how mean and cruel I am. She's probably telling him that the only reason you and I, dear Lindsey, have become friends is because as soon as everyone else is out of sight I make you carry my bag like a packhorse."

Lindsey grinned. "I would carry your bag if you asked me."

Eleanor laughed. "Promises, promises. Besides, there's no weight in it at all, especially from lunchtime onwards. No, I tell you, she'll not have a good word to say about any of us. She'll be saying how hard done-by she is, forgetting entirely that Simon himself has just been through the worst experience of his life. In fact if she hasn't already set her sights on Andrew I wouldn't put it past that conniving little strumpet to make a play for the poor jilted bridegroom. At the end of the day he is, after all, still very firmly a bachelor."

Lindsey swallowed. What could she possibly say that would make any sense to Eleanor about how the idea of Andrew and Bianca getting together made her feel?

"Do you suppose there's any hope that Simon and his fiancée might get back together?" Lindsey asked.

"He'd need his head examined," Eleanor replied. "But then, when have any of us been sane when it comes to love? Although let's face it, men are quite differently motivated than women. Some will go to extraordinary lengths to satisfy what the Victorians used to call the 'lusts of the flesh'. Who knows what motivates Simon? Perhaps a pretty face and the lure of a big bank balance might rank higher in the scheme of things than love and companionship. Then again, we don't know anything about his jilting bride yet, so how can we judge?"

Lindsey hid a grin at the phrase "yet". It seemed clear that before long Eleanor hoped to expand her knowledge of this particular subject.

"And what about you?" Eleanor asked, turning to give Lindsey the full benefit of her scrutiny. "I know you aren't the noisiest person but I thought you seemed uncharacteristically quiet last night. At one stage you had a very odd look on your face. I for one would like to know just what it was you were thinking about."

Lindsey felt tempted to lie, to tell Eleanor that it was nothing, that she'd imagined things. But for some reason Lindsey had never been a very good liar while Eleanor's openness and practicality seemed to invite or even demand confession. It seemed easy too when they were out in the middle of nowhere with no chance of being interrupted or overheard. The front group had opened up quite a distance on the two of them while Eddie and Vi had fallen further and further behind.

"To be honest, I was probably feeling a bit sorry for myself," Lindsey admitted. "I got to thinking that there are very few people to whom I really matter, who think of me and look out for me. I guess it was a sort of epiphany in a way, and not a particularly nice one."

"Hmm. And what brought on this wondrous revelation?"

"Watching Andrew and Bianca. Something about her absolute confidence in herself and in her rights made me feel inconsequential. And then I realized that, to all intents and purposes, I am inconsequential. If I'd vanished right there and then, who really would have minded?"

"Me for a start," Eleanor said sharply. "You know, your words do make me think so many things all at once, feel so many things all at once. I have to say it makes me angry to hear you talk like that. Please, please, Lindsey, don't ever feel sorry for yourself. I've seen things in this life that would curl your toes: injustice, poverty, oppression. Anyone that travels widely will see things if they open their eyes, things that could make them stagger. I know you've had a difficult upbringing. I don't mean to diminish what you've been through. In fact knowing you've been mistreated at all is another thing that makes my blood boil, but we all have a choice. At least in most cases we do in the western world."

"Not when we're younger, we don't," Lindsey said feeling every bit as sad as she sounded.

Eleanor thought about this for a moment. "No, that's true. I guess what I mean is that now, as an adult, you have a choice to make a change. You have to look at *why* you feel inconsequential, *why* that makes a difference and *what* you could do if it's something that's important to you. But Lindsey, please, don't whatever you do use someone like Bianca Caton as your yardstick of judgment, especially where confidence and importance are concerned. A person like Bianca is all show. She has plenty of confidence, that I'll grant you, but not a lot of substance. From what I've seen, she doesn't really care about anything other than what interests and motivates her. In that respect, she's the inconsequential one because there doesn't seem a lot behind her petulant, prissy facade.

"You, on the other hand, have depth and talent and compassion. These things do have consequence. They have the potential to influence people, to help people. All you lack is the belief in yourself and the confidence to step out of the shadow of your past to be all that you could be."

Lindsey grimaced. "When you put it like that it sounds so simple."

"Well, no, overcoming problems is never simple. But to not take any action is worse I think. If you were to compare life with walking, like we are now, out in this beautiful environment, problems are like a stone in your shoe. If you get a stone in your shoe what do you do?"

"Take off your shoe and get it out?"

"Of course. But to do so you have to actually stop and not just keep going in the hope that it'll go away. Because if you do keep going - try to ignore the stone - chances are you'll end up in even more trouble."

Lindsey thought about this. If she thought about her life her shoes had been full of stones, perhaps not quite as many as some people, but enough. Mostly she'd tried to keep going but maybe Eleanor had a point. Maybe keeping going without addressing the problem did make things worse in the long run. Maybe Lindsey had used certain situations and friendships like Band-aids, protecting her wounds from the stones but never actually doing anything about removing the stones themselves.

"And I tell you another thing," Eleanor said. "The funny thing about stones in your shoes is how enormous they feel. Sometimes you'd swear you were carrying around a great boulder only to find the stone to in fact be minute. I think problems can be the same. Often, if you actually look at them, problems can be far more simplistic than we realize."

Lindsey shook her head. "You make it all sound so easy."

"Not easy, just doable. You can do it, Lindsey, whatever 'it' is. I know you can."

Their conversation had drifted off at this point onto less weighty matters. They followed the route as Dennis had described, complete with unmolested signposts. They chose to stop at the little park as he had suggested, to enjoy their lunch. By the time they arrived they found no sign of the preceding group and no evidence remaining to suggest they had stopped at all. Eddie and Vi appeared on the horizon just as Eleanor and Lindsey were about to make their way again, but by now they knew better than to wait for the older couple. Eddie and Vi were content to set their own pace and could not be hurried.

Both Eleanor and Lindsey found the walking more enjoyable and relaxing once they left the main road to thread their way across country even though the roadway gave them a hard, flat surface to walk on and the lack of substantial traffic had made for an easy morning. The black asphalt seemed to reflect the heat back up on them while the green rolling fields that dipped and meandered over the local terrain brought with it a freshness and vitality they had missed. The breeze seemed more in control here, coming in wafts from the northeasterly direction that they headed, bringing with it yet more hints of the unseen ocean and the vibrancy of farm life.

Once again the laminated maps proved their worth for off-road traveling and Eleanor and Lindsey found Price Cottage without delay or difficulty. The cottage itself nestled by a band of old oak trees and overlooked green farmland that fell away gently from the bottom of the cottage garden into a valley that seemed to stretch without end. The cottage itself was constructed of greying weatherboards under a burnished red corrugated iron roof. It looked cozy and old, the gardens well established with mature trees.

From a distance the house barely looked large enough to accommodate their party even though it was two storied. However, once Eleanor and Lindsey made their way through the white picket fence and down the cobbled path bordered by wildflower gardens they could see the building had an annexed wing attached to it that wasn't initially visible. Toward the bottom of the garden and to the right lay a series of small outbuildings that clearly housed some sort of animals. On the left a gazebo had been erected by a small paved area. There a large table and collection of chairs sat ready for afternoon tea. Over the back hedge a velvet brown horse eyed Eleanor and Lindsey with interest as they made their way to the open farmhouse door.

Eleanor stuck her head inside the door and called out a greeting. Moments later a woman appeared from around the side of the building to greet them while another woman appeared seconds later from within the house itself. The two women exchanged a friendly laugh with one another, almost as though they were surprised at the coincidence of seeing one another even though both were clearly at home.

"Well," said Eleanor, "quite a greeting party."

The woman who had rounded the side of the house laughed. She had an open, hearty face that matched her hearty laugh. She wore a tie dyed dress with fluorescent pink leggings under it. Her short-cropped hair seemed to stick out in a thousand unlikely directions. Lindsey thought she looked like a real character.

"Yes, double trouble at your service," she said. "I'm Cybil Burrows and this is my partner, Maryanne Silver."

Lindsey and Eleanor turned to smile at Maryanne. She too had short-cropped hair that had turned as silver as her name suggested. She had a thin, clever face with thick wire framed glasses that gave her a look of a librarian from a bygone era. As though to reinforce this picture she carried a book with her that she tucked under her left arm in order to shake their hands.

Eleanor introduced herself and Lindsey.

"Good trip?" Maryanne asked absently.

"Great thanks," Eleanor replied. "The walk from the road was especially lovely. The countryside somehow takes on an English appearance around here."

"You don't have to extol its virtues to us," Cybil said with a broad smile. "We absolutely love it here. Couldn't imagine living anywhere else, could we, M?"

"No," Maryanne said with the same vague tone.

"Have the others arrived?" Eleanor asked.

"Some. Three men and a young woman," Cybil said. "Oh, and Dennis. He's getting the men settled. They're in the annex. You're both in the main house along with whatever her name is and that other couple that are yet to arrive. Sorry, but I'm hopeless with names. Lucky I remember my own most of the time. Still, you're only here one night so no sense in overtaxing the synapses is there, M?"

Maryanne shook her head. Lindsey wondered if Cybil called everyone by their initials that she'd have more success in remembering who people were. But she was such an open, friendly person that she supposed most people forgave her idiosyncrasies. She was the sort of person you couldn't help liking.

Except Bianca. Cybil showed Eleanor and Lindsey to their rooms upstairs while Maryanne floated away with a dreamy expression on her face and her nose back in her book. Eleanor and Lindsey followed Cybil through a maze of rooms filled with antique furniture - rooms crowded with books and ornaments and old sofas covered in the sort of cushions that looked as though the stuffing had been squashed out decades ago - up the stairs to their rooms which all lay off a central passageway. Once they were safely ensconced Cybil disappeared with a cheery wave.

Moments later Bianca appeared in Lindsey's room.

"What a dump," she said, flopping down without invitation onto Lindsey's bed. "Isn't this place just positively hideous? Aren't those two old bats just the limit? You really have to wonder that Dennis hasn't gone broke before now if this is his idea of a good place to stay."

Lindsey stifled a sigh. "I suppose it's not easy to find places big enough for all of us to stay within walking distance of one another. This house might not be as modern or big as Redpath Lodge or Christian House but I thought, on first impression, that it had a lot of character. It's the sort of character that reflects the house's owners."

Bianca rolled her eyes. "Those two? Did you see the way the one without the glasses was dressed? That's not character, that's insanity."

Lindsey shrugged. "They seemed very friendly to me."

"Of course they would to you. I can't imagine you've ever had enough guts to say a bad word about anyone. I bet they're lesbians, you know. What else do they mean when they say 'partner'? If that isn't a euphemism for 'gay as a picnic basket' I don't know what is."

"As I recall you've thought that before, and look how that turned out," Lindsey said with uncharacteristic vigor.

Bianca gurgled with laughter. "Well," she said, getting off the bed, "there are some times in this world when I don't mind being proved wrong one bit. At least there's now some hope that this trip won't be a total waste of time."

And with that Bianca flounced out of the room leaving Lindsey to contemplate just what she might possibly mean.

CHAPTER SEVEN

After Bianca's departure Lindsey eased off her shoes, flopped on the bed and closed her eyes. She suspected she could feel a headache coming on. The summer sun made for very warm walking conditions and she wondered if she'd got a bit dehydrated. Her room, being directly under the roof, seemed a little airless so Lindsey forced herself off the bed and went over to open the window before practically sprinting back to the bed to lie back down.

She must have drifted off to sleep but got disturbed when the sound of voices floated on the gentle breeze that now meandered its way into Lindsey's room. She could hear snatches of conversation and the occasional laugh. Curiosity got the better of her and she went over to the window once again.

Her room's aspect looked out over the paved courtyard where afternoon tea had been set out. It seemed clear that Eddie and Vi had lately arrived and had sunk straight into chairs without venturing into the house. Their daypacks sat abandoned and Eddie had taken off his socks and shoes. He currently prodded his feet in a speculative fashion as if trying to discern whether they yet still lived. Everyone else had also congregated – even Simon and Andrew – and sat sipping cold drinks and eating the nibbles that either Cybil or Maryanne had prepared.

Lindsey experienced an unfamiliar sensation as she realized she actually wanted to go down to join the group. She could not think of the last time she'd felt the desire to socialize so strongly. Under normal circumstances the very idea of making her way downstairs and intruding on a group of people she did not know well would have made her nearly physically ill. Yet in a matter of five short days she had begun to bond with some of these people and regarded herself as a legitimate member of the group.

After pulling her shoes on and giving herself a cursory glance in the mirror she set off downstairs. At the bottom of the stairs she paused to re-orientate herself. The temperature on this level of the house felt considerably cooler than upstairs. The afternoon sun had begun to dip and cast elongated shadows on the easterly walls, its rays highlighting eddies of dust motes. The rooms had an echo about them as unoccupied spaces often do. It made Lindsey stop in her tracks and she hovered on the threshold of the main lounge. It wasn't hard to picture such a homely room filled with people talking and sprawled comfortably on the sofas. It was a room with character that spoke volumes about its owners.

The occasional table beside the spot where Lindsay stood groaned with a collection of items - silver photo frames with shots of Cybil and Maryanne in foreign locations, a vase with some dried bunny tail grass heads. A group of Murano glass paperweights competed for space with a committee of ornamental thimbles. At the back a cameo locket on a chain had been artistically draped over one of the photo frames.

The sound of Eddie's booming voice brought Lindsey back to reality. She took a deep breath and got herself ready to take the plunge.

When Lindsey had made her way outside she had been welcomed with genuine warmth by the group. Andrew had leapt to his feet and indicated that Lindsey should take his chair beside Eleanor since no free seats remained. He'd disappeared for a few moments then returned with another. Eleanor had poured Lindsey a drink and given her a small *sotto voce* running commentary on what she'd missed of the discussion so far. Vi looked on the verge of falling asleep. Bianca's expression spoke volumes about her opinion of proceeding. Simon's eyes had glazed over in a way that suggested he'd become so used to his own company that he'd nearly reached saturation point. Cedric said nothing at all and looked like a man who'd been told on no uncertain terms to shut up.

In the end the group had broken up not long after Lindsey's arrival. Eddie finally noticed Vi's drooping eyelids and elbowed her back to life. He'd then suggested it might be time for them to find their digs for the night and get a bit settled before dinner. Simon had stood up as though someone had just scalded his crotch with a cup of hot coffee and said he thought he'd do the same. Before Lindsey knew it only Eleanor remained.

"Hope you don't mind," Eleanor said, " but I think I might follow suit. Will you be all right if I leave you to your own devices?"

"Of course," Lindsey said. "I inadvertently had my rest already. I'll just have a mooch about the place and see if inspiration strikes."

Once Eleanor departed it occurred to Lindsey that having her sketchbook with her might be handy so she went back upstairs to retrieve it. She had in mind that she'd have a go at sketching the cottage, although to what end she did not know. When she re-emerged from the house she crossed the courtyard and headed for the outbuildings in order to make her way down to the valley below to get a better view of the house.

When she rounded the corner of the largest shed she found yet another building sheltering in its lee. As she approached it she realized it housed a small collection of animals. The low-roofed building had been divided into four sections. The lower half of the building fenced the animals in while the upper half remained open to the elements so Lindsey could look in.

The first enclosure contained a fat pig who nosed about in a pile of straw. His curly pink tail almost wagged with delight. Beside him lived a colony of exotic looking rabbits enjoying their evening meal. This seemed to consist of a lot of ends of vegetables – probably from tonight's dinner – and a few scoops of some sort of pellets. From the look of their luxurious black pelts they appeared to be thriving.

The rabbits had a kid goat for a neighbor. As Lindsey peered into his enclosure he commenced a staring competition with her and stood still as a statue. He looked rather less well cared for which made Lindsey speculate on whether he may have been recently rescued from somewhere. He appeared unaccustomed to the presence of a stranger so Lindsey left him to his own devices and moved on to look at the next pen. She found this empty and yet it looked ready to house a new inhabitant at a moment's notice.

Lindsey decided to abandon her plan of sketching the house in favor of capturing the likeness of the pig and the rabbits. She returned to the pig's enclosure for no other reason other than to put a bit of distance between herself and the goat. If she hung around long enough he might tolerate her presence better and she might be able to draw him as well. It wasn't easy to find the right angle to work from, or a comfortable place to stand to do so, but once she'd positioned herself the old magic took over and she scarcely gave her body a thought.

Just as she began to make the finishing touches on her first sketch someone rounded the corner from the opposite direction. She hastily stowed her sketchbook behind her body then let out a relieved sigh when she saw it was Andrew.

Andrew smiled as he approached and said, "Ha ha, caught you."

Lindsey found herself grinning. "Guilty as charged."

Andrew looked into the enclosures then back at Lindsey. "Let's see then," he said.

Lindsey handed over her sketchbook without argument. Andrew came close and took it from her.

"That's some pig," he said. "You've captured his likeness perfectly."

"Not perfectly," Lindsey said. "Where we artists are concerned, perfection is a mirage. We learn to be content with 'good enough'."

'You wouldn't be saying that if people had trouble recognizing a stick figure when you drew one."

Lindsey had never felt comfortable with praise of her work so withdrew her sketchbook gently from Andrew's grasp and changed the subject. She said, "Simon seems to be doing a little better."

"In fits and starts he is," Andrew said. "Now that everyone on the tour knows what's up with him - and have generally been pretty great about it - I think he's able to see more clearly what I've been saying this whole time."

"Which is?"

"That people are far more likely to be sympathetic to his plight than they are to regard him as some sort of failure."

"Is that what he's been thinking?"

Andrew nodded. "I guess you probably had to be there to fully experience the drama in technicolor, but Simon's level of humiliation registered off the Richter scale. I think he thought every person from now til the end of time would be pointing fingers and laughing. And while it might be some time before he's back to being the life and soul of the party, I think he doesn't feel the need to be in hiding any more. With not even a week having passed since the whole fiasco erupted I'd say that's a reasonable amount of progress."

"Poor guy," Lindsey said with feeling. Under similar circumstances she would probably not let her face see daylight ever again.

"Not to sound too unsympathetic or anything but I am hoping this shocked-and-stunned phase doesn't last too much longer. I'm hoping it'll be like the stages of grief and that he'll soon move from shock, bypass guilt and get right to anger. After what Arabella did to him he should be livid and come out fighting."

Lindsey must have let her antipathy for violence show on her face for Andrew quickly said, "I don't mean literally fighting. But I do think a bit of anger on his part might make him realize that what she did wasn't fair and that he deserves better. Right now I think he feels as though he's never going to get over this during his lifetime."

"Some things do leave lasting scars," Lindsey said softly. "And there are some things you don't ever get over even when you do get through them."

Andrew tilted his head to one side and went to reply when another person rounded the corner.

"Aye aye," Vi called out. "What do we have here?"

"Hi, Vi," Andrew said as she approached. He seemed unruffled by her unexpected appearance while Lindsey felt sure her cheeks had turned sunset red. She tucked her sketchbook behind her once again.

"What are you two doing lurking here?" she asked suspiciously.

"Looking at the animals," Andrew replied.

Vi looked where Andrew pointed. "Gawd," she said. "It's a pig."

"I thought you were going to have a rest," Andrew said, his tone jovial.

"Hmph. Eddie's crashed out on the bed and wouldn't wake if you paid him. His snoring is like the combination of a bandsaw and a panicked elephant caught in quicksand. You'd have to be stone deaf to sleep with that racket. So I thought I'd take a quick look around these buildings and get a better lay of the land. Not that I really want to be walking another step further."

"How are your feet?" Andrew asked.

"I think if it weren't for the fact that I've started to lose sensation in them they'd be feeling like they were on fire. My blisters have started getting blisters."

"That doesn't sound good," Andrew said. "Maybe we should all head back to the house. At the very least you could have a rest in the lounge."

And so they made their way back to the main house without Lindsey having uttered a word to Vi whatsoever.

The group gathered around in the courtyard the following morning to get the day's instructions from Dennis. Lindsey thought most people looked far from refreshed even though they had all enjoyed a nice meal the previous evening and a hearty breakfast this morning. They stood about listlessly, waiting for Dennis to appear. For Lindsey's part she had slept well and felt ready for another day out in the wild blue yonder. She felt keen to see how the land would unfold today and what their next accommodation would be like since they were scheduled to spend two nights there.

Dennis finally emerged from the house with Cybil in tow. Cybil had swapped her dress and pink leggings for a white shirt and lederhosen. She'd completed this outfit with a waistcoat, braces and a little felt hat crushed down on her riotous hair. If she had suddenly started yodeling nobody would have been surprised in the slightest.

"Here we are folks," Dennis said. "Sorry for the delay. I just had to iron out a couple of administrative matters. Before I hand out today's walking instructions I wanted to give you the opportunity to say goodbye to Cybil. Hopefully you've enjoyed your brief time here."

A canon of affirmative comments echoed around the courtyard although none came across crystal clear. Cybil did not seem to mind this lack of clarity and smiled broadly.

"Sorry Maryanne couldn't be here to see you off," Cybil said. "Duty calls elsewhere. But we've enjoyed having you here immensely and hope that if you are ever passing this way again that you might feel free to pop in for a cup of tea. Any supporters of De Vine Tours are friends of ours."

Dennis bestowed Cybil with his most grateful smile and started to clap in appreciation. The rest of the group followed suit.

Cybil said, "Unfortunately, I need to get going as well so I will leave you in Dennis's most capable hands and wish you bon voyage."

With that she turned on her heel and disappeared back into the house. As she retreated Eleanor leaned over toward Lindsey and said, "I can't imagine where she might be going in that get-up. Off to Grindelwald to take a look at the Eiger maybe?"

Lindsey smiled then turned her attention back to Dennis as he busily passed out the day's information sheet. Upon receiving hers Lindsey set about studying it.

"Now today's route continues to head in a northeasterly direction as we make our way further toward the coast. We are heading for a very pleasant house called Whittaker's Rest where we will be staying for the next two nights. The homestead is owned by Graeme and Evelyn Barclay. You've got a free day tomorrow and so can rest up by the Barclays' pool, have a look around their most excellent gardens or even walk to one of the neighboring vineyards."

Eddie gave a groan. "More walking? Not bloody likely."

"It'll be your choice," Dennis said, quite unperturbed. "Now the majority of your route will take you across farmland today. You'll retrace your steps back to the main road and then walk for about two kilometers until you get to a collection of mailboxes on the right hand side of the road. They stand at the beginning of a little service road that trails out to several farms and ultimately right out to the coast. One of the boxes has the name 'Van Dooren' on the side. There aren't any signs so you will need to keep your eyes peeled.

"You need to start off down the service road which takes you up and over the brow of a small hill. Directly as you come over the hill you will see the Van Dooren's farmhouse on the left hand side. Continue past this. About two hundred meters after the farmhouse, on the same side of the road, you will see a stile over a fence. Hopefully you can all see this spot marked clearly on your maps."

The group peered at their maps. Eddie pointed the spot out to a confused looking Vi.

"Your route will then take you right across Van Dooren's farm. This eventually joins the back boundary of Whittaker's Rest. There's a row of trees on the boundary line and, at the far right end, a small access gate so you can pass from one property to another. It's then another three kilometers or so up to the house itself, first through an apple orchard and then through a small area of vines. Any questions?"

"Any good spot for lunch?" Eleanor asked.

Dennis squinted at his copy of the map. "About half way across the Van Dooren farm there's a small stream and a cluster of native trees. That's probably as good a spot as any. Don't drink the water though, people. It could contain farm runoff. I'm sure none of you will want a healthy dose of effluent with your lunch, will you?"

Bianca looked ready to be sick on the spot.

"And while we are on the subject of farms, don't forget to close any gates you need to open. Oh, and I nearly forgot. I talked with Mr. Van Dooren last night about conditions and he said to tell you that the sixth paddock you come to currently houses a bull of cranky disposition. He said you had best come one paddock along and cross there just to be on the safe side."

"Thanks for telling us," Bianca said heavily, clearly not impressed with Dennis's "Oh by the way," attitude to such a matter.

"And don't forget to let me know if you need first aid assistance," Cedric reminded them.

"Go the FATO," Eleanor whispered to Lindsey.

Lindsey clamped down a laugh.

Eddie and Vi continued to pore over their map with some consternation.

"Do you have more questions?" Dennis asked them.

Eddie looked up. "Me and the missus have just been trying to work out how long today's trek is going to be. It seems to be a mighty long way."

Dennis nodded. "I'm not sure that I would describe it as a mighty long way, but it is true that this leg is one of the longest you'll undertake. Is there a problem?"

"It's me feet," Vi said. "I only have to look at the map and they start complaining. What they'll actually do if I take them on this journey, Lord alone knows."

"I don't suppose there's any chance we could cadge a ride in the mini bus, is there?" Eddie asked.

A look of faint shock passed over Dennis's features, as though the very idea of anyone on a walking holiday bunking out on the walking portion of the holiday had never occurred to him. He looked from Vi's face to Vi's feet several times and then said,

"I guess you had better then."

Vi could scarce contain herself and flashed the biggest smile Lindsey had seen her make during their brief acquaintance.

The group – minus the walking wounded – collected their packed lunches and set off up the gravel driveway that snaked its way back up to the main road. As they reached the top of the slope Dennis puttered up the incline in the mini bus. He gave them a cheery wave and smile. In the back Eddie and Vi had commandeered the first set of seats and wore grins the size of the Cook Strait. Both waved regally as they made eye contact with the group as though they'd had as much practice at such an action as the Queen and the Duke of Edinburgh.

"What a cop-out," Bianca said. "I bet you they've been laying it on thick about their feet in order to pull just such a stunt."

"Not everyone has to resort to such drastic action to get attention," Eleanor said from behind her. "Besides, if you're ever fortunate enough to get to Eddie and Vi's age I'm sure you'll feel quite entitled to some extra consideration."

"That seems very charitable on your part," Bianca said in reply. "After all they can't be much older than you."

Lindsey watched outrage pass over Eleanor's face. Bianca knew full well that a whole decade stood between Eleanor and Eddie. To suggest otherwise could only be seen as a thinly veiled insult.

"Let's be careful crossing the road," Cedric sung out, thus preventing Eleanor from making any sort of stinging retort. "And don't forget that we need to walk on the same side as oncoming traffic and not stray all over the road too much. It's Friday today so there could still be plenty of working vehicles coming and going."

This seemed extremely unlikely. The road out to Price Cottage could hardly be described as arterial. Lindsey felt sure it wasn't often used by anyone other than the residents who lived off it. But since the group seemed to be sticking together today everyone conceded that he probably did have a point. Better to be safe than sorry.

Cedric tried to position himself in the middle of the group but kept coming too close to Bianca for comfort. Instead he opted for a spot at the front. Simon also seemed inclined to want a buffer between him and the rest of the pack and so walked alongside Cedric. Lindsey could see Cedric experimentally trying out some conversation with Simon and getting absolutely nowhere for his trouble.

As usual Eleanor and Lindsey tried to stick together and fell to the back of the pack, the spot usually reserved for Eddie and Vi. This left Andrew at the mercy of Bianca. Today she had donned a tank top of the brightest of whites - probably new off the hanger from some designer clothes store - and a miniscule pair of red shorts. In spite of the impracticalities of heat and the risk of perspiration from the exertion of walking, Bianca had applied a full face of make up. She quickly engaged herself in the task of batting her mascara-encrusted eyelashes at Andrew. With all of that exposed flesh Lindsey could only hope she had also taken the time to trowel on the sunscreen.

The road threaded its way up another incline toward the main road. Before them, on the ridge that lay on the other side of the main road, the ground rose more steeply. Craggy rocks could be seen at odd places beneath a group of pine trees that clung tenaciously to the terrain. The tips of the pines angled against the breeze. Lindsey wondered whether the fact that the wind had picked up might indicate a coming change in the weather even though the skies were still relatively clear.

As the climb required slightly more oxygen than the flat, Lindsey and Eleanor abandoned any attempt at conversation. They often chatted as they walked along but were equally comfortable with silence. Bianca, on the other hand, seemed determined to make the most of her captive audience. Her voice carried on the wind.

"Have you done much traveling?" she asked Andrew.

"A bit," he replied. "I went to Thailand last August with some friends. I went over to the States the year before that. Otherwise I've just done trips across the ditch – Melbourne, Brisbane, Sydney."

"You haven't been to the UK and Europe?" she asked with the sort of incredulous expression that inferred he'd never lived. When Andrew shook his head she said, "You must. Such great shopping and nightlife, so many things to do."

"Some of the greatest historical treasures and sites on the planet and Bianca reduces them to 'so many things to do'," Eleanor said to Lindsey in a low voice. She shook her head in dismay.

"I'm sure I'll get there one day," Andrew said. "My holidays tend to be with other people so I usually go wherever they suggest."

"Then it's time to take the bull by the horns and suggest somewhere yourself for a change," Bianca said. "Don't let yourself be walked all over. Suggest Venice. You can't go past Venice. I've been several times and never get sick of the place. It's fabulous."

"I can assure you I haven't been walked over and don't have any intention of starting now," Andrew said in a good-natured manner. He dropped back a pace or two and said, "You've been to Italy, haven't you Eleanor?"

"Been? I suppose you might say 'been'. I've lived there for an extended period a couple of times in my life."

"A full immersion experience then?" he asked. "Not just a fleeting visit?"

Eleanor laughed. "Oh yes, full immersion all right. I can assure you I've experienced every aspect of Italian life you might be able to think of – the food, the wine, the scenery, the men. I've had many wonderful adventures."

"And would you agree with Bianca's recommendation of Venice?"

"Oh mostly. Venice is an exceptionally unique destination and is unlike anywhere else I've ever been. But is it very commercial and unless you get out of the Saint Mark's square area into some of the other parts, such as Cannaregio district where true Venetians live, then it can be quite touristy. For a real Italian experience you'd want to go and stay in a little village, maybe somewhere south of Florence. I could recommend a couple of divine places off the beaten track if you ever get as far as seriously looking to go."

"Thanks," Andrew said. His genuine reply made it clear that if he ever needed tourist advice for Italy he'd definitely take her up on the offer.

Bianca looked miffed to have been usurped in her area of expertise. She made a huffy little sound, shook her head as if shaking the dust off her sandals and sped up, perhaps in order to save Simon from Cedric.

"I'm thinking you've had a very interesting life," Andrew said once Bianca had flounced away. Lindsey found herself feeling pleased to see that he seemed unconcerned at the loss of Bianca's company.

"I've had a very *fortunate* life," Eleanor said. "It has been interesting, no doubt, but my good fortune has been in getting to experience these things in the first place. I had a couple of quite liberal thinkers as parents and they liked to travel. Even as a young girl I got taken away on holidays and got given new experiences and opportunities to broaden my mind. Such a stroke of luck to have been given such a solid start in life. Not everyone is so lucky, believe me."

She sent a little sidelong glance at Lindsey but did not expand on this statement further, much to Lindsey's profound relief.

"Then I went into school teaching until I got married and had Sebastian. And while school teaching is not lucrative, it is - or can be - stimulating. These days I think they've coined the phrase 'lifelong learners'. What a wonderful concept. If I had to dole out advice to young things such as yourselves it would be to embrace the idea of lifelong learning. Keep learning. Always be on the lookout for new experiences and adventures."

"I think we've been having a few of those of late," Andrew said.

"Ha ha," Eleanor said. "Yes, so far De Vine Tours has proved to be most educational, although perhaps not entirely as Dennis might have foreseen. And who knows what might be around the next corner? But what happens when you get home? Or what happens in five years? Or ten? As young people we seem to all get programmed with the idea of trying to attain. We get an education, we start a career, we meet a life partner, we buy a house and we have children. It's all about building. But once you've done these things what comes next? We retire? I'll tell you what happens if you don't work at it – stagnation."

"And you think travel is the best way to do this?"

"It's the easiest," Eleanor said. "Travel can take you into uncharted territory, expose you to new ideas, new sights and sounds faster than almost anything else. But it does require the necessary capital – yet another area in which I have been fortunate. However, it's by no means the only thing you can do to keep going and keep growing. You just have to stop and think about it. Be deliberate, my dear Andrew."

Andrew laughed. "I can't say deliberateness is something I've been particularly famed for up til now. On the outside it probably looks as though

I've been quite intentional about things. In reality I've just drifted along until I've settled on something that seems a lesser evil than another choice."

"You sound like someone who hasn't entirely known his own mind. Perhaps this is something that comes with age. Maybe you haven't had too much pressure or expectation on you and have been able to rely on your God-given talents without the need to expend excess energy."

"You might be right," Andrew said. "But I will say this. Recent events have made me begin to question a lot of things. It's fair to say I feel some change coming on."

Lindsey's curiosity had been awakened at Andrew's intriguing remark but she did not have the courage to ask him more about it. Eleanor might have done so had it not been for the fact that they had finally reached the top of the rise where the road from Price Cottage joined the main road. Simon, Bianca and Cedric had waited for the rear party to catch up so they could carry on together. After a brief flurry of conversation they regrouped and set out once again.

It seemed clear from Simon's expression that he'd already had enough of Bianca and Cedric. He fell in beside Andrew and didn't appear to be about to let his friend stray too far away. Cedric had started to wear an almost permanent expression of pain. After yet another dose of acerbic comments from Bianca he seemed determined to stay as far away from her as possible. The feeling was completely mutual yet Bianca looked torn. She faced the uncomfortable choice if the group split up again of either forcing her attentions on Simon and Andrew or joining up with Eleanor and Lindsey. She hadn't really endeared herself to either party but the alternative would be to either walk alone - or worse - walk with Cedric.

In the end it proved to be a moot point. For whatever reason the group did not split apart. Once they started to walk down the main road they needed to walk in single file to be safe from passing traffic. Andrew and Simon walked at the front of the pack but Andrew kept looking over his shoulder to see how the rest of the group progressed and occasionally slowed their progress to let the others catch up.

Lindsey thought the group might break up once they reached the Van Dooren's mailbox. Instead they stopped there for five minutes so that everyone could have a breather and catch up on their water intake. The road had led them to the other side of the ridge and the spot seemed to be in the lee of the hill. But while they enjoyed a small reprieve from the windier conditions they had no let-up from the heat of the sun. Lindsey could see the heat haze shimmering off the surface of the tarmac as they stood by the battered collection of mailboxes that congregated together at the start of the road.

As they stood about, Cedric fussed pointlessly over everyone's wellbeing. Andrew suggested they try to push through from there to the point Dennis had suggested might be good for a lunch stop. Bianca withdrew some sunscreen from her daypack and smeared it on her arms before asking Andrew to apply some to the part of her back not covered up by her tank top. A strange look passed over his face as he contemplated her request but he acquiesced nonetheless. While he undertook the ministration Bianca closed her eyes, her face a picture of ecstasy. If she'd started purring Lindsey would not have been surprised. The spectacle made Lindsey feel intensely uncomfortable. She felt relieved beyond measure when Simon hurried them all up and they got under way once again.

The ground rose just past the mailboxes as Dennis had said but then leveled out as it stretched out toward the northeast. Some rolling hills in the far distance prevented any sight of the sea. Even though temperatures were bordering on being too warm, no carloads of beach-goers went by. All school-aged children were currently sweating it out in classrooms all over the country longing for the lunch bell, or even better, the end of the school day. Somewhere in amongst this verdant countryside farmers and agricultural workers slaved away in their fruitful endeavors and probably dreamed of the coming weekend.

There wasn't any sign of life as they passed the Van Dooren's modest weatherboard farmhouse save a motley looking dog who sloped out of the house and started barking at them. The house and the dog both looked a little neglected and in need of some sprucing up. The sky blue paint on the weatherboards of the farmhouse could easily have been slapped on around about the time the Beatles were breaking up. The dog wore a coat of dust over his ragged fur as though he had writhed around on an area of bare ground somewhere. He bounded over the unmown front lawn and peered through a gap in the weeds that choked the fence, watching them intently as the group trailed by.

"Did you know that cats have over one hundred vocal sounds while dogs only have about ten?" Cedric said.

No one made comment to this. They left the dog to his own devices.

They soon came across the stile Dennis had mentioned. Cedric went over first, followed by Simon, then Andrew. When Andrew had scaled the stile he stopped to help Bianca over it. She took his hand with relish and then lavishly thanked him. He then helped Eleanor who managed to make the act of climbing over a stile graceful. When it came time for Lindsey to climb over, the prospect of having to put her hand into Andrew's unnerved her but she couldn't see a way of avoiding it without looking churlish. It was an odd and unfamiliar moment for someone so used to avoiding physical contact. Andrew flashed her a bright smile as he took her hand and Lindsey found herself smiling shyly back. If she didn't know better she could have sworn he slightly squeezed her hand before letting it go.

They then set off across the uneven terrain of Van Dooren's farm. The group fanned out now that they were away from the constraints of the road. Their path took them across an open stretch of land beside the farmhouse. This land did not look as though it had been used for farming in a while. The ground beneath their feet felt like concrete and had cracked in places. There were also signs that suggested the soil might just as easily turn into a bog if enough rain fell. What grass that grew there looked reluctant and lacking the sort of nutrition required by livestock.

After walking for about ten minutes they came to a gate. Cedric rushed forward to open it and stood gallantly by while everyone filed through. This gate led into much richer pasture. On the far side of the field a group of cows stood chewing the cud. The cows watched without much interest as they made their way across to the next gate. The field proved something of a mine-field and required careful study to avoid floundering into excreta.

Five minutes later they reached the second gate. Cedric sprinted forward once again to do the honors. Only Eleanor and Lindsey bothered to thank him for his trouble.

The following field seemed without end and it took them quite some time to cross. As they reached the far side they could now see a group of native trees in the distance. When the group finally made their way up to this grove they found the small stream that Dennis had described. Here they halted for lunch.

"It seems funny to be here without Eddie and Vi," Eleanor commented as they got themselves settled.

"I bet they're sitting at a fabulous dining room table and having lunch off bone china plates and drinking out of crystal glasses," Bianca said with as much resentment as she could muster.

"This lunch looks more than adequate," Cedric said, waving about his kaiser bread stuffed with ham and an assortment of salad vegetables.

"One would hope for more than adequate on a trip like this," Bianca countered. "Especially for the money you pay."

"I was under the impression you didn't have to pay at all," Eleanor said to her. "Maybe if you had done, you'd appreciate the whole thing a bit more."

Bianca looked away but said nothing.

Simon got his cell phone out of his bag and started waving it about but didn't appear to be able to get any reception.

"Did you know that more than fifty percent of the world's population have never made or received a telephone call?" Cedric said.

"Really?" Simon said, stowing his phone away again. "I couldn't imagine that."

Bianca scowled at Simon for encouraging Cedric.

A few bees buzzed about the wildflowers that grew in amongst the rocks down toward the stream. The flowers' untamed and fragile beauty had captured Lindsey's attention as soon as they had settled. She longed to examine them in more detail and to make some rough sketches but there wasn't any way she'd do so in front of such a large audience. One of the bees flew up and headed for Andrew's face. He waved his arms about to deflect its trajectory.

"I hope you aren't allergic," Eleanor said.

"You can't be too careful," Cedric added. "The honeybee kills more people world-wide than all the poisonous snakes combined."

"What would you know?" Bianca countered. "New Zealand doesn't have any snakes."

"I find snakes quite fascinating," Cedric said. "For instance, did you know that the poisonous copperhead snake smells like fresh cut cucumbers?"

"Who cares?" Bianca said leaping to her feet. "All this excess of useless information has taken away my appetite. Who's coming?"

Simon said to Andrew, "I wouldn't mind seeing if I can find a spot with some cell phone coverage. There might be some if we get away from these trees."

Andrew's gaze flickered over to Eleanor and Lindsey then back to Simon. In weighing up his options he didn't seem to have much choice in the matter. He gave a small shrug and scrambled to his feet.

"You'll be okay?" Andrew asked Eleanor and Lindsey.

"Of course," Eleanor said pleasantly. "And besides, how can we go wrong when we've got Cedric with us?"

After Simon, Andrew and Bianca departed a silence ensued. Lindsey had expected Cedric would relax and start chatting again but he seemed to have lost his enthusiasm for the sport. Lindsey had also expected Eleanor to make some disparaging comments about Bianca, for no other reason than to cheer Cedric up a bit, but she simply packed away the remnants of her lunch and leaned back against the trunk of the tree she sat under and closed her eyes. Lindsey tried to think of something to say to Cedric but failed completely.

She wished she felt less constrained and thus free to get on with sketching but could not bring herself to do so in front of Cedric. She tried to think of a good reason that Cedric might be persuaded to go on his merry way. In the end she figured that taking some photographs might have to suffice so she took her camera out and went to examine the flowers in more detail.

After about twenty minutes Cedric started to sigh heavily. This prompted Eleanor to open her eyes. When he saw that she'd returned to the land of the living Cedric said, "Shall we get going shortly?"

"Oh, I don't know," Eleanor said. "It's very pleasant here. And besides, we must already be at the half way mark for the day, if not further. There's no need to rush, is there?"

Cedric squirmed. "I suppose not," he replied. "I just don't want there to end up being too big a gap between us and the forward party, in case they need me."

"Hmm, good point," Eleanor said, clearly trying for the diplomatic approach. The chances of any of them needing Cedric seemed remote at best. "Lindsey and I would hate to think we were holding you back though. Isn't that right, Lindsey?"

"Oh, yes," Lindsey said.

"And yet I don't think we're ready to move on yet, are we Lindsey?"

"No," Lindsey said. If Cedric left she would be able to abandon the camera in favor of her sketchbook. Here in this sheltered spot they were quite isolated. The sun beat down and yet the trees provided shade. The smell of native trees hung in the air and the babbling brook provided some background music.

"Maybe you should set out," Eleanor said. "Try to keep an even distance between us and the others."

Cedric's face portrayed his indecision as he weighed up the pros and cons of this idea. In the end he started gathering up his belonging in preparation to leave.

"Well if you're sure you'll be all right?" he said.

"Perfectly sure," Eleanor said. "We may only stay another twenty minutes or so anyway. We'll be right behind you."

With a last look of uncertainty Cedric hitched his daypack onto his back and gave them a strange little salute. He turned on his heel and set off.

In the end an hour passed before Eleanor and Lindsey departed. Eleanor said she felt perfectly comfortable right where she was and that Lindsey should take as much time as she wanted to make her sketches. Lindsey took her at her word and tuned out completely. She got quite a surprise once she'd finished to realize how much time had passed.

As they went to leave Lindsey pulled out her map in order to study it. They still had four more paddocks to cross before they would get to the boundary. It all seemed quite straightforward. Eleanor came over to examine the map for herself over Lindsey's shoulder.

"Do you remember what Dennis said about the bull?" she asked.

Lindsey suddenly wished she'd paid more attention. "I'm pretty sure he said the bull was in the sixth paddock and that we were to go one paddock over to avoid him."

"Sixth? I'm afraid I wasn't listening at all. How many have we been through so far?"

Lindsey counted. "Four. Or is it three? Do you count the land we went through directly after we crossed the stile? It didn't look like a paddock at all. If you count that, it's four. If not, then we've crossed three and have two more to go before we need to make a course correction."

"Oh dear," Eleanor said with a small laugh. "Maybe we shouldn't have been so hasty in letting Cedric go on without us."

Lindsey failed to see the humor and felt her stomach tighten.

"What shall we do?" she asked.

"Carry on," Eleanor said. "Maybe if we set off it'll all become quite self evident. We might even be able to see tracks to show which way the others went."

"What if they got it wrong?" Lindsey asked.

"Imagine if they had," Eleanor said, laughing even harder. "With Bianca wearing those bright red shorts she'd make a magnificent target for a bored bull with pent up aggression to spare."

Lindsey couldn't help a half smile at this. "You're terrible," she told Eleanor.

They set off. They jumped the stream at its narrowest point and continued in the northeasterly direction as indicated by the map. After ten minutes they came to a gate and paused to recount.

"So this is either paddock four or five, but we don't know which," Eleanor said. "Either way, it's not number six and we can see straight across it anyway. Wherever Mr. Van Dooren has got his livestock, it's not here."

Another ten minutes saw them reach the far side of that paddock and they paused at the next gate once again. From here the ground fell away into a shallow gully. They could see a band of poplar trees swaying in the breeze on the far side where they presumed the next fence would be.

"Hmm," Eleanor said. "So here the dilemma begins. Is this paddock five or is it paddock six? Let's have another look at the map."

Lindsey drew it out of her bag again and they both pored over it.

"So we are here," Eleanor said, pointing at the map. "And if this is indeed paddock six the advice is to walk all the way down here and cross the next paddock. I'm useless at scale. How much extra distance would that be?"

Lindsey pondered the question. "Quite a way. That's one big paddock. It'd probably add twenty minutes onto our journey and even longer if we decide to skirt around the following paddock as well."

Eleanor made a little huffing sound. "It's got very warm. I'm not sure I relish the prospect of an extra long walk, especially if we're wrong. It's a shame this paddock isn't flat like the others. Then we might've been able to see if trouble lies ahead. As it is, the field looks completely deserted – what we can see of it at least."

"So what do we do?"

"I think we should take the risk," Eleanor said. "If this field proves to be empty then I think we should definitely skirt around the one after."

"And if not?"

Eleanor gave a glamorous shrug. "Run? Besides, what are the chances that a lone bull would be lurking in the one place we can't actually see?"

Lindsey felt torn but she could see Eleanor's flushed face and did not want to be responsible for adding to Eleanor's fatigue by making her walk further than she needed.

"Okay," she said. "Let's do it. This field isn't as wide as some of the others so hopefully we'll be fine."

They opened the gate and ventured forth. High above a skylark wheeled about, chirping merrily as he flew. The grass grew longer in this paddock and the heads danced in the breeze. The sun beat down with fresh intensity. It felt as though they could have been the only two survivors left on earth.

They reached the middle of the field without incident and started down the gentle slope into the gully. They could now see the gate on the far side just up a short rise from the valley floor at the spot where the row of poplar trees started. It felt such a relief to be able to see their end destination. As they began to walk down the hill all seemed well but suddenly, on their left where the ground fell away more sharply, they spied their nemesis. There the bull stood, a fine specimen of bovine magnificence, a couple of thousand pounds of hulking strength with two impressive horns protruding from either side of his head.

The bull caught sight of Eleanor and Lindsey at precisely the same moment as they saw him. He immediately looked at them with an intensity that made shivers go down Lindsey's spine. He appeared immensely unimpressed to see them and the feeling was mutual.

Eleanor and Lindsey froze on the spot.

"What should we do?" Lindsey whispered.

"Act naturally," Eleanor said out of the side of her mouth, "or in your case try to man up a bit and not be too afraid. No offence, but animals can smell fear."

"None taken," Lindsey said, knowing it was completely beyond her to comply.

Eleanor took her hand and they started slowly forward. As soon as they took two steps the bull's whole body tensed and by the time they had taken another two steps he had begun to move with malice in their direction.

"Run," Eleanor said, dragging Lindsey forward. "Quick."

The two women sprinted down the remainder of the slope and into the gully and then had to apply extra energy to make it up the incline on the other side. All the while the bull came nearer and nearer. Lindsey felt sure she could feel the ground tremble beneath his thundering hooves. But he also required extra energy to get his bulk up the hill, giving Eleanor and Lindsey a chance to keep ahead of him.

"We're going to have to jump the gate," Eleanor yelled. "We can't risk opening it. We won't have time."

Paces lay between them and the gate. Lindsey's legs were beginning to feel like lead as her muscles burned up energy. She willed herself to go faster and to stay upright and at about the same time she could feel Eleanor begin to flag. Lindsey dug deep and tugged Eleanor toward the gate. She could feel the hairs on the back of her neck bristle as though the bull breathed right on her.

Just when it seemed as though they were about to run out of luck and energy, they reached the gate. Both women threw their packs over and then scrambled over as fast as they could. The bull still came at them and just as they made it to safety he charged the fence. Eleanor and Lindsey stumbled away from the gate and collapsed onto the ground. They lay on their backs gasping for air while the bull snorted and tossed at head at being denied his quarry.

Eleanor and Lindsey turned to look at one another. Eleanor made an O with her mouth but then started to laugh with hysterical fervor. And when Lindsey thought about the situation, about how fortunate they were to have got out of that paddock unscathed, she became overwhelmed with an astonishing lightness of being and started to laugh too.

If only Robyn and Will could have seen Lindsey at this precise moment they would have been utterly amazed and quite disbelieving.

CHAPTER EIGHT

Bianca stood before the mirror in her assigned room at Whittaker's Rest and preened. She admired herself and the outfit she had selected and knew she looked mighty fine. She gave a little twirl. The black dress she'd donned had an exposed back and a plunging neckline. It showed off her assets to best advantage.

In spite of having to undertake this god-awful trip at short notice she had nonetheless packed with care. She also knew that compared to the others on the trip she would look overdressed but in all honesty she'd already worn all of her less glamorous outfits. Now only the best remained.

From what Austin had led her to believe about the trip, her days would be filled with leisurely walks through spectacular scenery, her nights with fine dining and sophisticated company. Accordingly, Bianca had packed day outfits designed to accentuate her long slim legs and fine figure and eveningwear befitting the sort of exclusive clientele with whom she would be dining.

Instead she had found herself on the hack's tour of no man's land with boring landscapes, annoying co-travelers and average food both during the day and at night. In her mental picture there would be fine conversations with kindred spirits, she would glide along rather than have to exert herself during the walks and there wasn't a cowpat in sight. Having mostly experienced the great outdoors through the medium of television, Bianca had now discovered the truth of the matter. Nature stank.

The sight of Whittaker's Rest had cheered her considerably. The house sat in the middle of a sea of pristine green lawns that would be the envy of any self-respecting bowling club. Its vast lower storey had verandahs all around it while the upper storey had been built under a massive sloping metal roof and looked as though it could easily contain eight bedrooms. The exterior of the house had been painted white with grey trimmings, to match the color of the roof. Where the lawns finished, lush gardens had been planted and were a riot of flowers.

When they had approached the house, Evelyn Barclay had emerged from its immaculate interior looking smooth and sophisticated, her clothes clearly bespoke, her makeup carefully applied. She wore a beautiful set of pearls and gorgeous shoes and oozed class and wealth. Here at last was the sort of person Bianca had expected to encounter, the sort of person Bianca knew what to do with.

Evelyn had clearly been brought up in equally elegant surroundings. Her superior manners and good taste were so innate as to be natural. Unlike Eleanor, who Bianca thought to be full of false airs and graces, this woman didn't have to try at all. It also didn't hurt that she was tall, blonde and enviably thin for her age which Bianca estimated to be somewhere in her late forties or early fifties. With such superb clothes, posture and make up she could indeed be considerably older and no one would ever know.

Evelyn had greeted the advanced party with careful warmth, her eyes scanning and cataloguing them, Bianca thought, for social status and worth. She eyed their shoes with elegant disapproval and upon asking for their removal, shepherded them into the house and into a hexagonal lounge with magnificent views out toward the pool complex. Although she had a delicious array of snacks and cold drinks laid out she offered to show them to their rooms. Bianca had jumped at the chance. They had left Simon and Andrew to it, giving Bianca the opportunity to bond with their hostess and get an exclusive guided tour.

The room to which Bianca had been assigned met with her complete approval. She had her own en-suite bathroom with shower and toilet. She had since spent a long time under the jets of the shower, reviving her hot and wilted body and washing her hair with the luxurious shampoo provided.

She'd then had a rest on the most comfortable bed she'd come across so far and rejoiced in the fact that they would be here in this fabulous place for two whole nights. It was enough to make her almost happy, but for the fact that she still had to contend with her traveling companions: with that ridiculous pair Eddie and Vi whose social standing couldn't get too much lower; with Eleanor and her patronizing comments and superior airs; with that wet blanket Lindsey whose circumspect ways were starting to grate; with that buffoon Cedric and his endless inane comments.

Simon and Andrew were of course the exceptions. But Simon wasn't that easy to talk to with all his noble moping. Under the circumstances she could both understand and forgive this, but in Bianca's opinion he seemed more embarrassed than truly sorry about the situation. With a complete witch of a fiancée - who'd been prepared to ditch him at the altar like that - what he should really be feeling was relief. Bianca knew she might be capable of many a fine act of romantic terrorism but even she would not stoop so low as to leave a man in the lurch like that.

As for Andrew, well, he had so far proved to be a bit elusive. Bianca knew that he had come on the trip for the express purpose of supporting his friend through his hour of need and thus wasn't completely free to suit himself as to how he spent his time. This meant that Bianca's opportunities to monopolize him were few and far between. But he had proved to be very gallant today when he had helped her over the stile and she had relished their first physical contact to date. It gave her hope of more to come. Much more if Bianca had anything to do with it. It seemed a shame that Simon and Andrew had so far had to share digs all the way along. The chances of being able to slip along to Andrew's room in the middle of the night seemed remote.

So now she was about to go down for pre-dinner drinks where she would hopefully get the opportunity to spend more time with the boys and further hook her prey. She smiled to herself. Let the games begin.

Just before the allotted time for pre dinner drinks a knock came at the door. Lindsey opened it to find Eleanor hovering on the threshold looking elegant in black and grinning like a Cheshire cat.

"All rested?" she asked.

Lindsey gave a lopsided smile. "I'm afraid to say I had to have a little lie down. For a while there I feared I might start shaking."

"I had to have a scalding hot shower and a cup of tea with lots of sugar," Eleanor confessed. "I felt much better after that."

They looked at each other and erupted into laughter afresh.

"Ready to go downstairs?" Eleanor asked. "Ready to take the 'bull' by the horns?"

"After this afternoon I think I'm ready for almost anything."

Eleanor looked aghast. "Could this be the same Lindsey I met nigh on a week ago?"

Lindsey grimaced. 'Well, perhaps I couldn't tackle quite anything," she said, "but I think I can manage a pre dinner drink without quailing too much. Just 'steer' me in the right direction."

"Ha ha," Eleanor said as she led the way.

They found Eddie and Vi in the lounge hovering by the drinks trolley while Bianca lurked over by the window studiously ignoring the pair. For the evening Eddie had chosen to wear a particularly obnoxious Hawaiian shirt covered in images that looked suspiciously like beer mats with slogans from island-based drinking establishments. Its loudness could easily induce a hurricane-sized migraine. Not a millimeter of material remained unembellished. Vi had put on what might colloquially be known as a leisure suit and looked like an escapee from a seventies convention. Bianca appeared to be expecting some Hollywood A-listers and had dressed for the red carpet.

Eleanor and Lindsey's arrival brought a palpable reprieve to both sides, but by her fake smile and welcoming comments Bianca won the "Most Relieved" award.

"Eddie and Vi," Eleanor said with a warm smile, ignoring Bianca altogether. "How are you? Had a good day?"

"It was ruddy marvelous," Vi said. "I barely walked a step and feel much better for it. I even took the opportunity to have a little swim."

"Cor, that was quite a sight I can tell you," Eddie said with a smirk. "Haven't seen the old girl in that bathing costume since the late eighties. I have to say that it fitted her a little better then."

He made waving motions with his hand over his midriff to indicate that she'd gained some extra rolls of fat since then. Vi elbowed him in his own prodigious gut. "You're a fine one to talk," she said. "When he jumped in the pool, half of the water flew out."

Eddie guffawed.

"We missed you," Eleanor said. "It wasn't the same without you."

"Ah well, I expect we'll be back on the trail come Sunday," Eddie said. "I don't think Dennis was altogether impressed with us bunking off the walk today."

"Surely not," Eleanor said. "Where is he by the way? And Cedric for that matter?"

Vi said, "He and Cedric took the mini bus and went off at about four o'clock. Cedric had a hankering to see Whittington Bay and badgered Dennis into take him. I'm not sure they're back yet."

"Thank God," Bianca said.

"I do rather think you could be a little kinder to poor Cedric," Eleanor said to her. "It seems hardly fair that the man should be harried by your uncharitable comments every five minutes. He is, after all, paying good money to be here."

Bianca scowled and went back over to look out the window.

Eleanor rolled her eyes and focused her attention back on Eddie and Vi. "And what is the attraction of Whittington Bay?"

"Fur seals," Eddie said. "They've got a fairly new colony established there, so Cedric said, and he wanted to see it for himself. It sounds as though this is the closest we'll get to the spot. Bit of a case of now or never."

"And you weren't tempted to go too?"

Vi gave a snort. "It involved a walk from the car parking area to the beach."

"Plus we hear that seal colonies reek," Eddie said. "Neither of us was about to leave this perfumed paradise for a whiffy bunch of seals, no matter how cute or endangered they might be."

"I see. And what else did you two do today?" Eleanor asked.

"I had a bit of a scout around," Eddie said. "We were here pretty early so we've had plenty of time to get the lay of the land. Might be a bit bored tomorrow."

"And what did you discover?" Eleanor asked.

"The house is massive," Eddie said quite uselessly since they had all seen it for themselves. "These people have got some serious money. Gawd knows where it comes from though, because it feels to me as though they're just dabbling with agriculture. They've got the apple orchard but it seems to be on quite a small scale. And then there's the wine but they're only just getting into that."

"Oh?"

"Oh yeah," Eddie said. "I got an up close and personal look at the winemaking side of things when we were at Redpath Lodge. Keith Gressingham gave me the guided tour. They had winemaking equipment for Africa. This lot here send their grapes offsite for pressing and they've only planted out a few hectares so far. It seems much more of a hobby than an occupation."

"Interesting," Eleanor said.

"What about you lot? Good day?"

"On balance I would say yes, wouldn't you Lindsey?" Eleanor asked, sending her a meaningful look.

"Oh yes," Lindsey replied. "But I do think you did the right thing in getting a ride with Dennis. The first section of the walk was pretty hilly."

"Indeed it was," Eleanor said. "And then the walk across the Van Dooren farm wasn't without it challenges either, and that's no cock and bull story."

Lindsey stifled a giggle. She had a mental picture of the bull chasing after Eddie and Vi. Going with Dennis was the smartest move they'd made to date.

"And what happened to the boys? Lost them, did you?"

"They're outside," Bianca said, pointing out the window.

Lindsey took a couple of steps across the room to stand beside Bianca. There on the lawn, over by an ornamental fountain, stood Simon and Andrew. They appeared to be having an in-depth conversation. Simon wore a pained expression on his face and kept raking his hand through his hair. Shadow obscured Andrew's face but his stance looked sympathetic and calming to Lindsey.

It all of a sudden struck her that she might be witnessing a pivotal moment on the tour. Maybe Simon had reached the end of his rope. Maybe rather than finding the trip cathartic he might be finding the intense scrutiny and constant company too much to bear. Maybe being on the tour without his new bride made for a daily reminder of his torment. Maybe his need for cell phone coverage today signaled a decision made and the desire to resume his normal life. He could be at this very moment telling Andrew that he'd had enough and wanted to leave.

This unexpected thought struck Lindsey like a blow. She felt herself physically sway as she considered the prospect of Simon and Andrew departing. And while she would never verbalize her sense of dismay nor express her desire for the two of them to remain with the tour, she knew that she would feel their departure keenly if they went.

And such a sentiment shocked her. It made her realize that she had started to entertain the notion of getting to know Andrew better, something that had never happened to her before. She knew the likelihood of him feeling the same way - of him thinking of her as anything other than a traveling companion and acquaintance - to be unrealistic. And yet the prospect of him disappearing before the tour had finished practically brought tears to her eyes.

"Bloody hell," Bianca said in a quiet voice. "When is Simon going to get a grip? All this endless wringing-of-hands and gnashing-of-teeth is not doing him one bit of good. He should be in here with us, putting his troubles aside and trying to have a good time. He should have a drink, or two, or three. Get hammered, celebrate his freedom. Anything other than all this perpetual angst."

"It hasn't even been a week," Lindsey said. "I know if it had been me I'd take considerably longer to recover from what he's been through."

In fact she would never recover. Lindsey knew this with absolute certainty.

Bianca gave Lindsey a look that suggested the chances of Lindsey even getting as far as an engagement ring were about as remote as the moon, let alone making it all the way to the altar. Thus her argument could be dismissed as a moot point without uttering so much as a word.

Instead she said, "I'm surprised at Andrew. He ought to put his foot down and make Simon snap out of it. He's not seeming such a successful friend to me."

At this point Eleanor had joined them and when she heard Bianca's comments her face darkened.

"And I'm surprised you'd know anything about friendship," Eleanor said. "With your people skills I would imagine you to be a short-term specialist. I would imagine most people consider you to be someone to spend time with in extremely small doses."

"How dare you?" Bianca said. "I'll have you know I have plenty of friends."

Eleanor opened her mouth to make a retort but at that moment Dennis and Cedric arrived with the Barclays in tow.

"Here we are, here we are," Dennis said, his face beaming, "ready to announce that dinner will be served in five minutes and to introduce our hosts, Graeme and Evelyn. But wait, we are short in numbers. Where are Simon and Andrew?"

"They're outside," Bianca said for the second time that evening. "I'll go and get them."

Bianca sprinted for the door as fast as her designer outfit would permit, taking with her a cloud of tension. Lindsey could only be glad that Dennis had arrived before things had erupted into a full scale spat.

Had Graeme and Evelyn Barclay been magically transported to a fine country house in rural England a hundred years ago they would have fitted in without a lot of unnecessary adjustment. Both had changed for dinner and seemed keen to conduct the evening with a reasonable amount of pomp and ceremony. The only thing missing from proceedings seemed to be either the appearance of a kilted Scotsman to pipe them into dinner or the ringing of some enormous dinner gong.

Graeme and Evelyn led the way to the dining room. Evelyn hung off Graeme's arm in a most regal fashion and the pair walked at such a sedate pace that trumpets should have been playing a fanfare. This all seemed very much to Dennis's taste. He smiled widely and enthusiastically as he beckoned the rest of the party – including the now rounded up Simon and Andrew – to follow in their hosts' wake.

The dining room lay on the opposite side of the house from the room where they had assembled for drinks. It had also been constructed in the same hexagonal shape. This made the perfect backdrop for the enormous circular table that had been installed in the centre of the room. The table's proportions were so large as to make Lindsey wonder how it had ever been brought into the house in the first place. Arthur's knights would not have felt hard done by had they been made to sit at its magnificent acreage.

As they entered the dining room Graeme and Evelyn stood to one side as though making their very own receiving line. Eleanor went first, followed closely by Eddie and Vi and then Lindsey. The table had been luxuriously decorated with flowers and candles, crystal glasses and elegant place settings. They had even been assigned seating with each tour member having their own calligraphed place card set upon the table at their assigned spot.

Lindsey saw Eleanor make a quick assessment of these arrangements and frown. She turned to Vi and whispered something in her ear. Vi then turned, elbowed Eddie in the side and whispered in his ear. The pair then made a beeline for the Barclays and distracted them by asking a question about a painting on the far wall. With their attention occupied elsewhere Eleanor took the opportunity to make a quick rearrangement of these place cards before standing to one side and looking as innocent as a rose with thorns.

Graeme and Evelyn clearly did not want to have their attention diverted at such an important juncture in the evening's proceedings but answered the Joneses' question with an attitude that didn't quite make it all the way to haughty. When Vi saw that Eleanor had completed her mission she lost complete interest in the painting and turned to the table.

"Oo, where am I sitting?' she asked with enthusiasm.

Before Graeme or Evelyn could intervene and add yet another layer of formality to the evening, Vi had found her seat and the rest of the party followed suit. Lindsey observed a wrinkle in Evelyn's brow when she saw everyone sit down in places she had not assigned. A brief look of panic flitted across her features but she managed to keep her composure. In Eleanor's reshuffle Lindsey found herself sitting on Eleanor's left and Simon's right.

As they all got settled Graeme said, "Welcome one and all to Whittaker's Rest. We are delighted to have you here and look forward to a wonderful evening together and hopefully a special day tomorrow."

"Oh yes," Dennis said. "A special day tomorrow."

Eleanor leant toward Lindsey and said, "Sounds as though Dennis has been swigging back the bonhomie again on the quiet."

Evelyn coughed. Dennis was now saying something about the weather. "So I guess we'll have to wait and see what the morning brings," he said. "With the bit of luck those forecasters will be quite wrong and we'll have another marvelous day. If not, well, we might have to have a bit of a rethink. We should convene after breakfast – say ten o'clock – and see how things have developed."

At this point a man in a butler's uniform appeared and collected two bottles of wine off the sideboard.

"There's red and white," Graeme said. "Both from our own humble vines. Both of excellent vintage. We're exceptionally proud of them."

"He rather makes it sound as though he crushed the grapes with his own bare feet," Eleanor said in a quiet voice to Lindsey.

"Did you have a preference?" Graeme asked Eleanor, clearly not liking her lack of attention.

"I was just wondering to my dear friend Lindsey here whether it might be possible to try both. It would be a shame to have come so far and not sample all that there is on offer."

Graeme looked a little confused at this comment but rallied by saying, "The white will go wonderfully well with the first course, and the red with the second. However I will turn over to Evelyn for details on tonight's menu."

"Ah yes," Evelyn said. "Now we have drawn up tonight's menu selection on a card which you will find beneath the plate in front of you." Evelyn drew her own out with a flourish.

The menu had been formally printed on dense stock paper and headed with a crest that might have caused the Queen to get quite envious.

"As you will see, we have a poppy seed seared tuna with spicy beet salsa for entrée and for main a rare roasted eye fillet with pumpkin mash and exotic mushroom sauce. For dessert we are having honey and orange pastry pears. We even have a dessert wine you can sample with that, don't we darling?"

"We've got a first-class Sauternes-style wine you can try, made from our own late-harvest grapes. Fear not, it's far from sweet. My sommelier here will give you more particulars should you need them."

The man dressed as a butler gave a small bow at this. Lindsey could see his neck had flushed around the collar of his suit. The heat of the day still lingered. Lindsey felt grateful she had not been required to dress up in such a stifling fashion. The man looked distinctly uncomfortable. Lindsey had to wonder whether he harbored some reluctance at having to play such a subservient role in this day and age.

As the sommelier went around the table to ask people for their preferences Lindsey took the opportunity to look around her. Next to Simon sat Evelyn and then Bianca next to her. Eddie sat sandwiched between Bianca and Cedric. After having aided and abetted Eleanor to swap places he had not ended up sitting next to Vi. Lindsey wondered if he might be upset about this but he and Cedric were already engaged in conversation. Lindsey could hear Eddie asking Cedric about the trip to Whittington Bay.

"Worth it then, was it?" Eddie asked Cedric.

"Oh my, yes," Cedric replied. "Such magnificent creatures. Did you know that the New Zealand fur seal dives deeper – and for longer – than any other seal?"

"Get away," Eddie said. "I don't fancy that. I like to keep my head above water at all times."

"I expect they're designed for it," Cedric said. "It probably makes them very happy. Of course they're all lucky to still be here what with all the hunting that went on in the days of the early settler. Even today man remains the fur seal's greatest predator."

"Fancy that," said Eddie.

"It's outrageous," Cedric said.

Andrew sat between Cedric and Graeme Barclay with Dennis on Graeme's other side. The three of them had started to discuss wines although they were too far away for Lindsey to hear anything with precision. Lindsey could see Andrew's place setting between a gap in two bowls of flowers and a rather fine set of candle sticks. She couldn't help noticing that Andrew's place card, which had all been folded to make a little tent so that they stood up unaided, had been doctored. On the inside of his card she could see where another name had been written, a name that looked suspiciously like it said Arabella. She could only hope the flowers and candlesticks safely obscured Simon's view of this in case it set him off again.

Vi sat next to Dennis, with Eleanor beside Vi. They were choosing their wines. Eleanor suddenly remembered Lindsey and drew her into the conversation. Lindsey knew she didn't have the capacity for a lot of alcohol - in fact could live without it entirely - so chose a white that she would nurse along for the remainder of the evening. Some people found food and wine matching most essential but Lindsey wasn't one of them.

After the suffering sommelier disappeared a young woman, wearing the closest thing to a French maid's outfit that Lindsey had ever seen, appeared with the first course. All the plates were on a hotel-style serving cart and the young woman whipped them all on the table in a practiced manner. Lindsey couldn't help recalling the young woman at the Golden Sands motel with her surly looks and lanky hair. This young woman looked as though she'd bathed in milk by comparison.

A small lull in conversation came over the group as they began to eat but Evelyn and Graeme were much too urbane to tolerate the undignified sound of mastication and so each commenced talking. Graeme continued his discussion with Andrew and Dennis while Evelyn engaged Bianca in conversation. After a few minutes they discovered a number of mutual Wellington-based acquaintances and set about running them down with panache. Eddie and Cedric started talking again as did Eleanor and Vi.

This left Lindsey and Simon bereft of conversation partners and with only one another for company. While Lindsey found Andrew set her at ease, Simon seemed to have the opposite effect on her. He may as well have been an alien from another planet. She couldn't think of anything they had in common. Simon's good looks and obvious intelligence and sophistication made Lindsey feel like a country bumpkin. Try as she might she could not think of a single thing to say to him. She didn't even feel as though she could ask him about his opinion on the tour lest it prompt him to declare he was leaving.

She noticed after a while that he wasn't eating. He gave the appearance of doing so but instead had engaged in a dismantling exercise which saw him rearrange the food on his plate rather than ingest it. She could feel the pain radiating out of him and felt very sorry. It prompted her to swallow her fear, hope she didn't have teeth laced with poppy seeds and say,

"I hope you don't mind me asking, but do you not like tuna?"

Simon turned to look at her. Several expressions cascaded over his face but in the end he just looked at her as though he'd never seen her in his life.

'I…tuna's fine I suppose. I prefer salmon. I'm just not feeling particularly hungry. Maybe it's the heat."

Lindsey thought it might have been a lot of things but heat probably wasn't one of them.

"Do you have a favorite food?" Lindsey asked, feeling a bit lame for doing so.

"Scallops," Simon replied. "I could eat them by the truckload."

"What about Andrew?"

"That's easy. Chocolate cake. He'll be a bit disappointed there's no chocolate for dessert."

"You've known one another a long time?"

"Twelve years. We met through a tennis club. I suppose you could say we just hit it off, if that's not too bad a pun."

"Oh that's right," Lindsey said. "I think Andrew might have mentioned that."

She wasn't fond of the game with its peculiar scoring system and uncomfortably revealing outfits. It also had a need for strength and a reasonable amount of aggression. The two times she'd been enticed to play she could scarcely get the ball over the net and didn't care enough to persist. Lindsey couldn't think of anywhere to go with that particular thread of conversation.

She glanced over at Andrew who looked up and over at her just at the same moment. He gave her a smile, perhaps to thank for her making the effort to talk to Simon. She smiled back and resolved to try another tack.

"And do you have siblings?" she asked.

"A sister. Justine. She's about three years younger than me and is a vet. Maybe that's why she likes Andrew. He's sort of like a puppy. She's hoping they'll get married."

Lindsey started coughing and felt in danger of inhaling a lungful of poppy seeds.

"Is that likely?" she managed to say.

Simon gave a short laugh at this but it was a sound completely devoid of humor. "She's got no chance. Andrew does like her, but not in that way."

The French maid and sommelier returned at this point. The young woman began whisking away their empty plates. The sommelier began circulating to take wine requests for the second course. Lindsey hadn't even touched her glass at this point. The young woman disappeared with her trolley, no doubt headed for the kitchen. Lindsey was reminded of Pamela Gressingham laboring away in her kitchen to produce the fabulous meal they'd eaten without her. Evelyn undoubtedly had a bevy of staff beavering away in the kitchen thus enabling her to sit majestically at her table and hold court. Sometimes the world felt very unjust.

Ten minutes after the French maid disappeared the sommelier finished his second round and also left the room. The young woman returned on cue moments later with the trolley and proceeded to distribute the main course. Lindsey had to admit it looked a real restaurant-quality dish. It brought out a number of approving comments from her fellow travelers, comments that clearly made Evelyn happy. Dennis was most vociferous with his praise, losing no opportunity to remind his tour party of their great fortune to be in this place and be part of such a fine experience.

In the interim Bianca had claimed Simon's attention and included him in her discussion with Evelyn. She made it perfectly obvious that there wasn't any room in the conversation for Lindsey. Eleanor and Vi were still talking in depth on Lindsey's right. When she listened a little she found they were discussing their sons.

"The thing is," Vi was saying, "he may have got himself into a spot of bother with one of his more entrepreneurial ideas. He reckons he hasn't done anything wrong but fears the long arm of the law might come after him anyway."

"That's no good," Eleanor said.

"Na. The problem with people like Jack, with people like Eddie as well, is that they're too happy-go-lucky. It can rub people up the wrong way sometimes. People either don't like to see others so happy or they suspect it hides something. Either way, it makes them a target."

"Hmm," Eleanor said.

Vi said, "Your son's a lawyer, right? Sebastian? Me and Eddie were sort of wondering if Sebastian might do Jack a favor and give him a bit of legal advice. They are both in London after all."

"He's a barrister," Eleanor corrected gently. "And a pretty busy one at that. Remind me again at the end of the tour and I'll see what I can do. No promises, mind you, even though I know how to make a pretty good case myself."

"That'd be ruddy marvelous," Vi said.

Lindsey tuned out of their conversation and looked down the table to where Andrew still talked with Graeme and Dennis. Graeme, it seemed, was still in full flight about the virtues of his vintages and offered to provide Andrew with a price list should he want to buy a few bottles to take with him.

"It isn't as if you have to carry it," Graeme boomed. "Old Dennis here can take the wine in the mini bus where it would be safe as houses, wouldn't it Dennis?"

Lindsey could hear neither Dennis's response nor Andrew's.

As she ate her most delicious meal she kept her eyes on her plate but let her ears tune in to Eddie and Cedric's conversation. Cedric appeared to be doing most of the talking and failed to notice the imbalance. Eddie had got his "hmm" and "ah" comments down pat and made up for his lack of real interest by drinking a vast quantity of wine. When the sommelier came around for a top-up Eddie beckoned the man over as though he'd just crawled off the edge of the Sahara Desert.

During the course of Cedric's diatribe Lindsey learned a whole pile of new interesting facts. She learned that the average human body contained enough potassium to fire a toy cannon and enough phosphorus to make 2,200 match heads; that human thighbones are as strong as concrete; that the electric chair was invented by a dentist. The way in which Cedric managed to interweave all these relatively useless pieces of information could very well be some sort of undiscovered art form.

After a while - and a bit more wine - Eddie started to find almost everything Cedric said highly amusing. The sound of Eddie's laughter drowned out a lot of other conversation but also made Cedric take a second look at Eddie. It prompted him to say, "Did you know it's estimated that at any one time zero point seven percent of the world's population is drunk?"

Eddie laughed even louder at this.

All the while Lindsey was feeling more and more isolated. She didn't mind not talking and didn't mind not been included in any of the conversations but for the fact that she could not leave the table without drawing attention to herself. It felt odd to be sitting there in a room full of chatting people while she remained silent. Even Simon, who'd imbibed his fair share of wine as well, seemed to have discovered the resources necessary for conversation with Evelyn and Bianca.

At one point, as the young woman started to lay out dessert, Eleanor did turn around to see if all went well for Lindsey but Lindsey didn't have to heart to tell her that she'd not experienced a more miserable time on the trip to date. Vi started tapping Eleanor on the shoulder and Eleanor's attention soon got diverted once more.

For a while Lindsey closed her eyes and thought about her sketches and pondered her story. She hoped to find some time tomorrow to make further drawings of the Barclays' vines but this idea did depend on the good weather holding fast. And when she thought about it, she did need to remind herself that this trip was meant to be about work and not having a good time. Lindsey had actually started to lose sight of this as she'd relaxed and made some new acquaintances.

It suddenly occurred to Lindsey that she did not need to sit at the table any longer. All three courses of the meal had been served and consumed. She could be using this time much more productively. No one – and she meant this without feeling sorry for herself – would really be disadvantaged by her absence.

She leaned around Simon and said, "Excuse me, Mrs. Barclay."

Evelyn Barclay turned to look at Lindsey. Lindsey thought she might be more excited to see a reminder letter from the dentist than she was to look at Lindsey.

"Yes, dear?" Evelyn said.

"I just wanted to say thank you for a lovely meal. I'm going to get along now."

And with that Lindsey stood up and began to walk out of room. She willed herself with every step not to run.

Lindsey returned to her room but did not stay there long. A strange restlessness had overtaken her and even though she'd already covered a lot of ground that day she had it in mind to go for a walk. Even just a small stroll in the grounds around the house and some fresh air might help. She needed time to think and to let her creative brain ponder a little. Lindsey's assigned room had been tastefully decorated but was about as creative as factory assembly line. She needed sky and open spaces.

Lindsey pulled on a cardigan and let herself out of her room. She went down the corridor that ran the length of the top storey, down the staircase at the opposite end of the building and out through a side door that led out onto one of the verandahs. She then skipped down the verandah stairs, across the gravel path and out into the night.

Looking away from the house, the countryside had been veiled in a velvety blackness since Lindsey had last seen it. Yet light poured out from the windows of the Barclays' home so that the darkness wasn't complete. Lindsey walked a little further away and let her eyes adjust. As she got used to her new surroundings she began to make out definable shapes and realized she had come out of the house near to the ornamental fountain where Simon and Andrew had stood together just a few short hours ago.

The sound of tinkling water grew louder as she drew near. It spurted from the top and fell into a giant goblet then out of this into a second and even larger goblet before cascading into the pool below. This was like an enormous paddling pool with wide shallow sides that came up to form a rim wide enough to sit on. It all looked perfectly dry so Lindsey sat down.

The wind came along in little gusts bringing with it the fragrances of the garden. Although she could not identify any flowers in the gloom she could smell the presence of daphne and a hint of lavender. Lindsey could hear the sound of crickets in the vineyard while some creature snuffled nearby. Lindsey idly wondered if it might be a hedgehog.

Clouds obscured one half of the sky while the other half remained clear. Here in the dark, away from the illumination of the house, Lindsey could see a million stars with the sort of clarity she'd never seen before. Some seemed so close it might surely be possible to reach out and touch them. She breathed in the fresh air and felt great pleasure in being an insignificant little grain of sand on the beach of the cosmos. After all, being insignificant wasn't a rare or particularly uncomfortable feeling for Lindsey.

After a few minutes Lindsey heard the sound of footsteps on the gravel pathway. She hoped she might not be visible. She hoped that whoever wandered around the house might simply wander away. As the footsteps neared she heard them halt. This made her feel a little vulnerable so she turned to see who had come out of the house.

To her complete surprise it was Andrew.

When he saw her looking his way he waved and came over.

"There you are," he said. "I wondered where you'd gone."

"Did you?" Lindsey said, feeling every bit as shocked as she sounded.

He waved at the fountain edge. "Mind if I join you?"

Lindsey didn't need to give it a second thought. "Please do."

Andrew sat down and arranged his long legs.

"What are you doing out here?" he asked.

"Philosophizing," Lindsey replied. "Enjoying the serenity."

"You've picked a nice spot for it," Andrew said. "And what have you concluded?"

Lindsey shrugged. "Not much. I had been eyeing up those clouds, though. Do you think they're coming in to rain on our parade?"

"Probably. Dennis said as much, didn't he?"

"Hmm." Lindsey hadn't really been listening at the time.

"But then Dennis says a lot of things when given the chance," Andrew said. "He certainly had a lot to say at dinner."

"Maybe he gets lonely driving the mini bus. Maybe he'd much rather be out in the wilds with all of us."

Andrew laughed. "I can just picture him staggering down the road in an attempt to carry all our luggage. And I think he'd try it too, if he thought it would do any good. I think he'd try just about anything for his baby, De Vine Tours."

"It was a nice meal though," Lindsey said.

"Very nice. Evelyn's chef did a lovely job. I thought you didn't look too happy throughout proceedings. That's why I came to find you. To see if you were okay?"

Lindsey sighed. So it was a sympathy visit.

"I wasn't unhappy," Lindsey said quite truthfully.

"But you weren't happy either," Andrew concluded.

Lindsey said nothing. She could think of nothing to say that wouldn't promote a fresh wave of pity from Andrew, something she neither needed nor wanted.

"I saw Bianca leave you out of the conversation," Andrew said.

"She and Evelyn were talking about Wellington, about people they knew and places they go. It turns out that Simon also spends time in Wellington as part of his job and that set off a lengthy discussion to which I couldn't have added a thing."

"And then Eleanor and Vi talked up a storm."

Lindsey nodded. "Vi wants Eleanor's boy Sebastian to meet her boy Jack. They both live in London."

"Do they? My brother lives in London."

"Does he?"

"Sure. Mark's been over there for about two years, living and working. I think his visa's about to expire though. Mum's hoping he can't renew it and that will force him to come home. She misses her baby. Come to think of it, we all miss him."

"And do you think it's likely that he will come back?"

"Hope so. But if not, he could always get together with Sebastian and Jack. They could have a grand old time together."

Lindsey laughed. "I'm not sure he would want to go. One of them needs some legal advice and other is supposed to supply it."

"No prizes for guessing who might be who in that equation."

"Probably not."

After a moment Andrew said, "Anyway, I'm sorry you got left out. I don't think it was deliberate."

Lindsey pictured Bianca's scheming face and couldn't be too sure about that.

"Not to worry," she said. "I'm not a wildly social person anyway. I…let's just say it was pretty much business as usual for me."

Andrew made a funny sound that Lindsey could not interpret. Out in the gloom she could not see his face clearly either.

"But you did try to talk to Simon?"

"I did," Lindsey said. "Not very successfully, I'm afraid. He did tell me you were getting married though."

"What?"

"Ha ha," she said. "Just joking. What he actually said was that his sister is in love with you and wants to marry you."

"You had me going for a minute there," Andrew said. "I hope he told you that while I like Justine there isn't any chance of me proposing, ever. She's really not my type. Besides, I'm thinking about giving my heart away to someone else entirely."

Lindsey felt her mouth go dry and could not respond.

"What else did Simon tell you?" Andrew asked.

"That you met through tennis."

"You already knew that," Andrew said with a smile. "Do you play?"

Lindsey gave a short laugh. "Let's just say that sports and I don't really see eye to eye."

A silence fell as Andrew pondered this. After a while Lindsey felt she just had to know the lay of the land.

"I hope you don't mind me asking, but does Simon want to leave?" she asked.

Another silence. At length Andrew said, "He does. He got in contact with his father, just to check in and let his family know that he's doing better and that they shouldn't worry. When he asked his father how things were going his father confessed that a number of wedding related issues had come up. Apparently Arabella's family hadn't been quite as diligent as they should have been in sorting out the ramifications of the cancelled wedding. While the De Villes are as rich as Croesus they didn't get that way by being generous. I gather they have refused to pay for a number of things since the services weren't used. Trouble is brewing. These companies are then trying to track Simon down to be recompensed. Simon hates to think of having left his parents in the lurch and feels he should go home."

"How awful, especially on top of everything else."

"I know. But on the flip side I don't think Simon is ready to face the music just yet. He has improved, but the week of the tour that remains would still do him a world of good."

"So you don't want to go?"

"Me? Certainly not. While I hadn't ever planned on coming on this trip it has been a most unexpected and charming delight."

"You do surprise me," Lindsey said. "I would have thought you'd found us all a bit of a motley crew."

Andrew laughed. "Not at all. People are interesting, don't you think? You have to admit that Eddie and Vi are real characters and that Eleanor is most charming and maybe even a little mysterious. And think of the things you must have learned from Cedric. Where else could I have found out that a quarter of the bones in my body are in my feet or that the strongest muscle is the tongue? Who's to say when such information might come in handy?"

"He told me today that it's physically impossible for pigs to look up at the sky," Lindsey said.

"Pity he hadn't told you that earlier," Andrew said. "We could have checked that out for ourselves back at Price Cottage."

They both laughed.

"And Bianca?" Lindsey asked.

"Ah, Bianca," Andrew said. "To know her is to love her. She reminds me of a number of girls I know at home."

Lindsey did not know how to interpret that remark.

"Anyway, back to your original question about going home. For now I've persuaded Simon to wait a couple of days and see what his dad sorts out. If things are still problematic we can always review it then. But it might be better if you keep that between the two of us. While everyone is getting along so well – apart from Bianca and Cedric – it would be a shame to start unsettling people needlessly."

"Of course," Lindsey said.

"And hopefully," Andrew added, "we can keep on enjoying the journey. What's to object to when your days are full of leisurely walks, good food and good company?"

"The walking wasn't so leisurely for Eleanor and me today," Lindsey said.

"Because we left you with Cedric?"

"Cedric? No, he wasn't a problem. It was after he'd gone that the trouble started. Eleanor and I sort of miscounted the fields. We didn't know whether the wilderness area from the road to the first paddock should be counted as a field and so we made the mistake of walking through the field with the bull."

Andrew looked at her with surprise. "You didn't?"

Lindsey nodded. "I have to say that the bull wasn't in the slightest bit pleased to see us. In fact Eleanor and I had to run for our lives. We only just made it out of there unscathed by the skin of our teeth."

"Oh, Lindsey," Andrew said. He looked as though he was tossing up whether to laugh or wag his finger at her.

"Don't tell anyone, will you? We both feel pretty embarrassed about it. I'll keep your secret and you can keep mine."

"Fair enough," Andrew said. "Let's shake on it."

He proffered his hand and for the second time in less than twenty-four hours Lindsey found herself holding the hand of a young man she had begun to like very much. After a brief shake Lindsey withdrew her hand in case she started getting silly ideas.

"I can see that in future I might need to keep a closer eye on you, Lindsey McIntyre," Andrew said.

Lindsey smiled. She couldn't help it. This was one of the nicest things anyone had ever said to her.

CHAPTER NINE

When Lindsey woke up and went over to pull back the curtains the following morning she found the sky shrouded by pewter clouds with a steady fall of rain coming down from the heavens. By the way the plants drooped under the weight of the water it seemed clear it had been raining for some time. The leaden look of the clouds suggested it wasn't about to let up any time soon. It certainly wasn't the slightest bit conducive to getting out amongst the vines for another session of sketching.

On top of this a strange melancholy had descended on Lindsey overnight. Where she had felt light and optimistic after talking with Andrew, she now felt unsettled and unsure of herself. All had seemed well while they were together. They had chatted for some time about nothing consequential – food, movies, art – before agreeing that the time had come to turn in for the night. When they parted he had smiled at her in a way that suggested all would be well and that she mustn't worry.

But worry she did, and wonder.

She wondered why he had bothered to seek her out in the first place. Why would he care whether she was all right or not? She wasn't anyone of importance, just a fellow traveler whom he'd never see again in a week's time. Lindsey could only conclude that he'd done it out of pity. This wasn't altogether surprising since they all knew him to be compassionate. After all, he'd only come on the trip in the first place to be a support for his friend. Not everyone would do that.

She wondered what he had meant by a lot of things that he'd said. Like loving Bianca for who she was, like mentioning he had contemplated giving his heart away to another, like offering to be an escort for Eleanor and herself. What did this all mean?

But most of all she worried about herself. She worried that she liked this young man far more than could be considered sensible. When she thought about him she saw someone so different from herself. He was the sort of person to whom things came easily. He'd been brought up in a good home, went to a good school where he used his good brain, he'd made good friends, had a good job, was good looking.

Someone like that would never be interested in Lindsey. She was a person from a dysfunctional home, had gone to a string of different schools as the family moved around, had few friends, a low opinion of herself and nothing in her looks to recommend her. And even if by some miracle he was interested, she had nothing to offer in return. She knew her deficits to the absolute nth degree and knew she'd make a far from worthy partner for anyone.

The whole idea bordered on being ridiculous. The very thought of it made Lindsey feel ashamed.

Lindsey quailed when it came to the idea of going down to breakfast. The prospect of seeing Andrew when she knew she liked him made her feel embarrassed, especially if he had a hint of it himself. Her despondent mood had killed her appetite anyway.

Instead Lindsey drew out her sketchbook and decided to spend the time between now and their rendezvous time of ten o'clock to review her work and to make some refinements to one or two sketches. The fountain had also given her a new idea for another work entirely. She figured she could make one of two drawings of some of the images she had in her mind before they got lost.

Eleanor came by to see how she fared and tried to persuade Lindsey to go down for breakfast. When Lindsey told Eleanor she wanted to work, Eleanor went away but came back a little while later with some breakfast pastries on a plate in case Lindsey felt hungry in a while. She then left Lindsey to her own devices.

At ten o'clock Lindsey figured she could hide no longer. Dennis wanted everyone to get together to discuss the plan for the day and although Lindsey couldn't imagine what that might be she would go down anyway. Obedience was, after all, a trait that ran deep within her.

When Lindsey descended the stairs she found everyone already congregated in the foyer. Lindsey caught sight of Eleanor and made a beeline for her. She studiously avoided eye contact with any other member of the tour party.

"Righty-o people," Dennis said. "Welcome to day seven of the tour, officially a rest day here at the beautiful and very aptly named Whittaker's Rest. Unfortunately, as forecast, the weather has packed in and so wandering around in the grounds or lounging by the pool seem off the cards for this morning at any rate. With any luck it may brighten up later today and you may be able to take a dip. In the meantime you're free to enjoy the house or if you would like to spread your wings a little I do have an alternative in mind.

"There's a little town about half an hour's drive inland from here called Waiata Junction. Its merits are reasonably humble but it does have a few shops and eateries and even a grocery store. It also has a gas station and since I need to fill the mini bus's tank up I thought I would make the offer and see if anyone would like to come with me for a small slice of civilization. Any takers? A show of hands?"

Eleanor looked at Lindsey to see if she'd like to go. Lindsey could see that Eleanor herself would like to so she nodded her assent and they both put their hands up. When Lindsey looked around at the group it was to find that all eight of them waved their hands in the air.

The group, it seemed, was off to town.

Dennis gave everyone fifteen minutes to get themselves organized and get to the mini bus. Lindsey and Eleanor returned to their rooms to collect purses and umbrellas and in Eleanor's case, the letters she'd written in her few quiet moments. She hoped to find a post office. Eleanor then came back to collect Lindsey from her room, an arrangement that suited Lindsey very well. Safety in numbers seemed highly desirable right now.

When they got to the mini bus they were the first to arrive so had their choice of seat. Lindsey indicated her wish to sit behind the driver's seat at the front. Eddie and Vi soon bustled along and claimed the two seats behind them. Vi had brought with her a voluminous beach bag into which she appeared to have packed half their belongings. Cedric and Dennis appeared together from around the side of the house. Cedric climbed into the front cab with Dennis. Simon and Andrew came dashing out of the house and claimed their usual seat at the back. As they did so Lindsey gazed out of the window on the far side. She could not bring herself to look at Andrew's face.

Of Bianca there wasn't a sign. Minutes passed. Lindsey could hear Dennis start to mutter under his breath and look at his watch. Finally, just after Eleanor had suggested they send out a search party, Bianca came waltzing out of the house with Graeme Barclay as an escort. He held aloft a large umbrella to shelter Bianca from the worst of the rain. Bianca had changed since they last had seen her into an outfit more befitting a trip to one of the capitals of Europe. She appeared to need all the sheltering she could get.

"Ridiculous," Lindsey heard Eleanor say under her breath. "Where on earth does she think she's going? And did you see the crazy heels on her shoes? The girl is mad."

With Bianca safely on board Dennis got under way. With windshield wipers on, he completed a quick maneuver to turn the mini bus around and then put on some speed to take them down the Barclays' very long driveway and out onto the road.

This was only Lindsey's third time in the mini bus and it felt strange to be back under motor power again. It seemed hard to believe that they could have walked all the way to Whittaker's Rest – a distance easily travelable by mini bus in no time at all – but walk they had. It seemed like a real achievement. The atmosphere in the mini bus felt different this time around. Last time, at the outset of the tour, none of them had known one another very well. Conversations had been stilted if they started at all. People had been watchful and wary. Simon and Andrew had kept completely to themselves with Simon's sad story yet untold. Now, at this juncture, they'd learned a whole raft of things about each other during the past week.

The atmosphere in the mini bus became even closer as they clocked up the miles. With damp conditions and multiple bodies the windows of the van had fogged up. Lindsey wiped a circle out of the condensation but it scarcely made a bit of difference to her view. The landscape outside sat sodden and uninspiring.

However, by the time they reached Waiata Junction the cloud cover had begun to lighten and it had stopped raining. The gas station lay at the beginning of the Waiata Junction shops. Dennis pulled the mini bus over into the car park adjoining the forecourt so they could all get out.

Dennis gathered them around for a final pep talk before setting them loose on the local populace.

"Here we are then, folks," he said. "It's stopped raining, thank goodness. Now Waiata Junction is not very big so I would say there's no danger of getting lost. Most of the shops lie along the main road here but there are a few down the side roads and down by the river. There's a riverside walk should any of you get inspired and the weather holds.

"In case you've all lost track of time, it's Saturday today. In a place like

Waiata Junction that means the shops will close at two o'clock. I suggest we meet back here where I can get a safe park at about..." he looked at his watch, "...at about two thirty. That should give everyone plenty of time to explore, have lunch, run any errands you might have and be safely back on time. If the weather's improved even more by then you might still get a chance for a dip in the Barclays' pool before dinner this evening. Any questions?"

"What should we do if we get lost?" Cedric asked.

"Stay that way," Lindsey heard Bianca mutter.

"You aren't planning on it, are you Cedric?" Dennis asked with a good-natured smile.

"Certainly not," Cedric replied.

"Good. I trust you all have my cell phone number. If you get into difficulties just give me a bell. I'll be round about the place. I think you'll find everything very straightforward and the natives more than friendly. See you all at two thirty."

Cedric hung back momentarily after Dennis's final announcement to see what everyone would do. As predicted, Simon and Andrew set off together with Bianca just steps behind. Cedric couldn't help feeling pleased about this. He almost didn't mind where he ended up as long as it wasn't with Bianca. Eddie and Vi had got into a little knot with Eleanor and Lindsey in order to discuss their strategy for setting forth. This left Cedric alone again, naturally.

Cedric had wondered if he might be able to tag along with Dennis for the day. After all, Dennis had to do something between now and two-thirty to fill in his time. That totaled three and a half hours to be whittled away. But earlier, when Cedric had mooted the idea of the two of them teaming up, Dennis had been very elusive. It seemed clear that whatever Dennis's agenda might be it did not include Cedric.

It occurred to Cedric that if he didn't get a move-on he would be caught standing about looking sheepish. He made a point of avoiding such social embarrassment. Dennis had already disappeared into the gas station shop and only the other four remained so Cedric turned on his heel and headed toward the shops.

Cedric's first observations on the town of Waiata Junction were that it bustled with people and that it bore a striking resemblance to their first stop of the trip, Brookfield. Like Brookfield, this town comprised of a main street laced with retail shops and several minor roads coming off that to provide access to businesses of a more industrial nature. Unlike Brookfield, Waiata Junction did not have a wide grass strip in the middle of the main road but the local council had established gardens at regular intervals down the main drag and these all look well tended.

And where Brookfield had been built on flat land, Waiata Junction had been constructed on a shallow ridge. Side roads to the left led west and dropped down to a plain that stretched as far as the distant Tararua Ranges. The roads to the right were slightly steeper and went down toward the river. Cedric presumed that if the river ever flooded the shops on the main road would be out of harm's way since they sat on higher ground.

Brisk traffic trawled up and down the main road. Competition for free car park spaces seemed fierce. The road glistened with rain. Almost every vehicle bore traces of agricultural life: muck spattered up mudguards and onto the rear of vehicles, utes loaded with collections of farm implements, even the odd sheep dog with his head hanging out of the window. As cars parked they disgorged an array of people: farmers young and old, families in town to run errands, even the odd passing tourist in a rental car.

The sidewalk bustled with pedestrians. Cedric saw two men greet each other like old friends - a meeting that involved a vast amount of pumping of hands - while further on three women stood swapping gossip while taking up the bulk of walkable space. Cedric passed a gift shop, a clothes shop and a furniture shop that appeared to specialize in country-style pieces and accompanying soft furnishings. On the other side of the road he could see another gift shop - one that looked as though it featured souvenirs – a hairdressers and a beauty salon. He came across a gourmet food shop, a bookshop, a shop that sold a dizzying array of items made from plastic and an antique shop.

Cedric ignored all of these shops for now. He was a man on a mission with only one destination in mind. He determined to keep walking until such time as he found what he was looking for.

Simon and Andrew set a cracking pace that Bianca found hard to keep up with. She didn't know what the hurry was since Dennis had only minutes before pronounced that they were to be marooned in this hellhole for three and a half entire hours. Since it appeared to be smaller than the size of a city block there really didn't seem to be any need to rush. If they went too fast they've done the whole town over in the first five minutes and then be casting about for things to do to fill in the time. There were a lot of things in life that Bianca couldn't stand. Pointless hanging about came very close to the top of the list.

"Where are we headed?" Bianca asked from behind them.

Both Simon and Andrew swiveled around with looks of surprise on their faces. Bianca could only conclude that neither of them had realized she'd come with them. Men really could be so dense at times.

"Well?" she said when neither of them replied.

"We're just getting our bearings," Andrew said.

"What we should be getting is coffee," Bianca countered. "Not that I would imagine this dump would manage anything better than filtered."

Andrew looked at Simon.

"Coffee?"

Simon shrugged. "I suppose so. It isn't as if we don't have plenty of time to kill."

"If I'd known Dennis had proposed coming for such a long time I might not have bothered coming at all," Bianca said as they walked along looking for any place that looked hopeful.

They passed one eating establishment still clinging on to the old coffee lounge tradition. Its gloom undoubtedly hid a multitude of sins, among them stodgy food, lukewarm beverages, utilitarian crockery and cutlery and tables smeared with a sticky patina of grime. The trio gave it a wide berth.

As they walked along there seemed little choice of other eateries. They saw a bakery and one Indian restaurant that didn't open until evenings and a greasy spoon takeaway. Then finally, when all hope of finding anywhere decent seemed lost, they came across a very pleasant looking café with fancy tables and interesting art on the walls.

They filed in and ordered coffee at the counter before claiming a table by the window.

"This isn't bad," Andrew said.

"I guess not," Bianca said. "Although I must say that after being spoilt by the Barclays, the benchmark has been raised a bit. That was a great meal last night."

"It was," Andrew said. "Although Graeme Barclay did lay it on a bit thick about the virtues of his wine."

"I don't know who was responsible for the seating arrangements last night but they didn't do a good job," Bianca said. "I'm sure if Evelyn had been responsible she would have deferred to Dennis as to a good fit for where people sat. To be honest I'm not sure which of you two boys I felt sorrier for. There you were, Andrew, stuck with Cedric, while you had to put up with Lindsey, Simon, mooning about the place as she does."

Simon said, "I think she's just shy. We did have one small conversation and she was very pleasant, in a mousey sort of way. She did seem concerned for my welfare."

"I'd say she's someone who takes time to get to know others," Andrew said.

Bianca rolled her eyes. "And I'd say it scarcely seems worth the effort. Anyway, I rescued you from having to talk with Lindsey after that. You have to admit that Evelyn Barclay is a superior hostess. Such charming and interesting conversation."

Their coffee arrived.

Simon said, "I would never have guessed that we knew so many people in common." To Andrew he said, "She knows my parents. Apparently she grew up in Auckland and moved in the same circles as my father. She even went to their wedding, although lost touch with them when she moved down here."

"Really?" Andrew said. "But then that's New Zealand for you. Much more two degrees of separation than six."

"I'm hoping that the rest of the tour can live up to the same standard of accommodation as Whittaker's Rest," Bianca said. "What Dennis seems to forget is that I'm here to review the tour for prospective clientele. If he thinks he's been pushing the boat out to ensure the utmost in deference and service then he's got another thing coming."

"It hasn't been so bad, has it?" Andrew asked.

Bianca made a scoffing sound. "The Golden Sands motel was beyond doubt the worst place I've ever stayed. Christian House had promise I will admit, but having us stay with those lesbians at Price Cottage was the limit."

"I thought those ladies were real characters," Andrew said. "And what about Redpath Lodge? I know we did have separate accommodation there but the rest looked nice."

"Nice? Hardly a word for an advertising slogan, is it? You aren't going to attract scores of new clients with that sort of wet-fish recommendation. Besides, I got bad vibes off Pamela Gressingham. She could do with a few lessons in hospitality from Evelyn."

Andrew drained his coffee and looked at his watch.

"I saw a book shop back there a way," he said. "I wouldn't mind having a browse, maybe find something to read for our downtime hours. Do either of you want to come?"

Simon and Bianca looked at one another. Bianca made a face that indicated she'd really rather not. Simon clearly felt the same way.

"Right you are, then," Andrew said. "I'll leave you to it. No doubt I'll catch you both up later."

And with that he stood up and took his leave.

By the time Andrew emerged from the café the clouds had started to disperse. The forecasted fine weather looked for once like playing its part in the prognostication. Steam rose from the road as the deposited rain turned to vapor. Thin sunshine cast a citrine glow on the town. The air felt fresh and clean in a way that it never did in the city. It felt good to Andrew to be somewhere different and to set out on his own to explore. He'd started to feel as though he couldn't remember how it felt to fly solo.

As much as Andrew sympathized with Simon and his plight, the burden of having to keep his friend's spirits up had begun to wear thin. He'd come on this tour as the only practical thing he could think of doing to ensure Simon didn't get crushed under the weight of his misery. It had been such a difficult time in the beginning, made even more so by the two of them having to share accommodation, but as the days passed Andrew had found himself enjoying the tour for its own merits.

Andrew had struggled with this. After all, he'd not come to have a nice time or to please himself but to be an ongoing support for Simon, whose moods continued to fluctuate. At times, when they were on their own, Simon still lapsed into melancholy silences or had outbursts of anger or wondered afresh how on earth he could ever bear to face people. But Andrew had long since run out of cheering speeches and platitudes. He now often felt tempted to leave Simon to his own devices.

Mercifully there were some signs of improvement. Andrew wasn't overly enamored with the charms of Evelyn Barclay but he did have reason to thank her. She had managed to draw Simon out during last night's dinner. For the first time there had been traces of real animation in Simon's expressions. This welcome improvement was tinged only with the fact that his friend had completely ignored the plight of his neighbor. There had been a couple of times during the evening when Andrew had wanted to shout at everyone and chastise them for their complete insensitivity. Even Eleanor, who Andrew liked very much, had left Lindsey to sit alone and unhappy while everyone else enjoyed themselves. He still felt sorry this morning that he'd not done anything about it.

Now, though, with Simon still reasonably buoyant from last night's dinner, and with him having found some common ground with Bianca, Andrew felt free to take some time out for himself. As they'd walked along he'd spied a bookshop on the other side of the road and upon seeing it had been struck by an idea. The fact that Simon and Bianca hadn't wanted to come with him suited Andrew just fine. He cut across the road opposite the antique shop.

Andrew opened the door of the bookshop to the smell of paper and the sounds of an old fashioned bell. And while it might have been an outmoded form of alarm in this day and age it proved just as effective as any modern contraption. The lady behind the counter put down the book she held and looked up to greet him with a dreamy expression on her face. It took him a couple of seconds to realize that he'd seen that dreamy expression before.

"It's Miss Silver, isn't it?" Andrew asked. "From Price Cottage?"

She gave a tinkling little laugh that sounded a lot like the doorbell. "It's been a long time since people have called me Miss Silver. You must call me Maryanne. Miss Silver always sounds to me like something that should be used in a science experiment."

Andrew smiled.

"I'm sorry," Maryanne said. "But do I know you?"

"Only vaguely," Andrew said, not in the slightest bit put out. "I just stayed at your house the night before last."

"Of course," Maryanne said, clapping herself on the cheeks. "One of the De Vine Tour lot. How silly of me. Cybil always says I can't see any further than book distance in front of my nose. She says I'd have more chance of recognizing Elizabeth Bennet or Jane Eyre than I would a real live person. I'm afraid I can't remember your name."

"It's Andrew," he said. "I suppose you see a lot of faces coming through on the tour?"

"Not so many," Maryanne replied. "We usually have a group to stay about every six or eight weeks, sometimes even longer over the winter months."

"That's not too often at all," Andrew said.

"I think Dennis's business is only at the fledgling stage. He would like to be running tours every two or three weeks - more or less back to back - but the numbers just aren't there at the moment. I'm afraid I don't think we help matters much. Our property is reasonably humble compared to some you get to stay at. We don't have a lot with which to recommend ourselves. It must drag the overall rating of the tour down considerably."

Andrew thought of Bianca's unfavorable comments on the subject and said, "I wouldn't say that at all. I found my stay at your place to be quite charming."

"How kind of you to say so, especially since you were one of the young men we popped in the annex. As I recall, you were supposed to be on your honeymoon."

Andrew made a face. "Not me. My friend, Simon. Unfortunately, his bride failed to turn up at the church. I'm the best man."

"Oh, how sad," Maryanne said. "Almost as sad as poor Jane Eyre turning up to marry Mr. Rochester only to find at the eleventh hour that he was already married. Still, that all turned out fine in the end, didn't it? Apart from poor Mr. Rochester's eyesight, that is."

Andrew had never read *Jane Eyre* so really couldn't comment. Instead he said, "I'll be sure to tell Simon that he shouldn't lose all hope. I didn't realize you worked here."

"Oh, I don't," she said, despite of all evidence to the contrary.

"No?"

Maryanne seemed to comprehend Andrew's confusion and laughed again. "A dear friend of ours owns the bookshop. She's gone to Wellington for the weekend and so I'm filling in. Lord alone knows why she trusts me, but there it is. I have conquered the terrible job of learning how to use the till and the card machine thingy and know to watch for people shoving things up their jumpers. I can even point people in the direction of a good book or two. Whether I'm actually any good at any of these things is another matter."

"I'm sure you do just fine," Andrew said.

"How was the walk yesterday?" Maryanne asked.

"Good for my part," Andrew said. "Although maybe not everyone would agree. Two of the party got chased by a bull."

"Oh my. How alarming. I hope they are both none the worse for the experience."

"Not that I could tell," Andrew said, hoping Lindsey wouldn't mind his having mentioned the adventure to Maryanne. Thoughts of Lindsey reminded him of his true purpose for visiting the bookshop.

"This might seem a bit of a strange question but I was wondering, do you have a children's section?"

"Of course," Maryanne replied. "It's in that recessed area over there. Go and have a look for yourself. Let me know if you have any questions."

Before Andrew had even turned away Maryanne had her nose back in her book. He moved off. Andrew wondered what the chances were of finding Lindsey's book in a remote shop like this. He had no idea whether she was a household name or yet another writer in the firmament of obscure authors.

The children's alcove contained three main sections: a good selection of picture books, a number of shelves for junior readers and a section for teens that seemed to be crammed with books about vampires and fallen angels. The walls had been decorated with images of ladybirds and bumblebees and flowers. A few beanbags had been scattered about in the middle of the alcove but the area, like the rest of the shop, was mercifully unoccupied at present.

The picture books had been stacked several deep in shallow shelves fronted by plastic coated wire and all faced out. Andrew had no idea what he was looking for so began on the top shelf by flicking through and looking at the author's names. When he got down to the bottom shelf he thought the chances of coming up trumps seemed very slim but there, to his surprise, he found a book written and illustrated by Lindsey McIntyre.

She'd entitled it *Gilbert's Outing* which had been embossed in raised letters on the front. Under the title stood a small mouse dressed in a cute little outfit, his rucksack on his back. He had a wonderful expression of expectancy and fear on his face and had been cleverly drawn. Andrew ran his hands over the embossed title and felt almost reverential. He didn't know what it was about Lindsey that brought out strange emotions in him. He'd started to feel a bit crazy.

He turned the pages until he reached the beginning of the story and there he read the tale of Gilbert the mouse who sets off to go to the beach for the day and who ends up collecting a whole lot of animal friends on the way. In Andrew's inexpert opinion on such things the book's illustrations seemed exquisite and the story a simple but clever lesson on different animals and on how friends enhance a person's life. He loved the way she'd written about Gilbert's new friends, most of whom are far from perfect, but who in the end make Gilbert realize he can have a much better time with them than he would by himself.

The story could almost be prophetic. Lindsey, like Gilbert, appeared to have set out with very few friends and had gathered more on the way. Andrew didn't always find Lindsey easy to read but he could see that she appeared almost surprised to be enjoying herself at times. Then something seemed to happen in her thought processes, perhaps something that told her having a good time might be unwise, and she'd retreat back into her quiet ways. He'd seen that in her this morning. After their nice chat the previous evening Andrew had felt as though he'd made some progress in getting beneath the brittle veneer she wore much of the time. This morning, however, she'd quite deliberately not even glanced his way and her protective defenses were back up again.

Andrew found her to be such a dichotomy. On the one hand she seemed shy and vulnerable and a bit like a whipped dog. He found this brought a strange streak of protectiveness out of him as it had last night as he'd watched her struggle valiantly through the interminable meal. The desire to help her - to somehow ease her discomfort - had been very strong.

On the other hand she could be warm and funny and caring. Her talent just blew him away. If her relationship with Eleanor could be used as a yardstick then she clearly knew how to make friends, given the right sort of person. And when he looked at her book Andrew had to review his assessment that she needed help. Not if she could assist children to understand the world around them in such a simple yet eloquent fashion. It was enough to make him feel like he'd not achieved anything in his own life worth mentioning.

No, he just could not figure her out. He could only conclude that something had happened to her to make her so diffident. She was so different from all of the girls he knew at home, many of whom were like Bianca with their cynical outlook and obvious charms. He found himself intrigued enough to want to know more. All he had to do now was convince Lindsey that she could trust him.

When Eleanor, Lindsey, Eddie and Vi emerged from their huddle they found no sign of the rest of the tour party. Lindsey had seen Simon and Andrew stride off with Bianca trailing in their wake but she hadn't seen Dennis and Cedric disappear. The foursome agreed that Dennis and Cedric must have gone off together somewhere since they seemed fast friends these days.

Their huddle had achieved precisely nothing. Since none of them had a faintest clue as to the charms of Waiata Junction they'd ended up talking around in circles about what they might do depending on what they found. In the end the most sensible thing seemed to be to set out and see what there was to be seen and where their meanderings might take them.

Eleanor's number one aim lay in finding a post office, preferably before it closed for the day. Just because most of the shops stayed open until two o'clock they couldn't assume that the post office would adhere to the same rules. They started off down the main street where there seemed to be plenty of activity happening. The busy sidewalk meant they could not walk close together and Vi's bulky bag also proved a bit of a hindrance. This caused Eddie to use a voice at the volume akin to a bullhorn. For the first time since they started the tour his voice was as loud as his shirt.

"This town's quite nice," he hollered. "Bit of a step up from Brookfield. Let's hope the natives are a bit friendlier too."

Eleanor cringed and said, "I wonder where the post office is."

"We should ask someone," Vi suggested.

"Eh?" said Eddie.

"I said we should ask someone where the post office is," Vi shouted.

"Good plan," came the loud reply. "What about asking that man?"

The man in question had just got out of his car. He turned to look at them, probably on account of Eddie's booming voice. As they came into focus the man's face crinkled into a smile of recognition.

"If I'm not mistaken it's the poor bereft out-of-towners," he said looking at Eleanor. "I don't know if you remember but we met in Brookfield last weekend? As I recall you were in search of somewhere to eat?"

Lindsey watched Eleanor's face light up and with just cause. Although well into middle age, the man remained very good-looking. Somehow the word "dashing" sprang to mind.

"We were indeed," Eleanor said. "We even lived to tell the tale. Fancy meeting you again. Aren't you a little out of your way here?"

"Not at all," the man said. "My property is about half way between Brookfield and Waiata Junction so sometimes I mix it up a bit."

"You devil," Eleanor said, almost batting her eyelashes. Lindsey found Eleanor in full flirty mode to be quite entertaining.

"And what about you four? What brings you to here?"

Eleanor said, "When you last saw us we were about to commence a walking tour that goes from Brookfield through to Gordondale. We're staying at a nearby property and have come into town to run errands and fill in some time until the weather clears."

"I see," the man said. "Where are you staying?"

"At Whittaker's Rest," Eddie said before Eleanor could answer. "Gawd, what a place. Do you know it?"

"Of course," the man said. "Evelyn and Graeme Barclay are friends of mine."

"Cor," Eddie said. "It really is a small world round here, ain't it?"

"I suppose so," the man replied. "It's often the same in rural communities. Everyone gets to know everyone else, one way or another."

"That sounds quite delightful," Eleanor purred. "I'm Eleanor by the way. And this is Eddie and Vi Jones, and my young friend Lindsey."

"Charmed to meet you all. I'm Tom. Tom Aughton."

They all shook hands. Eleanor almost purred when her turn came.

Tom said, "So are you keen to sample the delights of Waiata Junction? Are you in need of a café recommendation?"

"We might be a bit later," Eleanor said. "But first I need to find a post office. I don't suppose you know where it is?"

"I do indeed," Tom said. "Let me show you the way."

Eleanor smiled widely. Lindsey felt certain that if Tom had offered her his arm she would have taken it immediately.

Tom and Eleanor set off at the front of the group with the rest of them trailing behind as space on the sidewalk allowed. Lindsey couldn't help likening Tom to the Pied Piper with them having fallen under his thrall. All he lacked was the two-toned coat and the pipe. He led them along past half a dozen shops before leading them across a pedestrian crossing then past more shops and a cafe until they came toward the end of the ribbon of businesses. He then led them into a shop selling magazines and stationery. There at the back they saw the post office agency.

Eleanor beamed. "Well," she said. "I think we would have had a hard time finding this without you."

Tom smiled. "Somehow I doubt that," he said. "I suspect you are a most resourceful person even though I do have a weakness for a damsel in distress."

Eleanor looked even more pleased. Eddie looked at Vi and said, "Blimey."

Eddie, Vi and Lindsey partly turned away to leave the smitten pair to stare into each other's eyes.

"I have to get going now, I'm afraid," they heard Tom say.

"That's a shame," Eleanor said. "You could have joined us for lunch."

Tom laughed. "Alas, as tempting as that sounds, I fear I'm not able to. If you're looking for somewhere nice there's a café down by the river. The food is good and the outlook is very pleasant."

"Thanks," Eleanor said. "We'll be sure to check it out."

A small silence followed and then Tom asked, "How much longer are you in the area for?"

"A week," Eleanor replied.

"Hmm," said Tom. "Maybe I should give you my cell phone number. That's twice now that I've come to your aid. Who knows how many more emergencies you might have in the next seven days?"

It was Eleanor's turn to laugh. "None, I hope, but that does sound like a very sensible idea."

She then drew a cell phone from her handbag that Lindsey had never seen Eleanor use to date. The pair proceeded to exchange numbers.

"Don't hesitate to call," Tom said to Eleanor. To the rest of the group he said, "Nice to meet you all. Enjoy the rest of your tour."

And with that he was gone.

Lindsey, Eddie and Vi browsed around the stationery shop while Eleanor joined the short but very slow moving line at the post office counter. The heavy-set woman behind the counter sounded ratty and not inclined to either hurry or be obliging. She looked the sort of person who had not been happy for a very long time and in consequence had lost the skill entirely. It wasn't hard to picture some poor hen-pecked man at home awaiting her return with about as much enthusiasm as a prisoner on death row.

Eddie and Vi went off to look at the racks of magazines. Vi declared herself to be passionate about magazines, especially those that were gossipy in nature. They'd been on the road for one week and all sorts of scandals in tinsel town and amongst the royals could have taken place in that time. The opportunity to have a top-up on trivia seemed quite a gift. Eddie could be quite partial to the odd issue of *National Geographic* but mostly liked technology magazines, even though he could only understand one word in five. His favorite magazine, he told Lindsey, used to be the *Trade and Exchange* before it went the way of the dinosaur. All those lovely bargains to be had at the end of his fingertips. He still lamented its demise and found the online alternative a very poor substitute.

"You can't just browse online," he told her. "You have to know what you want and search for that. With the old paper version you could look at it all. You never knew what might jump out and take your fancy."

Lindsey left them to it and went to meander around the items of stationery. As an artist she was by necessity most passionate about stationery but she found the selection here to be pretty inferior. Other people evidently had shared her assessment. A number of journals and notebooks had fade marks on them and had clearly been overlooked by half a decade's worth of prior customers. The pencils and drawing materials were suited for school students and amateurs.

At length Eleanor came to the head of the line. Since she only wanted a few stamps she concluded her business in no time without having passed one single unnecessary word with the woman behind the counter.

As they regrouped Eleanor said, "She's definitely been to Adolf Hitler's Charm School. Wouldn't want to meet her in a dark alley on a night with a real grumpy on."

Eddie laughed and as he did so Eleanor's phone beeped from within the recesses of her handbag. She drew it out, read her text message, had a little giggle, stabbed out a reply and put her phone away again.

"That was Tom," she said with a coquettish expression on her face. It seemed clear she wasn't about to disclose the contents of her text or her response.

"You've found yourself a boyfriend," Eddie said.

Eleanor waved an elegant hand. "Oh I doubt that," she said. "How old do you suppose he must be?"

"Late fifties, I'd say," Vi said.

"In which case," Eddie said, "you've got yourself a toy boy. What does that make you these days?"

"A cougar," said Vi, her magazine knowledge suddenly paying dividends.

Eddie gave a faux roar. "I knew we needed to watch you," he said.

"No need to get excited," Eleanor said. "He's probably married and just a bit bored. It's all harmless fun. Shall we move on?"

They emerged onto the main street and since they had already walked the length of the shops they agreed to retrace their steps and see what they'd missed on the way. The first shop they came to sold gourmet food and since they had no need of fat rolls of salami or little containers of haloumi cheese or tabouleh or anchovies they moved on. The shop next to that sold clothes and the one after sold second hand goods to fundraise for one of the local charities.

Next to this the shop sold sweets and chocolates which proved too much of a temptation for Eddie and Vi. They entered the shop with childlike enthusiasm and began ooh-ing and gaa-ing over the wonderful selection on offer. Eddie asked if there were any free samples but got politely told no. He and Vi seemed undeterred by this in a way that suggested deep familiarity with asking for free stuff and coming away empty-handed. They set about making their choices with gusto.

The smell of chocolate and sugar permeated so strongly it seemed a wonder a person didn't gain weight just by standing there. Chocolate reminded her of Andrew and of Simon's comments on his fondness for the stuff. It also reminded her of Robyn who'd declared herself to be a chocolate aficionado. It occurred to Lindsey that she should think about buying both Robyn and Will something to give them on her return. But then the weather had been so warm and would probably continue that way. The chances of chocolates making it home in a recognizable shape seemed slim at best. She dismissed the idea but then on impulse bought a little box of chocolates for Andrew. She did not know if she would have the courage to give them to him but she did appreciate his concern for her last night and figured this could be a way of expressing her thanks. At best she would manage it, at worse she would have wasted only a few dollars of her money.

Back on the street once again they wandered by a clothes shop – for grannies, so Eleanor said – and a pharmacy, before coming to a side street that led to a vast grocery store surrounded by an acreage of car park space. On the lamppost a sign had been attached to show the way to the Waiata Junction museum. Eleanor brought them all to a halt at this junction and looked at her watch.

"Half past eleven," she said. "What time do we want to have lunch?"

"Now?" Eddie suggested optimistically.

"It's a bit early isn't it?" Eleanor said. "You don't want lunch yet, do you Lindsey?"

Lindsey shook her head. "I don't mind waiting a while."

Eleanor worked her mouth about. "I'm wondering about the idea of visiting the little museum. We could have a look through and then go for lunch after that. I can't imagine it would be very big, but it might be interesting to take a gander. Lindsey?"

"I don't mind," she replied. "I'll go with the group consensus."

Eleanor looked at her as if to say she would much rather Lindsey had an opinion of her own and express it.

"Eddie and Vi?" Eleanor asked.

"Er, I've got a bit of an allergy to museums if I'm truthful," Eddie said. He coughed. "I think it must be all that dust. Old places like that always have plenty of dust."

"And I'm a bit parched," Vi said, transferring her bag from one shoulder to the other. "I'd kill for a sit down and a cup of tea right about now."

"And I could murder its companion, the cream bun, too," Eddie said. "Better watch out for us, you two ladies, me and Vi are trained assassins when it comes to cups of tea and cream buns."

"What about lunch?" Eleanor asked.

Eddie patted his prodigious gut. "Plenty of room," he pronounced. "I also need to try to track down some new shoelaces. We're pretty sure Dennis isn't going to stand for us cadging a ride in the mini bus tomorrow, in which case some running repairs will be in order. Why don't we split up and meet back here at twelve thirty? We can then go and see if we can find the café your boyfriend mentioned."

"Far be it from us to stand between you and your killing spree," Eleanor said. "We'll see you here at twelve thirty."

CHAPTER TEN

The Waiata Junction Museum sat on the left of the side road that sloped off toward the west, recessed half way between the main road and the giant grocery store. Lindsey and Eleanor had both expected the museum to be installed in a small house built at the turn of the previous century. Instead they found a substantial, purpose-built edifice of some standing. It had clearly been architecturally designed with a double storied entranceway and two wings fanning out at an angle on either side. The colossal sloping entranceway roof stretched out to provide a covered area outside the massive entry doors. It had a modern wooden façade and big plate glass windows over which wide eaves had been built, presumably in an attempt to provide adequate shade for the exhibits inside. It glistened as the sun came out in full force and began sucking up the deposited rain with humid eagerness.

"This is a surprise," Eleanor said as they stood and stared at the building. "Did you expect this?"

"Certainly not," Lindsey said. "Not for such a small town as this."

"This smacks of serious money," Eleanor said. "Probably government money. It would take several decades to fundraise for something like this, if not longer. Shall we go in?"

The massive entry doors glided silently open as they approached and they found themselves in a large foyer. In the middle of the foyer sat a reception desk. On either side of the desk, tables had been laid out with a collection of souvenirs, gift items and books along with the almost obligatory selection of stuffed toys. To one side of the entry doors a notice board stood advertising a guided walk on offer for eleven o'clock tomorrow morning.

"Shame we'll miss it," Eleanor said, pointing out the sign to Lindsey.

Lindsey thought Eleanor didn't sound very sorry at all.

They approached the reception desk behind which sat an ancient looking man dressed in an equally ancient looking three piece suit. Even in the air conditioned splendor of the building the temperature still sat in the early twenties and yet the man looked like he wouldn't say no if someone offered him a blanket. He had a skeletal thinness about him. His blue eyes watered while his skin had developed a papery look. He had enough excess flesh on his face to make an origami animal.

Nevertheless he welcomed them with as much warmth as his cadaverous body allowed.

"Good morning," he said. "And a very fine one at that now the blessed rain has taken its leave. How are you ladies?"

"We are very well," Eleanor said.

"Keen to look through the museum?" he asked, as though there could be some doubt as to the purpose of their visit.

"We thought we might," Eleanor replied. "Is there a charge?"

"We just ask for koha," he said. He leant toward them over the desk and said, "That means 'donation' in case you don't know."

"Of course," Eleanor said. She fished in her bag, drew out her purse and handed over a twenty-dollar note. Lindsey had also drawn her purse out but Eleanor waved it away. "My treat," she said.

The man took the offered money with an unsteady hand and looked at Eleanor with surprise. "Would you like some change?" he asked in a voice that indicated his familiarity with koha in the form of coins rather than the folding stuff.

"Certainly not," she said.

"Here's a guide to the museum," the man said, producing it with that same unsteadiness. Lindsey noticed both hands were flecked with age spots and that the veins behind the surface looked as though someone had inserted pipe cleaners beneath them.

"Now," he said, opening the brochure, "there are two wings, one on either side of this point, with two sections in each wing. The wing to your left houses a section on pre-European times at the front, and a section on the pioneer days at the back. The wing on your right has displays about local flora and fauna at the front and an exhibition room at the back. Our current exhibit is an art display with paintings by local artists from the mid eighteen hundreds right through to the present day."

"Wonderful," Eleanor said.

"I'd start on your left," the man said. "Leave the art until last." He leaned over the desk again in that same conspiratorial way. "Between you me the old stuff is far superior to the new stuff. At least with the old paintings you can actually tell what they are."

He gave a funny little snigger.

Eleanor and Lindsey smiled politely and moved away. Eleanor leaned toward Lindsey for her own turn at conspiratorial speech. "If that man plays his cards right he could go straight from receptionist to exhibit. What a fossil."

Lindsey laughed. "He seemed very nice," she said. "And it's good to see someone of that age still active."

Eleanor rolled her eyes. "It's a wonder they let him out of the rest home," she said. "He probably had to climb a barbed wire fence or dig himself out with a teaspoon. Come on, let's go and see the marvels of the museum."

The first room had been tastefully laid out with displays about life for early Maori. Someone with some skill at art had painted backdrops to the display cases that livened them up. Each of the exhibits had small easy-to-read reference cards with pertinent information printed on them. There were displays on Maori and their way of life, customs and art. One display told about the rudimentary use of plants as medicines and as building materials and about the people's interaction with the natural world.

"It says here," Eleanor said, "that they think Maori might have been here in the late thirteen hundreds. They are thought to have moved away from the area and then come back at some stage. It says there were several tribes who intermarried and that another tribe came invading in the late eighteen hundreds."

Lindsey said, "I was just reading about what they ate. They apparently lived off small birds, kumera, fish and seals."

"Seals? Best not tell Cedric. He'd be horrified."

Lindsey grinned. "Still," she said, "there probably wasn't a lot of choice in those days."

"True," Eleanor said. "There wouldn't have been an enormous grocery store back then I suppose."

"I suppose not," Lindsey said, well used to Eleanor's sense of humor by now.

They moved to the room at the rear to look at the displays on the life and times of early Europeans who had started trickling into the area from 1770 onward. Interesting exhibits of furniture and fashions had been laid out, complete with a couple of fully dressed mannequins.

"There could be more life in those two than the man out the front," Eleanor said.

They looked at a collection of jars and cooking implements and old irons and old toys. A group of photographs showed some of the early pioneers in the days when smiling seemed strictly prohibited and the more pinched and rigid a person looked the better.

"I just can't imagine it," Lindsey said. "No proper roads, no medical facilities, no shops, no electricity."

"And to think the women still went about in corsets," Eleanor said. "It does make you realize there has been at least some progress in the world for women since then."

They returned to the foyer to move over to the other side of the building. The ancient receptionist had slumped on his seat and looked as though he might nod off at any second so the women did not disturb him. In the first room on the other side they looked at the collection of stuffed native birds and at the butterflies and other insects that had been harpooned in their middles with pins. They looked at information on the devastation introduced pests had wreaked upon the native species. They also looked at a display about seals that would have been enough to make Cedric salivate.

They moved in to the fourth and final room to look at the display of art. As advertised a whole swathe of different art from different periods had been hung in chronological order about the room. They went around the room to see all the art and then Lindsey returned to the earliest pictures. And while she found almost all of the paintings to have some merit – whether old or new – the ones that most captured her attention were the portraits from the early days.

Lindsey had always admired portrait painters and their ability to capture a look about a person. One of the artists in particular had painted several of the pieces, both of Maori and Europeans. The Maori figures all seemed to have such a nobleness about them and yet many had a sadness too as though they had seen a glimpse of the future and did not like what appeared to lie ahead. The featured Europeans had about them a determination to be here and make progress in a new land, and yet a dedication to retain the ways they had brought with them.

At length Eleanor said, "We had better get moving. We're supposed to be meeting Eddie and Vi in five minutes."

Lindsey had been quite lost in her own little world and moved away with some reluctance.

"Inspiring?" Eleanor asked.

"I don't have a great gift for oils," she said as they emerged back into the foyer. "I'm very envious of the ability to speak volumes with simple brushstrokes. It's masterful."

Eleanor eyed her with interest and went to reply but the emaciated receptionist spied them and said, "Are you finished already?"

"I'm afraid we must be on our way," Eleanor said. "We are due to meet up with some friends."

"Shame," the old fellow said. "Do enjoy the rest of your day."

They passed some more punters ready for their turn in the museum as they exited. Lindsey turned to see the man getting ready for their arrival by straightening things on the already straightened counter. As they walked back up the road Eleanor said, "I fear the old guy couldn't believe we'd done justice to his fine institution in such a short time. Of course the fact that he slept through half an hour of that time probably didn't help much."

When they walked up the slope and reached the corner Eddie and Vi were nowhere in sight.

"We are a bit early," Lindsey said, looking at her watch.

"Shall we kill five minutes in the antique shop over the road?" Eleanor suggested. "Maybe we could find the old guy's wife on sale there and send her off down the road to join him."

"Okay," Lindsey said with a grin.

The antique shop looked as though it could easily have been there since the days of the early pioneers. Its dim interior seemed crammed with a plethora of treasures of a decrepit and dubious nature. A smell of rust and mothballs assailed the nostrils. The place looked as though it hadn't been dusted any time in this millennium.

As they looked around Lindsey saw furniture and china and ornaments and old toys. There were platters of tarnished silver, a mahjong set that appeared old enough to have been owned by Confucius and some enormous brass pots that had been fashioned in the shape of elephant feet. In one cabinet lay a whole collection of harmonicas in varying states of repair. Lindsey even saw a few things that were down in the museum as exhibits.

A woman in her mid fifties sat on a stool behind the counter. She was in the process of knitting what could easily have been a carpet since its proportions were so large. As they approached, Lindsey saw a pattern for a sweater sitting on the counter top and concluded that something had clearly gone terribly awry. The knitting seemed to be getting the better of her. She worked the needles as though the chances of dropping a stitch were large. Her face had a clenched look and her tongue protruded from the side of her mouth with the effort of concentration.

She glanced up at them then back to her creation.

"Looking for anything in particular?" she asked.

"No," Eleanor said. "We'll just have a little browse about, if that's okay."

"Fine with me," the lady said, making a maneuver with her needles akin to a fencer parrying a sword.

As they started to go around the shop for a second time the door opened and in walked Andrew.

"Fancy seeing you here," Eleanor said.

Andrew smiled broadly at the pair of them.

"You two are a sight for sore eyes," he said. "I was starting to feel as though I might be the only tour member left in Waiata Junction."

Eleanor's elegant brows shot northward. "What happened to your friend?"

Andrew shrugged. "I'm not sure, to be honest. We went for coffee and I left to go to a shop I'd seen. When I went back he and Bianca had gone. I haven't seen hide nor hair of them since."

"Curious," Eleanor said. "You'll have to tag along with us then. We're about to go to meet Eddie and Vi."

"Are you folks tourists?" the lady behind the counter asked, her face a picture of incredulity. If Lindsey didn't know better she could have sworn their encounter with Andrew was the most exciting thing to have happened inside the walls of this shop in a very long time.

"Indeed," Eleanor said. She told the lady about the tour.

The lady gave a little snort. "Funny to think of people coming here for their holidays. For those that live here we can only think of one thing and that's leaving. In fact I'm getting on a plane tomorrow."

"Where are you going?" Eleanor asked.

"Brisbane," the lady said. "I'm going for eight days to stay with my daughter and see my grandchildren." Then she mysteriously added, "Hence the knitting."

Eleanor and Lindsey both looked at the monstrosity she'd deposited on the counter and made murmuring sounds that might have passed for approval.

"I can see Eddie and Vi," Andrew said from his spot by the window.

"Well, that's us then," Eleanor said. "Do have a nice holiday."

The lady smiled to show two rows of tea-stained teeth. "I will," she said. "And you enjoy the rest of yours."

"Don't worry," Eleanor said. "We fully intend to."

Eddie and Vi stood on the corner of the street looking a bit lost, almost as though they'd mistaken the right place to wait. When they saw the others coming their faces lit up like Christmas trees.

"Look who we found," Eddie said as they approached, indicating Cedric who lurked at a short distance behind them.

"And look who we found," Eleanor said, pointing at Andrew.

They all laughed.

"Where are your pals?" Vi asked Andrew.

He shrugged. "Your guess would be as good as mine. You wouldn't have thought it possible to lose someone in the town this size but there's me being proved wrong yet again."

On hearing this Cedric came over to join the group. It seemed his lurking had been on account of Andrew's presence. Now satisfied that Bianca wasn't about to make a grand and unwelcomed entrance Cedric could then join the rest of the group without concern.

"What happened to Dennis?" Eleanor asked Cedric.

Cedric screwed up his mouth. "I don't know," he said. "I haven't seen him since we left the mini bus. For all I know he might have left town entirely."

The others digested this information. It seemed strange to think of Dennis driving off and leaving them even though he did so every day.

"Time for lunch?" Eleanor asked.

"I should think so," Eddie said. "I'm ruddy famished. We saw the place down by the river so can show you the way if that still suits?"

"Lead on," Eleanor said.

Eddie and Vi turned on their heels and led the group across the pedestrian crossing and down to the right a bit toward a side road that led off to the east. This cul-de-sac street ran for a couple of hundred meters before petering out into a car park. Beyond the car park lay a children's playground area and beyond that the river. A boardwalk had been constructed on the bank along which people meandered, enjoying the sunshine and fresh air. Eddie and Vi then led them left along this until they arrived at a giant glasshouse of a building that housed the café.

Although the place looked busy it wasn't so overrun that it couldn't accommodate six more people so the group sauntered in and lined up to peer into the self-service cabinets. Eddie went straight to the front of their group in the line while Vi went off to claim some tables. She found a couple over by the far window and set about noisily dragging one over to the other and arranging six chairs so they could all sit together.

Eventually they all sat down with their lunches before them. As Eddie sat down he made a great performance of tucking his trouser legs into his socks.

"What on earth are you doing?" Eleanor asked.

Eddie jabbed a finger at the river. "Protecting meself against mosquitoes. With water around there's bound to be a million of the bloomin' things swarming about. Nothing worse than having them fly up your trouser legs and bite you in your sensitive regions."

No one quite knew what to say to this and no one followed suit.

"I would have thought repellant to be a better option." Eleanor said.

"Actually," Cedric said, "technically mosquito repellents don't repel. The spray blocks the mosquito's sensors so they don't know you're there."

"Aren't scientists clever?" Vi said. "I'd have never thought of that in a million years."

"This is the life." Eddie said around a mouthful of pie. Little shards of pasty fluttered down into his lap.

"Indeed," Eleanor said. "So what did you two get up to in our absence? Did you have your cake and eat it?"

Eddie guffawed. Some of the shards of pasty made it as far as the table.

"Naw," he said. "In the end we moseyed around a bit to get the lay of the land and wandered into a few shops. The place is bigger than it looks. There are quite a few businesses off the main road and even a collection of emergency services down one of the other side streets. There's a fire station, a police base and a small hospital of sorts. And then I had to talk Vi out of wanting to get her hair done."

Vi fingered her hair. "This trip's playing havoc with my do," she said.

"And did you find some shoelaces?" Eleanor asked.

"Sure did," Eddie said.

"There wasn't a cobblers," Vi said, "but we found an emporium that sold everything from axes to Zimmer frames. What you couldn't buy in there probably isn't worth talking about."

Cedric said, "Did you know that the collective noun for a group of cobblers is a drunkship?"

"Really?" Andrew said.

"How was the museum?" Vi asked, changing the subject before Cedric could get going.

"Interesting," Eleanor said. "The man at the reception desk was by far and away the oldest thing in the building but some of the exhibits were quite informative. Lindsey enjoyed the art exhibition. The museum building is also very impressive. Not a speck of dust in sight."

"We'll take your word for it," Eddie said.

"I didn't know there was a museum," Cedric said, his eyes widened just at the thought of it.

"What did you do, Cedric?" Vi asked.

"I tracked down the pharmacy," he said. "I'd taken an inventory of the first aid kit Dennis issued me and found it to be woefully inadequate. I took the liberty of buying some supplies to top it up. Do you suppose he'll give me a refund?"

Eddie shrugged. "You can only ask."

"I've got the receipts," Cedric said. "Of course I didn't realize there was a great big grocery store off the main road or I might have gone there first. I probably could have got things for a lot cheaper. I might even have got some free stuff if I'd known there was a hospital. "

"It's good to support the local businesses," Eleanor said. "Big chain stores and grocery stores are often the death of the sole trader."

Cedric looked more concerned about whether his lack of thrift might jeopardize his chance of getting his money reimbursed.

"And what is our assessment of Waiata Junction?" Eleanor asked the group.

"I like it," Vi said. "They seem to have everything here you could want, it has a spark of life to it and it's all nicely set out."

"I found out a bit more about the origins of the town's name," Cedric said. "As you might know 'waiata' is the Maori name for a song or chant. The words and expressions are supposed to be a way of preserving the knowledge and wisdom of the ancestors."

"Just as well Cedric doesn't have such a tradition," Eleanor whispered to Lindsey. "It'd take him two weeks to belt it out."

"There are all sorts of different waiata," Cedric continued, quite oblivious. "Some are meant as lullabies, others as laments and some are love songs. Some are even a challenge of sorts."

Eddie said to Eleanor, "Is that what was in your text? A waiata of love?"

Andrew and Cedric looked confused so Vi said, "Eleanor's got herself a boyfriend. Tom is his name."

"Impressive," Andrew said, "considering we've only been here what, just over two hours. That's pretty good going."

Eleanor gave a tinkling laugh. "It's a long story," she said. "I'll tell you all about it later."

"Anyway," Cedric said, not best pleased to have his tale thus diverted, "apparently one of the early settlers here was sympathetic to the plight of local Maori. He helped them out in a number of different ways and as a gesture of thanks the local iwi wrote a waiata just for him. Thus, the place became known as Waiata Junction."

"And just where did you learn all this fascinating information?" Eleanor asked.

"I came across a community notice board," Cedric said. "Someone had put up a whole information sheet on it."

Everyone pondered this for a few moments and then Vi asked Andrew, "What do you think of the place?"

"It's nice," Andrew said, "but I'm really a bit more of a city man myself. I think the smallness of it would drive me crazy after a while. I'm not sure I'd pick it as a holiday destination either but it makes a change from walking."

Vi gave a heavy sigh. "I'm dreading tomorrow," she said.

"Cheer up, love," Eddie said. "I'll keep you going. We could spend the time as we walk making up some waiata of our own."

Eleanor's phone beeped. Once again she withdrew it from her bag, smiled a secret smile and made a reply.

"Cor," Eddie said. "He really is keen. Who knew that coming on this tour could be a pathway to love. People should give up dating sites and go on holiday."

"They reckon thirty five percent of people using personal ads for dating are already married," Cedric said.

"Always the prophet of doom, aren't you Ced?" Eddie told him.

"Anyway, enough of all this," Eleanor said. "By my reckoning we've got just over an hour until we need to be back at the mini bus. What are we going to do to occupy our time?"

"I wouldn't mind checking out the riverside walk," Andrew said. "Anyone want to join me?"

Eleanor and Lindsey exchanged glances. "We will," Eleanor said.

Andrew said, "What about you, Eddie and VI?"

Vi shuddered. "Voluntary walking? You must be joking."

"We thought we might check out the antique shop," Eddie said. "Want to come Cedric?"

"I've already been," he said. "I thought I might go and have a look at the museum."

Everyone looked less than surprised at this.

Eleanor said to Eddie and Vi, "Well, if you want to get yourself a new harmonica then the antique shop is the place to go. They've got plenty."

"Really?" Vi said. "How odd."

"Did you know that in Belgium children have to learn the harmonica at primary school by law?" Cedric asked them.

Eleanor shook her head. "Where do you learn these things, Cedric?"

Eddie made a hmphing sound. "Bloody glad I wasn't born in Belgium then. Of course they are right next to France so I suppose you couldn't expect total sense out of them."

"Come on, Frankie," Vi said, getting up and hoisting her bag onto her shoulder. "Let's get going."

They all stood up with a scraping of chairs and Andrew dragged their second table back where it came from. When they emerged from the café they bid each other a fond farewell and promised to see one another back at the mini bus in an hour.

As Andrew, Lindsey and Eleanor went to set off down the boardwalk Eleanor suddenly stopped.

"You know," she said, "I think I've changed my mind about the post-prandial walk. I think I'd rather go and check out some of those lovely look-ing craft shops. You don't mind, do you?"

And before Lindsey could say a word, or express an interest to come too, Eleanor strode away leaving Lindsey on her own with Andrew.

As Lindsey and Andrew watched Eleanor make her way back toward the main road Lindsey had to stop herself from running after Eleanor yelling, "Don't leave me," at the top of her voice. The prospect of spending time with Andrew made her squirm. She could feel her face flushing with embarrass-ment and she longed for the safety that numbers provided. Here with him, in broad daylight, there wasn't anywhere she could hide.

Andrew, on the other hand, looked far from fazed by the departure of Eleanor. But then he did seem to have a knack for taking things in his stride that Lindsey lacked entirely.

"Shall we?" he said, indicating the path along the boardwalk.

Lindsey gave a small shrug and started walking. She told herself to stop being stupid. She'd already had several conversations with Andrew by herself and all had gone well. He wasn't a demanding companion and seemed to know how to put her at her ease. She would just have to trust he would do it again this time.

"Did you enjoy lunch?" Andrew asked.

Lindsey thought of her chicken salad and its exceptional ordinariness. "Yes," she said.

"You were very quiet," Andrew said. "By my reckoning you never said one word."

"It doesn't matter," Lindsey said. "I didn't feel in the slightest bit left out."

Andrew glanced at her with a searching look.

"Besides," Lindsey said, "it's not as if a person can get a word in edgeways with some of our tour companions, is it?"

Andrew laughed. "You've got a good point there. Eddie, Vi and Eleanor are what you might call natural conversationalists. And as for Cedric, well, what can a person say about Cedric?"

Lindsey smiled. "I know," she said.

"I suppose he's made it to the museum by now and is absorbing all those new facts like a sponge."

Lindsey smiled again. "He'll be as happy as a pig in mud."

Andrew laughed. "Yes, apart from that terrible deficit of not being able to look up at the sky. Where do you think he learns all those bits of trivia? And more to the point, how does he remember them all?"

"Some people have a photographic memory," Lindsey said. "Or maybe it's the necessity to share that compels him."

"What, because he's interested he thinks everyone else will be too?"

"Something like that," Lindsey said. "I do feel sorry for him, though. He tries so hard to fit in."

"Whereas you don't?"

Lindsey considered this. "Abraham Lincoln once said 'Better to say nothing and be thought a fool than to open your mouth and remove all doubt'," she said.

"Ha," Andrew said. "I can think of quite a few people to whom that might apply but I'm pretty sure you're not one of them."

"It's kind of you to say so," Lindsey said, "but it does seem to me that a lot of energy gets expended in trying to make quiet people noisier and noisy people quieter. Wouldn't it be better to just leave everyone as they are?"

Andrew shot Lindsey another appraising glance. He appeared on the verge of saying something to rebut this but seemed to change his mind. Instead they walked for some time in silence. Strangely, Lindsey did not find this silence uncomfortable in the slightest.

The boardwalk hugged the western shore of the river. A number of people were out walking its length. Some sat on park benches in the shade of willow trees. People were also enjoying the river. They passed a boat shed where a muscular man sat in a deck chair waiting for customers to come along and hire the canoes he'd laid out. At various intervals along the river Andrew and Lindsey came across people who'd done just that. Some managed the paddle with a deal of proficiency while others struggled to row in a straight line. They saw one older couple laugh over their spectacular failure to make a decent amount of headway. Further down the river a young couple also struggled with the skill and bickered about who was most at fault for their lack of progress.

Eventually the boardwalk petered out. From there a gravel path trailed off into the distance. A park bench had been erected out of the same wood as the boardwalk right at its very end. Andrew and Lindsey halted here and wordlessly contemplated their next move. Andrew pulled his phone out of his pocket to check the time.

"Do you want to sit here for a bit?" he asked.

Lindsey looked at her watch too. It seemed too early to turn back and too late to go on.

"Okay," she said.

Andrew sat down and lifted his face up to the sun. "Ah," he said. "This is the life."

"It's very pleasant," Lindsey agreed.

Andrew looked her. "What would you normally be doing on a Saturday afternoon at home?"

"Hmm. Nothing very exciting. Robyn – she's one of my flatmates – she'd probably have us doing some cleaning if we were all home. If I've got commissioned work I could be doing that. I'd probably be at home. You?"

"The usual weekend stuff," he said. "Cleaning the house or the car. Going out sailing. Visiting my olds. Getting together with friends. Whatever comes along, really."

"Have you got your own house?" Lindsey asked.

"I live in an apartment on the outskirts of the CBD," Andrew said. "Mercifully it does not take a lot of looking after. It's got a nice view but absolutely no garden. I look out on greenery but don't have to do a thing to maintain it. That's a recipe for success in my book. How many flatmates have you got?"

"Two," Lindsey said. "Robyn and Will. They've been the best friends a person could hope for."

"And do you often work in the weekends?" Andrew asked.

Lindsey gave a small shrug. "It depends," she said. "If I've got a freelance job to do in a hurry, or if I have a deadline to meet then I will. Sometimes you just have to work when the inspiration strikes."

Andrew reached for his backpack at this point and opened it. He drew out a brown paper package, put his thumb under the seal and drew out a book.

"*Gilbert*," Lindsey said with surprise. "Where did you get it?"

Andrew smiled. "At the bookshop," he said.

"Goodness. Fancy my book being in a small town like this. Fancy you finding it."

"That wasn't all I found," Andrew said. He told her about meeting Maryanne Silver.

Lindsey shook her head still feeling quite disbelieving to see her book in Andrew's hands. She wanted to ask him what he thought of it but did not think she could handle any potential reply. Instead she asked, "What on earth are you going to do with it?"

Andrew laughed. "You think I'm a bit past this?" he asked.

"Just a tad," Lindsey said.

"I'm going to keep it," he said. "It isn't every day a person meets a famous author. I'm going to get you to sign it for me. One day it might be worth a fortune."

"Or it might come in handy to put under a table leg if one of the four is a bit short," Lindsey said.

"Now, now," Andrew said. "I think this book is thoroughly charming and I think you should be tremendously proud of it."

His comment made Lindsey feel a little contrite and she did not know what to say to him. In truth she did feel proud of all her work. She just seemed to lack the ability to show it in any way.

Lindsey wondered if Andrew could sense her change of mood as he didn't press her further. Instead he said, "How is your latest project coming on?"

Lindsey attempted a small smile. "Not too bad," she said. "I'm hoping to get a bit more sketching done this afternoon once we get back to the Barclays. In truth I won't know how it's going until I get home and start working on the project in earnest."

"I'd be very interested to see how it all shapes up," Andrew said.

Lindsey could not think of a single thing to say to this either. When the tour finished she fully expected to not ever see him again. But she did feel grateful for his interest and for the fact that he seemed willing to try to overcome her natural reticence. It made her think of the chocolates she'd bought. In a small fit of madness she decided she would give them to him after all.

"I got you something," she said as she fished around in her bag.

"Me?"

Lindsey drew out the little cellophane bag and gave them to him. "I wanted to say thank you for taking the time to see that I was all right last night. As you might have guessed, I'm not very good at verbalizing such things."

Andrew took the package off her with a look of such astonishment that Lindsey said, "Simon said you like chocolate."

Andrew shook his head with an action that looked suspiciously like disbelief.

"Did he now?" Andrew said. "Well, he was quite right about that." He cradled the package in his hands and said, "Thank you so much. I'm touched. There really wasn't any need."

"I think there was," Lindsey said. If Andrew only knew how little she came across gestures of friendship and caring he wouldn't think so either. Most people just thought Lindsey to be a bit strange and were happy to leave it at that.

"And what else did Simon say about me?" Andrew asked. "From what you indicated last night, he appears to have said a great deal."

Lindsey's face fell momentarily as she remembered the horrors of the previous evening.

"He just said you liked chocolate and that his sister wants to marry you," she told him. "That really is the sum of it."

Andrew laughed. "What more does a person need to know?" he said.

"Whatever you care to tell me," Lindsey said.

Andrew pondered this. "Okay then," he said. "My father is called Allen and my mother is called Doreen. She hates her name but clings on to the hopeful thought that it could have been something even worse. Something like Mildred or Maude. My father sometimes called my mother Mildred when she gets a bit antsy. It usually makes her come right."

"They sounds funny," Lindsey said, thinking of her own austere parents. The only smile her mother knew seemed to come out as she said cruel things. Her father never smiled at all.

"They are," Andrew said. "I think you'd like them."

"And you've got a brother in London," Lindsey said.

"He's called Mark. No other siblings. I went to Auckland University and have a degree in business studies. I've got a nice circle of friends mostly from those days. I work as a business analyst which basically means I'm paid to be logical in order to save people money. I'm good at problem solving, I drive a Peugeot and I like the color terracotta. How's that for a summary?"

"Not bad," Lindsey said. "I'm impressed that you like terracotta."

Andrew's blue eyes sparkled with humor. "I tell you all about my wonderful life and illustrious career and the best you can say is that you like my choice of favorite color?"

"One has to get their priorities right," Lindsey said. "And besides, despite your assertion that you have a lack of creativity and that you have a liking for logic, you have nevertheless proved otherwise. Most people, if asked their favorite color, usually go with blue or red. They'd never dream of coming up with something as unusual as terracotta."

"So there's hope for me yet?" Andrew asked.

Lindsey nodded. "I would say so."

"Your turn then," Andrew said. "I want to hear your potted history."

"There's not much to tell. My parents are both alive. They are both retired. My mother never worked anyway but my father changed jobs quite often during his working life. We moved around a lot."

"Didn't he like what he was doing?" Andrew asked.

Lindsey screwed up her nose. "I don't believe it was always his choice. He is, how would you say, very strong-minded. I think his employers often found his brand of critical thinking to be just a bit too far on the critical side."

Andrew gave her a penetrating look as he attempted to divine more out of what she said than her words betrayed. She wasn't about to elaborate. The less she thought about her parents the better.

"I don't really see them," Lindsey said. "They find me both a trial and a disappointment, I'm afraid. Whereas my sister – she's called Denise – can't do anything wrong. She makes them blissfully happy and so it seems much better to just leave them to it. I last saw them three years ago when Denise married her odious boyfriend, Scott."

Andrew looked appalled. Before he could say anything Lindsey said, "I went to art school and that's where I met Robyn and Will. If it weren't for Robyn I probably wouldn't be published. She took my work to one of our tutors and they handed it on to someone else and it all just fell in my lap. When I think of how difficult most people find getting published, it makes me ashamed. What else? I love passionfruit – even the seeds – and my favorite color is violet."

Andrew blinked several times and frowned. "I scarcely know where to start about that summary," he said.

"Please don't," Lindsey said, meaning it. She glanced away and watched a dragonfly hover about over the pads of some lilies growing by the bank.

He took her hand and she looked at him. He gave her fingers a brief squeeze then put her hand back in her lap.

"Okay," he said. "For now. Do you plan to keep writing children's books?"

"As long as I have ideas and they keep selling," Lindsey said. "My publisher wants me to start going into schools to do talks but every time I think about it I get the chills. I think I'll stick at what I'm best at for now."

"I hope that is you conceding you are the best," Andrew said. "Do you have more ideas?"

"I got a new one last night, by the fountain," Lindsey admitted. "I need to think about it more, see if it's viable. You?"

"The world is full of choices," Andrew said. "I sometimes don't feel like I've ever made a conscious one in my entire life. Maybe it's time to change that."

"I'm hopeless at choice," Lindsey said. "I get a bit paralyzed by the fear of the consequences. You know what they say about a butterfly flapping its wings. You never know where choice might take you."

"Ah, chaos theory," Andrew said. "I suppose there's plenty of truth in it. Every action has equal and opposite reaction. But you know, I don't think you're as bad at making choices as you think you are."

"Oh?"

Andrew smiled. "You chose to come on this trip, didn't you? You weighed up the options, your finances and your need to come and you made a choice. That seems a great example of choice in action to me. And hopefully one you are not regretting."

Lindsey considered this. She looked around her at the beauty of the countryside. She thought about the people she'd met and the places she'd seen and the things she'd experienced and knew that he was right. She looked at Andrew's face and gave him a little smile of concession. Indeed she could not think of anywhere she would rather be.

By the time Eleanor had her fill of the various craft and souvenir shops – having bought nothing whatsoever – she only had ten minutes to spare before being due back at the mini bus. By this stage Eleanor felt as though she'd quite had her fill of the delights of Waiata Junction. She decided to go straight back to the rendezvous spot even if it meant being early.

On balance Eleanor decided she liked the place. It wasn't unattractive and seemed to have everything a country person might need for day-to-day living. Moreover the river area seemed quite charming and was hopefully proving to be a inspirational spot for two young people to spend a bit of time together.

Eleanor stifled a laugh. The look on Lindsey's face when she, Eleanor, had announced her intention to look at the shops rather than walk could have won prizes. Lindsey would definitely have been a shoe-in for "Most Shocked" category and might have even gained a place in the "Most Terrified" section too. And while a small bit of Eleanor did feel just the tiniest bit guilty for the way in which she'd so innocently connived to get Andrew and Lindsey on their own, sometimes a person just needed to think of the greater good and put culpability to one side.

Besides, there wasn't the slightest bit of doubt in Eleanor's mind that Lindsey liked Andrew as much as she would probably deny it if confronted. She also suspected Andrew liked Lindsey although she couldn't really say she knew Andrew enough to be sure. She also knew that if the pair was to have any chance at a budding romance Lindsey could not be relied upon to make this happen. When God handed out the gumption he appeared to have overlooked Lindsey McIntyre entirely. And since this was the case someone needed to intervene. And who better to step into the role of fairy godmother than Eleanor herself?

But then Eleanor wondered if she'd not been a bit uncharitable to God regarding his handing out of gifts. Lindsey's references to her past and her family made Eleanor know that some bad things had happened to Lindsey.

She had deliberately not asked Lindsey for any of the details but figured perhaps the time had come to stray into this territory and find out more. Eleanor held a suspicion that Lindsey might need to get over some of the things from the past in order to move on with her future. Eleanor resolved to look for an opportunity to prompt some discussion in this direction.

As Eleanor neared the gas station she could see the De Vine Tours mini bus parked to one side. Dennis had slid along the door to the rear compartment and sat in the shallow stairs with a book in one hand and a banana in the other. It gave him an incongruous look, half wild and half educated. He glanced up and saw Eleanor approaching and threw both the banana and the book into the front cab.

"Hi hi," he said. "Found your way back all right, then? You're the first."

Eleanor smiled. "I thought I might be."

"The others aren't too far behind you?" Dennis asked, as though she'd been assigned as their keeper.

"I expect so," Eleanor replied. "Eddie and Vi are somewhere in the shops, a couple have gone off for a walk along the river and Cedric took himself off to the museum."

Dennis's face darkened at the mention of Cedric. Eleanor couldn't tell whether that had more to do with the picture of Cedric in a museum (and taking forever about it) or Cedric in general pontificating about stuff (and taking forever about it).

"What have you been up to?" Eleanor asked.

Dennis gave a little shrug. "Ah you know, odds and ends," he said. "There are always things I need to attend to."

Eleanor looked at Dennis. His good-natured mask sat firmly in place but Eleanor couldn't help thinking that maybe all wasn't entirely well beyond the façade.

"And what about yourself?" Dennis asked. "Enjoyed Waiata Junction, did you?"

A picture of Tom Aughton's face came into Eleanor's mind. It had been a while since Eleanor had met anyone for whom she felt an instant attraction. Plenty of men expressed an interest in Eleanor but they were usually old, bald, paunchy and completely delusional about the breadth of their own charms. Here now came a man with potential. Of course she knew next to nothing about him and that would need rectifying before too much longer. He might just as easily be married. But even potential brought with it a number of delicious feelings that Eleanor fully intended to bask in while they lasted. The fact that Tom had mentioned being friends with Graeme and Evelyn seemed so fortuitous as to make it a gift. And while Eleanor found the Barclays' brand of sophistication to be bordering on pretention – and Evelyn's interest in Bianca to be almost unforgivable – she wasn't above getting over these facts in order to go on a bit of a fishing expedition. Some things were, after all, worth making sacrifices for.

"I found the place to be full of surprises," Eleanor told Dennis. "It's been a most unexpected and enjoyable day. Look, here come Eddie and Vi."

Eddie and Vi came puffing along as though they'd been running.

"We aren't late, are we?" Eddie asked. "We got a bit held up in one of the shops."

"No," Dennis said, "you're dead on time."

"That's no good," Eddie said with a wry expression on his face. "Didn't anyone ever tell you it's better to be late than dead on time. Dead on time." He laughed. "Get it?"

Vi rolled her eyes. "The only thing round here that's dead are your jokes."

"Where's everyone else?" Eddie asked. "They'd better look lively or they'll miss the bus."

Dennis said, "We'll just wait for everyone. I'm sure they'll be along shortly."

"I thought you were going for a walk with Lindsey and Andrew," Vi said to Eleanor.

Eleanor waved her hands in the air. "Plans change, Vi," she said. "Sometimes you've just got to go with the flow. Here they are now anyway."

As Andrew and Lindsey walked toward the mini bus Eleanor could see Lindsey's cheeks were flushed. She looked as though she'd been caught illicitly drinking communion wine or at the very least smuggling cocaine. Before Eddie, Vi or Dennis could start asking questions that might make Lindsey's discomfort even greater, Eleanor said to them, "Have you seen the others in your travels?"

"I haven't seen Simon or Bianca since this morning," Andrew said. "And as for Cedric, he's probably still at the museum, isn't he?"

"Bloody hell," Eddie said. "We'll be waiting all bleedin' day for him to come back."

"What about Simon and Bianca?" Eleanor said. "Doesn't it seem strange to you that none of us have seen so much as a glimpse of them since about eleven thirty this morning? It isn't that big a town."

"Let's have a bet on who'll be back next," Eddie said. "If we're going to be waiting around we might as well make it interesting."

"It has to be Simon and Bianca," Eleanor said. "The equation of Cedric plus the museum can only come up with one answer and that's Cedric being late. Andrew?"

"My money's on Cedric being last," he said. "What do you think, Lindsey?"

"Maybe they'll turn up together," Lindsey said. "Maybe the three of them are at the museum."

"But if you had to choose?" Vi asked.

Lindsey's face looked troubled, as though making a decision could affect the very fabric of time and space. "Oh, all right," she said at length. "I'll say Cedric will be last."

Dennis had busied himself in the front of the mini bus during this discussion so nobody bothered him about it. Eleanor figured he was probably way too diplomatic to commit himself either way.

Eddie looked sulky. "There goes my opportunity to make a bit of money," he said. "If everyone bets the same way that makes for terrible odds. It's hard for us senior citizens to make ends meet, you know."

"Poor you," Eleanor said.

Five minutes went by without any sign of the three missing tour members. Dennis started to fuss with bits of paper and mutter to himself as he considered the best course of action. Just as he went to address the group about what he'd decided Andrew said, "Here comes Cedric."

The group all watched as Cedric came striding toward them. The way his long legs walked it made it look like Cedric had hopped on some stilts. He had a look of keen concentration on his face as he willed himself to go as fast as he could without actually breaking into a run.

"Sorry, sorry," he said as he neared. "I completely lost track of time. Such a fascinating museum. So much to look at and read and study. I could have spent all day there."

Eleanor looked over at Lindsey and they both exchanged a knowing smile. Only Cedric could have said something like that about so small a place.

Dennis frowned but then said, "As it turns out you are not the last. Simon and Bianca are still AWOL. I don't suppose you've seen them in your travels?"

"No," said Cedric. "They certainly weren't at the museum."

"I'll give Simon a call," Andrew said, getting out his cell phone.

The group watched as he punched some numbers and waited for the connection to be made. After a bit Andrew said, "It's going straight to his voice mail."

"I'll try Bianca," Dennis said, rifling once again through his sheaf of untidy papers. After trying her number he said, "Same deal. No answer. I wonder where they could have got to?"

Lindsey said, "Here they come."

They all turned to watch the progress of Simon and Bianca as they weaved their way along the sidewalk. Simon had his arm around Bianca's shoulder and Bianca had her arm around Simon's waist. They appeared to be singing but so poorly as to make that an insult to the art form. Eleanor took one look at them and knew instantly what they were about.

Both of them were drunk as skunks.

CHAPTER ELEVEN

The housekeeper at Whittaker's Rest was a glacial woman named Bridget Tunstall who, with one look, could turn the average man's heart to ice. She practically gave Dennis tremors every time he needed to deal with her. He made a point of avoiding her as much as possible but there were always things that needed sorting out on leaving day, not the least of them collecting the packed lunches for the ongoing journey. He had organized to see Mrs. Tunstall at nine thirty and now, at nine twenty, had to walk a fine line between not wanting to be late and not wanting to see her for a second longer than necessary. He milled about by his mini bus and marked time.

Dennis let out a deep sigh. When he'd come up with the fabulous idea to start De Vine Tours it had all seemed so romantic. Amiable guests strolling through wonderful scenery, enjoying great food and wine. It seemed like a recipe for success. Once the route had been finalized and the stops all sorted out Dennis just had to sit back and wait for bookings, drive the tour members to the starting point and set them off on their merry way every day. It seemed so simple.

But Dennis kept discovering the elusive qualities of simplicity. Bookings were slow to come in and didn't seem to be having the cumulative effect he imagined once things had got going. Some people who booked cancelled at the last minute and then tried to get out of paying so much as a cancellation fee. Dennis never realized the world contained so many difficult people until he started meeting them up close and personal. Nor had he pictured having to cope with so many different sorts of faults and foibles. He certainly had never imagined feeling embarrassed on account of his clientele and yet just last night he'd been mortified by the drunken antics of Simon and Bianca and ashamed when Bianca had been violently sick into one of Evelyn Barclay's prize winning rose beds.

The property owners weren't always easy to deal with either. In spite of the fact that they were paid quite handsomely for having the small party to stay, they weren't always as hospitable or obliging as Dennis would have liked. They did not seem to realize that part of offering accommodation required them to be accommodating. Some were fine but Dennis had begun to suspect that several owners of the properties on their route were beginning to re-evaluate their participation in De Vine Tours. Dennis could not afford for this to happen. He'd invested everything into making this venture work. He also feared for his marriage if he did not manage to pull it together. The complaints were already coming thick and fast from that direction.

Then there'd been the perplexing call from Allyson Green from Christian House just last night. An Egyptian amulet of some value had gone missing. They had only just discovered its absence and couldn't think what might have become of it. As part of their ruminations on its current location someone had brought up De Vine Tours and although Allyson didn't want to cast aspersions she did feel she should raise the subject with Dennis.

"Leave it with me," Dennis had said. And yet he had no idea what he meant by that or even what he could say to his tour members without it coming out as an accusation.

It was all very troubling indeed.

With just under half an hour to go until they needed to meet up with the group and be given their day's instructions, Eddie and Vi still lurked in their room. Vi had packed up all their belongings and Eddie had already been out to the mini bus and stowed their stuff inside. Now all that remained were their daypacks and their walking shoes. Vi had put hers on a chair by the door where they sat looking reproachfully at her. She dreaded the moment of having to put them on so currently sat on the bed eating some of the chocolates she and Eddie had brought the day before.

Eddie had decided that maybe some warm-up exercises would be helpful. He'd already twirled his arms about this way and that, had goose-stepped around the room a few times and had just begun a series of squats. Every time he bent his knees and lowered his backside small trumpeting sounds echoed forth.

"That's romantic," Vi said after the fifth such explosion. "Maybe you should do that outside. I don't want to be gassed before the day's even begun."

"Just call me old bugle butt," Eddie said good-naturedly.

"I could sit here forever if it wasn't for that," Vi said, popping yet another chocolate in her mouth.

"You're only saying that because you don't want to walk today," Eddie said, trying and failing to touch his toes. "But we have to keep moving. There are ever more vistas to be checked out."

"I always think that vistas without blisters are a much better combination though, don't you?" Vi asked.

"Probably," Eddie conceded. He gave up entirely and flopped on the bed.

"I've been thinking," Vi said.

Eddie rolled his eyes. "I wondered what those creaking sounds were."

"Seriously," Vi said. "I really don't know that this trip was a good idea. It's starting to feel too risky. At our age we can't afford to take chances. Neither of us is as young as we once were. Maybe we should pack it in, leave while the going is good."

Eddie sat up and looked at Vi sharply. "You don't mean that, do you?"

Vi shrugged. "Maybe," she said. "I've just started to get a bad feeling."

"What sort of bad feeling?"

She shrugged again. "Just an inkling, like a cloud on the horizon," Vi said.

Eddie took Vi's hand and patted it. "Now don't go getting all soft on me," he said. "You've had these feeling before and they've come to nowt."

Vi pursed her lips but then gave a little sigh. "Okay," she said. "You win."

"That's me girl," Eddie said. "Everything will be just fine. And now, I think I might have one more quick scout around the place before we leave, see what everyone's up to. I'll come back and get you in ten minutes."

And with that he was gone leaving Vi alone to finish her chocolates and consider the future in peace.

Andrew sat in one of the chairs by the pool and quietly fumed. He clenched his jaw and considered the monumental argument he'd just had with Simon. In the wake of this argument Andrew felt as though he had no choice but to leave even though it felt petulant to stalk out and leave Simon to stew in his own juices. But it was all so irritating and Andrew had had enough of Simon's mercurial moods, self-pity and surliness.

It had begun to occur to Andrew of late that maybe Simon had brought some of his misfortune down upon himself. Maybe not all the blame could be laid at Arabella's feet. Maybe painting her as a black-hearted witch was more convenient than any sort of self-contemplation whatsoever. Maybe Arabella's reason for failing to turn up to the altar had more to do with an enormous case of cold feet than it did with being a heartless cow. And maybe Simon's massive depression had more to do with shame than it did with having lost the love of his life. Andrew just didn't know.

What Andrew did know was that his friend wasn't quite the person he thought him to be. They had lived in close quarters for eight days now and every day had brought some fresh insights into the character and personality of Simon Ellery that had never been apparent on the tennis court or at parties. And it was fair to say that Andrew didn't entirely like what he saw. Here, stripped from his possessions and his portfolio and his family of excellent pedigree, Simon had revealed his selfishness, his pride and his disdain for his fellow human being in a most alarming way.

It occurred to Andrew that Lindsey had not helped matters. Simon and Lindsey seemed to Andrew like polar opposites. Simon usually lived his life with a large degree of entitlement iced with confidence that bordered on arrogance. Lindsey lived her life almost as an apology, with a lack of confidence and a sweet humility. For all that Simon had achieved and attained, it seemed meaningless in the face of Lindsey's life. Her struggles produced works of worth, Simon's produced money and things. She seemed like a delicate bird with a fine song that needed protecting and nurturing. Simon seemed like King Kong blundering about in New York oblivious to the damage left in his wake. The contrast between the two had made Simon's deficits seem even greater. Andrew wondered if he wouldn't have noticed – or minded – so much had he not been shown another slice of life.

After the spectacle that Simon and Bianca had made of themselves the previous evening something in Andrew had snapped. This morning had suddenly felt like the prime time for a few home truths to be delivered to Simon and so he had set about giving vent to all of this thoughts and feelings. On balance he did wonder if some of the things he'd said might have benefitted from a bit of editing but it was too late now.

Only time would tell what effect, if any, Andrew's words might have had.

Bianca had reason to feel glad at the complete lack of focus of her eyes as she stood in front of the bathroom mirror. That way she couldn't see the great bags under them or the way they had become all bloodshot. She couldn't see her blotchy skin or zombie-like expression and freak out about how she would ever be able to show her face in public again.

Yesterday had been a great day up to a point. When Andrew had ditched them to go and run his mysterious errands Simon and Bianca had been at a loss as to what to do or even what to say to each other. They'd not wanted to go with Andrew but hadn't factored on the vacuum his presence would leave behind. It felt weird. In the end Bianca had suggest they walk about a bit more and during this time they'd come across the pub at the far end of town. One drink had led to two then three then goodness knows how many more. Too many.

Liquor had loosened both their tongues and they'd ended up having a whale of a time. For a while Bianca had even looked at Simon with fresh eyes and wondered whether he didn't in fact have "potential" written all over him. But then she'd reminded herself that he did have an awful lot of baggage and worse, was on the rebound. She also hadn't given up on trying to snag Andrew so knew she had to walk a fine line. In the end she settled for giving him a snog and leaving it at that. For now anyway.

Things had seemed so great in the light of her alcohol-fueled haze. But by the time the group gathered for the barbecue dinner around the poolside, Bianca's sense of equilibrium had begun to feel rather wobbly. After ingesting a large portion of flame-grilled meat and sumptuous salads her stomach had also joined in the game. Too late she realized the degree of her malaise and she'd ended up ignominiously regurgitating the lot into Evelyn Barclay's garden.

After that she could tell her popularity was at an all time low so she'd sloped off to bed. Now, in the harsh light of morning, everything seemed to have sobered up, even Bianca's mood. What was more she still needed to find it within herself to walk umpteen kilometers today and act as though nothing was amiss.

Bianca wasn't really concerned about the opinion of her fellow travelers but she did care about what Evelyn thought of her. So Bianca resolved to have a shower, get packed and go and make amends before they had to leave. It went against every personal ethos Bianca had, but sometimes a girl just knew when she needed to do the right thing.

Simon's head pounded as though the All Blacks were training in his temporal lobe. He could feel the sprigs of their shoes were cutting up the grass of his brain. It had been ages since he'd got that hammered. On reflection it probably wasn't the smartest decision he'd ever made. But then he had just felt so pissed off with everything that when the chance to check out for a while came along he'd grabbed it with both hands. He'd then grabbed as many glasses as came his way with both hands and at one stage he'd even grabbed Bianca with both hands.

Simon closed his eyes and groaned. It all seemed like a fiasco. And of course just to top it all off Andrew had to go and get his wand in a knot over Simon's behavior of late. Simon might have only been half awake when Andrew let him have it but some of the accusations that Andrew leveled at him had stung. Andrew was his best man, had come along to make things better, not make things worse. To be accused of being shallow, self-pitying and uncaring seemed way too harsh. To be told he'd probably brought his misfortune on himself seemed beyond the pale.

But then a little part of Simon had to acknowledge that Andrew might be right, especially where Arabella was concerned. He'd had quite a few guilt elbows nudged into his conscience of late and it had occurred to Simon that he might not have been all that a groom should be. For a start he'd probably only chosen Arabella as his future bride because she met every criteria on his list: she came from an influential family, would come with a sizeable potential inheritance portfolio and had a great set of legs. Beyond this he did love her, but all things being equal he guessed that this fact should have been first on the list rather than just a nice bonus tacked on the end.

He swore. Just what was he supposed to do now?

Eleanor put the final touches on her packing and closed her case. She'd managed to spread herself around in an exceptional way over the course of the last two nights and it had taken her a while to corral all her belongings once again. She double checked the bathroom and looked pointlessly into the drawers beside the bed and even looked under the bed to make sure she'd not missed anything. She then triple checked she had her purse, her phone and her phone charger. All the things of vital importance were present and accounted for.

Eleanor went over to look out the window. Her room looked down into the pool area. She could see Andrew sitting there by himself. He'd flopped down into one of the poolside loungers and had his head laid back with his hands tucked in behind his skull. Eleanor might be getting a bit long in the tooth but wasn't beyond admitting to Andrew's good looks. Both he and Simon were fine specimens. At first Eleanor had thought that both Simon and Andrew seemed a little too assured of their outward attributes for their own good. And although she had yet to revise her opinion on Simon, she felt Andrew had the potential to be a nice young man. No doubt another six days in one another's company would bring more opportunities for divining such things.

But it wasn't what lay beyond the handsome features of Andrew Powell that occupied Eleanor's mind. Her thoughts lay much farther afield to a certain silver haired gentleman by the name of Tom. Last night had proved most interesting. While Bianca set about making a complete spectacle of herself Eleanor had set about gleaning some facts about Tom Aughton.

It seemed clear from the outset that Evelyn and Graeme held Tom in pretty high esteem, to the point where Evelyn had questioned Eleanor on how she might possibly know the man. She'd learned he was a screenwriter and spent time traveling around the globe as his work dictated. She learned that he been widowed some fifteen years earlier and that, after a decorous passage of time, many of the local single ladies of an advanced age had begun the process of landing themselves a lovely fish. She learned that Tom had avoided all attempts to be hooked and was still fancy free, clearly, Evelyn said, not ready to put his toe back in the sea of romance.

Eleanor would have begged to differ had she held the desire to do so. It seemed quite clear that Tom Aughton wasn't above being caught. He just hadn't met the right person yet. Perhaps until now. Only time would tell about that.

And when Eleanor gazed into the vista that was the future she couldn't help doing so with great expectation.

Cedric went out to the mini bus with his bag. He'd hoped to find Dennis but there wasn't a trace of him. He could see that Eddie or Vi had been out with their bag. Eddie's very large, very thin old suitcase couldn't be mistaken for anyone else's. Cedric stowed his bag and then stood with uncertainty beside the mini bus. He looked up at the sky. The beautiful blue they'd been so used to seeing was this morning partially obscured by a thin veil of cloud through which the sun still penetrated, causing a filtered effect and a most unusual light. Somehow this seemed to suit the day. Cedric could detect a funny vibe in the air this morning. The atmospherics just added to that ambience.

Since Cedric had already moved out of his room he did not feel inclined to return. Instead, and perhaps in an attempt to throw off the strange feeling that had settled over him, he decided to go for a walk around the grounds of the fine house. From the area where Dennis had parked the mini bus a path led away around the house, first toward a kitchen garden then over to a small collection of outbuildings that housed various items of rural import, and from there around to the main gardens at the rear of the house.

The gravel crunched under Cedric's feet as he walked. He breathed the fresh morning air into his lungs and reminded himself of his good fortune in being here. In a week's time he would be laying out his clothes ready to go back to work on the following Monday morning. He would get up on that said Monday morning and perform his standard list of preparatory tasks before catching the bus to his place of work. There he would find his desk buried under a mountain of paperwork that people would have shoved heedlessly onto it with him not around to direct it elsewhere. Cedric would probably feel equally buried for the first couple of days but would eventually bring order to chaos. Usually such a prospect would not have concerned Cedric. Bringing order to chaos had to be one of his most favorite things. Today it just made him sigh.

As he came around through the formal gardens he neared the pool area and saw Andrew sitting there. Cedric hovered for a few moments but then decided to make an approach. He could do with someone to talk to and maybe Andrew might feel the same.

"Morning," Cedric said as he neared.

Andrew looked up. "Hi, Cedric," he said, his tone so neutral as to make Cedric second-guess his own desire for company.

"Interesting light this morning," Cedric said, sitting down on one of the loungers beside Andrew.

Andrew looked up at the sky as if for the first time in his entire life. "So it is," he said. "I can't say I'd noticed."

"How's your friend this morning?" Cedric asked. "A bit the worse for wear after his bender yesterday?"

Andrew scowled. "Bloody fool. How on earth he'll manage the walk today, I don't know."

"Make sure he keeps up his fluid intake," Cedric said. "Alcohol is very dehydrating. Not to mention the fact that his liver will probably need a good wash out."

Andrew said nothing to this.

After a while Cedric said, "It's my mother's birthday today."

Andrew looked at him. "Really?"

Cedric nodded. "I've already talked to her this morning. I gave her a call to wish her many happy returns."

"That's nice," Andrew said.

"I'm afraid the only return she'd be happy with is me," Cedric confessed. "I hadn't realized when I booked the tour that I'd be missing Mum's birthday. When she told me I felt terrible. But by then I'd paid my non-refundable deposit so it was too late."

"Shame," Andrew said. "Is it a birthday of significance?"

"Aren't they all at her age?" Cedric asked.

"I guess," Andrew replied. "I suppose you can understand her wanting you home. We all like to be made a fuss of on our special day."

Cedric said, "That's a bit of a myth. These days you share your birthday with approximately nineteen million others. You could hardly call that special. Not only that, the world's population grows by over two hundred thousand people per day so it's only going to get worse."

"Really?" Andrew said. "That's insane."

Cedric thought about the world, its people, its oddities and all those seven billion unfathomable personalities.

"I couldn't agree more," he said.

Once Lindsey had taken her bag to the mini bus she figured she might as well just go to the meeting spot and wait for ten o'clock. It all seemed very leisurely. She'd expected they'd all be required to get up at the crack of dawn and be dispatched every day before the dew had even evaporated from the grass but it hadn't been like that at all.

Lindsey felt quite refreshed and ready for another day of walking – and most likely talking – with Eleanor. The day's break had made all the difference to Lindsey's outlook on life and in spite of the uncomfortable dinner she'd endured on the first night here, her relationships with others had continued to grow and improve. Lindsey might even go so far as to say that she herself had grown and improved as a result.

Eddie and Vi were already waiting when Lindsey arrived at the rendez-vous point. Eddie had evidently gotten through his vast collection of hideous shirts and had donned one that Lindsey had seen before. Vi too wore a familiar outfit but sported a new hat that she must have bought the day before. Its straw brim had been trimmed with miniature plastic bananas, apples, oranges and strawberries so that she looked like a walking fruit salad.

They exchanged pleasantries. Vi confided that she wasn't looking forward to today at all. Eddie whispered that Vi had already eaten a dozen chocolates that very morning and could do with all the walking she could manage. Cedric turned up, followed closely by Simon and Andrew – both of whom wore expressions like a long wet week – then Eleanor. Bianca came strolling along with Evelyn. They were deep in conversation. Bianca looked pale and perhaps just a little bit sorry, probably mostly for herself.

Dennis came striding along with his usual paraphernalia and their lunch packs for the day. He wore a very business-like expression on his face this morning and set about handing out their maps and information with brisk efficiency and barely a greeting. It seemed so unlike him Lindsey had to wonder whether he was entirely well.

"Now," said Dennis, once all the cards and lunches were handed around. "Today is a bit different from usual for two reasons. The first is that today you get a choice of route. One route takes you mostly along backcountry roads. The going is pretty easy, the traffic will be light and the scenery nice but not spectacular. The other route joins up with a coastal walk and takes you out to Hunter's Cove and Mills Point Lighthouse before winding back toward your ultimate destination for today, Thomas Peak. It's a lovely walk with some stunning views."

"Stuff the scenery," Vi said. "Which one's shorter?"

"There's a big difference between the two walks," Dennis said, "so I suggest you choose carefully. The first route I mentioned should take you about two and a half hours to walk, three with a stop for lunch. The coastal walk will take more like five and a half hours including a lunch break."

The group immediately started discussing this amongst themselves.

"Bear in mind," Dennis interjected, "you do have two nights at Thomas Peak so will have time to recover if you choose the longer walk."

"What do you think?" Eleanor asked Lindsey.

"I don't mind either," Lindsey said. "It's up to you."

Eleanor's expression bordered on exasperation. "You can do better than that," she said. "I want you to have an opinion."

Lindsey shrugged. "I really don't mind," she said. "The longer walk sounds more interesting."

"Right," Eleanor said. "The long walk it is."

In the end Eddie and Vi opted for the short walk. Simon and Bianca had also both chosen this route. After their recent inebriation neither of them had the wherewithal for a longer journey. Lindsey could see Andrew struggling to choose but in the end his loyalty to Simon won out and he opted to go with the short-walk party.

Cedric was equally torn and didn't really have anyone else to consult anyway. To the group he said, "My preference would be the longer walk but if the group divides how will I be able to execute my duties as First Aid Treatment Officer?"

Dennis made a sound that could have been impatience. "Why don't you take the longer route?" he said. "Since the short route is mostly all on roads I can easily turn back and come to the aid of anyone who might legitimately need it."

His use of the word "legitimately" implied that he would have no sympathy for recovering drunkards, malingerers or quitters. They were there to walk, and walk they would.

"Is everyone clear about who to call in an emergency?" Dennis asked.

They all nodded.

"You said there was a second thing," Eddie reminded.

"And there is," Dennis said. "I was just getting to that. Rather than setting off on foot this morning we will be getting in the mini bus. The first part of the journey between here and Thomas Peak is along a busy stretch of road and I would rather drop you off than risk any of you getting skittled. The short walk group will be dropped off first then we'll drive another ten minutes to the start of the coastal walk for the remaining party. Any other questions?"

No one had a single question, not even Cedric.

"Great," Dennis said. "Now a small word about the weather. There are some storm conditions forecast for overnight tonight. As the day progresses some thicker cloud is expected to roll in over the ranges but you shouldn't have any difficulty today. It's already raining on the west coast of the North Island but all the bad stuff is expected to stay on that side until the early hours of tomorrow. So it's hats and sunscreen as usual today, folks."

Everyone looked at Vi's hat.

"Great, isn't it?" she said.

They all murmured false niceties.

"I fear this trip is turning me into a terrible liar," Eleanor said softly to Lindsey.

"So now all that remains," Dennis said, reclaiming their attention, "is to thank our hostess for a lovely stay and be on our way."

Evelyn managed a smile that barely altered her face.

"I wish you all the best with your onward journey," she said after the short cannon of applause. She then gave a faux regal wave and left them all to it.

Dennis drove the mini bus out of the long driveway of Whittaker's Rest to join up with the road. He then turned left and headed west toward the main state highway as though heading back to Waiata Junction. They then joined the flow of traffic heading north which seemed rather busy for a Sunday morning in a sleepy backwater. Lindsey wondered if they would end up passing through Waiata Junction again but a couple of kilometers south of the town Dennis turned right into a minor road and set them off on a more north eastern course. This took them back into the familiar territory of fields and farms with the odd farmhouse dotted at regular intervals.

After about five minutes Dennis pulled the mini bus over to the left hand side of the road and swiveled around in his seat.

"All those for the short walk, this is your disembarking spot," he said.

A scramble followed as the five for the short walk jostled one another to get out into the fresh air. Vi waved at Eleanor and Lindsey as she departed and wished them luck. Andrew threaded out last and turned to give them a wistful look, still torn between loyalty and inclination. Lindsey couldn't help feeling wistful herself. The morning thus far had passed without them exchanging so much as a single word.

Dennis hopped out of the cab, got the group going with their final instructions and jumped back in the mini bus again. He tooted the horn as he drove off, leaving the five in a small cloud of dust. Cedric, Eleanor and Lindsey waved.

After another ten minutes Dennis pulled the mini bus over to the side of the road into a small lay-by area where two other cars were parked. On the left a couple of ancient picnic tables had been provided under the shade of a grove of trees. On the right hand side a large display board had been erected with details of the coastal walk.

"This is it, folks," Dennis said.

They all hopped out and regrouped by the map board.

"Right," Dennis said, "so no prizes for guessing that this is the start of the walk. As you can see, the track meanders from here down toward the coastline, then follows the shore north a ways before coming slightly inland again. You'll go over the brow of a small hill and the view on the other side will look down into Hunter's Cove. The land sticks out there on a small promontory upon which sits a lighthouse. Tricky reefs jut out from there so the lighthouse is still in use, although all automated these days.

"It should take you about two hours to get to the top of the hill and another half an hour to get down to the cove itself. You could either have lunch at the lookout spot at the top of the hill or carry on down to Hunter's Cove. If the tide is out you can cross over to the lighthouse itself. Both the time for lunch and the time to get to the lighthouse are factored in the five and a half hours. Stick to the track. There are bluffs on the right hand side of the track in some places. We wouldn't want you to come a cropper."

"No problem," said Cedric.

"Good," Dennis said. "Hopefully you should have a lovely day."

The trio watched Dennis get in the mini bus and drive away and then turned to set out on the day's adventure. At the beginning the track was wide enough for the three of them to walk abreast but after a while it narrowed so that only two could walk side by side. This made conversing quite tricky so they talked in fits and starts.

The trail wended its way at first alongside a field of wheat that had not yet been harvested. This prompted Cedric to tell them that each year insects eat one third of the world's food crop. After they had walked the entire length of two wheat fields, the track veered off to the right past a field of cows.

"Not bulls," Eleanor remarked to Lindsey.

"Thank goodness," Lindsey said.

"Did you know that boanthropy is a disease in which a person thinks they're a bovine?" Cedric asked.

Neither Lindsey nor Eleanor had known that which made Cedric look rather smug.

They walked for another half an hour before the trail left the farm altogether and headed off into an area of regenerating bush mostly made up of tea tree, flax and native pittosporums. The track narrowed, making conversation virtually impossible. Little wind blew under the shade of the trees but the temperatures remained pleasant. At one point Lindsey looked up through the thin canopy and could see that the cloud cover had thick-ened slightly.

They stopped a couple of times for a breather and some water and then, after another hour, finally got a glimpse of the sea. It made for an arresting sight. Its ultramarine depths stretched away as far as the eye could see. Toward the horizon the water sparkled like a tray of diamonds.

"The Pacific Ocean," Cedric said quite pointlessly. "If you set off swimming from here you'd end up in South America."

"If I set off swimming from here I'd end up dead," Eleanor told him.

The trail here then started to follow the coast in a northerly direction just as Dennis had said. It was wild country. At times they found themselves back under the cover of trees only to then re-emerge and follow the trail where the grass grew rampant and unchecked in big drifts. The trail then left the coast and threaded inland and began to gradually climb.

At the top of the hill they came to a lookout from which they got a spectacular view looking northeast. Down below they could see Hunter's Cove, a wide sweep of golden sand. On the right of the beach the sand gave way to a rocky area as the promontory started to push its way out to sea and there, at its end, sat the spire of the lighthouse.

"There's something very romantic about lighthouses," Eleanor said. "A heady mixture of solitude, isolation, danger and the smell of the sea."

"The last lighthouse to be de-manned in New Zealand was in nineteen ninety," Cedric said. "They're all automated now. Nothing romantic about that."

Eleanor gave a snort. "There's nothing romantic about *you*, Cedric," she said but Cedric just gave a small shrug.

They debated whether to stop for lunch but decided to push on down to the cove. After five minutes they came to a side track that led off toward the west. A sign announced a thirty-minute loop track to a stand of ancient kauri trees. Cedric halted.

"I read about this at the museum," he said. "Apparently the grove holds one of the biggest kauri trees in the country. Shall we go?"

Eleanor and Lindsey looked at each other. Eleanor screwed up her nose and said, "I'm not keen. I'd rather save my energy and make it out to the lighthouse. Lindsey?"

"I'm with you," she said. "I'd feel a bit cheated if I came all this way and didn't touch the lighthouse."

Cedric's face fell.

"Don't let us stop you," Eleanor said to him. "We'll be perfectly fine. If they say thirty minutes you'll probably do it in twenty and catch us up before we've even finished lunch."

The conflict showed plain as day on Cedric's features but his desire to see a tree mentioned by no less than a museum proved too much to resist.

"Well, if you're sure," he said.

"Of course," Eleanor told him. "Now get going."

As they watched him depart Eleanor said, "I'm not sure that Cedric doesn't have a bad case of boanthropy himself. He's certainly full of bull."

At one o'clock Eleanor and Lindsey reached Hunter's Cove. The descent from the lookout point had been steep and both women commented how pleased they were not to be doing the walk in reverse. The track at times snaked down the hillside like a coiled serpent and at other times came down via long flights of stairs, all under cover of dense bush. The light under the thick canopy seemed to have a strange green tinge to it. In certain places tree roots and fallen branches meant they had to pick their way carefully to avoid twisting an ankle or falling flat on their faces.

By the time they completed their descent the sun had ceased shining. A heavy blanket of cloud shrouded its magnificence and the wind had got up. But when they turned to look to the west they discovered they'd dropped so low down as to not be able to see beyond the hill itself.

"I guess this is all a precursor for tonight's storm," Eleanor said as they walked over toward the beach. There wasn't a soul in sight. Waves rolled and crashed then eddied. A group of seagulls argued over some spoils that had been found. On their left hand a huddle of pohutukawa trees clung to the bank above the beach. On their right they could see a path leading over the rocks out toward Mills Point lighthouse.

"Lunch at the lighthouse?" Eleanor suggested.

Lindsey nodded.

The pair made their way over the rocks via a path that had been cleverly constructed amidst its uneven terrain. This ran for about ten minutes before they came to a set of stairs that led down to a small horseshoe of sand framed by a steep rocky cliff on one side and the surging sea on the other. They made their way across the sand and then climbed up an identical set of stairs on the other side.

Once up the second set of stairs the going became easier as the land flattened out. As they approached the lighthouse it occurred to Lindsey that constructing it in the first place must have taken some doing. As they approached Eleanor and Lindsey stopped to admire the lighthouse in all its glory. It rose straight up into the air, tapering only gradually as it neared the top. At the bottom a closed red door showed the way in. Windows punctuated the column at three different levels on the way up. Toward the top a perilous looking catwalk had been added. Atop this they could see the windowed room where the lens and lantern were housed, and then finally a vent ball on its utmost peak.

"A lone sentinel," Eleanor said. "Who knows what heroic exploits have happened here?"

They wandered nearer and found a plaque had been fixed to the lighthouse with details of its history. From this they learned that the lighthouse had been prefabricated in England and shipped out in pieces, then transported and assembled on site in a process that took two years. They learned that it had been de-manned in 1960 and now operated via computer from Wellington. They also learned that the light functioned with only a fifty-watt bulb and could be seen from thirty kilometers away. The lighthouse keeper's cottage had long been demolished.

"I've got higher wattage bulbs in my lights at home," Eleanor said. "How on earth does that work?"

"I think it's all done by refraction and reflection," Lindsey said, "but it does seem incredible."

"I've never been to a lighthouse before," Eleanor said. "I'd love to spend the night in one some time. Yet another thing for my bucket list."

They decided to have their lunch on the east side of the lighthouse, looking out to sea. This gave them a bit of protection from the prevailing wind that blew in ever increasing gusts from the west.

When they got settled Eleanor said, "I didn't feel too sorry to leave Whittaker's Rest today, did you?"

"What?" Lindsey said. "Even though your journey will take you further away from the marvelous Tom?"

Eleanor laughed. "Distance is no object these days," she said. "Besides, from what Evelyn told me, he's hardly ever around with all his globe trotting. In my book that makes him even more attractive. It gives us very compatible lifestyles."

Lindsey smiled.

Eleanor said, "Speaking of compatibility, how was your walk with Andrew yesterday?"

Lindsey could feel herself flushing. "It was nice," she said. "But there's no 'compatibility' about it. We're just friends and maybe not even that. I fully expect to never see him again once we get home."

"And why would you expect that?" Eleanor said. "If you like each other there's no reason to suppose you won't see each other again."

Lindsey recoiled at this. "I don't think he really likes me," she said. "I think he just feels sorry for me because I'm so pathetic. Respect is an essential part of friendship and no one respects someone like me. All they feel is pity."

"What rubbish. You make it sound as though you're the Elephant Man's less attractive kid sister," Eleanor said, looking cross. "I don't think I've ever met anyone who sees themselves less clearly than you do. Even Bianca, for all her visions of grandeur."

Tears welled in Lindsey's eyes and she blinked them back, determined not to make the situation worse by crying.

"Who or what has made you this way?" Eleanor asked in a gentler tone. "Won't you tell me?"

"No one," Lindsey whispered. "I just wasn't born good enough."

"Is that what you've been told?" Eleanor asked.

Lindsey said nothing.

"Tell me what it was like for you growing up," Eleanor said. "Tell me from your perspective, not from what you've seen and been told."

"I don't know what to say," Lindsey said, her stomach churning like an angry ocean. "Everything that happened to me I brought upon myself. My father and my mother and even my sister all tried to help me improve myself, to be as they were, but I just never could measure up to their expectations."

"And what was it that they wanted from you?" Eleanor asked.

"Academic excellence, sporting prowess, sharp decision making, a killer instinct," Lindsey said listing them off like a litany. She found she could no longer hold back the tears and cursed herself for her weakness. "All the important things," she said. "I tried, Eleanor, I really tried, but I wasn't ever good enough."

"Good enough for what?" Eleanor asked. "And who made your family the arbiters of what's good and what's not?"

Eleanor's words confused Lindsey. She felt she had no right answers for these questions and that made her feel more inadequate than ever.

"And what, exactly, did your family do to you in order to 'help' you get better?" Eleanor asked.

Lindsey's mouth went dry and she felt as though she couldn't see any more as blackness closed in around her. "I don't speak of it," she whispered. "I'm not allowed to speak of it."

Eleanor turned Lindsey around to face her. "What aren't you allowed to speak of?" she pressed. "Did they spank you?"

"There wasn't a law against it then," Lindsey said softly.

"What else?"

Flashes of Lindsey's childhood came to her through the darkness, of the things her parents did until she learned her lessons, things she strove hard never to think on.

"Please, Eleanor," Lindsey begged. "I can't…"

Eleanor scrutinized Lindsey's face, wanting to divine the truth. Whatever she saw there slowly made her soften. Rather than saying anything else she just pulled Lindsey into an embrace and hugged her tightly.

"Okay," she said at length, gently pushing Lindsey back from her. "You don't have to say anything. Not to me, at least. But Lindsey, I really think you should tell someone. I think you need to get it out of you. And then you have to have someone tell you how wrong your parents were to try to make you into someone you weren't. If you want my opinion I don't think there's anything wrong with you that they didn't cause in the first place. I also think that if you could have a better perspective on yourself you would have a much happier life. Will you consider it?"

Lindsey looked out to sea and felt a wave of emotion wash over her. She could not help but speculate what her life might have been like if she'd had someone like Eleanor for a mother. Someone who believed in her, who thought good things about her and encouraged her to think good things about herself. But could she do it? Could she find the courage to speak the words and recall the memories and uncover the sins of the past? Lindsey just didn't know.

At that moment a few drops of rain began to fall so they tidied up their lunch things and donned their raincoats. The sky had darkened considerably while they had talked but both women had been so engrossed in their conversation that neither had noticed. Nor had they noticed the wind pick up even more or the way the sea had begun to roil and foam with whitecaps.

As they rounded the lighthouse and came out from behind its protection they saw a terrifying sight. Here, at a remoter distance from the cliffs they'd descended, they could see further west and the angry slate clouds that bore down on them. Lightning flashed and in seconds the rain went from a few heavy droplets to a driving sheet coming right at them.

"Quick," Eleanor shouted, taking Lindsey by the hand and pulling her forward.

They started running for the stairs that led across the small beach, rain stinging their faces. Both of them knew how imperative it was to get across that thin strip of sand and up the stairs on the other side. Failure to do so would see them trapped for the duration of the storm with virtually nowhere to shelter.

As they ran Eleanor fell heavily, knocking all the wind from her lungs. Lindsey crouched down to see if she was all right and could see at once that all wasn't well. She helped Eleanor into a sitting position and could see her friend struggle to see straight. When Eleanor brought her legs out from under her Lindsey could see she'd sustained a nasty cut on one of her shins from which blood rushed freely.

"Can you stand?" Lindsey said.

"I think so."

Lindsey helped Eleanor to her feet after quite some effort. Once upright, Eleanor sagged against Lindsey as she fought to regain her sense of equilibrium. Once stabilized they slowly made their way together across to the stairs only to be greeted with another appalling sight. During the half hour they had spent at the foot of the lighthouse the tide had come in. All sign of the white strip of sand had now been obliterated. Instead, pounding waves crashed without mercy on the rocky cliffs making the way impassable.

"We're trapped," Lindsey cried out. "What do we do?"

"Go back to the lighthouse," Eleanor said loudly over the noise of the storm. She leaned heavily against Lindsey. "It's the only protection we've got. Can you manage to get me there?"

Lindsey nodded and the two of them set off in the opposite direction. The rain lashed down so hard now that even the lighthouse looked much further away than it actually was. Lightning flashed at regular intervals and the ground shook beneath their feet as the thunder unleashed its answering echo.

Once they reached the lighthouse there still seemed nowhere to go. Large waves now crested the end of the promontory and pelted salt spray onto the place they had sat to eat their lunch. Lindsey maneuvered them instead toward the red door that had the smallest of recesses and there they collapsed, clinging to one another for dear life and wishing for it all to be over.

CHAPTER TWELVE

Eleanor and Lindsey huddled miserably in the doorway of the lighthouse with their backs to the ferocious wind and driving rain. Lightning continued to flash at close intervals and thunder echoed all around them, reverberating off the tower of the lighthouse. The briny smell of the sea filled the air as fierce wind whipped salt spray off the ocean.

Lindsey did her best to shelter a pale and shocked Eleanor, without much success. Within minutes both women were drenched. Their raincoats were no match for the torrential downpour that lashed them like a whip. The temperature had dropped markedly. It seemed cruel to think that shelter lay just on the other side of the locked door, so near yet so far.

They had tucked their daypacks in front of them in a vain hope of protecting their possessions. After a while Lindsey fished around in her bag for her phone in the hope of calling for help but could find no signal whatsoever. She didn't want to bring the phone out of her bag or wave it about a bit for fear it would be ruined. Instead she had pulled out her cardigan then re-zipped the bag, praying her sketchbook wouldn't turn to pulp.

Her immediate concern lay with Eleanor's leg. The gash she'd sustained continued to bleed but the punishing rain made it impossible to see just how badly. Red rivulets ran down Eleanor's leg, leaving Lindsey feeling most uneasy. She took her cardigan, already soaked with rain, and wrapped it around Eleanor's calf as tightly as she could. Eleanor's face creased with pain but it couldn't be helped. Lindsey had to try to stop the bleeding.

Every so often Lindsey would glance over her shoulder back toward the Hunter's Cove beach but visibility remained so poor that she couldn't make anything out. At one point a large bush that clung to the cliff face below the track they'd descended came crashing down onto the rocks below. Lindsey could only imagine that the track itself had turned into a waterfall by now and was most likely treacherous.

Lindsey began to lose track of time. Half an hour might have gone by, maybe an hour. The sky above remained dark and threatening with no promise of abatement on the horizon. Both she and Eleanor had begun to shiver, although in Eleanor's case Lindsey wondered if shock might be playing a factor. She'd fallen so heavily. Lindsey drew her in closer and Eleanor sagged against her chest. When Lindsey looked down she could see Eleanor had closed her eyes. Watching enough episodes of hospital dramas with Robyn had taught Lindsey that this wasn't a good thing.

"Hang on," Lindsey said in Eleanor's ear.

Eleanor's eyes fluttered open and she managed the weakest of smiles. "I'm just resting," she said. "Never fear."

But Lindsey did fear. And there wasn't anything she could think of to make things better. The lighthouse door remained impenetrable, there wasn't a single other place they could go and the noise of the storm made talking virtually impossible. All they could do was wait it out and hope and pray for the best. In the end Lindsey too closed her eyes for no other reason that to keep the rain from running into them.

A particularly loud crack of thunder roused Lindsey and she turned her head once again to look back toward the beach. There, to her surprise, she saw a lone figure. Visibility still remained so poor that for a moment she thought the figure might be a mirage. Then the person started waving with both arms and Lindsey knew that salvation might be at hand. At the very least someone knew they were there.

"Look, Eleanor," Lindsey said loudly, shaking her friend. "Someone's over there."

Eleanor pushed herself up with considerable effort. "Do you think it's Cedric?" she croaked.

Lindsey looked into Eleanor's face. She'd never seen her look in the slightest bit ruffled but now she looked so vulnerable. "It could be. It's too hard to tell. But whoever they are, it is a real person. A real person who can go and get some help."

Eleanor and Lindsey both began to wave back and when their savior saw them respond he turned on his heels ran off, quickly disappearing from sight.

They turned back and hunched together once more. Rescue was surely now only a matter of time.

"If that was Cedric," Eleanor said, "I don't think I've ever been happier to see him. In fact I don't think I've been happier to see anyone in my entire life."

$$\rightarrow$$

More time elapsed. The euphoria of possible salvation began to erode as reality set in. Even if rescuers came no one would be foolhardy enough to brave the current conditions. Their own lives would be in peril if they attempted to cross the stretch of water between the stairs. By now the tide would be full in. Lindsey could just hear the sound of the sea above the cacophony of the wind as its might whipped up the waves. All Eleanor and Lindsey could do was hunker down and wait for reprieve.

Lindsey felt tempted to check on Eleanor's leg but didn't want to take pressure off the wound by removing the cardigan to look. She felt tempted to peek at her phone again to see if she could get a signal but that seemed pointless and risky. She felt even more tempted to slump down on the ground and cry but knew she had to stay strong for Eleanor's sake. Eleanor continued to hunch into Lindsey's chest with her eyes closed.

Finally, after what felt like another hour, Lindsey realized the wind had started to abate just a little. The rain no longer drove in horizontally but had eased to an energetic pelting. When Lindsey looked up she saw the sky had lightened from a dark slate to battleship gray. Where once it had felt as though the storm might never pass, Lindsey could now see real signs of subsidence.

When the rain eased just a little more Lindsey said to Eleanor, "Will you be all right if I leave you just for a minute?"

Eleanor seemed to barely have the energy to answer but didn't object so Lindsey left her slumped over their bags and set off to survey the scene. She found it hard to stand as her muscles had chilled and gone rigid with sitting in one spot for so long. Her legs felt shaky. She picked her way carefully over to the stairs and gazed down to where the small beach had been, hoping that the way would now be clear. She saw to her dismay that while the waves no longer pounded the rocky wall with the same degree of ferocity, they still swelled against them with an intensity that prevented the idea of being able to simply wade across. There wasn't a hope of the two of them being able to ford such a difficult stretch, especially in Eleanor's current condition.

Visibility had improved but the constant rain meant that Lindsey had to keep wiping water out of her eyes. It proved a thankless task since every square inch of Lindsey had long since become saturated. The stairs on the far side were so tantalizingly close, and yet with the surging water in between they may have been on the far side of the moon. When she realized there wasn't anything to be gained by looking at a gap that could not be breached by simple willpower she returned to Eleanor.

Sitting back down again proved harder than Lindsey would have thought. She felt terribly stiff and had begun to ache. She'd also started to shiver with greater intensity and did not take this as a good sign. She wondered if keeping moving might not be the better option but at the same time she wasn't about to leave Eleanor on her own so returned to her former spot to wait some more.

Lindsey had lost all track of time. She had no idea how long they'd been there and the weather prevented gaining visible clues as to how late in the day it had become. Her brain began to feel foggy. Although the noise of the storm had now passed neither she nor Eleanor had the heart or energy for conversation. They just stayed slumped together. The world around them might have ceased to exist, right along with their interest in it.

After a while it occurred to Lindsey that she could hear something. When she thought about it she realized it sounded very much like an engine. When the noise grew even louder, Lindsey began to wonder if the sound might actually be real so she left Eleanor once again and went to look. When she couldn't see anything or anyone over on Hunter's Cove it occurred to her that the sound might be coming from the sea. And when she looked out through the rain eastward she saw a small fishing boat pitching and rolling its way precariously through the choppy sea toward them.

She immediately stood up and started calling out for help. She waved her arms about in order to get their attention but soon realized she need not have bothered. A man in a bright yellow raincoat stood in the bow of the launch on the lookout for her and waved back. It soon became apparent that the boat had come just for them. Rescue seemed finally at hand, if not just a little too far away to be true.

"Eleanor," she called, "there's a boat here."

Eleanor opened her eyes and gave a little smile.

Lindsey watched as the boat came to a halt at a safe distance from the shore. The man in the bow lowered the anchor and the boat captain in wet weather gear emerged from the wheelhouse. The two of them stood right by the prow and appeared to be having a discussion with one another. Lindsey watched as they pointed and generally weighed up the viable options for rescue under the current conditions. The two men then disappeared into the cabin of the boat which made Lindsey fear they'd come to the conclusion that no rescue could yet be attempted. She felt her spirits fall and realized how desperately she wanted to be saved.

After a few minutes the two men re-emerged. While one of them still wore his heavy yellow raincoat the other had donned a wetsuit. He came straight to the front of the boat and dove over. He then set off swimming into the area between the stairs with slow, measured strokes. He paused for a moment just a bit out, needing to judge it correctly to avoid a lethal combination of waves and rocks. He then struck out again. Before Lindsey knew it he was climbing the stairs and coming toward her with a big grin on his face. He was a tall man in his late thirties with a craggy face, an unruly mop of hair and shaggy beard.

"Need a ride?" he asked jovially.

Lindsey felt her shoulders sag with relief. She managed a watery smile. "I don't think I've ever wanted transport so much in my entire life," she said.

"Are you both all right?" he asked.

"My friend fell and cut her leg," Lindsey said. "I couldn't tell how seriously because it wouldn't stop raining but I wrapped it up as best I could. She's been very quiet. I've been quite worried."

"Hmm," the man said, going over to examine Eleanor. She sat watching his approach with a dreamlike expression on her face.

"Hello, young man," Eleanor said with a reedy voice as he bent down to peer at her and examine her leg. "Has anyone ever told you what a beautiful face you have? It's like a work of art."

"Is she delirious?" Lindsey asked.

The man grinned up at Lindsey. "Nothing wrong with her if you ask me. Great eyesight and wonderful taste. I'd say her leg might not be too bad. Sometimes those surface cuts bleed like buggery without actually having done much damage. I can see you're shivering. Are you okay?"

"Fine," Lindsey said. "Just cold and stiff. I'd love a hot shower."

"Not hot," her rescuer said. "Just warm. And plenty of warm fluids too. Let's see what we can do about getting you two off this rock. You certainly picked a hell of a day for a picnic."

"How can we get out to the boat?" Lindsey asked.

"I'm going to swim you out one at a time," the man said. "We figure the two of you probably couldn't get any wetter than you already are and the sea is pretty warm even in these conditions. It always is at this time of year."

"What about our things?" Eleanor asked. "We've tried our best to keep our bags a bit dry. They've got our electronic stuff in them."

"You two are from Auckland, right?" the man asked. "Only city folk would worry about stuff like that."

"Please," Eleanor said. She looked at Lindsey. "My phone's the only place I've got Tom's number."

"Right-o," the man said. "I'll take you first then, young lady," he said to Eleanor, "then come back for your friend with a big plastic bag for your stuff. If we wrap it up with tape it should be as right as rain. Although perhaps that's not the best expression under the circumstances."

"No," Eleanor agreed.

"Now the tricky bit is going to be getting off the stairs and away from the rocks," the man said. "Once we get away from there I want you to float on your back and let me tow you out. It's imperative that you don't try to swim yourself out and very important for you to stay calm. Concentrate on breathing in and out. I can't save you if you start flailing around. Got that?"

Eleanor nodded.

"And I'm thinking you might need to ditch the shoes and the raincoat. We don't want you wearing anything heavy or that might drag you down. And before you start panicking we can leave both here with your little friend and we'll bring it all over when I come back to get her. Okay?"

Eleanor nodded again.

To Lindsey the man said, "You stay right here and carry on trying to keep your bags dry." He looked at the sodden bundles behind Lindsey with skepticism. To Eleanor he said, "Now madam, let's see if we can't get you up."

The man put his large arm around the middle of Eleanor's back and hoisted her to her feet. He gave her a moment to steady herself and looked at her closely. "All right? Or do I need to swim back to the boat and radio for the rescue helicopter?"

"I'm okay," Eleanor said. "I've tried to stay calm and conserve my energy."

"Very Zen," the man said. "I suppose you've also got your yoga mat tucked in your bag, have you?"

"Of course," Eleanor said. "It's right next to my latte. Now enough with the Aucklander bashing." She stood on her own and took off her coat and shoes then said, "Okay, I'm ready as I'm ever going to be. Get me out of here."

Before she could object the man scooped Eleanor into his arms. She peered over at Lindsey and said, "See you soon."

Lindsey attempted a smile but said nothing. She suddenly found her throat had dried out like a sponge in the sun. The man carried Eleanor off toward the stairs. As she watched them withdraw and leave her behind, a wave of panic threatened to overwhelm her. She had to resist a very strong urge to get up and run after them. She feared they might have some difficulty getting away from the stairs. She feared something might happen to them on the way out. But most of all she feared something might prevent the man from returning and Lindsey would find herself marooned on her own at the lighthouse for the duration, even overnight. She did not think she could manage that.

But then, she reminded herself, she had endured worse. All she needed to do was to recall the coping mechanisms from the past. All would be well. Didn't Will always say that every cloud had a silver lining?

The pair was soon out of sight. Lindsey found the job of having to stay with the bags burdensome indeed. It meant she could not get up to watch proceedings and see how far they had progressed. She had no way of knowing how they fared. All she could do was wait some more.

Lindsey closed her eyes and made herself count her blessings. First off she was still alive and seemed in no immediate danger of losing that status. She surely hadn't survived the incident with the bull only to perish in a bit of rain. The weather wasn't as bad as it had been. Help was at hand and rescue only a matter of time. Eleanor would be well. Lindsey recalled some of the great experiences and wonderful things she'd seen over the last week or so. She had made some new friends and had managed to push herself out of her comfort zone. Her work had started to come together and she had made some great sketches provided they survived the ordeal. When this was all over she would be warm and dry and at the end of the trip she would return to Robyn and Will once again.

See, she told herself, plenty to be thankful for.

She made herself think about her story, playing with words in her head. She loved to use alliteration in her children's stories and focused on pairing words together and testing out some rhymes. She visualized her illustrations and tried to form it all together in her mind. Anything to keep the panic at bay.

She felt her muscles groan with sitting in one position and contemplated her need to get up when a voice in front of her made her open her eyes with a snap.

"I thought you might have gone to sleep," the man said.

"I'm still here," Lindsey said.

"Good," he said. "It will be much easier for me to get you to the boat if you're still conscious."

"How's Eleanor?" Lindsey asked.

"Fine," he said. "She got a bit bruised being dragged out of the sea and into the boat and the process made her leg start bleeding again but Pete's onto it. She's more worried about you than she is about herself so I'm taking that as a good sign. If either of you has hypothermia it's only mild. Here's the plastic bag."

He proffered a large thick bag that had a roll of industrial tape shoved in the bottom. Lindsey withdrew the tape and started stuffing their possessions into it.

"Your shoes and coat too," he said.

Lindsey shed both and tried to flick the worst of the water off her coat. After stowing everything away the man folded the plastic numerous times over at the opening and then used vast quantities of tape to seal it up. He places the remnants of the roll on the lighthouse doorstep.

"That'll probably make someone wonder," he said looking down at it.

"Lucky you had these things," Lindsey said.

"It's a boat," the man said. "You set out prepared for water. You never know when you might have occasion to keep things dry. Are you ready?"

Lindsey nodded and before she knew it found herself up in the man's arms. Lindsey found such proximity quite disconcerting especially since she tried so hard to avoid contact with strangers. She started worrying that she might weigh a ton but the man gave no sign of struggling. He walked them slowly over toward the steps. Lindsey looked forward. The sea had calmed even more since Lindsey had been over to look at it but in her opinion it still seemed quite perilous.

The man descended the stairs and put Lindsey down on the last exposed one. Cold water rushed over her feet. She feared her idea of mild sea temperatures and his might be poles apart. She did not relish the prospect of getting even colder. But in one respect he had been right. She certainly could not get any wetter.

"Right," her rescuer said. "We've got to time this just right. We need to hold hands. As soon as I say jump you need to propel yourself straight out as far as you are able then get ready to flip onto your back. You then need to let me take you under the chin and drag you out to the boat. If you've got the strength to kick a bit at first that would be helpful. The more distance we can put between those rocks and ourselves the better. As soon as you get tired just stop. Got it?"

"Got it," Lindsey said.

The man took her hand and stood watching the waves. He seemed to be assessing how the breakers came in and looking for a calm spot between the waves. Once he seemed satisfied he said, "Right, on three. One, two, three."

As instructed, Lindsey jumped as far out as she could manage. Her impact on the water made her brain momentarily freeze but she reminded herself of her rescuer's instructions. She flipped over onto her back. The man put his left hand under her neck while balancing the bag of possessions on her chest with his right. He started to tow her. She could feel a breaker coming toward her and started to kick as hard as she could. She could feel the man also start to kick with a vast amount of power. In spite of getting a face full of sea water as the wave crested, to her surprise they started to head in an easterly direction and out to the boat. She kept kicking for while and then felt the muscles in her legs start to burn with the exertion so stopped.

"You're doing well," the man said. "Just stay calm."

Lindsey concentrated on her breathing and took comfort from the fact that the man did not appear to be struggling with this task at all. She took the plastic bag off him and clung on to it to make it even easier for him. And then, almost before she expected it, she found that they had arrived at the boat. The man took the bag off her and tossed it up to the captain and then spun her around so she could cling on to the edge of the boat.

"Put your feet here," the man told her, "and stretch your arms up. Pete will pull you up and I'll push you. I'm assuming you won't be offended if I touch your derriere?"

Lindsey couldn't have cared less. She followed the man's instructions and after one enormous pull and corresponding push she found herself slumped on the deck of the boat.

Eleanor, who'd been draped in a silver thermal blanket, came forward at once.

"Thank God," she said, helping Lindsey to her feet and pulling her into her arms.

"We're saved," Lindsey said.

"Praise be," Eleanor said with an enormous and very relieved smile.

Their rescuer had now made it on board and shook himself like a dog. Water flung in all directions from his beard and shaggy hair. He reached for a towel to wipe his face. When he removed the towel he grinned at them lopsidedly.

"How can we ever thank you?" Eleanor said.

The man waved his arm dismissively. "Nothing like a bit of an unexpected adventure," he said. "Or a dip in the sea. It makes you know that you're alive. Wouldn't you agree?"

After introductions were made – the captain Peter Nodder and their rescuer Alan Freel – Peter led them into the cabin of the boat and sorted them out with some emergency clothes. The blue and orange work overalls he supplied weren't exactly the height of fashion but under the circumstances neither woman cared a jot. To be out of their wet things and into something dry seemed heavenly. Once they were changed Peter suggested Eleanor kept wearing the silver thermal blanket and produced a second one for Lindsey. He poured them tea laced with sugar from a flask and then disappeared. Both women were still a bit shaky. Moments later they heard the scrape of the anchor and the sound of the engine being coaxed back into life.

Alan reappeared, fully dressed and looking no worse for wear for his efforts. He continued to wave away their attempts at thanks as though they were grateful for nothing more serious than him having bought them an ice cream. He told them that he and Peter were neighbors, that they lived at the end of Thomas Peak Road which ran from the coast and right past their next destination and out to the main highway north. Peter farmed goats and Alan was having a go at growing organic vegetables and living sustainably. The two men were great friends, shared the boat and often turned out in case of emergency without any funding, training or recognition. Eleanor said they should both be getting medals. Alan laughed at that but Lindsey could tell Eleanor meant it. She certainly wasn't above petitioning the Governor General for some sort of honor to be bestowed.

Their boat trip turned out to be a relatively short one, emphasizing yet again how rescue had been so near and yet so far. By the time they reached the boat ramp at the end of Thomas Peak Road the rain had almost stopped falling and both women had warmed up a degree or two. Alan said they should keep it that way. Peter navigated the boat as far up onto the boat ramp as he dared and Alan jumped out into ankle deep water. Peter then helped lower first Eleanor and then Lindsey into Alan's arms and he carried them to shore to save them getting wet once more.

There Dennis waited, umbrella in hand. Lindsey could tell that his concern for them had been very great. His face had taken on a pinched look that barely relaxed upon seeing them safe and well. Lindsey suspected he would have hugged them but his main priority lay in bundling them in the mini bus and out of the last of the rain as fast as possible. Lindsey and Eleanor had no such compunction and would not be rushed. They both hugged Alan and waved at Peter before getting out of the wet. Once Dennis had them safely stowed along with the plastic bag containing their belongings he exchanged a few words with Alan before getting in the cab and firing up the engine.

Before he drove off he swiveled around in his seat and said, "I can't tell you how relieved I am that you are both here and have come out of your ordeal reasonably unscathed. You've given us all some very anxious moments, I can tell you. Everyone has been so worried."

Eleanor took Lindsey's hand and squeezed it. "I don't think you're quite as relieved as we are, Dennis," she said. "It's been quite a day. Have we far to go?"

"Only about ten minutes up the road," Dennis said. "I'll have you there in a jiffy."

True to his word, Dennis drove the short distance in about ten minutes. The windows of the mini bus had fogged up with the moisture in the air so neither Eleanor nor Lindsey had any chance of getting their bearings or seeing where they were headed. Neither minded about that either. They sat close together in grateful silence. And before they knew it Dennis was swinging the mini bus into the driveway to Thomas Peak House.

Once they arrived Dennis parked close to the entrance to the house where they were bundled in through a columned front porch and into the foyer where the entire tour party stood waiting to greet them. Vi came rushing forward to hug them and it seemed clear that she'd been crying.

"Gawd love you," she said. "If you two ain't a sight for sore eyes. I've been having heart palpitations with wondering how you were ever going to be saved."

Eddie came over hot on Vi's heels. He drew the line at actually hugging them but instead fingered Lindsey's silver thermal blanket with interest.

"You two look like you're ready for a trip into space in that get up," Eddie said.

"Or maybe a penitentiary," Eleanor said, patting the front of her blue and orange overalls with bemusement. "There's something rather penal about these outfits."

Dennis said, "I can't tell you how sorry I am about all this. I should have triple checked the weather forecast. If I'd known there was any chance of the storm coming in early I would not have suggested the longer walk."

"Weather forecasts always seem half a day out to me," Eleanor said. "Please don't think any more about it. We certainly don't blame you."

Cedric stepped forward looking pale and mournful. "I too let you down very badly," he said. "I should not have left you alone to go to see the trees. I shouldn't have got talking to the people I met there or taken so long to get down the hill to see if you were all right."

"But it was you who raised the alarm?" Eleanor asked. "It was you we saw waving?"

Cedric nodded.

"In which case both Lindsey and I will both consider you a hero until the day we die," Eleanor told him. "If it wasn't for you we might still be stuck by the lighthouse. Isn't that right, Lindsey?"

Lindsey nodded but found herself unable to speak. True to form she found herself a lot more troubled by the scrutiny of numerous sets of eyes than she did of the storm itself.

A woman they didn't recognize stepped forward to stand beside Dennis. She appeared to be in her early forties and wore a smart black dress and a profusion of gold jewelry. She had the same auburn colored hair as Lindsey but wore hers in a style made famous by Princess Diana.

She said, "There should have been a sign at the top of the stairs that lead across the little beach as you go out toward the lighthouse. It's supposed to warn people to double check the tide times before proceeding." She made an apologetic face as though responsible for the sign herself. "I'm afraid you aren't the first people to ever be stuck out there, I'm sorry to say."

Eleanor gave an elegant little shrug. "We didn't see a sign," she said. "In fact I'd put money on there not being a sign at all. But in all honesty I do wonder if it would have mattered. The gap between the stairs didn't look very big and we weren't intending to be out at the lighthouse for very long, just long enough to eat some lunch. If the tide had come back in a little we would have just figured on taking off our shoes and socks and wading back across. What we didn't count on was a storm surge with dangerous waves and pelting rain, nor that I would fall over and get injured."

"Speaking of which," Dennis said, "I think we should get you both upstairs for warm showers and fresh clothes and some hot tea or coffee. Then when you are a bit warmer and drier I think we should take a little trip back to Waiata Junction and let the folks at the hospital take a look at you both."

Eleanor went to object but Dennis said, "No, I insist. If anything more serious should develop I would be held liable. You must let me take you for medical attention so I can put my mind at rest."

And with that Eleanor and Lindsey were taken away up the very grand staircase for what would possibly be the best showers of their entire lives.

Three quarters of an hour later Eleanor and Lindsey had showered and changed into the warmest clothes they'd brought with them and were downstairs ready to set off with Dennis for Waiata Junction Hospital. Eleanor still protested that it wasn't necessary and that all she wanted now was a nice lie down in bed. Dennis remained adamant that they should be checked over by qualified medical personnel. And, as if to give credence to the necessity of going, Cedric had weighed in to the discussion as First Aid Treatment Officer and insisted on coming along for the ride.

In the interim their hostess, whose name turned out to be Elizabeth, had taken all of their wet things and their rescuers' overalls to clean and dry them as best she could. Both Lindsey and Eleanor's phones had reacted to moisture exposure by acting a bit strangely but Elizabeth felt sure that popping them in a bag of rice for a night in her airing cupboard would work wonders. Lindsey could see this bothered Eleanor greatly but there wasn't anything she could do to speed the process up. Elizabeth came to wave them off, promising them a hearty meal on their return. Eddie and Vi, Andrew, Simon and Bianca also came to the foyer to form a little farewell party mostly, it seemed, because Eleanor and Lindsey's departure appeared to be the most interesting thing happening.

As Lindsey went to head toward the mini bus she caught sight of Andrew stepping forward. As she walked she turned her head to look at him. He looked like he might like to say something but judged it to be the wrong place at the wrong time and halted in his tracks. Lindsey sent him a shy smile and kept walking. As much as it would be nice to speak with Andrew she certainly wasn't about to do so with a captive audience.

On the trip into Waiata Junction Cedric regaled them with his tale, of how he had met a lovely British couple who had walked all the way to Hunter's Cove and were then on their way back to the starting point where they'd left their rental car. While they were talking (which Lindsey understood as "while Cedric was talking", especially as he regaled them with every sentence of their conversation) the first signs of a change in the weather appeared with the darkening of the sky. It had taken on that same green tinge as Eleanor and Lindsey had observed. Five minutes later both parties decided it might be time to get moving. By the time Cedric and his new friends had threaded their way back to the lookout point the rain had started to fall with a vengeance.

The trip down the steep path had proved a perilous one. The heaviness of the rain and the gradient of the track meant that water soon ran in great cascades where Cedric tried to walk. But since there wasn't another way down Cedric had to content himself with going as fast as he dared, which wasn't very fast at all. In several spots he'd had to stop entirely in order to fashion a makeshift bridge over sections of the path that had been dry when Eleanor and Lindsey had walked on them but, with rushing water upon, them looked too dangerous to ford.

"There was so much lightning," Cedric said. "Not to mention thunder. It was pretty scary. I didn't want to end up like the man from Virginia who got struck by lightning seven times between nineteen forty two and nineteen seventy seven."

When Cedric finally drew breath Dennis said to Eleanor, "Oh by the way, some man keeps calling asking about you. Some chap called Tom."

"Tom?" Eleanor said, livening up considerably. "What did he say? What did you say?"

"I didn't know who he was or how he'd got my number but he explained about knowing the Barclays and having met you," Dennis said, talking loudly over his shoulder. "He wanted to check that you were fine and wasn't at all happy to learn how the two of you had been marooned by the lighthouse."

"Do you have his number?" Eleanor asked, leaning forward with interest. "I should let him know I'm okay."

"No need," Dennis said airily. "He called once we'd got you back to Thomas Peak House and he knows you're fine. I told him we were going to head for the hospital just to be on the safe side."

Eleanor leaned back into her seat at this news and let out a contemplative sigh. Lindsey looked at her and raised her eyebrows questioningly. Eleanor gave a little shrug.

Five minutes later Dennis negotiated their way into a deserted looking Waiata Junction and pulled in to the rather busier car park at the hospital. It seemed strange to be back in a town Lindsey wasn't expecting to see again on this trip. The rain had ceased altogether now. Some small patches of blue sky could be seen to the west, letting in filaments of late afternoon sun.

They made their way into the main entrance of the medical facility. Since neither Lindsey nor Eleanor looked on the verge of collapse they were given forms to complete by a severe looking receptionist and directed to a bank of uncomfortable plastic chairs in the foyer. Judging by the amount of other people milling about Lindsey assumed they might be in for a long wait. The bad weather had evidently brought with it a number of minor catastrophes of a medical nature.

While Lindsey and Eleanor filled out their forms Cedric said, "Did you know that the longest wait on a hospital trolley was seventy seven hours and thirty minutes?"

Eleanor looked sharply at Dennis. "I am not waiting that long," she said. "If we are here more than an hour I am going to have to insist you take us home and the consequences be damned. I'll come back in the morning if I have to."

Lindsey suppressed a grin. She felt very relieved to see Eleanor's spark had returned.

"I don't suppose they have much staff in the first place," Cedric said. "Not a small field hospital like this."

"Thanks for the encouragement there, Cedric," Eleanor said.

"Well, it could be worse," Cedric replied, looking quite indignant. "Malawi has the fewest physicians per head of capita – only one for about every fifty thousand people. At least you don't live there."

Everyone ignored him. When Eleanor and Lindsey had finished filling in their forms Dennis took them over to the receptionist to hand them in. They could see him having a lively discussion with the matronly looking woman behind the counter after which he returned.

"Apparently," he said, "they're a bit swamped. Some man got crushed when a tree branch fell on his house and two British tourists got injured when they ran off the road due to poor visibility. I explained what you've been through so I think I've persuaded Bloody Mary's meaner half sister over there to see that you are given priority."

"I think Bloody Mary was the meaner half sister," Eleanor said, "but thanks."

"Did you say some British tourists had been injured in a car accident?" Cedric asked. "Imagine if it's the people I met today? Wouldn't that be terrible?"

Before they could stop him he went over to talk with the formidable receptionist.

Dennis said, "He won't get much joy there, I can tell you."

"Poor Cedric," Eleanor said. "From now until eternity he'll be torturing himself about how he had it in his control to prevent disaster for two lots of people and failed on both accounts. If he'd come with us we might have made a different decision about going to the lighthouse. If he'd not gone to see the kauri trees those poor people might have been underway long before the storm hit and not been affected at all."

"It would have taken them hours to make it back to the car park," Lindsey said. "Surely by then the rain would have eased."

"I wonder if someone should check on them," Dennis said. "Imagine if they got into trouble. No one would necessarily be wondering where they were."

He looked troubled so Eleanor said, "Why don't you go next door to the police station and report it to them? They might send someone out to make sure the car park is empty."

"Good idea," Dennis said. "As long as the two of you will be okay?"

"Okay?" Eleanor asked. "Compared to where we've been today this place couldn't get any safer. Besides, we've still got Cedric."

Reassured, Dennis decided to take up Eleanor's suggestion. They watched as he made his way over to the main exit. As he went to leave another man came in. Eleanor jumped to her feet at once. Tom had arrived.

Tom covered the distance between himself and Eleanor with remarkable speed before pulling her into his arms and whirling her around. He then placed her back down and stared into her face as though she was the most precious, most amazing thing he'd ever seen. Then, with great deliberation, he kissed Eleanor for all she was worth.

Eleanor's objection to waiting evaporated with Tom's arrival. She became perfectly content to wait for as long as it might take to be seen and processed. But Bloody Mary proved true to her word. As soon as the more severe cases had been dealt with, Eleanor got called and then Lindsey not long after. Both women were pronounced fit for discharged without need of further intervention or overnight observation. A nurse re-bandaged Eleanor's leg but the gash she sustained wasn't deep enough to require stitches. What signs of mild hypothermia they'd displayed had all but vanished. Alan's advice had been reliable and they'd already done everything recommended. The only prescription given was for a good night's sleep somewhere more conducive than a noisy hospital.

When it came time to leave, Eleanor and Tom were reluctant to part from one another. Tom gave Dennis a look that suggested he'd be wise to take much better care of his charges in future. Dennis, whose bewilderment over the whole romance knew no bounds, didn't know what to do or say in response. Cedric couldn't have cared either way. His every attempt to establish the identity of the British tourists had been thwarted. He bore his immense disappointment over this with a face worthy of a martyr.

In accordance with the tour's itinerary, tomorrow would be a free day. Tom promised to come to see Eleanor at Thomas Peak House in the morning. This made parting not quite such a sweet sorrow. The promise of tomorrow lingered in the air as the new couple parted. From Lindsey's perspective she would let tomorrow take care of itself. All she wanted now was a good night's sleep.

Elizabeth Carr set her alarm for five thirty a.m. From experience she knew this would give her enough time to get up, shower, dress, do her hair and makeup then do a sweep of the house to ensure perfection. She would then head to the kitchen. At six thirty she would start a series of preparations for the day that were many and plentiful. She had a buffet breakfast to lay out for her guests – large bowls of cereals, cut up fresh fruit, yoghurt, warm croissants and sweet rolls, jams and honey, tea and coffee. She had a Mexican themed lunch planned for whichever guests chose to hang around today. She also needed to be ready to pack some lunches for those who chose to go further afield. Then she needed to get tonight's dinner under way since the Provencal chicken stew she'd planned as a main course needed at least eight hours in two large slow cookers.

She had to pack two school lunches for Julian and Olivia and have them on the school bus by seven fifty. She also had to get them out of bed on a Monday morning. She knew both children would be reluctant to leave while so many interesting guests were around, especially in light of yesterday's dramas. She wouldn't put it past either of them to come down with a mystery illness that would preclude school but somehow exclude staying in bed. Jeremy would also need guiding out the door so he would be at work on time. Like most husbands, he often needed pointing in the right direction with anything from what to wear, ("Not that!") to where he'd left his car keys.

There would be other things she did not expect, just as there had been yesterday with the two ladies who'd required rescuing. The pair had been most fortunate in their saviors since Peter and Alan were a couple of adrenaline junkies who had probably attempted their rescue when others would consider it too risky. It all seemed a most unfortunate business but mercifully all had ended well.

Yet Elizabeth wasn't in the slightest bit fazed by the mountain of tasks that lay before her. While some people would be daunted by it, Elizabeth would thrive. And while most people would consider time to be their enemy, Elizabeth embraced time as her friend. She knew how to manage it, how to make the most of it and above all how to thwart it by means of vast lists and contingency plans. If she couldn't make this the best stop on the De Vine Tour itinerary she'd eat her hat.

At ten a.m. Dennis made his way to the Carr's kitchen to check in with the hostess. He found Elizabeth looking fresh and immaculate as though she'd just sprung out of bed after the best night's sleep anyone had had in a century. She'd donned a white chef's apron over her expensive blue calf-length dress but worked so neatly it seemed surplus to requirements. A myriad of mouthwatering smells assailed his nostrils and yet the kitchen seemed clear from the sort of detritus required to make such wonderful aromas.

"Ah, Dennis," she said. "Is everyone done with breakfast?"

"Eddie and Vi just left," Dennis said. "Simon, Andrew and Cedric finished some time ago. Bianca almost never has breakfast. If we haven't seen her by now then she isn't interested. As for Eleanor and Lindsey, well, I don't know what to do about either of them. I want to know they are okay but don't feel I should disturb them if they're still sleeping after their ordeal."

"You can rest easy there," Elizabeth said. "I discussed the morning with both ladies yesterday and suggested I take them a breakfast tray at about nine thirty. When I popped in to see them, both ladies were awake, had slept well and weren't feeling too bad apart from the odd muscle ache."

Dennis breathed out an enormous sigh of relief. "You are a wonder," he said. "I've been agonizing over what to do."

"No need on that front. All is well. How are your other tour members this morning? Any planning a jaunt up Thomas Peak?"

"I think they're all going to stay here today," Dennis said. "To be honest everyone seemed in a very strange mood this morning. Andrew was fine, but determined not to go anywhere. His friend Simon - the jilted bridegroom I told you about - had been making progress and had seemed a lot more cheerful of late. This morning he's like a bear with a sore head. Cedric's still fussing about the fate of the British tourists he met yesterday. Even Eddie and Vi, a couple as cheerful as the day is long, aren't in top form either. Vi looks like she's been having palpitations over something while Eddie's mood borders on crotchety. The storm appears to have driven everyone a little batty."

"It's a shame," Elizabeth said. "There are such excellent views from the peak. It's such a beautiful day today in the way it often is after a storm. Everything is crisper and cleaner somehow."

"A bit like your kitchen," Dennis said. "I've never known anyone who could produce such great results with so little evidence of effort."

Elizabeth smiled. "My mother says I'm like a swan. I glide on top of the water but my feet are going like the clappers under the surface. It's easy really. Break things down into manageable chunks and keep things tidy as you go."

"You'll be all right with having a full house for lunch?" Dennis asked.

"Of course. It will probably make things easier in a way. At least I don't need to make any picnics for those going out," she said. "Maybe lunch together will be just what the doctor ordered. With the ladies taking straight to their beds on their return from hospital last night and a few no-shows at breakfast, lunch will be the first time your group has been together for a while. If they all get on okay with one another, a bit of camaraderie might do wonders."

Dennis frowned. "I hope you're right," he said, "because at the moment things feel all wrong. I've never had a tour like it. Let's just hope yesterday's fiasco is the last disaster of the trip. I'd hate to think that more calamity might lie just around the corner."

Elizabeth, who clearly did not have the word "calamity" in her personal dictionary, gave him a reassuring smile and said, "I'm sure everything will turn out just fine."

CHAPTER THIRTEEN

Lindsey couldn't remember the last time someone had brought her breakfast in bed. It had probably been Will on her birthday the September before last. As she recalled, his well-intentioned efforts had not gone according to plan. For a start Lindsey had not been awake enough to appreciate his gesture. Will had by necessity made her breakfast before he set off for work, at an hour far earlier than Lindsey normally rose. She'd stayed up late the night before working on some illustrations and had left some reference books strewn on the floor. In the half-gloom Will had not seen these obstacles. As a result Lindsey had ended up with a bed full of limp toast, sticky jam and the contents of a glass of orange juice.

Elizabeth Carr, on the other hand, had the process of delivering breakfast in bed down to a fine art. She helpfully plumped the pillows and cracked open the curtains. She placed the immaculate tray to one side where it sat handily without being restrictive. She made enquiries as to Lindsey's health and wellbeing without conducting the Spanish Inquisition. She could tell Lindsey that Eleanor fared well and had enjoyed a wonderful night's sleep. Not only that, the well-provisioned breakfast tray was a wonder to behold.

Lindsey discovered she'd regained her appetite overnight. When they returned from the largely pointless trip to the hospital last night Lindsey could barely keep her eyes open. According to Elizabeth the rest of the tour group had already been served dinner. As such she could either serve a second sitting in the dining room for the four of them or she and Eleanor could have a tray in their rooms. Eleanor had wondered about the possibility of soup and before Lindsey knew it she was ensconced in her room with a hearty chicken broth and some fresh crusty bread. She'd consumed this at a rapid rate before falling straight to sleep.

Now that Lindsey had breakfasted and dressed ready for the remainder of the day she felt a little tentative about setting off from her room. Her recollections of the property from yesterday were blanketed in fog. She knew the house looked very grand and sat on flat land, tucked in the lee of Thomas Peak. She'd seen that the grounds looked lush and welcoming and that the Carrs had a very impressive tennis court somewhere to the right of the house. In fact when Lindsey thought about it, she could hear the sound of a ball ricocheting off rackets at that very moment. This made her feel tempted to see what lay beyond.

The Carr's residence was quite sumptuous. The painted walls and lighting had been cleverly designed to give off a golden glow that added an immediate warmth. The furniture, mostly antiques, looked expensive and both well chosen and well placed. Some fine pieces of art hung on the walls. The cream carpets were embellished with wonderful Turkish rugs.

Lindsey wasn't entirely sure where she was going as she descended the stairs so just followed the sound of voices. This led her to a fine looking lounge area with elegant white couches positioned around the unlit fireplace. On one of the couches sat Eleanor and Tom, starring into one another's eyes and giggling like teenagers.

Eleanor caught sight of Lindsey and came rushing over. She embraced Lindsey as though they hadn't seen each other for fifteen years rather than fifteen hours.

"There you are," she said. "I was about to send a search party for you." She laughed at this. "Well, perhaps not a search party. I don't know about you, but I don't have the smallest intention of ever needing rescuing again."

"No," Lindsey said. "Me either."

"Come and sit down," Eleanor said, shepherding Lindsey onto the couch opposite Tom and then returning to his side.

"Morning, Lindsey," Tom said.

"Hi," Lindsey said.

"Ellie's been telling me all about how heroic you were yesterday, so brave and so comforting," Tom said.

Lindsey could feel her face flushing. "No…I…"

"You can't deny it," Eleanor said. "I won't let you. If it weren't for you I probably would have gone out of my mind. I will always be extremely grateful for your support in my hour of need."

"How are you today?" Lindsey asked, determined to steer the conversation away from such a mortifying and baseless subject. "Elizabeth said you were well."

"Elizabeth," Eleanor gushed. "What a wonderful woman. If she wasn't already married I would propose immediately. Such a treasure."

Tom made a sound of protest at that. "Well," said Eleanor, patting his hand, "maybe not propose. I would however offer her a tidy sum to enter my service for the rest of her natural life - or mine - and make all things domestic hum like a symphony."

Lindsey couldn't help thinking at this point that love had done something strange to her friend Eleanor. Her satisfaction with everything appeared to know no bounds.

"But you," Lindsey said. "How are you?"

"Absolutely fine," Eleanor said. "I slept like a log, ate an enormous breakfast and feel happy to be safe and dry and inside."

"And your leg?"

Eleanor waved her hand. "Oh, just a little twinge here and there. Nothing to write home about. It's probably just as well that today was another rest day though. You?"

"I feel fine. I wouldn't be surprised if I needed a little nap this afternoon but I'm good for now."

"Oh, an afternoon siesta," Eleanor enthused. "Doesn't that sound heavenly, Tom?"

Eleanor and Tom commenced staring into one another's eyes. After a couple of uncomfortable minutes Lindsey said, "Where's everyone else?"

"Cedric insisted Dennis take him back to Waiata Junction so that they could find out what happened to Dennis's report about the British tourists. I don't think he'll rest until he knows they are fine. Eddie and Vi decided to go back to their room. Apparently they've got an enormous wall-mounted television in their room and were going to indulge in a bit of channel surfing. Cedric told them that you burn more calories sleeping than you do watching television but neither seemed concerned by this."

Lindsey smiled. Good old Cedric. A fact for any occasion. "And the others?"

"Simon and Bianca are playing tennis. I don't know where Andrew went. Simon and Bianca probably press-ganged him into being their umpire. I don't envy him a jot. It would not be difficult to imagine Bianca giving John McEnroe a run for his money in the tantrum department. One can only hope that Simon is gracious enough to let her win."

Lindsey suppressed a smile. Eleanor's bountiful outlook on life did have limits after all. Lindsey thought she might like to see this tennis game for herself and since she had been trying to think up an excuse to leave the lovebirds to their own devices, this seemed like a wonderful excuse. Neither Tom nor Eleanor put up much of a fight when she announced her intentions.

Lindsey went back out into the foyer and let herself out through the commanding front door. This led to a portico-covered area wide enough for cars to drive through. Royalty wouldn't object to being dropped off here should they have been in the area. She then set off through a hedged formal garden toward the continuing sound of tennis. Just as she neared the gap in the hedge that led the direction she wanted to go, Andrew came around the corner and nearly bashed into her. He quickly steadied her by the arms, realized who he'd careened into, then pulled her to him in a warm but fleeting embrace.

Lindsey could feel her face burning once again but wasn't altogether displeased with his gesture.

"You can't imagine how relieved I am to see you alive and well," he said. "We were all in ten types of agony yesterday when the storm hit and we knew you were out in it with no protection. Then when we heard you'd got stranded at the lighthouse - and there wasn't any let-up in the weather - we really feared for you."

Lindsey gave him a shy smile. "That was kind of you," she said.

"Kind?" Andrew said. He shook his head. "That's not the word I'd use. Dennis said you're none the worse for wear?"

She nodded. "Apart from Eleanor's leg, two damp cell phones and some ruined sketches we really were pretty lucky."

"I wish I'd not stuck with Simon yesterday," he said. "Sorry to hear about your sketches. If it's a matter of doing them again I'd be more than happy to bring you back by car after the tour is over. We could retrace our steps so that you could recapture the magic, as it were."

Since Lindsey had already convinced herself that she would never see Andrew again after next weekend, his offer came as something of a surprise. She felt touched by his kindness and said so.

"There's that word again," he said. "Helping an old lady across the street is kind. Giving up your seat on a bus is kind. Donating some used goods to a charity shop is kind. They are all acts of strangers, not of friends."

Lindsey considered his words and their effect on her. "Is that what we are?" she asked in a small voice, half fearing his answer.

"Of course," Andrew said. "And if I've got anything to do with it, we'll go on being friends for a very long time to come."

Before he could say anything else Simon and Bianca rounded the corner of the hedge, bickering in a mostly good-natured way about their game.

"I won," Bianca said with triumph. "And now I'm starving. What time do you suppose we'll be fed lunch?"

Elizabeth served lunch in the informal lounge at the back of the house. She'd decorated this room to be like an exotic bar in far-flung Singapore with warm reds and oranges, with cane furniture and potted kentia palms. It seems the perfect setting for the Mexican lunch she'd made. She'd laid out a variety of items: a creamy burrito casserole, guacamole, some Mexican rice, a dish of chicken enchiladas and another of mini tacos, a couple of fresh salads. Her guests - including Tom - were encouraged to help themselves from the buffet and sit anywhere, eating off their knees. After so many picnic lunches and dinners of a more formal nature everyone seemed to enjoy this as a bit of a novelty. Not only that, as people went back to the buffet table to try other things they often ended up sitting in a different spot afterward and so mingled far more than they were used to. This didn't seem a problem as long as Bianca wasn't in danger of sitting next to Cedric. But since Cedric took great pains to avoid Bianca there wasn't much chance of that happening anyway.

The only person to suffer some discomfort at lunch was Lindsey. Eleanor had got it into her head that everyone should know how brave and true and caring Lindsey had been during their ordeal. As a result Lindsey found herself the focus of so much unwanted attention and praise that she did not know how to cope. Elizabeth, who kept coming and going during the course of the meal, seemed to notice Lindsey's uneasiness and took the opportunity to draw Lindsey aside at one point.

"It sounds as though you were very brave," Elizabeth said.

Lindsey blushed. "I wasn't," she said. "I was pretty terrified most of the time. I really didn't do anything except not lose it."

Elizabeth put her hand on Lindsey's arm. "While that might be true, no one is ever going to believe it," she said. "People have a fundamental need for heroes and this is your turn. My advice, if you'll allow me to give it, is to be as gracious about it as you would about receiving a compliment. My mother, God rest her soul, taught me that if someone gives you a compliment the best thing to do is accept it with grace, not deny its veracity and be defensive. Instead she told me to smile politely and say, 'Thank you,' or tell them it's kind of them to have said something."

Lindsey looked at Elizabeth while she processed this information, unsure of what to say.

"Trust me," Elizabeth said. "You'll feel a lot better if you learn how to receive praise, and you'll notice it has a great effect on the bestower as well. Besides, if you get used to accepting accolades, one day you might actually start to believe what people tell you."

She then gave Lindsey a conspiratorial wink and moved quietly away. After this one or two more comments of a complimentary nature came Lindsey's way and, with Elizabeth's wisdom echoing in her ears, she forced herself to bite down what she wanted to say in favor of smiling shyly and being thankful. Lindsey could soon see that her hostess had given her sage advice if for no other reason than it cut the conversation short. If she didn't try to tell the person how wrong they were in their assertions - which inevitably meant them reasserting their original comment - talk soon moved on to something else.

At one point Lindsey realized that only twenty-four hours ago she and Eleanor had feared they were never going to be safe or comfortable ever again. It already felt like a fading recollection in the same way action from a film feels. At the time it's all so powerful but before long the intensity fades and the whole thing gets consigned to memory. What wasn't quite so easy to overcome was the physical repercussions. By two o'clock, while everyone still lingered around in the lounge, Lindsey felt utterly exhausted. She could also see the strain on Eleanor's face even though she tried hard to fight it. Tom might be a great elixir for now but Lindsey thought Eleanor might crash if she didn't rest soon.

Mercifully, when Lindsey begged to be excused so she could go for a nap, Tom came to his senses and made Eleanor go too. He vowed to take a walk or read a newspaper or find someone to chat to – anything other than leave.

Lindsey ended up sleeping much longer than she'd intended. In fact she realized she probably should have set the alarm on her phone and napped for a controlled amount of time. Now she felt groggy, as though someone had stuffed her head full of cotton wool. She wondered when she would ever learn her lesson where resting was concerned. Since it was already after four thirty she decided to change into a floral dress for dinner, plait her hair rather than wash and dry it, then head out for a walk in the garden. She had a hankering to take some photos of some of the flowers she'd seen before the light faded too much.

Once she was ready she headed down the stairs and out through the front entrance, pleased no one seemed to be around to hamper her progress.

She then threaded her way through the formal garden to a gap in the hedge on the opposite side from the tennis court. There she found another garden laid out like the dial of a clock, set around a tinkling fountain. Large trees had been planted around the perimeter. These provided a bit of late afternoon shade but also made the garden very sheltered. Scent from the flowers and the warmth of the sun made for a heady mixture. The fountain played a sweet, romantic song.

Lindsey set about taking the photographs she wanted. Elizabeth had grown some wonderful plants that had flowered with riotous color: salvia, portulaca, phlox, catmint, celosia. Lindsey was so absorbed in her endeavors that at first she didn't realize she wasn't alone. When she became aware of someone watching her she looked up to find a young girl standing in the gap in the hedge, observing Lindsey carefully. This, Lindsey presumed, must be Elizabeth and Jeremy's daughter, Olivia. Lindsey waved and gave a little smile, unsure of the girl's intentions. Whatever the reason for such scrutiny, Lindsey's smile seemed enough to break the ice. Olivia waved back and started to walk toward Lindsey.

Lindsey guessed Olivia's age to be about eight years old. In spite of her youth she did not seemed to be suffering from a deficit of confidence or identity. She had a similar sort of forthright way about her as her mother but lacked her mother's auburn coloring. A mop of jet-black hair covered her head. She had sparkling blue eyes and a smattering of fetching freckles. She held in her hand a thin book. As Olivia neared, Lindsey saw it was a copy of her second book, *Charlie's Neighbors*. A desire to run suddenly overtook her.

"Sorry to disturb," Olivia said, sounding much more like her mother than an eight year old. "It looks like you're busy but I wanted to ask you a question."

Lindsey could pretty well guess the question. She made herself stand her ground and said, "All right, then."

"I want to know, are you Lindsey McIntyre? The Lindsey McIntyre, author of '*Charlie's Neighbors*' and '*Gilbert's Outing*'?"

Lindsey made a funny little grimace. "I am," she said.

Olivia's mouth went into an O. "I thought you must be," she said. "I *told* Mum you must be. I saw your sketchbook, you see, all those great drawings, and when Mum said your name, I guessed right away."

"You're very clever," Lindsey told her.

Olivia swelled with pride. "I loved your books when I was younger," she said, as though that might have been at least a century ago. "'*Charlie's*

Neighbors' is really funny, but '*Gilbert's Outing*' was always my favorite until my brother threw it in the bath and it got ruined."

"That's a shame," Lindsey said.

"Brothers," Olivia said heavily, once again doing an uncanny impression of her mother. "They really are the limit. Are you writing a new book?"

"I will be," Lindsey said.

"Are you doing research?" Olivia asked. She made it sound like Lindsey's next work might be the equivalent of *War and Peace*.

"I've been sketching," Lindsey said. "As you saw. Hopefully my sketchbook didn't get too ruined."

"Oh no," Olivia said. "It's all dried out now. Perhaps not quite as good as new but your drawings are fine. I hope you don't mind that I looked?"

Lindsey shook her head, not really trusting herself to answer that question with complete honesty.

"I've never met an author before," Olivia said. "I think I might quite like to be an author. It would be great to write something that helps people and entertains them. In fact books do all sorts of things, don't they?"

"I guess that depends on the book, but yes," Lindsey said. In truth she considered herself more of an illustrator than a writer, even though she'd done both on her two books to date.

"I think your books are great like that," Olivia told her. "They're funny and clever and they use interesting words. Is it fun being famous?"

Lindsey laughed. "I'm not famous at all," she said. "For instance only two people on this trip know that I've written some books, and only because I chose to tell them."

"If it were me," Olivia said, "I would tell *everybody*. Besides, those are all the wrong people. You need to meet more children. Then you'd be famous as."

Lindsey didn't have the heart to tell the girl that she found the notion of personal fame repugnant. Olivia then said, "I think other children would love to meet you. You could answer their questions and inspire them. You could read the stories with the voices you gave them. You do funny voices, don't you?"

Lindsey felt sure Olivia would sign her up for a world tour if she didn't bring the conversation to a halt. She searched for something to say but then realized they weren't alone. Andrew had appeared and stood grinning as he watched Lindsey in the process of meeting what appeared to be a bona fide fan.

"Hi," he said. "I've been dispatched to find you. There are some pre-dinner drinks on offer and Dennis is keen that everyone attends. It appears he wants to talk to us all."

Lindsey could have hugged both Andrew and Dennis with relief but at the same time she didn't want to hurt Olivia's feelings.

"It was nice to talk to you," she said. "Thank you for your kind words. If you like I could send you a replacement copy of '*Gilbert's Outing*' even though, as you say, you are too old for it now."

"Would you?" Olivia beamed. "That would be great. None of my friends are going to believe I've had you to stay at *my* house. They're all going to be so jealous."

Everyone assumed that Dennis wanted to give all tour members an update on plans for the following day as they were due to move on once again. And while he usually saved such speeches for the morning of their departure - when it was in everyone's best interest to listen or risk getting lost - they figured recent events had promoted Dennis to be a bit more thorough. But from the way he stood in front of them, wringing his hands and pacing up and down, it seemed clear that this wasn't about to be an ordinary debrief.

Once Dennis realized his audience were getting restless he started to clear his throat, more, it appeared, to avoid talking than for any reasons of health.

"Erm," Dennis said, "thanks all for coming. Dinner will soon be served, another sumptuous feast for you to enjoy. But first, a rather serious little matter has come to light. It's a bit difficult to know how to phrase this, but it appears that some items of value from each of the houses we've visited to date have gone missing. An Egyptian amulet has vanished from Christian House, a pair of ivory figurines from Redpath Lodge, a cameo locket on a chain from Price Cottage, and a pair of silver candlesticks from Whittaker's Rest."

Cedric sat next to Lindsey. He swiveled in his seat and said to her, "We saw that amulet, didn't we?"

Lindsey nodded. "And I saw the cameo necklace at Price Cottage."

Cedric said, "I'm pretty sure I saw those figurines at Redpath Lodge. Two Oriental ladies, they were, and they sat beside a figurine of a mother and child."

Dennis's brows rose skywards. "And you all saw the candlesticks," he said. "Evelyn Barclay used them on the night we all had dinner at her giant round table."

"Maybe the items have since been misplaced," Bianca said. "Maybe somebody moved them out of their usual spots."

"Alas," Dennis said. "As it happens, all four items are present and accounted for. Each has turned up in an antique shop in Waiata Junction. The question that remains unsolved is how the items got from their usual locations to Waiata Junction. I'm wondering if anyone knows anything?"

Tom, who had yet to leave, said, "I assume that the items were sold by someone and therefore purchased by someone. Couldn't you just check with the antique shop owner and ask him or her for a description of the person or persons who brought the goods in?"

Eleanor said to him, "The lady who was on duty the day we went in was about to fly off to Australia."

"And therein lies the problem," Dennis said. "The salesperson in question is currently away and isn't due back for almost a week. And while the owners all have their property back, money did change hands and questions need answering."

"You mean you think one of us did it," Bianca said angrily, "and you're just pussyfooting around trying your best not to come right out and make an accusation."

"No, no," Dennis said with haste. "All we are looking for here is a bit of clarity. Even the fact that some of our tour party saw the items in question is helpful."

Bianca let out a sound of exasperation. "You've certainly spent most of the trip talking things up but this just takes the cake. Things went missing from places we visited. Those things turned up in an antique shop in a town we spent time in. Ergo one of us took the items and flogged them off and you just can't bring yourself to ask us which one of us did it. How's that for a summary?'

Dennis did his best deer-in-the-headlights impression and stood blinking owlishly.

"Just as I thought,' Bianca said, her face flushed with fury. "Well I for one am not going to sit here and be accused either directly or indirectly. I've had it with your stupid tour."

And with that Bianca flounced from the room. She left everyone bewildered, no one any the wiser and Dennis with no room to maneuver.

Where Bianca went no one did find out but she didn't appear at dinner or at breakfast the following morning. Both meals were conducted with a somberness more befitting a silent order convent than a party of tourists. The mood had even put a dampener on Eleanor's burgeoning romance. Tom had taken himself off home not long after dinner and seemed to have no plans to come back the following day. Lindsey wondered if Bianca hadn't left entirely but in the end she turned up wearing a stony expression in time for the pre-departure chat at ten o'clock the next morning.

Whatever agonies Dennis might have suffered overnight had been carefully hidden behind his trademark enthusiastic expression. He'd evidently decided on pretending that nothing unpleasant had happened - or was likely to happen - even though the mystery of the fenced items had yet to be answered.

"Onward and upward today, folks," he said with a cheery grin. "Our next destination is Strachan Ridge where we'll be staying for one night. Today's walk is a reasonably easy fifteen kilometers through wine country, with the majority of the route being on quiet country lanes. The weather forecast shows not so much as a cloud on the horizon and I estimate the chance of danger, storms or life-threatening peril to be zero percent."

Dennis gave a little laugh at this last pronouncement but failed to get anything more than a weak smile out of his audience.

"As usual, here are the maps and your lunches," he continued, passing them around, "and just to let you all know that Cedric has comprehensively restocked the first aid kit. Don't hesitate to speak up if you need assistance. If you suddenly find yourself requiring an iron lung en route I'm sure Cedric will have one."

Eddie guffawed at that. "Good one, Dennis," he said.

Lindsey noted that Eddie sported a red and white Hawaiian shirt that she hadn't seen before and wondered if it had been dragged out from the recesses of his bag. Vi, she saw, looked rather subdued, most likely dreading another day of slogging along on her feet.

"Now I've spoken with Eleanor and suggested she ride in the mini bus with me," Dennis said. "Other than that you should all be good to go. Any questions?"

Vi's hand shot up. "Could Eddie and I go in the mini bus too?" she asked.

Dennis's enthusiastic expression slipped a little but he quickly recovered himself. "I suppose so," he said, "although strictly speaking this is supposed to be a walking holiday."

Bianca made a sound of distaste. "Holiday? You must be joking. It's more like a test of endurance."

Eleanor turned to Lindsey. "Sorry to desert you," she said, "but my leg could really do with another day's rest. That way I should be good for the rest of the trip. I hope you don't mind."

"Of course not," Lindsey said, although she suddenly felt far from certain about the day.

"You'll look after her, won't you, Andrew?" Eleanor said to him as he hovered to one side of where they stood.

"It would be my absolute pleasure," he said. "And don't you worry one bit, Eleanor. I'll keep Lindsey out of mischief."

They said their farewells and expressed gratitude to Elizabeth Carr. Eleanor and Lindsey were particularly thankful for her help in their hour of need. The two groups then went their separate ways.

"Are you sure you shouldn't be going with Eleanor?" Cedric asked Lindsey as the walking group made its way down toward the main road.

Lindsey could feel everyone's eyes on her, scrutinizing her every movement. She might well have been a china doll ready to shatter at any moment into a thousand pieces.

"I'm fine," she said. "I might take it easy and not walk too fast, but otherwise I really don't feel bad at all."

Bianca made yet another one of her scoffing sounds. She had made it clear in numerous little ways that Eleanor and Lindsey's little drama had not impressed her one jot. Lindsey couldn't be certain whether this had more to do with the fact that it took attention away from Bianca or that she considered the whole thing to have been blown out of proportion in the first place. After all, a little rain never killed anyone, did it?

"Well, I've got no desire to crawl along at a snail's pace all day," Bianca said. 'Maybe we should split up."

She looked meaningfully at Simon and Andrew. Simon looked at Andrew, trying to assess what he wanted to do. Andrew looked at Simon and then at Lindsey then back at Simon.

"I promised Eleanor," he said to his friend.

"Oh, for God's sake," Bianca said. "You two can get by without one another for one day. Let's get going, Simon. Let Andrew play nursemaid if he so desires."

"What about me?" Cedric said.

Bianca's eyes narrowed. "You'd better walk in the middle," she said. "You wouldn't want to neglect your first aid duties by favoring one party over another."

Thus, in a single sentence, Bianca doomed Cedric to a day entirely on his own. As he processed this his mouth worked like a fish's. He went to say something but then appeared to realize he'd made way too much out of being First Aid Treatment Officer to debate the issue.

Bianca towed Simon away by the arm. After a rather wistful look in Andrew's direction, he turned on his heel and set off at the brisk pace Bianca seemed determined to set. Lindsey watched Cedric count the seconds in his head, like a person gauging the proximity of a storm by the gap between lightning and thunder. He then set off at an appropriate pace to create space between the two pairs.

Andrew and Lindsey watched him go. When Cedric had got into his stride Andrew gave Lindsey an encouraging smile. "Shall we?" he said.

Lindsey nodded and they started walking. She could scarcely believe that she was setting off into the unknown with a young man she'd not known for at least half a decade, or that she felt so glad about it. She figured Robyn and Will would be even more amazed by that than by Lindsey's encounter with the bull or by her having to be rescued out of a storm.

"Not to harp on or anything," Andrew said, "but are you quite sure you're okay?"

"I really am," Lindsey said. "I did mean it though, about not going too fast. In fact I am sort of hoping the opportunity to stop a few times might arise, if that's okay by you. Dennis said we'll be passing through more wine country. If there's anything worth sketching I might need to make the most of it. We haven't been past as many vineyards as I'd envisaged."

"Fine with me," Andrew said. "Just prop me under a vine and I'll either read my book or have a snooze. We can take all day if you like. By the way, I gather young Miss Carr was a bit of a fan of your work?"

Lindsey put her hands on her cheeks. "Oh dear me," she said. "I scarcely knew what to say to her. She was so complimentary, so confident. What could I possibly do with that?"

"Lap it up," Andrew said. "Bask in the glory."

Lindsey laughed. "As you may have gathered, I'm not exactly the basking sort."

"That's true," Andrew said. "So you didn't get anything out of your encounter?"

"I…she said I needed to meet more children so that I could inspire them," Lindsey confessed. "I can't seem to get that idea out of my head. It seems to me that some children could do with all the inspiration they can get."

"Interesting. You mentioned before that your publisher is keen for you to do school visits. Perhaps you could try one or two and see how it goes."

"Perhaps," Lindsey said, knowing she sounded as doubtful as she felt.

They walked for a few minutes in silence before Andrew spoke again.

"So what do you make of Dennis's revelations last night?" he asked.

Lindsey shrugged. "It's all so baffling. I definitely saw three of the four missing items so there doesn't seem to be any denying that these things weren't already lost by the time we came to stay. Somewhere between then and now those items were taken and then on-sold at the antique shop. On the one hand I can easily see why people would conclude one of us was responsible. On the other hand, knowing everyone, it just seems so unlikely."

"I know exactly what you mean," Andrew said. "One of us is the most likely suspect. We all had the opportunity to take things and we all had the opportunity to dispose of said things in Waiata Junction. It could have been any of us – well, apart from you and me and Eleanor. We were in the antique shop together. I didn't do it, and I certainly didn't see you or Eleanor offer to sell stuff to the lady with the crazy knitting project."

"Eddie and Vi went after lunch," Lindsey said. "They invited Cedric to go with them but he said he'd already been."

"And Simon and Bianca went in before they went and got hammered in the pub," Andrew said. "Simon told me last night."

"I'm surprised he remembers anything about that day at all," Lindsey said.

Andrew laughed. "Me too."

"What about Dennis?" Lindsey asked.

"Hmm. While my guess is that his little tour business isn't going as well as he'd like it to, it's not in his best interests to steal off his hosts in order to make a fast buck. Besides, he's got one of the most transparent faces I've met in a long time. You could see his genuine shock over the whole thing, not to mention the fact that it's created quite a quandary for him."

"So it isn't you, me, Eleanor or Dennis," Lindsey said. "And it can't be Eddie and Vi. At the outset of the trip I lost twenty dollars and Eddie found it and gave it back to me. They're as honest as the day's long."

"Really? I also don't think it's Cedric. He's a bit eccentric but completely harmless. Not to mention the fact that he compulsively tells everyone everything. If he'd done it you'd have known about it within the hour, with statistics to prove it. He wouldn't have been able to help himself."

"That only leaves Simon and Bianca. Or should I say Simon or Bianca. I know they've got a bit friendly but I don't see them working together."

"I'd eat my hat if it was Simon," Andrew said. "For a start he's pretty well off. Stealing stuff and selling it would be pointless. If he got caught it would jeopardize his whole career. On top of that he and I have been together for the majority of time and often by ourselves. We had separate accommodation at Redpath Lodge and were in the annex at Price Cottage. We barely set foot in the main house at either place. I definitely didn't see any of the objects other than the candlesticks. I doubt Simon did either."

Lindsey pondered this.

Andrew said, "I know that grief can do strange things to a person, make them act out of character, but I really don't think it was Simon. Then again, in my opinion I don't think Simon is grieving anyway. He's more sorry for himself and embarrassed than he is heartsick over the loss of Arabella."

"So are we saying we think it's Bianca?" Lindsey asked.

Andrew shrugged. "It does seem highly unlikely. She also doesn't need the money. And while she isn't the most willing tour member ever, she'd risk losing her job if she got caught doing anything untoward. On the other hand I guess she isn't beyond a bit of sabotage. She could just as easily have done it to make Dennis look bad and ruin his reputation. She isn't a great fan of De Vine Tours, that's for sure."

"Do you think there's anything in the fact that she got so angry about the implication one of us were involved?" Lindsey asked.

"'The lady doth protest too much, methinks'," Andrew said with a quirky smile.

Lindsey shook her head with disbelief. As much as she'd never warmed to Bianca, the idea of her being a petty criminal seemed ludicrous. Still, it could not be denied that four items had been stolen from places they'd visited and that one of them was most likely the perpetrator. It simply beggared belief.

Strachan Ridge came as something of a surprise to Lindsey. While most of the homes they had stayed in had quite a grand exterior, Strachan Ridge's exterior aesthetic bordered on boring. It had been constructed out of large white concrete blocks with little style save a pitched roof and very large windows. It had a squat main section in the middle with two equally dull wings mirrored on either side.

The gardens around the house had a lot more style and were well established. Most gardens were bordered by buxus hedging and contained interesting sculptures and statues. A riot of summer clematis covered a pergola attached to the house. The table beneath it appeared to contain the remnants of afternoon tea but by the time Andrew and Lindsey arrived there wasn't a soul in sight nor anything left worth eating.

As they neared the front door a trio came around the corner from the other side of the house, an older couple with a young boy. The woman, a sharp looking lady in her late sixties, peered at them through her rimless glasses in much the same way as a scientist examines something under a microscope. Then she smiled and her features softened.

"You must be our lucky last guests," she said. "Welcome. I'm Anne Burton. This is my husband, Victor, and our grandson, James."

Victor also had the look of a scientist about him. His neatly trimmed grey beard, pale skin, milk-bottle glasses and slightly disappointed expression made him appear as though he'd spent his entire life inside dreaming up hypotheses and ultimately disproving every single one of them. He'd dressed in a brown shirt with brown corduroy trousers and all that seemed missing was the lab coat with a row of obligatory pens in the coat pocket. He shook hands with them in a vigorous sort of way and smiled but never said a word.

James, who looked about ten, also never said a thing. Instead he leered at them in an unsettling way. He didn't look past conducting experiments of his own of an unsavory nature. His surly features announced his vast opinion of himself and his subsequent low opinion of everyone else. Anne made no reference as to why James would be with them and not with his parents but Lindsey wouldn't be surprised to learn it involved something remedial.

Anne said to Lindsey, "Come. I'll show you to your room." She turned to Victor. "You can take the young man to his room. You do know where that is, don't you? With the other young man."

"Yes, dear," Victor said in a robotic sort of way.

Anne shook her head but said nothing further. She led the way inside. Once indoors Lindsay quickly saw that the large windows came into their own. Light poured in to the white-walled rooms that had been furnished most elegantly with antiques and collectables. She followed Anne down a corridor paved with terracotta tiles then up some carpeted steps to the top level of the house. Anne quickly dispatched her new guest and left Lindsey alone to get settled.

Two minutes later, as Lindsey went to ease off her shoes, she heard a knock at the door.

"Surprise," Eleanor said, beaming on the threshold. "I just had to come and see you. I must say it's been a terribly long day without you. I'd begun to give up hope you were ever going to arrive."

Lindsey smiled, waved her friend inside and closed the door.

"I didn't feel like rushing and Andrew seemed happy enough to go at my pace. We stopped quite a few times, twice so I could sketch, once for lunch, and once at one of the vineyards on the way. We even did a little bit of wine tasting."

Eleanor looked at her with eyes like saucers. Lindsey might well have told her they'd gone horse riding without any clothes on.

"Well," Eleanor said. "That's progress."

Lindsey had no idea what Eleanor meant by this so asked, "How was your day?"

"Apart from being long, boring, and bereft of both you and Tom? Fine, I suppose. You have met our hosts, I presume. They are quite dull sort of people. Vi got a headache and had to go and lie down. Eddie's been watching television non-stop. Dennis dropped us off and then drove away again to goodness knows where. Simon and Bianca arrived a couple of hours ago, heard about a vineyard down the road and headed off there. I haven't known where to put myself."

"You didn't mention Cedric," Lindsey said.

"He convinced me to walk around the gardens for a bit," Eleanor said, "but while he might know a lot of trivia he knows next to nothing about gardening. When I admired the Burtons' rather nice selection of delphiniums the only thing he had to add to the conversation was that the pupil of an eye expands as much as forty five percent when looking a something pleasing. The only surprise was that he didn't whip out a ruler to measure my eyes for their pupil to enjoyment ratio."

Lindsey laughed.

"I don't think you missed me at all," Eleanor said accusingly.

"I did," Lindsey said, although in truth it had been a most enjoyable day. "You could have added your thoughts to our discussion on the likelihood that one of us is involved in the thefts."

"I could have," Eleanor said. "Oh to have missed out on that. What, pray, did you conclude?"

Lindsey gave a little shrug. "That any one of us being involved just seems so unlikely. We know it isn't you, me or Andrew. Andrew's sure it isn't Simon. I told Andrew about Eddie and Vi and my twenty dollars. That only leaves Cedric or Bianca. We didn't think Cedric had it in him, if for no other reason than he lacks the ability to self-censor. If it had been him, he'd have told everyone."

"Hmm," Eleanor said. "And yet he is a bit of an unknown quantity in a way. Apart from the fact that he loves trivia, is divorced and lives with his mother, what else do we really know about him?"

"He's a civil servant," Lindsey said, "although I can't say I've got a clue about what he does."

"What else?"

"I can't think," Lindsey said.

"Precisely. He could be the Norman Bates of the antique thievery business for all we know, going around permanently shoving things up his jumper."

"Do you really think so?"

Eleanor let out a little laugh. "It isn't very likely, is it?"

"And so we get to the same point as Andrew and I got to. That only leaves Bianca."

Eleanor frowned. "Well, it's no secret that I haven't got much time for that little snippet. But even I wouldn't have added burglary to her list of ills. Why would she do such a thing?"

"Andrew wondered if she might have it in for Dennis and want to see his business go to the wall," Lindsey said.

"I suppose, as theories go, that's about as good as any," Eleanor said. "Of course it could be someone else entirely. Maybe our presence in each of these locations provided a clever ruse. On the other hand maybe I've seen too many murder mysteries on television and am overcomplicating things. Any minute now we'll all be called into the drawing room with the butler. Then Miss Marple will pop out of the woodwork to tell us whodunit."

"I hope it turns out to be the butler," Lindsey said, not wanting to think ill of anyone in their group.

"What is strange, though," Eleanor said, "is that there hasn't been any sign of a police investigation. If they've been brought in to look at the case then you'd expect we'd have got wind of it by now. I know it isn't the exactly the crime of the century - and the local constabulary have probably got other more pressing things on their minds - but you have to wonder why they aren't involved."

"Maybe they are and we just haven't seen any evidence of it," Lindsey said. "Maybe none of the items taken were worth very much. Maybe they've decided to wait for the batty lady from the antique shop to come back and do their job in one fell swoop."

"Hmm," Eleanor said. "And yet she told us she'd be away eight days. That means she'll be home this coming Sunday. We'll all be heading home come Saturday. In theory, if one of us is the perpetrator, that person could get away with it scot free."

"Did Eddie and Vi say anything about it in the mini bus today?" Lindsey asked.

"Not a word. Eddie kept up a constant stream of conversation about anything and everything but neither of us would have raised the subject in front of Dennis. I think we're all aware that Dennis is pretty cut up about the whole thing. As Andrew quite rightly premised, the big loser here might in fact turn out to be our esteemed tour leader. As time's gone on I've become more aware of just how tenuous De Vine Tours is as a business. All it would take is for one of the hosting parties to pull out and his carefully constructed route would be no more."

"Poor Dennis," Lindsey said. "He tries so hard to make everything perfect."

"He certainly does," Eleanor agreed. "But if one of us does end up being responsible I fear all the best efforts in the world might not be enough to pull the whole endeavor back from the brink. Let's just hope the whole things turns out to be nothing more than a storm in a teacup."

CHAPTER FOURTEEN

The group had departed the following morning just after ten a.m. as usual. As Eleanor's leg had benefitted from the previous days' rest and yet another solid night of sleep, she had no hesitation in rejoining Lindsey on the walk. They were headed for Needham Park House where they were due to stay for two nights. Dennis had been voluble about the delights of Needham Park house so they set off with quite high expectations. Tomorrow, he'd told them, would be a free day when they could either climb the nearby Scout Hill or visit one of the local wineries. The day after that the group would walk to the little town of Gordondale for one final night before returning to Wellington and thus dispersing.

The group's stay at Strachan Ridge had come and gone in a flash. They'd enjoyed an uneventful stay apart from the unsettling presence of the Burtons' grandson. No explanation was ever offered as to why James wasn't with his parents but it seemed clear that the move had been both recent and expected to be of some duration.

"If that boy doesn't end up in prison in future I'll eat my hat," Eleanor had said to Lindsey over breakfast prior to their departure.

Lindsey, still struggling with the whole concept of apportioning blame, wasn't in a rush to agree, especially given his young age. Yet even she had to confess that she found the boy's coldly assessing gaze quite chilling.

"Maybe there are mitigating circumstances," she'd replied. "Maybe he witnessed some tragedy or got caught up in some terrible situation."

Eleanor raised one delicate eyebrow. "Alas," she said, "you forget I spent some time as a teacher. I've only ever seen a few children like that before and not one of them turned out any good."

Simon and Andrew set off together at a brisk pace and had soon left everyone behind. Eddie and Vi didn't seem to be able to get up much steam and dragged their heels at the rear. Vi seemed a little quiet and Lindsey had observed Cedric sending her darting little glances to make sure she was well. Perhaps because of this he had fixed himself firmly to the couple and looked intent on staying there for the day. Bianca wasn't walking. She'd gone off to Waiata Junction with Dennis in the mini bus for some unknown purpose. That left Eleanor and Lindsey in their usual spot in the middle of the pack.

"I really don't know what it is," Eleanor said as she and Lindsey set off together. "There's just a strange mood in the air. I keep wondering if it's because of this whole mystery of the vanishing items or whether it's more because everyone's starting to think about the tour coming to an end and the imminent return to reality."

"I guess it could be either," Lindsey said.

"Why do you think Bianca's gone to Waiata Junction?"

Lindsey shrugged. "Maybe she needs some urgent supplies. Maybe she's sick of walking and dreamed up some excuse to have a day off."

"Or maybe Dennis had to take her in because the police want to question her over the thefts," Eleanor suggested with an arch look.

Lindsey stared at her friend. "You don't really think so, do you?"

"There seemed something very clandestine about the way the two of them set off this morning. It certainly made me suspicious enough to wonder."

Lindsey shook her head. "I still hope there's some other perfectly rational explanation for all of this," she said. "Or that the butler did it."

Eleanor laughed. "Maybe we'll never find out either way," she said.

They were walking once again through wine country under a clear blue sky. The sun seemed to throw all its strength down upon the land. Only a mere hint of a breeze blew to alleviate the heat. When it was quiet Lindsey felt as though you could almost hear the grapes ripening as they passed by.

Eleanor went to great pains to tell Lindsey that she would happily stop as many times as Lindsey required for further sketching.

"Thank you," Lindsey said, "but to be honest I feel as though I have enough drawings of canes, cordons, spurs, shoots, laterals and leaves, not to mention the fruit itself."

"You sound like a real expert," Eleanor said.

"Not me," Lindsey said. "Andrew. He and Simon seem to have learned far more about the whole process of vine management and viticulture than you and I have. He pointed out lots of things to me yesterday that I hadn't a clue about."

"I fear I shall be a very poor substitute today," Eleanor said. "Just how has he managed to glean all this exciting information?"

Lindsey smiled. "I think it's because they walk faster than us. They're usually the first to arrive at a new destination. They catch the property owners when they're fresh and enthusiastic and willing to talk. By the time we crawl in a good portion of that happy hospitality has been used up on Simon, Andrew, Cedric and Bianca."

"Charming," Eleanor said. "You'd think Dennis would have arranged little talks along the way to cover all that sort of thing. I sometimes feel he's at his happiest when we're out of his hair. He could just as easily call it Own Devices Tours rather than De Vine Tours."

Lindsey smiled again. "Maybe it's all still a work in progress," she said.

"I'm sure," Eleanor said, "that you could represent New Zealand at the World 'Making Up Excuses' games."

"I think it must be a reflex," Lindsey said. "In my growing-up years I never got the opportunity to explain things from my perspective. Everything was always my fault regardless of the situation. I know so well how things can look one way and yet be another. As a result my mind seems to seek out plausible explanations to mitigate others' behavior."

Eleanor looked at Lindsey with an expression akin to wonder. "Perhaps there's something quite laudable about that," she said. "Maybe we're all too prone to jump to the wrong conclusions."

"Maybe," Lindsey said. "It has also made me feel as though everything is my fault which isn't very laudable at all. How's Tom?"

Eleanor let out a sigh of contentment. "Ah, Tom," she said. "He's like a dream and a mirage and a fantasy all rolled into one. Or at least he is at the moment. I'm not so naïve as to think that he'll stay that way in a long-term sense. For now all I can say is that he has great potential and I find that quite exciting. Whether he lives up to that potential is another matter entirely. But hopefully finding out will be fun and interesting. At my age fun and interesting don't come along every five minutes. It's nice to feel optimistic about the future."

Lindsey didn't quite know what to say to that. At her young age she supposed she should feel the same way about her own future. And while there were some things that made her feel more positive about life than she had in a long time, Lindsey knew that her biggest barrier to enjoyment stared out at her every day when she looked in the mirror. If she could only work out a way to get over herself she'd feel a whole lot better about the things that might be yet to come.

Eddie, Vi and Cedric stopped for lunch at twelve noon precisely. They'd already had two brief water stops along the way and so had not made great progress. Vi could tell that Cedric's patience with her and with Eddie had begun to wear a bit thin but it couldn't be helped. Her feet had never recovered from the early stages of the walk which meant she dared not walk any faster. On top of that, extended sun exposure seemed to have given her a permanent headache. Frequent hydration and rests were the only antidote.

She thought yet again of the folly of them coming on this ridiculous trip in the first place. How on earth they had managed to convince themselves that walking day after day after day in the blazing summer sun was manageable given their age, stage and general lack of fitness she did not know. She could only put it down to yet another of Eddie's great ideas, where the potential benefits far outweighed any possible risks or disadvantages. Why she hadn't shot him down in flames when he'd first mentioned the idea she would never fathom. And why they'd chosen a trip like this that lasted two weeks she'd never know either.

Vi did concede that there'd been some good things about the trip. She and Eddie had enjoyed some lovely accommodation, great food and a few laughs. The scenery had been nice and she hadn't needed to walk every day. They'd also made some nice friends along the way, although whether Cedric was actually one of them could be debated. If Cedric could just shut up for five minutes she might be able to make up her mind.

Vi tuned back into reality to find Eddie and Cedric looking at a trail of ants that marched right through the middle of the spot they'd chosen to stop at.

"I wonder where they're going," Eddie said. "They look very certain."

"They're probably off to a new food source," Cedric said.

"Can't blame them for that," Eddie said. "I'm quite partial to new food sources myself." He peered into his lunch bag. "This isn't too bad, is it, Vi?"

"Calzone seems a funny thing for a picnic lunch," she said, prodding the pastry with her finger. "It needs heating up to be really edible. And I'd like a chocolate bar but all I've been given is a muesli one."

Eddie laughed. "You're getting fussy in your old age," he said. "And if you had a chocolate bar it would only melt in this heat. Then you'd really have something to moan about."

"Maybe not," Cedric said. "Chocolate stimulates the release of endorphins in the body. Endorphins enhance a person's mood and block pain."

"Shame you can't have it intravenously," Vi said.

Eddie laughed but went back to looking at the marching ants.

"They're very polite," he said. "No stampede for ants. It's a nice orderly line for them."

"Technically," Cedric said, "they aren't walking in a line at all. They're following the trail set down by a scout ant so that they get to the new food source safely."

"Really?' Eddie said. "That's clever."

"Ants are pretty amazing," Cedric said. "Did you know that they are able to lift fifty times their own weight and pull thirty times their own weight too?"

"Did you know that drawing a breath now and then is good for general health and wellbeing?" Vi said as the pounding in her head increased.

Eddie frowned at Vi. She knew he wasn't accustomed to hearing her speak so sharply but every aspect of this ridiculous trip was starting to get to her.

"Actually," Cedric said obliviously, "during a twenty four hour period the average human will breathe twenty three thousand and forty times, will exercise seven million brain cells and speak about four thousand eight hundred words."

Vi stared at Cedric and tried to figure out just how many brain cells he'd ever exercised on anything other than trivia. How could anyone with so much knowledge show such a lack of awareness? She also figured he used up far more than his daily ration of words just by lunchtime, let alone in twenty four hours. It made something inside Vi shriek for release. It had all got too much for her which was strange given all that they'd been through with the earthquakes. Her desire for new vistas and for being in a place untouched by the destructive forces of the planet had evaporated entirely. In the aftermath of the quakes she had forgotten the feeling of being truly safe in her own home. Now she felt as though it might just be the safest place on earth. If she never left again it would be too soon.

At the front of the pack, Simon and Andrew were getting close to Needham Park House. While they might have made good walking progress they had quite some way to go to make significant inroads into their daily word count. In fact much of their walk had been conducted in absolute silence. Simon knew the largest portion of the blame lay at his feet for this as it had done for the entire trip. His anger and embarrassment over the whole wedding saga had sapped him of his ability to be cheerful or to pass the time of day with any sort of civility, especially when he and Andrew were alone. The effort required to exchange inane remarks and generally be happy had deserted him. He felt, in short, that he'd been jilted by far more than his erstwhile bride. He felt as though the lighter parts of him had departed entirely and he'd started to wonder if they would ever return.

He'd started to wonder other things as well. Ever since Andrew had got stuck into him at Whittaker's Rest he'd been trying to persuade himself that he wasn't the villain of the piece, that his past actions had been the only right and proper ones for a man of his background and standing. He'd tried to hammer down those filaments of his feeling that attempted to suggest otherwise. He'd dreamed up justifications, defenses and vindications for his conduct, had tried to reassure himself of the purity of his motivations. The more he realized the truth, the more angry and sulky he'd become.

Simon found it hard to man up and take responsibility for his mammoth failures and lack of insight into his own arrogance and folly. It was far easier to apportion the blame elsewhere. Arabella came top of the list since she had so publicly rejected and humiliated him. If she had found him lacking in certain respects, could she not have found time to tackle this before the big day, before everything had been bought and paid for?

Andrew had also incriminated himself by the unfeeling way in which he had slung around his accusations. His criticisms had made Simon out to be the lesser man, and in comparison Andrew to be the more superior being. Not only that, the more Andrew bonded with the rest of the group, the more he showed Simon up by comparison. On top of all that Andrew's friendship with the mousey Lindsey was beyond comprehension. What on earth did he find to talk about with her? Surely Andrew couldn't be serious about having her as a friend? That he appeared to prefer her company over Simon's own stung almost more than anything else.

Simon's unfamiliarity with navel-gazing left him at a loss as to how to move on. He knew he'd come full circle - had gone from thinking himself the victim to realizing the want of authenticity in his own actions to feeling the victim again – and knew his thoughts had taken him on a dishonest journey. It all seemed such a complete waste of time. He knew now that he needed to make some changes in his life in order to move forward. He also knew this interminable tour was making things worse and the sooner the whole thing came to an end the better off he'd be. He could only be grateful for one thing. He was relieved beyond measure that this wasn't his honeymoon. This tour would have been a terrible way to start a marriage.

All in all Bianca felt very satisfied with her time in Waiata Junction even though she'd had to spend more time with Dennis than she'd prefer. There'd been a number of loose ends she wanted to tidy up and things she wanted to achieve before she could put her plan into action. She now felt in a much better position to be able to do so. The fact that only two more full days of the tour remained weighed heavily upon her. Time was running out. Bianca needed to make the most of it and fully intended to do so.

Andrew and Simon were welcomed to Needham Park House by Diane Finlay and by her little children, Jack and Ashleigh. Simon ignored the children. His first question had been his standard one, asking whether any chance existed of he and Andrew getting separate sleeping quarters. As usual the answer was a resounding if not slightly apologetic no. This meant an ongoing lack of privacy, the need to toss a coin to see who got the bed, and Andrew having to put up with Simon's despondent demeanor and general lack of charm. Andrew had started to fear for the long-term viability of their friendship. Their honeymoon was most definitely over.

Once they had been shown to their room, Andrew lost no time in freshening up and leaving Simon to it. He couldn't wait to get away from the cloying presence of Simon's wounded ego. He let himself out of the room, headed down the corridor, descended the stairs and made for the great outdoors.

Andrew had to concede that Dennis had not oversold Needham Park House. Nestled beneath the conical-shaped Scout Hill, it sat in magnificent grounds, surrounded by stately oak, beech and pine trees and verdant lawns of bowling-green precision. The house itself had the look of a stately home, as though it had been transported stone by stone from Mother England. The massive cream brickwork had a look of marble but when Andrew ran a hand over it he realized it felt more like limestone. His guess was that it came from much closer to home, from the South Island, and more specifically, Oamaru.

The house had lovely bay windows, a very grand entranceway flanked by two massive columns and a covered verandah enhanced with smart black wrought iron work around which a single grapevine curled and unfurled.

A white gravel path led away from the house and down a leafy avenue. Andrew decided to follow it to see where it led and soon found himself on the banks of an ornamental lake edged by lush gardens and weeping willows. A wooden jetty had been constructed and a couple of rowboats had been tied up at either end. Andrew decided a bit of a turn on the water might be just the ticket. He walked the length of the jetty, untied the rowboat and jumped with practiced ease into it. He sat down and went to make himself comfortable when he heard a voice calling his name. He looked up to see Bianca running down the jetty, heading his way. She stopped at the end, and stood looking down at him, one hand on her hip, the other holding what looked suspiciously like a picnic hamper.

"You aren't thinking of going off in that thing without me, are you?" she asked.

Andrew gave a little shrug. "It doesn't appear so," he said.

"Permission to come aboard, captain?"

Andrew regarded her. She looked undeniably fetching in a white summer sundress that showed off smooth skin that had turned golden under the sun. She looked as though she'd just had her hair styled and seemed more ready for a garden party than a spot of rowing. Still, after his day with Simon any willing company might be better than none at all.

"Permission granted," he said, "but don't get mad if you end up getting your dress dirty."

Bianca shook her head dismissively. "Help me down, then," she said.

Andrew steadied the boat on the side of the jetty while he helped Bianca in. She made the rookie mistake of standing too close to the edge. The craft tilted dangerously causing Bianca to step forward and propel herself into his arms.

She smiled up at him coquettishly. "You saved me, Captain," she said.

Andrew quickly got her seated in the prow and sat down in the middle.

"Now, now," he said. "A good standard of behavior is required on my ship. A captain has the right to ask infringers to walk the plank, you know."

Bianca looked at the greenish water with suspicion.

"You wouldn't," she said. "It's probably full of diseases."

"I doubt that," Andrew replied as he began pulling on the oars. Within moments he'd set them on a course for the middle of the lake.

"You've done this before," Bianca said.

Andrew smiled. "I grew up on and around the water. I don't get out as much as I used to but it's a bit like riding a bike."

"Fun," Bianca said, batting her eyelashes. "The only thing this trip lacks is a few bubbles."

With that she opened her picnic hamper and drew out a couple of fine champagne flutes and a half bottle of bubbly. "Champers?" she asked.

Andrew watched Bianca for signs of a trick, bearing in mind her penchant for getting drunk and then getting up to high jinks. Her expression was as innocent as a dove. It made him feel bad for picturing her as the spider and him as the fly. Besides, she could be quite fun when she put her mind to it.

He considered her offer for only a moment and concluded there'd be no harm in it.

"Go on," he said. "Don't mind if I do."

Out of all the properties that they'd visited on the tour, Needham Park House was by far Lindsey's instant favorite. The commanding building set in a pleasant aspect safely tucked at the foot of Scout Hill had about it a permanence and security and serenity that spoke volumes to Lindsey. She figured the joy of coming home to this place must be immense indeed. She certainly envied six-year old Jack and three-year old Ashleigh their childhood, being raised somewhere solid and dependable like this. A child could grow up here breathing fresh air into their lungs, running around the beautiful grounds and letting their imagination run wild.

The earliest owners of the house had clearly appreciated a good fire. Many of the rooms had ornate and original fireplaces, including one in the enormous kitchen. This sat on the opposite side of the breakfast bar from workings of the kitchen itself. A couple of comfy chairs had been positioned around the fireplace on top of a luxurious rug that was almost obscured by a mountain of toys for the children to play with while their mother cooked dinner.

This was where Lindsey found Diane and the children when she went to ask about the possibility of borrowing some scissors, needle and thread to make some running repairs to her daypack. Jack sat playing with the toys but Ashleigh clung to her mother's skirts, grizzling in a pitiful way. The poor mother looked hot and a little harassed.

"Hello," Diane said, wiping the back of her hand across her forehead and promptly transferring flour onto her fringe. "Sorry about the racket. Ashleigh's teething at the moment. She seems to be birthing the most spectacular second molars known to mankind."

"Oh dear," Lindsey said.

"Teeth," Diane said with the sigh. "They give you trouble when you get them, are trouble to maintain, and if you're so unfortunate as to have to part with them, then their absence becomes the bane of your existence. I'm afraid all Ashleigh's efforts to bring them forth will be in vain too. She'll probably have to have some extracted when she gets older and require braces that cost the same as the national debt of a small country."

"Double oh dear," Lindsey said. "Can I help? Would taking the children out for a walk be helpful?"

"Be my guest," Diane said. "Ashleigh's not a great one for strangers, but if you can get her to go it might distract her for a couple of minutes. I'm afraid I've started to run hideously behind with dinner."

Lindsey bent down and smiled at Ashleigh. "Have you got sore teeth?" she asked.

The solemn little girl nodded. Her tear stained face had developed a red and puffy look.

"Would you like to go for a walk?" Lindsey asked her. "We could clean your face and you could show me your favorite spots."

"*I'll* show you," Jack said from behind Lindsey. "She's just a dumb girl and doesn't know anything."

"Jack," Diane said in a warning tone. "I've told you before, just because Ash doesn't know as much as you that doesn't mean she's dumb. She's just little. And it's got nothing whatsoever to do with her being a girl."

Jack didn't look so sure about this but said nothing further on the matter. Lindsey said to him, "Why don't you come too, to make sure we don't get lost?"

Diane wiped Ashleigh's face with a cloth she produced from somewhere in the magical way that mothers often seemed to.

"Have fun," she said. She looked at Lindsey. "You are an angel," she said with a grin.

The temperature outside felt considerably cooler. The late afternoon sun caressed the trees and caused long shadows to stretch across the immaculate lawn. The scent of pine drifted in the air. Cicadas basked and chirped merrily. It all felt like a little slice of heaven.

Jack led the way across the grass. Ashleigh slipped her hand into Lindsey's in a gesture so touching and so trusting that it brought a lump to Lindsey's throat. Even though she wrote for children she'd never thought much about having some of her own. Ashleigh's confident dependence made her wonder why anyone ever found significance in anything else.

"Have you been at school today?" Lindsey asked Jack.

'Yes," he said.

"And do you like school?"

Jack shrugged so hard that his shoulders nearly touched his ears. "It's okay. My new teacher is a bit old and she's not very good at coloring in."

"Really?" Lindsey asked. "What does she color in that's so terrible?"

"Her lips," Jack said. "She doesn't seem to know where the edges are and she always puts her lipstick on outside them. That's a bit strange, don't you think?"

Lindsey suppressed a smile. "There must be some good things about school," she said. "What's your favorite thing?"

She expected him to say "lunch time" but instead he said, "Math. My dad says I'm really good at it."

"Clever you," Lindsey said. "Where are you taking us?"

"Down to the lake," Jake said. "Did you know we've got a lake of our own?"

"No," Lindsey said. "How lucky."

"We aren't allowed to go there without an adult," Jack said. He peered sideways at her. "You are an adult, right?"

"Yes," Lindsey said, although truth be told she didn't feel that way. She wondered how many people ever did.

"Great," Jack said. "It's this way."

He led them off down a tree-lined path, walking slowly enough to accommodate the speed of his sister in a way that suggested he was more than used to doing so. Ashleigh had stopped grizzling and now sucked her thumb in a mindless sort of way. She had yet to utter a word but Lindsey figured the longer Ashleigh went without thinking about things the longer Lindsey might be able to keep her entertained. Everybody's dinner tonight might just depend on it.

The path down which young Jack led them had thick hedging down the right hand side. Lindsey got quite a surprise when they rounded the corner at the end of the path to find the lake right in front of them. She was even more surprised by the view that greeted her. There, in the middle of the lake sat a rowboat containing Andrew and Bianca. Andrew, with glass in hand, was standing up in the middle of the boat and looked as though he might be reciting poetry or telling a joke or even pronouncing his undying love while Bianca looked on with rapt attention, laughing at his every move. They were too far out to hear what Andrew said but he looked happy and relaxed. In fact they looked every inch the golden couple.

The sight of them caused Lindsey's heart to contract so painfully she found herself pressing a hand against her chest in a vain hope that she might calm its agitated fluttering. Jack was also less than impressed.

"Someone's in my boat," he said crossly.

Lindsey took him by his hand and turned him back in the direction from whence they came.

"Never mind," she said. "It's nothing to worry about. Why don't we go somewhere else? Somewhere even more special."

Jack thought about this for a moment then said, "I know just the place."

He then pulled Lindsey away back toward the house and within seconds they were screened from the view of the lake by the trees. For Lindsey's part she didn't really care where they were going as long it was away from the lake, away with no chance of being seen, and away from the specter of her own jealousy.

After Jack had shown Lindsey every inch of the grounds Lindsey suggested she could maybe read the two of them some stories. They returned briefly to the kitchen to check this idea out with Diane and then went upstairs to Ashleigh's room to get comfortable. Lindsey spent a most charming hour reading stories to her little charges. One of the selection included *Charlie's Neighbors*. Lindsey never mentioned a thing about her authorship of the book but reveled in seeing how much the children enjoyed the tale. She knew the memory of it would be something she'd treasure for a long time to come.

Reading the stories proved beneficial on two other fronts. The purity of it lessened the impact of her feelings on seeing Andrew and Bianca looking so happy together. It also gave her a crash course in what other authors were up to. She found much to admire in the work of others and some inspiration too.

Eventually it did feel as though all of them had had enough. Lindsey returned the children to a most grateful Diane and then went back to her room with the scissors, needle and thread she'd requested. By this stage her enthusiasm for fixing her pack had reduced to nothing so she set the things aside and threw herself onto the bed. What she needed right now was to give herself a stern talking-to and to pull herself together. For while the presence of the children had been a sweet distraction she still needed to get her thinking straight in order to carry on.

It occurred to Lindsey that the biggest issue she faced was the folly of false hope. Somewhere along the line she had let herself believe that Andrew liked her as much as she liked him, that his friendship could be the first step in a longer and a much deeper relationship. Given Lindsey's poor opinion of herself she didn't know whether to be pleased or penitent about this.

On the one hand the fact that she had entertained the hope of a relationship did suggest progress of sorts. Before the tour Lindsey's expectations regarding romance had been so low as to be negligible. On the other hand Lindsey should have known that a man like Andrew, who had a confidence and sophistication that Lindsey could only dream about, would never be seriously interested in someone as insecure and uninteresting as herself. To indulge in such a crazy idea had been extremely foolish and had led precisely where it was always destined.

She also had to remind herself that one ride in a rowboat wasn't necessarily a recipe for romance. Just because there had been a rightness about the way that Andrew and Bianca had looked together out on the lake, that didn't mean they had started a holiday romance at the eleventh hour. And while Andrew's tolerance of Bianca seemed much greater than that of some others on the trip, this did not automatically imply a partiality on his side. So while Lindsey needed to remind herself to guard her heart and not be so stupid, she also didn't need to conclude at the same time that Andrew and Bianca were now together.

An hour later, after much daydreaming, dithering and diffidence, Lindsey made her way down to dinner at the last possible moment. By this stage everyone had already been directed to go through to the impressive dining room so that Lindsey was the last to arrive. Mercifully, Eleanor had saved her a seat. She found herself sitting down one end of the table with Eleanor on her left and Cedric on her right. Andrew and Simon sat down the other end with Bianca between them. Lindsey realized with regret that she had way too clear a view of them for comfort and would spend the time during the meal watching them talk and laugh together. They already looked quite chummy. Bianca wore a revealing black evening dress that begged for attention. Even Simon seemed more animated than usual. It wasn't quite what the doctor ordered.

The room had been papered with a William Morris print detailing birds and pomegranates that Lindsey recognized from a project she'd done at art school. The dining room fireplace had been painted forest green. Over it hung an ornately framed mirror that made the room feel even larger than it was. The dominant furniture pieces were a mahogany sideboard and the great stretch of the twelve-seater oak table. Diane had placed several vases of dark blue hydrangeas around the room and decorated the table fit for royalty.

"All well with you?" Eleanor asked.

Lindsey smiled. "Of course," she lied. "I had a very enjoyable couple of hours with the Finlays' children and got my own personal tour of the grounds from the perspective of a six-year old. It was a very nice way to pass the time."

"I wondered where you'd got to," Eleanor said. "I came knocking but there wasn't any answer. I thought perhaps you'd been commandeered by Andrew."

Lindsey made herself laugh at this. "Oh no," she said. "My male companion for the afternoon came from another generation entirely."

Eleanor looked sharply at Lindsey after this comment but Lindsey kept her face neutral. To break the spell she said, "What do you think of the house?"

"It's heaven," Eleanor said. "When Tom and I marry we must buy a place like it immediately and then you can come to stay for the weekend whenever you like."

Lindsey's eyebrows shot up. "When you marry?"

Eleanor put her hand on Lindsey's arm. "Just a little joke, dear," she said. "Although if it came to pass I wouldn't be sorry."

"I hope it does," Lindsey said. "You deserve to be happy."

"Indeed," Eleanor said. "But you know what they say. If wishes were horses, beggars would ride."

Diane appeared with the first course, a porcini mushroom soup with parmesan wafers. Lindsey looked down at the appetizing bowl and around the room that seemed like something out of a fairy tale and at all her tour companions. She said, "I've reached the conclusion that going back to reality is going to much tougher than I ever expected."

Eleanor lifted her glass in a mock toast. "Amen to that," she said.

Dinner proved to be a gastronomic treat. Lindsey marveled over what Diane managed to produce given the chaos she'd seen in the kitchen and the added impediment of two small children. The most excellent soup got followed by a char grilled beef fillet with potato puree, caramelized onions, baby carrots, a confit garlic butter and a red wine jus. For dessert they were served a lemon mousse so light it seemed surprising that it didn't just float out of its delicate glass and straight into their mouths.

Diane and her husband Paul also ate with them. She'd initially seated herself between Cedric and Eddie but after the soup asked Cedric if he'd mind swapping so she could sit next to Lindsey. Lindsey felt immensely flattered by this and was most delighted. She found Diane an interesting dinner companion and from then on had little trouble keeping her eyes away from the opposite end of the table. A couple of times during the course of dinner Bianca had laughed loudly at something either Andrew or Simon had said, drawing everyone's eyes to her. Every time Lindsey looked down the table, Bianca had her own gaze fixed firmly on Andrew's face.

After dinner, Diane and Paul invited everyone through to the lounge for coffee or tea or to sample yet another dessert wine with some cheese. Lindsey couldn't eat another bite but trailed along with everyone else. Eddie and Vi excused themselves. Vi said she had a bit of a headache and wanted to lie down for a short while. Eddie patted his stomach and said he might need to process his dinner a bit and headed off to the bathroom. Dennis mentioned needing things from his mini bus and disappeared out a side door.

The Finlays' lounge seemed the least finished part of the house. It contained an eclectic collection of rustic furniture and old sofas that Diane had draped with interesting throws and cushions. A squat little potbelly stove with shiny brass flue crouched in one corner. French doors opened out into the grounds, hidden from view behind fine net curtains that ebbed and flowed like waves as the wind sucked them gently in and out. Along one wall sat a substantial bookcase made out of a light wood that looked to Lindsey like rimu. This looked custom-made in order to also house a moderate sized flat screen television and stereo. The rest had been liberally weighed down with books and ornaments, photos and vases.

Lindsey watched as Paul went over and flicked on the stereo. The room filled with the sound of modern but not unpleasant music the likes of which a person could buy on a compilation disc. He then went over and started chatting to Cedric, perhaps blissfully unaware that he might shortly start to lose the will to live. Diane had started circulating the room with a platter of cheese and crackers but had only got as far as Andrew and Bianca. Most uncharacteristically Simon had come over to talk with Eleanor and Lindsey.

"I know we've still officially got two nights to go," Simon was saying, "but it does feel as though things are already winding down."

Eleanor said, "I know what you mean. I find my mind already casting itself into the future. And although the prospects that lie before me are pleasant indeed I have to keep reminding myself to keep my mind on the here and now. There will still hopefully be some most enjoyable moments. What do you think, Lindsey?"

Lindsey gave a shy smile. "I suppose it's like I said before. When you are sitting in such a wonderful dining room and enjoying such a great meal, the idea of being back home seems unthinkably ordinary. But then work does await."

"Andrew said you write children's books," Simon said.

He said this in a way that implied that a very small amount of time and skill would be required in such a book's production, like the sort of thing one's quaint maiden aunt might do as a hobby.

"I do," Lindsey said with as much pride as her character could muster, "plus other graphic design work."

Eleanor looked faintly displeased with Simon's lack of enthusiasm over Lindsey's work. Perhaps because of this she asked him, "And are you going home to much chaos? I guess there must be some considerable carnage in the wake of a cancelled wedding?"

An unfathomable look passed across Simon's features. "My parents have dealt with all of the most pressing things," he said. "The things that are of much greater importance might take considerably longer to rectify. I fear carnage might be a very good word."

Eleanor's eyebrows shot up. "There speaks a man who sounds as though he has had a revelation or two," she said.

Simon gave a wry smile. "Bit of an understatement," he said.

"The philosopher Immanuel Kant said, 'Enlightenment is man's leaving his self-caused immaturity'," Eleanor said. "Unfortunately, all the most valuable lessons in life seem to come out of trials and tribulations."

"Shame," Simon said. "Fortune cookies would be a far easier and much less painful way to go about it."

Eleanor laughed. "Too true. Tastier, too."

Lindsey saw Diane excuse herself from Andrew and Bianca and come toward them with her cheese-laden platter. Bianca turned to Andrew and said something to him that made him grin. She then started dancing and tried to encourage him to do the same. He seemed less than keen on this idea but allowed himself to be swirled around. The pair got closer and closer to the French doors. Lindsey saw Bianca take Andrew by the hand and lead him out through the net curtains and into the rapidly fading twilight.

Almost immediately after this Dennis came bustling into the room carrying a stack of laminated pages. He went straight over to Paul, who in turn went straight over to turn off the music. Dennis then commenced to cough politely to get everyone's attention.

"Sorry to interrupt the fun," Dennis said, as though they'd all been swinging from the chandelier just moments before. "I thought I'd take the opportunity to run through a few things regarding tomorrow so that you can give some thought to what you might like to do."

He looked around at the room and suddenly realized they were a bit thin on the ground numbers wise.

"Where are Eddie and Vi?" he asked.

"Vi went upstairs to rest," Cedric said. "She's been complaining of a headache all day."

"And what about Andrew and Bianca?"

Everyone looked blankly around forcing Lindsey to say, "They've gone outside."

Dennis frowned. "Cedric, if I could dispatch you to find the Joneses, that would be most appreciated. And Lindsey, if you could go and find the others?"

Lindsey almost quailed at that but didn't feel as though she could refuse without turning the whole matter into a federal case. Eleanor could see her hesitation but gave a little shrug so Lindsey crossed the room and found her way out through the net curtains. The cool evening air greeted her. The scent of pine seemed even stronger as the day declined toward night. The chirping cicadas had been replaced by a cacophony of crickets.

There wasn't any visible sign of the pair so Lindsey turned left and set off in the direction of the main gardens that lay at the rear of the house. She hoped they hadn't gone too far afield and wouldn't be too hard to find. As she turned the corner she quickly revised that assessment and wished with all her heart that she'd never come across them. For there, under one of the beech trees, stood Andrew and Bianca in a passionate embrace, kissing as though their lives depended on it.

Lindsey's discovery must have made her emit an unconscious sound. The pair broke apart. Andrew looked dazed but Bianca's expression could only be described as triumph.

"Dennis wants us," Lindsey croaked, before turning on her heel and practically running back to the lounge. Her mind felt numb but she managed to clear her head enough to realize that Eleanor had settled herself on one of the couches. She stumbled across the room and slumped down in the chair. Every time she blinked she could see an image of the two of them stuck together like glue and felt anew the shock and pain of discovery. It had been one thing to suspect an affection as she had done this afternoon. Finding out just how deep that affection ran was quite another.

Cedric came through the door with Eddie and Vi close on his heels. Vi looked sleepy, as though roused from a nap. Eddie grinned broadly at Eleanor and Lindsey then rolled his eyes in a "What now?" sort of way. At the same time Lindsey could see in her peripheral vision Andrew and Bianca slink back in through the net curtains. Bianca went over to claim the last spare seat beside Simon, leaving Andrew to lurk by the doorway. This suited Lindsey. The less she could see of him the better.

Diane and Paul started clearing empty glasses away before leaving the group to it. They were doubtless headed for the kitchen to begin the mammoth task of clearing up. Dennis waited for them to depart then said,

"Well, folks, time is certainly ticking by. We've got one full day tomorrow, free for you to do with as you will, then the final walk out to Gordondale the day after. You'll stay the night at the Gordondale Hotel before our final trip back to Wellington in the mini bus. With a bit of luck we should have you back there by two o'clock at the latest and then you'll be free to wend your merry way home.

"I will say a little more tomorrow night, since that's our last official night together, but I sincerely hope you've enjoyed the tour to date, that you've enjoyed meeting one another, and that you're all prepared to overlook the odd hiccup or two along the way. Such are the joys of travel."

Bianca leaned over and said something to Simon. This caused him to laugh and put Dennis off his stride. Dennis frowned, but gathered himself to say, "In fact I would like to think that you would all recommend De Vine Tours to your friends and family. Word of mouth, after all, is the best endorsement a business could wish for. Now, as for your options tomorrow…"

Dennis halted mid-sentence as Diane opened the door and said, "Dennis, might I see you for a moment? I wouldn't interrupt but this is important."

Dennis stifled a sigh. He turned to the group and said, "Pardon me, folks. A short interlude follows while I deal with some pressing business. Just talk amongst yourselves. Don't go anywhere. I won't be a moment."

Dennis disappeared leaving them all in complete and mystified silence. Dennis came back less than three minutes later. He, like Diane, did not enter the room entirely but merely popped his head around the door. His face, Lindsey saw, had taken on a blanched look in the intervening minutes.

"Er, Eddie and Vi," he said. "Might I have a word with you, in private?"

Eddie and Vi looked at one another. Vi looked fearful, as though she strongly suspected she would shortly receive bad news. Eddie tried out a grin and attempted to look calm but Lindsey could see it was all an act. Lindsey hoped nothing untoward had happened to their son. Eddie shimmied himself to the edge of the sofa and heaved himself to his feet. He put his hand out and likewise pulled Vi upright. The two of them then made their way out the door looking every inch like lambs to the slaughter.

CHAPTER FIFTEEN

Another silence followed the departure of Eddie and Vi but after a few moments the group began to talk amongst themselves. Simon and Bianca got straight into a vigorous conversation about what might be up. Andrew started out in Eleanor and Lindsey's direction but got waylaid by Cedric. Lindsey averted her gaze from them, relieved to be spared the agony of having to face Andrew.

Indeed she felt perilously close to tears, a fact that Eleanor saw the instant she turned to talk to Lindsey.

"Ah now," Eleanor said. "Don't worry. I'm sure it will be nothing. Maybe Vi had asked for some headache medicine and Diane has finally found some. Maybe Vi's asked for a doctor and one's turned up to see her. Maybe it's Eddie's birthday tomorrow and Diane wants to know what to pull out the freezer in order to cook Eddie's favorite meal."

"Eddie's birthday's in November," Lindsey said with a weak smile. "He told me."

"Okay, so not Eddie's birthday then," Eleanor said. "The point is, there could be a million different reasons why Dennis needs to see Eddie and Vi. Those reasons don't necessarily have to be bad. There's no sense in getting upset prematurely."

Lindsey didn't quite know what to say to this since the truth would involve telling a tale far too painful to speak of. Instead she said, "You're getting as bad as I am. I've set you off inventing reasons and excuses."

Eleanor smiled. "Very true," she said. "Mine might need just a little bit of work, though, to be truly plausible. Yours, I find, are at least logical."

Time ticked by. Every minute that passed seemed to increase the seriousness of the situation. Lindsey saw Bianca yawn and Simon check his watch. Each of the little groups appeared to be finding it more and more difficult to find things to talk about. Eleanor and Lindsey started discussing the following day. Both were in agreement that they would attempt to climb Scout Hill if the weather didn't seem to bad and the trip wasn't billed as being too arduous. Eleanor began speculating what culinary wonders Diane might whip up for dinner tomorrow night. Lindsey pondered on, but did not verbalize, her concern over how to stay as far away from Andrew Powell as she could manage. She might have to borrow Diane's children again for protection and distraction. She might have to come down with an imaginary illness.

At length Dennis returned. Lindsey could tell at once that whatever had transpired had been of a serious nature. He looked like a man in shock. He stood for a few moments just staring at the carpet as though he'd lost the power of speech, his shoulders slumped, his gaze fixed yet unfocused. He held a sheaf of papers in his hands and she could see them trembling in his grasp.

"Well?" Bianca demanded. "What's going on?"

Dennis looked at her and shook his head. "I scarcely know how to tell you," he said.

"Find a way," Bianca told him.

Dennis shook his head a second time. "The police have just been here," he said. "To arrest Eddie and Vi."

Lindsey's stomach churned and she found herself taking a great gasp of air into her lungs. For the second time in less than an hour she felt as though someone had physically struck her in the solar plexus.

"What for?" Eleanor asked, her tone thick with disbelief.

"Unfortunately," Dennis said, "it appears that Eddie and Vi are responsible for the various thefts experienced along the way. Apparently the owner of the antique shop returned from Australia early. She has confirmed Eddie and Vi as the pair she bought goods off last weekend."

"There must be some sort of mistake," Eleanor said. "We met that lady. She was as batty as the day is long. Surely she's got confused. Surely she can't be considered a credible witness."

"I'm afraid there isn't any doubt," Dennis said. "Eddie and Vi have as good as confessed. What's more, they had taken other things along the way that they hadn't sold off. Possession of stolen property couldn't make things plainer."

Eleanor shook her head with disbelief.

"How serious is it?" Simon asked. "Taking a few trinkets is hardly appropriate but it isn't too significant, surely?"

"Alas, it appears that the items taken were far more valuable than I had thought. It seems as though Eddie and Vi were very clever in their selection of items."

"That's preposterous," Eleanor said. "Eddie and Vi are simple people. They wouldn't know a Fabergé from a bit of frippery."

"Maybe they were just lucky," Dennis said, "but the police have given me a list of all that was taken. Some things are quite valuable indeed."

"Such as?" Andrew asked.

Dennis produced a sheet from amongst the sheaf that he held. It vibrated in his hand as adrenalin continued to course through his body.

"The first item to go missing – from Christian House – was a rare ancient Sekhmet Amulet that had originally been part of Baron Empain's collection. It's made of Egyptian faience and looked quite worn but its approximate value is around seventeen hundred dollars."

Andrew whistled.

"From Redpath Lodge they took a pair of maidens made from ivory in Japan. They're quite sought after and worth around two thousand New Zealand dollars," Dennis continued. "Then there was the cameo locket from Price Cottage that's been valued at just over two hundred dollars and the pair of silver Georgian candlesticks from Whittaker's Rest that are worth a cool two thousand seven hundred dollars."

Cedric shook his head. "This is unbelievable," he said.

"It gets worse," Dennis said. "They had with them a copper Bas relief depiction of 'The Last Supper' that a quick internet search put at nearly five hundred dollars, while Eddie had stashed a large and very heavy item in his suitcase that beats them all."

"What was it?" Eleanor asked.

"It's an antique Patchen running horse weathervane, very rare in New Zealand. Indications are that it might fetch over seventeen thousand dollars to the right buyer."

"Wow. No wonder he always wanted to handle his suitcase himself," Simon said. "Presumably the weight of that would instantly make someone suspicious."

"He found it here," Dennis said. "Paul confirmed he's had it stored in one of their outbuildings for a couple of years. They've been thinking about putting it on the roof over the garage but had never got around to it. Don't forget Eddie's been in the scrap metal business a long time. He would have instantly appreciated the value of anything made of copper."

No one seemed to know what to say after that. Lindsey found herself too overwhelmed to speak. She didn't know whether the discovery of Eddie and Vi's perfidy was worse than the idea of them being dragged off in handcuffs. All this on top of her heartbreak over Andrew and Bianca suddenly became too much to bear. She knew she could not cope with hearing or seeing any more. Tears threatened and she knew she could not hold them back any longer. With shaking legs she got to her feet then bolted from the room before anyone could stop her.

Diane came to see Lindsey the following morning, bearing with her a breakfast tray. She found Lindsey awake but looking very pale. Her auburn hair fanned out over the pillow and she looked like a tragic figure from a feature film. She had a delicacy about her at the best of times but looked even more vulnerable in the thin morning light.

"I thought you might like to have breakfast in peace," she said. "Ashleigh keeps asking for you every five minutes but believe me, you're far better off staying where you are until you're ready to face the day. Eleanor told me you'd taken the news pretty hard."

Lindsey closed her eyes as if to block out the memory.

"I still can't believe any of it," she said. "Eddie and Vi might not be the most sophisticated people on the planet but they are decent, I'm sure of it. I suppose that's difficult for you to understand given they were about to make off with a valuable piece of your property."

"No," Diane said. "I'm with you. I would never have suspected them in a million years. In fact we wouldn't have been any the wiser if they had taken the weathervane. Neither of us has looked at it in a couple of years apart from moving it out of the way now and then."

"Is everyone else up?" Lindsey asked.

Diane nodded. "They're all having breakfast in the dining room and discussing the matter to the nth degree. Except Eleanor. Your friend's a woman of action it seems. She's already been on the phone to some man called Tom, drafting up legal help for the pair, and has demanded that Dennis take her into Waiata Junction to see Mr. and Mrs. Jones before they are moved."

Lindsey's eyes widened. "Moved? Where will they go?"

"Wellington, I expect," Diane said. "Waiata Junction has no court."

"Court? So soon?"

"My understanding is that it's standard procedure. After a person is arrested and questioned they are then formally charged. They then make a first court appearance, at which stage they will either plead guilty or not guilty. If they plead guilty the judge will most likely pass sentence then and there. Otherwise, they'll be bailed if they aren't a flight risk, and will have to return for a trial. You can only hope that everything will transpire this side of the weekend. Just as well it's Thursday and not Friday."

Diane watched Lindsey's face pale even further at this. The poor girl looked stricken.

"Eleanor wants to know if you feel up to going with her," Diane said. "She and Dennis are leaving in twenty minutes if you want to go."

Lindsey put her breakfast aside and rocketed out of bed.

"Tell them not to go without me," Lindsey said. "I'll be ready as quickly as I can."

Diane smiled. "I will," she said as she crossed the room back to the door. She paused, turned and said, "Oh, by the way, Andrew was asking after you this morning. I get the distinct impression he's looking for you."

Lindsey got ready in record time and bolted down the stairs and out of the door so no one could interrupt her. She did not know why she wanted to go so badly. Part of her needed to see Eddie and Vi to learn the truth, part of her wanted to know how they fared and why they'd taken things. Another part of her just wanted to get away somewhere where there wasn't any chance of seeing Andrew.

Eleanor and Dennis were already waiting for her.

"Sorry," Lindsey said, climbing in the mini bus and pulling the door closed behind her. "I rushed as fast as possible."

"Never mind," Eleanor said. She had dressed in a smart skirt and blouse and looked very serious, as though she might be off to broker a business deal rather than see a couple of accused felons. She turned to Dennis. "Let's just get going, shall we?"

Lindsey had feared there would be a small farewell committee gathered to see them off but mercifully there wasn't anyone else in sight.

When she said as much Eleanor said, "That's because I didn't tell anyone other than you that I was going. I suspect our presence at the Waiata Junction police station won't be altogether welcome. The last thing we need is for all of us to turn up and make things worse. It seemed easier to say nothing than to have to turn people away."

"Thanks for inviting me," Lindsey said.

"Hmm. Don't thank me too soon. I suspect it might be quite a harrowing day."

"Diane mentioned you've been talking to Tom."

Eleanor managed a small smile. "He's been marvelous. He's got a friend who's a very successful barrister, a man who lives not far from Tom. He's often in Wellington for trials and suchlike but he's home at the moment. Tom's been in touch and drafted him in to help. We're supposed to be meeting up at the police station."

"The whole thing's such a nightmare," Lindsey said. "I hardly know what to think. It all seemed so much easier when we thought it was Bianca."

"Or the butler," Eleanor said. "Alas, we appear to have been wrong on both fronts."

"Do you really think they'll let us see Eddie and Vi?" Lindsey asked.

"Provided there's time, I don't see why not," Eleanor said. "Even the accused must have the right to see friends or family. We're the closest they've got to either."

"But do you think Eddie and Vi will want to see us?"

Eleanor frowned. "That I'm less certain about," she said. "I guess we can only wait and see."

The trip to Waiata Junction seemed interminable in the way that many outward journeys seem too. After their initial burst of conversation, Eleanor and Lindsey fell silent and let their own thoughts occupy them. Neither of them could talk about anything other than Eddie and Vi's situation and speculation seemed pointless. Dennis concentrated on driving and made no attempt to talk with them either. Lindsey could see from his face in profile that his features had taken on a pinched, tense look that bordered on becoming a fixed expression these days. She wondered if he feared this latest incident might see the complete unraveling of his fledgling business. The whole situation seemed both sad and quite irredeemable.

They hit the outskirts of Waiata Junction, a place that was becoming familiar in a way that Lindsey had not expected. Dennis drove along the main road past the antique shop. Both Eleanor and Lindsey looked at it as they went by. It seemed strange to think of such a place being a pivotal part of the unfolding drama, especially since Lindsey could not really separate her memory of it from thoughts of Andrew.

Dennis turned down the side street toward the emergency services block. The car park out the front contained a number of vehicles. No doubt the little hospital was as busy as ever. Some cars probably belonged to staff. One, with a bit of luck, belonged to Tom. Dennis found a free space and maneuvered into it with practiced ease. The three of them got out and then stood together for a moment, collecting their thoughts and preparing them for what might follow.

Inside the police station they found Tom sitting in the waiting area, perched on the same type of uncomfortable chairs they had sat in at the hospital next door just five days earlier. He leapt to his feet upon seeing them and came toward them with loping strides, his gaze fixed firmly on Eleanor's face.

"We've arrived," Eleanor said to him, managing a small smile.

Tom pulled her into an embrace and kissed her soundly. "We must stop meeting like this," he said as he stepped back.

"I couldn't agree more," Eleanor said, "however good it is to see you. What's the latest?"

"Rob and I arrived about half an hour ago. Rob had called ahead and so we were expected. He seems to know his way around the station here and the system in a way that I found deeply reassuring. As soon as we arrived Rob was taken through to see Eddie and Vi and that's the last I've heard."

Eleanor looked at the young officer who sat behind the main reception desk. "Should I go and ask?"

Tom shook his head. "Truly, Eddie and Vi are in good hands with Rob. All we can do is wait."

"More waiting," Eleanor said. "It's getting to be a bad habit on this trip."

As they moved over to the bank of chairs Dennis asked, "Are you sure there isn't anything I should be doing? I feel so responsible. And to be honest, although I'm deeply shocked by Eddie and Vi's reprehensible actions, it is incumbent on me as the tour leader to help to sort this mess out."

Tom's fleeting expression spoke volumes about his opinion of Dennis's ability to sort anything out. He said, "I guess you should let the officer know that you've arrived. As official tour operator, that is."

Lindsey watched Dennis swallow as though to prevent himself from either crying out loud or bringing up his breakfast. He looked like a man who heartily wished he'd kept quiet. He stood up and smoothed down his shirt in a way that suggested culpability rather than responsibility and made his way over to report in. When he stated who he was, the officer got up and disappeared out the back, leaving Dennis shuffling uncomfortably on the spot. After a few minutes the officer returned.

"The officer in charge wants to talk to you," the young man said. "You need to wait."

"Do you know how long this all might take?" Dennis asked.

The young man shrugged. "I'd say at least an hour."

Eleanor, who'd been leaning forward to listen, flopped back in her chair. "An hour," she said with a sigh.

Lindsey stifled a sigh of her own. Her concern for the plight of Eddie and Vi was being overridden by her growing sense of claustrophobia. Lindsey had begun to feel slightly nauseated by the paucity of fresh air in the waiting area and this, coupled with the lack of action, made it feel as though the walls were closing in.

"I think I might go for a walk," she announced. "Just far enough to get some fresh air."

Eleanor looked at Lindsey sharply. "Are you all right?" she asked.

Lindsey nodded. She felt so many things all at once and although all right wasn't one of them she knew she couldn't verbalize her state of mind if money depended on it.

"I won't be long," she said. "I've got my phone with me. You can always text me if things change in a hurry."

Eleanor smiled faintly. "Okay," she said.

She made no suggestion of joining Lindsey, just as Lindsey had expected. Eleanor wasn't about to leave Tom, and Tom wasn't about to leave in case his friend reappeared. Dennis looked as though he would rather be anywhere else on the planet but had been given instructions to wait. Lindsey felt momentarily pleased about this. Some time on her own would be wonderful.

Once outside, Lindsey stood for a moment or two and breathed deeply then headed in the direction of the river. A few puffy cotton-ball clouds floated across the sky, blown by a gentle wind that did little to allay the warmth of the sun. Thinking that it would be cooler down by the river - and not thinking she could bear the sight of normalcy as people went about their business on the main road - Lindsey turned left and headed down toward the boardwalk.

Lindsey let out a sigh of relief to see that the area was almost deserted. One mother pushed a pram along the boardwalk while another attempted to persuade her small charge that a swing might be fun. An elderly couple walked along in the sort of wordless way that a lifetime together brings about. Everyone else was working or in school or at the shops.

Lindsey's relief came to an abrupt end once she started to walk along the riverbank. Instead of bringing her comfort and ease, every step served as a reminder of the time she'd spent here with Andrew. It had been so enjoyable. He'd been very gentlemanly and had seemed to welcome her company. They'd shared things about their lives, he'd showed her that he'd bought her book and he'd taken her hand. There seemed such promise in the time they'd spent together. But it had been, as Lindsey might have known in her heart of hearts, a mirage. Instead, he had fallen for Bianca's much more obvious charms, ones that no one had to take the time to search for.

All these thoughts made Lindsey halt in her tracks. She knew she couldn't keep walking in the same direction she and Andrew had headed without it taking a toll on her already fragile state of mind. Instead she turned on her heel and set off in the opposite direction, past the playground and the café where they'd all had lunch and off toward the far end of town where a bridge traversed the river, taking the main road northward.

As she went by the café she couldn't help recalling the happy lunch they'd all spent together – apart from Simon and Bianca – and the memory of how Eddie and Vi had been so chirpy. The only fly in Vi's ointment had been the thought of more walking. Other than that they'd laughed and joked. None of them would have guessed that Vi's big bag that she'd brought along contained items of someone else's property that they were about to go and flog off at the antique shop.

Lindsey walked as far as the bridge and had a choice of walking back to the police station via the main road or back along the boardwalk. Her dilemma lay in the fact that there didn't seem to be anywhere to walk in the wretched town that didn't either bring up some sort of unwelcome memory or ruin those that lay unmolested in the recesses of her mind. In the end she decided that, difficult as it might be, the police station seemed the only place she ought to be. She turned back along the boardwalk, determined to take the fastest route back so she could wait with a growing sense of despair for news of the fate of Eddie and Vi.

Fifteen minutes after Lindsey arrived back, Rob Yealand emerged from the rear of the station. Lindsey had expected someone who looked a little like a walrus but was surprised to find the esteemed lawyer to be both younger and better looking than she'd imagined. He was very tall, with a shock of jet-black hair. He had an intelligent face with a gaze that suggested he missed very little.

He wore glasses over eyes that suggested he'd spent far too much time poring over weighty tomes with miniscule print, an impression further enhanced by slightly stooped shoulders. He emerged in the company of a senior police officer. It seemed clear the two were old acquaintances, if not friends. They laughed over something the policeman had said, a noise that felt so at odds with the seriousness of the situation as to make Lindsey momentarily question her current location.

The police officer detached himself from the lawyer as the pair neared the waiting group and asked for Dennis. All color drained from Dennis's face but he stepped forward.

"I need you to come and make a statement," the officer said. "This way please."

As Dennis followed the officer he glanced back over his shoulder looking more like the lamb already cooked and drenched in mint sauce than a man merely off to make a statement of fact.

Eleanor, Lindsey and Tom watched him go and then turned their attention to Rob.

"You must be Eleanor," Rob said, proffering his hand.

"I am indeed," Eleanor said, responding in kind. "And this is one of our other traveling companions, Lindsey."

"Pleasure to meet you," Rob said. "Now, you'll be wanting to know about your friends."

"Yes, please," Eleanor said.

"Right," Rob said. "The state of play is this. Mr. and Mrs. Jones have both been charged with theft and with selling stolen goods. Since there is no disputing these facts, Mr. and Mrs. Jones will be entering a guilty plea. They will do this in the district court, the closest of which is Wellington. Transportation is currently being arranged to take them there. They will probably leave this afternoon for a court appearance some time tomorrow afternoon."

Eleanor and Lindsey exchanged glances. It all sounded so terrible, put so baldly.

"Can't anything be done for them?" Eleanor asked.

Rob pursed his lips. "Only so much, I'm afraid. Even if they hadn't confessed, one only has to take a look at Mrs. Jones' face to see her guilt. I plan to travel to Wellington myself and represent them before the judge. In cases such as this it's all about minimizing the seriousness of the charges. Some things will stand in their favor. The main thing that will help is that the damage from their little spree is reasonably small. All the missing property will shortly be returned to their rightful owners since the items are no longer required as evidence. I need to contact each of the affected parties to confirm this, but my initial understanding is that none of them are interested in pressing charges against the Joneses."

Eleanor's elegant brows shot up. "If that's the case, why do they need to go to court?"

"Under New Zealand law, just because an individual party chooses to not press charges, this doesn't mean that the police stop pursuing the matter. There's also the fact that the antique shop owner is out of pocket for the money she paid out to the pair. The majority of the sum she paid them is still intact and can be returned which will also help."

"And I'd be more than happy to cover any shortfall," Eleanor said. "I'd do anything that would help. I have been thinking about that whole transaction, though. I'd have thought owners of antique shops would be wary about buying goods off complete strangers without some sort of provenance documentation?"

"Correct," Rob said. "However I understand that Mr. and Mrs. Jones had a plausible story and agreed to take far less than the items' true value. As this fell under the amount the shop owner had set as raising a red flag, there seemed no reason to ask further questions. Besides, the most valuable item taken was the weathervane and that hadn't technically even left the owner's property. As it is, such incidents happen more online these days. Many antique shops have gone the way of the dinosaur, I'm afraid."

"What plausible story?" Tom asked.

"Like all such tales, one grounded in a modicum of truth. They told the shop attendant that they'd been badly affected by the Christchurch earthquakes, that they'd packed up their things - including their most valuable items - and traveled north, looking for a new place to settle. They claimed to have run out of money and be desperate to improve their cash flow, that things were difficult while they waited endlessly for the insurance company to settle up. The shop attendant felt sorry for them, as many of us do over the plight of people from Christchurch."

"If Eleanor covers the shortfall, will this help?" Lindsey asked. "If so, I'd be happy to contribute too."

Rob turned to look at Lindsey, giving her the benefit of his steady blue gaze.

"At this point everything that reduces the damage will be useful. If none of the owners want to pursue prosecution, and if no one is out of pocket, this will reduce the severity of the charges. If Mr. and Mrs. Jones are contrite, which I believe they are, this will also help. Judges are remarkably fond of full and frank confessions that don't require lengthy trials and that are iced with lashings of remorse. Mitigating circumstances also help and it will be my job to tell the Joneses' story and hope for a lenient sentence."

"You don't think they'll have to go to prison?" Eleanor asked.

Rob shook his head. "Most unlikely unless the judge has just had a fight with his wife, has been left by his mistress or just lost a round of golf. Given their age, the minimal fallout and their circumstances, I'd say they're looking at the least punitive sentence available. It could be community service or a fine. We'll just have to wait and see."

"That's a relief," Eleanor said. "I'd hate to think of Eddie and Vi separated. The image of Vi behind bars is enough to make a person weep."

"I agree," Lindsey said.

"And what of your fees?" Eleanor asked.

Rob waved a hand. "Ordinarily I'm very expensive," he said with a devilish smile. "But the few hours I spend here today and the couple I commit tomorrow are inconsequential. I was off to Wellington after the weekend anyway. Going a day or two early won't make any great difference and may in fact allow me to ask a certain lady out for dinner. I owe Tom a favor or two anyway."

Tom grinned at this but it seemed clear the ladies weren't about to hear the specific nature of these past debts.

"You mentioned mitigating circumstances?" Tom said.

Rob smiled. "All of us have a tale to tell, do we not? As for Mr. and Mrs. Jones' story, I'll let them tell it to you directly."

"We can see them?" Eleanor asked.

"I need to clear it with Doug, but I can't see any reason why that wouldn't be allowed. Leave it with me."

Rob disappeared but returned a few minutes later with the junior officer from the front desk, saying that they could see Eddie and Vi for a short while as they would soon be departing for Wellington. Dennis had yet to return but neither Lindsey nor Eleanor felt inclined to wait for him in case the window of opportunity to see the pair closed. The officer punched in a number on the security door and led them down a hallway to an interview room at the far end of the corridor. He opened the door and stepped back to let them pass.

Eddie and Vi sat behind the interview room table, both hunched and still as statues. They looked up at the sound of the door and gasped at the sight of some faces they desperately hoped were still friendly. Vi took one look at Eleanor and burst into a fresh round of tears. Her face, already stained from previous bouts of crying, had taken on the appearance of a wizened apple.

"I'm sorry," she sobbed into her hands. "I'm so very sorry."

Eddie, whose loud Hawaiian shirt had never appeared so out of place, looked like a man defeated. His shoulders had slumped in an alarming way and his face had taken on a grayish tinge that no one in their right mind would associate with good health.

He put his hand on Vi's arm in a fruitless attempt to pacify her and said, "It's all my fault. You know it is. Me and my dumb ideas. Look where I've landed us now."

The mere thought of her surroundings had Vi sobbing with fresh vigor.

"This will be nothing compared to where they're likely to send us," Vi said. "We'll be locked up in hellholes at opposite ends of the country and will never see each other again."

Eleanor stepped forward at this point and said, "Please don't upset yourself, Vi. Your lawyer assures us that there's almost no chance of that whatsoever."

"We have a lawyer?" Vi asked, blinking rapidly.

Eleanor, Lindsey and Tom exchanged glances at this comment. Maybe Eddie's grey pallor wasn't the only thing they should be worried about.

"He was here before," Eleanor said. "Rob Yealand. He's going to do his best to get you the lightest possible penalty."

Vi shook her head as though unable to comprehend the matter. "Why would he do that?" she asked. "We will get what we deserve. We should never have taken those things. We will need to go to prison as punishment. How you must all hate us now."

"Please, Vi," Eleanor said, "please look at me. That's it. Are you listening? You need to understand that no one hates either you or Eddie. We might not understand why you did what you did, but we are all worried for you. That's why we've come, that's why we engaged the services of a lawyer. We want to make sure you are going to be all right."

Vi blinked through her tears. "You don't hate us?"

"Of course not," Eleanor said. "Look, here's Lindsey too, and Tom. We're all here to make sure you're okay."

"It was my idea," Eddie said, by way of explanation. "If anyone should be despised, it's me."

Eleanor shook her head. "Are you able to explain?" she asked.

Eddie slumped a little further. "I don't know if this will make sense to you, but things just got a bit too much to bear. See, me and Vi have always been good at pretending. We grew up with nothing and lived through some terrible times as youngsters. Did we mind? No, course not. We just got on with things, made the best of it, laughed our way through life. But after the Christchurch earthquakes we really couldn't pretend any more. Did you know there's been over twelve thousand quakes since that first seven point one jolt in September a couple of years back? Try pretending your way through that. Then there was the February one that devastated everything, where people died and others lost their homes and where even now it can take you twice as long to get anywhere as it used to because of road works and diversions. Every time you turn around another familiar landmark's been demolished.

"We had to fight for a couple of years to get a payout from the insurance company and once the money came through decided that we'd have a break somewhere quite different. Somewhere where we could be spoiled a bit yet where we could be out somewhere peaceful during the day, to try to come to terms with what we'd been through. De Vine Tours seemed just the ticket. But then, just before we were about to come away, we heard from Jack with news of his legal problems and we couldn't pretend about that either. He wants us to send him money we don't have. We'd never have booked the trip if we'd known but it was too late and Dennis wouldn't give us our money back.

"I'm afraid I just looked at those lovely houses and all the lovely things they owned and figured it would hardly matter if one or two things disappeared as we went along. I didn't say a word to Vi at first but we'd hardly brought any cash with us and so I made the decision to tell Vi and to suggest liquidating some of the things I'd taken. And then I found that weathervane, just sitting there, and I knew it would be worth a bit of cash just from the value of the copper alone. It was just too much to resist."

He then buried his head in his hands and started to sob every bit as loudly as his devastated little wife.

Hours later, when Eddie and Vi had left for Wellington, and after Eleanor, Lindsey, Tom and Dennis had gone for a late lunch - during which barely anyone ate a thing or said much either - the group returned to Needham Park House. Tom came too, following Dennis in his car. Diane and Cedric came out to greet them but the others were conspicuous only by their absence. This suited Lindsey just fine. After the harrowing time they'd spent with Eddie and Vi, the last thing she needed was to see Bianca draped triumphantly all over Andrew. She excused herself as fast as possible and retreated to her room.

An hour or so later there came a knock at the door. Lindsey froze as she contemplated who it might be and what they might want of her. Before she had time to consider whether to respond or stay silent, Diane's voice said, "It's only me."

Lindsey leapt off the bed and went to open the door to find not only Diane but Jack and Ashleigh as well.

"Sorry," Diane said. "I know you've been through the mill today. Tom and Eleanor have just been filling me in on how the day went. But I wondered if I might ask a rather giant favor of you."

Lindsey looked down at Jack and Ashleigh.

"You want me to look after the children?" she asked.

Diane let out a relieved sigh. "Would you? They've both been asking for you. Jack wants to take you to see the neighbor's horse. It's about a twenty minute walk at their pace, down the driveway and across the fields."

"Sure," Lindsey said, pleased to hear their trip would take them away from the main house. And she figured that even if she met any of the others she would be able to excuse herself on account of the children. "But on one condition."

"Name it," Diane said with a grin.

"Could I have dinner in my room tonight, by myself? I just don't think I could face anyone else right now or to hear the whole thing hashed over again and dissected."

"Of course," Diane said. "I quite understand. For you, anything."

In the end Lindsey spent hours with the children. After their walk she read them more stories, sat with them while they ate dinner, supervised their baths and read them more stories at bedtime. They were a wonderful diversion, so sweetly innocent and full of curiosity about the world and how it worked. She then retreated to her room. Apart from a short visit from Eleanor, and an even shorter one from Diane, Lindsey spent the rest of the evening and night in unmolested solitude. The only thing lacking was any sort of peace of mind, but it seemed far better to keep herself contained than exposed herself to any more upset at this point.

In the morning the children had come to see her before Jack left for the school bus that would take him to school. Realizing he wouldn't see her again, he clung to her leg and made her promise to return. Lindsey promised to try without actually promising that she would and he seemed satisfied by this. Their parting added to a growing toll of sorrows but the thought that she'd already said goodbye to Eddie and Vi, and that she would soon separate from Eleanor too, made it a little easier to bear.

A short time later Eleanor came bearing breakfast. She also carried under her arm a laminated card that looked suspiciously like their day's instructions.

"Things are in an uproar," Eleanor said. "Simon and Bianca have insisted Dennis take them into Waiata Junction. Apparently Bianca has arranged to pick up a hire car there -something she organized on her solo visit there a couple of days ago - and she and Simon are heading back to Wellington today. Andrew looks quite stunned over the whole thing but Cedric attempted to cheer him up by suggesting they walk the final leg together. I told the pair of them that there's no way either of us are going to rush today so they may as well leave without us. Dennis seemed very cross and handed out today's instructions without so much as a by your leave. He said he'll see us in Gordondale this evening."

"Gosh," Lindsey said. "Things are really falling apart."

"Rob is going to visit Eddie and Vi this morning and will phone me once he's seen them," Eleanor said. "If you don't mind, let's wait to hear from him before we depart."

"That's fine with me," Lindsey said, picturing Andrew and Cedric getting further away by the minute.

"I'll see you downstairs in half an hour?" Eleanor asked.

"In half an hour," Lindsey agreed.

By the time Diane, Paul and Ashleigh bid farewell to Eleanor and Lindsey the clock had already edged passed eleven. Diane tried to persuade the pair to stay for lunch. Paul offered to drive them to Gordondale and be done with walking. Ashleigh cried big tears and begged them to stay. As tempting as all three offers were, Eleanor and Lindsey knew this was their last walk together and that neither of them wanted to sacrifice it.

A veil of thin cloud had appeared overnight, brought in on a freshening breeze. It made for much more pleasant walking conditions than they'd had of late. At first they walked in silence but eventually Eleanor said, "I can't believe this is our last walk, in fact our last day."

"We've still got the trip back to Wellington in the mini bus tomorrow," Lindsey said.

"Ah, about that," Eleanor said. "Tom's asked me if I want to stay with him for a bit, once the tour is over. I've thought about it a lot and have told him I will. We'll probably see how things play out for Eddie and Vi, and will help them out further as things unfold. You don't mind, do you?"

"Not if it's what you want," Lindsey said.

"Do you think it's all too soon? Too much of a fairytale?"

Lindsey thought of Andrew and how easy she'd found it to like someone she'd not known for long.

"Under some circumstances, maybe. In your case, not at all. What's the worst thing that could happen?"

"He turns out to be an axe murderer and I'm never seen or heard from again?"

Lindsey laughed. "I doubt that," she said. "Besides, we've heard good reports of him from others. Even his online profile suggests he's an upstanding citizen. We've seen his kindness in action. I don't think you've got anything to fear."

"Except perhaps him turning out to be a dud," Eleanor said.

"I doubt that too," Lindsey said.

Eleanor let out a little sigh. "It's been a strange old journey," she said. "So many highs, so many lows."

"I know. It hasn't been at all as I imagined."

"Such is life," Eleanor said. "Things rarely ever turn out as we expect. Although some of my expectations for the tour did turn out as it happens. We stayed at some lovely homes, saw some wonderful scenery and ate some excellent food."

"And I came to do research for my book," Lindsey said. "I've got some great material to work from and have even thought of a few new ideas that might have potential."

"You've also gained some confidence, if you don't mind me saying so," Eleanor said. "I don't believe you'll be going home the same person."

Lindsey shook her head. "I hope that's true," she said. "And I do have you to thank for it. You've been very good for me, Eleanor Atkinson."

Eleanor smiled. "I feel as though you've been good for me too," she said. "And out of everything, that's the thing I'll take away from the trip as a biggest gain: the new friends I've made."

"Especially Tom," Lindsey said with a little smirk.

Eleanor laughed. "Ah, Tom. Yes, he is pretty hard to compete with."

"Don't worry," Lindsey said. "I won't even try. Of course on the other side of the coin we did nearly die in a violent storm."

"Not to mention nearly being gored by a bull."

"And then there's poor Eddie and Vi."

Eleanor gave another little sigh. "Poor Eddie and Vi. I keep thinking of them and wondering how things are going. I was encouraged when Rob said they were both very calm this morning until it occurred to me that's often how you feel after you've cried and poured out lots of emotion. Sometimes, no matter how you feel, there just aren't any more tears left to shed."

"I can't help thinking about this afternoon," Lindsey said, "and how scared Vi will be to stand in a courtroom in front of a judge and wait to hear their fate. Let's hope Rob is right about possible leniency."

"Funnily, I keep thinking about what Eddie said about all the thousands of earthquakes they've been through. Courtesy of Cedric we've been exposed to more trivial facts than I've heard in a lifetime but it's that one from Eddie that'll stay with me. The rest will be long forgotten."

"It's a horrifying statistic. It really makes you feel fresh compassion for those who've lived through it," Lindsey said. "Although one or two of Cedric's fun facts might stick with me too. Like the fact that the hummingbird is the only bird that can fly backwards."

"Or that babies are born without kneecaps."

"Or that an ostrich's eye is bigger than its brain."

They both laughed but the frivolity was fleeting.

Lindsey said, "I also keep thinking about what Eddie said about them having lived a life of pretending. It struck me as a very strange way to have lived."

Eleanor contemplated this. At length she said, "But when you think about it, a lot of people pretend their way through life. You have to wonder if civilized society isn't largely based on our ability to pretend things are otherwise. It doubtless helps many a person get through trying circumstances, deny horrors, even prevent people from saying and doing what their natural inclinations would dictate. You've had a difficult life. Was there no time when pretending made things better?"

"I think my imagination saved my sanity many a time," Lindsey said. "In fact, when I think about it, maybe my life could have been quite different had I been better able to pretend, both then and now."

"Hmm. Maybe. There also needs to be a balance though, between pretence and honesty. And a time for facing what's been, as well as facing what's to come. Don't forget what I said about having a stone in your shoe. At some point the stone has to come out."

"Striving for balance feels a bit never-ending," Lindsey said.

"But perhaps is the secret for a happy life journey? For that's what life is, a journey. Besides, some people could definitely benefit from a bit more pretence in their lives. Think of how much better Cedric's trip would have been had Bianca been able to pretend that she liked him."

"Right now I'd settle for pretending I'd never seen Andrew and Bianca kissing," Lindsey said with some fervor.

"What? No, surely not. When?"

"The evening before last. I found them together outside when Dennis sent me out to fetch them."

"I don't believe it," Eleanor said. "For a start I thought Andrew would have much better taste. And secondly, I had rather thought he'd developed a soft spot for you."

Lindsey's laugh contained no humor. "Fat chance."

Eleanor's gaze swung to Lindsey's face. "But it's a chance you would have wanted? You do like him?"

"No. Yes. At one point Andrew told me that we were friends now, that after the holiday he wanted to see me again. I supposed it did make me unrealistic in my expectations. But nothing more was promised or inferred so I shouldn't really be disappointed. If he wanted a holiday romance Bianca is a much more obvious choice."

"Which really just goes to prove that holidays – like weddings and funerals – bring out the best and the worst of us all," Eleanor said. "But no matter what happens from this point on, at least you can count on one thing. You and I will from this time on always be friends."

If Eleanor and Lindsey had been expecting another bustling little town like Waiata Junction, or even like Brookfield, they were to be sorely disappointed. Gordondale's settlement comprised of a few shops clustered around a T-junction and seemed to be on the road to nowhere. It baffled to imagine what held the place together.

On one corner of the junction sat the squat square two storied Gordondale Hotel, their temporary home for the night; on the other corner a gas station that looked as though it hadn't been modernized since the 1950's. A small park lay across from the incoming road, yet another rural memorial to the glorious war dead. A grand set of columns and gates had been erected in their honor at the entrance to the park, made quite redundant by the fact that no wall had ever been constructed to go with it. Lindsey suspected that these days population reduction came through young people leaving for the metropolitan areas. Probably anywhere would do.

Yet Gordondale wasn't completely without charm. All the buildings, some of which had clearly been around since the days of the early settlers, were well maintained and contained some smart shops hoping to entice the passing traffic. There were a couple of welcoming looking cafes, a couple of gift shops and a wine store stocking vast quantities of the local vintage. The Gordondale Hotel dominated the landscape and was typical of its ilk: a ground floor contained a maze of public and private rooms, the main bar and reception; upstairs guest rooms adorned with groaning, long abused wooden furniture, scant bathroom facilities and access out onto the covered verandah that encircled the entire upper floor of the building.

Two hours after they checked in Eleanor came to fetch Lindsey so they could go in search of somewhere to have dinner.

"Hopefully there'll be somewhere better than in Brookfield," Eleanor said as they descended the dusty stairs, "although somehow I doubt it."

They made their way through the fire door at the bottom of the stairs and found Dennis and Cedric standing together. Of Andrew there was no sign.

"Ladies," Dennis said. "I heard you had made it. Everything all well?"

Eleanor frowned. "The accommodation? It's adequate, Dennis, just adequate. After some of the beautiful homes we've stayed in this is a bit of a comedown. In fact, I may as well take the opportunity to say so before the tour ends, that I do feel you need to rethink your beginning and ending accommodation choices. Not the Stansfield, but the atrocious Golden Sands and this place. Both lower the tone of the overall experience, Dennis. I'd give serious consideration about the idea of dumping these stops entirely. Surely there's a better way around it?"

Dennis made some spluttering sounds, nonplussed at such unsolicited and negative feedback.

"Well…I…I guess I will take that into consideration for future tours."

"And you need to include something a bit more formal about wine growing and production, Dennis," Eleanor continued. "A few little talks along the way, perhaps? Leaving it up to us seemed less than satisfactory. I'm sure most of the vintners would be delighted to have a fixed opportunity to wax lyrical about their grand passion."

'Oh…I…good thought," Dennis managed.

"And maybe better vetting of your tour guests wouldn't go amiss either," Eleanor said.

Dennis did not know what to say to this. His mouth went slack and he stared at Eleanor as though she'd grown two heads.

"Only joking about that," Eleanor said, although Lindsey felt quite sure that if Eleanor had meant that anyone should have been excluded, it was Bianca.

Dennis, upon thinking about it, decided she must have meant Eddie and Vi for he said, "Any news of how things went this afternoon?"

"As it happens there is," Eleanor said. "Things went about as well as we could have wished for. For a start the charge brought before the judge was the lesser one of theft, and the Police Prosecutor remained neutral when it came to defence counsel recommending a lenient sentence. This left the judge free to exercise his discretion and impose the lightest sentence possible. In consequence they have been convicted and discharged."

"What does that mean?" Cedric asked.

"That they now have a criminal record that shows they have been convicted of theft, but that no punishment has been given."

"Goodness," Dennis said. "A criminal conviction still sounds severe. How will that affect them?"

"As they are New Zealand citizens it won't affect their residency or their ability to travel should they decide to return home to Blighty. They aren't likely at their age to be doing anything from which a conviction would preclude them."

"So this is great news?" Dennis asked.

"Given their undoubted guilt, the best," Eleanor said.

"So what will happen to them now?" Cedric asked.

"As it happens that may be a little bit up in the air," Eleanor said. "Tom's had a bit of an idea and we are going to drive down to Wellington tomorrow to see them and make a proposition. Tom's away a lot, you see, and his property left idle in his absence. He's going to ask Eddie and Vi if they would like to become caretakers. They could live in the guest quarters and take care of things, live rent free and, hopefully, earthquake free, although they don't call New Zealand the Shaky Isles for nothing."

"Gosh," Cedric said. "A whole fresh start."

Eleanor smiled. "We'll see. Who knows if they'll be keen? And speaking of keen, who wants dinner?"

In the end Eleanor, Lindsey and Cedric found a nice little bistro attached to the wine store. Dennis could not be persuaded to join them, although whether this reluctance stemmed from a desire to maintain the last vestiges of professional distance or avoid yet more critical analysis of his tour, Lindsey could not tell. It seemed strange to have been reduced to a party of three. Lindsey felt profoundly aware of the absence of Eddie and Vi. And although her relief at how things had transpired for the couple could barely be expressed, Lindsey could not help but wish that events had not taken such a dark turn in the first place. She even found herself filled with nostalgia for Eddie's loud Hawaiian shirts and astonishing knobbly knees. She also could not help but wonder where Andrew had got to and how he fared on his own.

Cedric tried to lighten the mood with a last ditch effort to impart some more facts and figures but neither Eleanor or Lindsey could get very interested in the fact that a million cells in your body die and get replaced every second, or that some lions mate over fifty times a day. They made short work of dinner, rejected the offer of dessert and were back out into the bustle of Gordondale within forty-five minutes.

The bustle of Gordondale consisted of one lone figure on the sidewalk: Andrew. Lindsey found herself taking in a great breath of evening air at the sight of him. Mercifully, Eleanor stepped forward, knowing precisely what was at stake.

"Andrew," Eleanor greeted. "How are you?"

Andrew gave a little shrug and darted a look at Lindsey.

"As you can see, quite bereft of company. I'm afraid the charms of this half horse town have quite overwhelmed me."

Eleanor gave a rather cat-like smile. Lindsey wondered whether she thought this state of affairs to be Andrew's just desserts.

"I heard you're going your own way yourself tomorrow," Andrew said to her when she did not reply.

"I am," Eleanor said. "Tom and I are off to Wellington to throw Eddie and Vi a lifeline."

"Dennis told me," Andrew said. "I'm actually going my own way too."

"Really?"

"I've decided to go back to Auckland via the scenic route," Andrew said. "Paul Finlay is traveling up to Napier on business tomorrow and he's going to swing by and take me with him. I've booked a hire car from there and am driving myself back to Auckland."

Lindsey felt her heart drop at this news, even though she knew she should be relieved at the prospect of not being cooped up in the mini bus with him tomorrow.

"Imagine," Eleanor. "Who would have thought when the nine of us set out that only three would return in the manner intended?"

"It's pretty astonishing," Andrew agreed.

He turned his attention to Lindsey. "I was wondering if I might be able to talk with you," he said. "There are things to say, I think."

Lindsey did not know what to do or say in response to this but found herself unable to tear her gaze away. If she had done so she would have seen Eleanor also carefully assessing Andrew's expression.

"That sounds like a good idea," Eleanor said. "Come on, Cedric. You can escort me back to our salubrious accommodation."

She leaned over and kissed Lindsey on the cheek.

"The benefit of the doubt may be required," she whispered. "I'll see you later."

Lindsey's gaze remained fixed on Andrew and Andrew's on Lindsey as Eleanor bundled a still-talking Cedric away. Once they'd gone it felt to Lindsey as though the rest of the world faded to the sort of indistinctness one associates with a dream, where little is defined and the rest lies waiting in the wings like sets in a play, just out of sight but ready to be brought into focus at a moment's notice.

At length Andrew said, "I think you, Lindsey McIntyre, have been avoiding me."

Lindsey felt herself blush. She felt sure her cheeks were now redder than her hair. She did not know what to say in response. How could she tell him that avoiding him had been a necessity, that the sight of him together with Bianca had been excruciating? That it had caused her to have many conflicting thoughts about herself, her past and her future? It seemed yet another situation of life where much could be said but the right words remained elusive.

"I would like to talk if you will let me," Andrew said. "Shall we go across to the park and sit for a while?"

Lindsey suddenly thought of all the crossroads they'd been faced with on the journey, places where paths diverged and roads went their separate ways. The choices then had been easy. Everything had been mapped out on laminated sheets so that the way forward lay without ambiguity. But here, with the need for maps at an end, she found herself faced with the most difficult crossroads of all. Her hurt feelings and the surety that Andrew had bestowed his affections in another direction made her feel justified in refusing him. The fact that Andrew wanted to talk and that Eleanor had urged her to give him an audience made her hesitate.

In the end the desire not to part on bad terms won out, even if it might require Lindsey to lie at little. "Okay," she said. "Just for a bit."

Andrew made a sweeping gesture in the direction of the little memorial park opposite the Gordondale Hotel. They crossed the traffic-free road and entered in through the pointless memorial gates. Several oaks had probably been planted at the time of the Great War, and beneath those old and generously mature trees some municipal organization had placed park benches. Andrew chose one whose view was obscured from the terrace of the Gordondale Hotel and that faced toward the decaying gas station.

As they sat, Andrew stashed his daypack on the ground and leaned forward, linking his hands together. Lindsey sat back and waited.

"First of all," Andrew said. "I think I need to clear up a bit of confusion that might exist after the last time you saw me, which, unfortunately, involved you seeing me with my lips attached to Bianca's. Could I just say here and now that the kiss you witnessed was not of my initiation, nor of my desire? It was Bianca who grabbed me, Bianca who kissed me."

"What?" Lindsey asked, scarcely believing what she was hearing.

"It's true," Andrew said. "I'm not sure what got into her. I don't know whether she thought that if she didn't make a last-ditch effort to secure my affections or have herself a holiday romance that the trip would shortly be over and all her careful flirting and obvious pursuit would be for nothing. It also crossed my mind that Bianca saw you coming and kissed me on purpose, just to upset you. Whatever her reasoning, it was all for nought. I am not, and never have been, interested in Bianca Caton."

Lindsey blinked several times as she took in this information.

"Not interested in her? I thought you liked her?"

Andrew gave a wry smile. "I don't dislike her," he said. "In fact I'd go as far as to say that I understand her, and I guess that makes me sympathetic toward her. She reminds me of so many girls I know, trying too hard, pushing to make things happen, willing to give themselves away in the hopes that attraction might be made to morph into something more. A guy could take advantage of girls like that every night of the week. No, Lindsey, in that sense I definitely am not interested in her, or any of the others. How could I be when a certain redheaded enchantress has ensnared attention? Don't you know that it's you I'm interested in?"

"Me?" Lindsey squeaked. "You can't be."

Andrew laughed. "Now, see, that's why I like you so much. There's nothing pretentious about you at all. You aren't vain or conceited and you appear to care much more about others than you do about yourself."

"But I'm a basket case," Lindsey said. "Dysfunctions at every turn."

"So?" Andrew said. "Who cares? We've all got faults and foibles, things that drag us down and things we have to work to rise above. It seemed to me that you need someone like me to remind you of all the wonderful qualities you possess, to counteract those voices in your head that continually tell you otherwise. Just as I need someone like you to remind me what life is really all about, and who will inspire me to want to be a better person."

Lindsey blinked again.

"I want us to be together," Andrew said. "To start seeing each other when we get home, to spend time together and talk about everything, the good, the bad, the past, the future. I'm hoping that you want that too."

"Want it?" Lindsey said. "Of course I want it. I can't think of anything I want more, although I'm having trouble saying so, just as I'm having trouble believing this could be true."

Andrew took Lindsey's hands in his own.

"Really?"

Lindsey nodded. "Really."

"Can we start before we get home?" Andrew asked. "Could I persuade you to consider the idea of coming with me tomorrow? Paul wouldn't object in the slightest if you came with us to Napier. We could then travel home together, set out and see where we get to."

"Just you and me?"

Andrew laughed. "Yes, just you, just me. No Eleanor, no Simon and most definitely no Bianca."

"That would mean Dennis returning to Wellington with only Cedric."

Andrew laughed a second time. "How bizarre. Lucky Dennis."

This time Lindsey laughed. "I should decline your offer if only to save Dennis," she said.

"But you're not going to?"

Lindsey hesitated for a shortest of moments. Launching out into the wild blue yonder with a man she had barely known two weeks would be the most radical and daring thing she had ever done in her entire life. The thought of not doing so made her feel bereft and a little bit desperate.

"No, I'm not going to," she said. "Dennis will have to fend for himself."

Andrew let out a whoop.

"Lindsey," he said. "You just made my day."

Lindsey laughed at his delight, feeling astonished and overwhelmed by degrees. This, then, would be the start of a whole new journey.

The Legend of the Vine Fairies

By Keitha Smith

If you were to take a walk one summer's day amongst the vineyards, your mind might not be thinking of the presence of fairies. Captivated by the arching sphere of brilliant blue sky overhead, the smell of grass underfoot heated by the sun or the sound of the skylark drifting in the breeze, you could easily be forgiven for missing them. But if you were to stop and stay a while, to study the gnarled branches of the vines and examine both leaf and plump fruit you might be surprised by what you could see. For, as all believers in fairies will tell you, the quiet observer will slowly perceive what others casually dismiss.

There, beneath the verdant canopy, live the Vinifera, almost as they have lived for thousands of years. Long ago, even as far back as the Stone Age, when vines grew wild as forest climbers, the Vinifera have lived in harmony with the vine. Amongst the canes, shoots and tendrils the Vinifera have set up home, living in twist and hollow very merrily indeed.

The Vinifera are, of course, extremely small and move at such speeds as to be difficult to detect. They have tiny, perfectly round faces, intense green eyes and noses like ski jumps. Above their pointed ears they wear their hair jauntily, in the style of a strawberry hull. They dress in blouse and leggings of earthy tones except on special occasions. Then the males don saffron coloured waistcoats and the females wear purple ribbons in their hair. Their shoes are made from cordons, that part of the vine that supports the fruiting spurs.

As a people they are cheerful, hard working and adaptable. Most transitioned long ago from wild to cultivated vine and have slowly moved across the globe in step with the growing dominion of man. But while man has no time or belief in their race, the Vinifera take a great deal of interest in mankind. They consider man a quaint species, if not a little arrogant or misguided. It is the source of much amusement that man prides himself so much on his abilities with the vine without realising the intense work carried out by the Vinifera under their very noses.

The Vinifera live in family groups, marry and raise children. Many live to ripe old ages of two hundred years. They have a great thirst for knowledge and development and place a high value on education. A young Viniferi will be sent off at the age of four to attend Vindergarten, then on to Vinary School until, in their teens, they attend Vingh School. Those with exceptional ability might then progress to Vinerversity where viticulture, photosynthesis and phenolics are the most popular subjects. Some even take oenology, mesoclimatology or organoleptics.

So while man blithely takes credit for his success with the fruit of the vine, the Vinifera busily work their magic out of sight and out of mind. It is they who ensure healthy growth, bumper crops and successful propagation. It is they who wage tireless wars against downy mildew, mealy bugs and phylloxera long before man becomes aware and swoops down with his arsenal of chemicals. It is they who nurture the grapes while the fruit sets and the berries develop, and who watch with tender care while the grapes go through the arduous pubertal change known as veraison.

Mid spring to late summer are the busiest times of the year for the Vinifera. The warmer days of spring rouse the vine from its winter slumber. At first, one by one, minute buds swell and burst, sending out the most delicate of shoots from the deadest looking canes. The Vinifera are ever vigilant with their new charges, guarding against blister mites and powdery mildew while praying for fine weather and for no late frosts.

Within days those new shoots are growing at a great rate, up to three centimeters a day. There the Vinifera remain, warding off blackspot and deadarm disease. Tiny flower clusters appear, like miniature bunches of green grapes, until the cap covering each floret detaches and falls, exposing anther and ovary. This, with a combination of luck and hard work by our small friends, will result in the formation of a grape.

So things continue until, around three months after bud burst, flowering and fertilizing begin. Within two weeks the fruit becomes set. Then, as summer starts and the berries develop, the Vinifera take a well-earned rest. They celebrate with feasting and frivolity, their most auspicious calendar date, that of St. Vitus Day. Sumptuous food is prepared. The most delicate wines are served from early evening until late into the night. All the families from an entire vineyard come together, the women to swap gossip, the men to tell bragging tales of victorious battles over bugs and mold. Young Viniferi observe the young women from a distance until, as night falls, musicians take up their instruments and the dancing commences. Shy introductions are made as young love bursts forth.

But the cycle of the vine is not yet over. The Vinifera support the vine as the grapes mature, guarding against thinning skins, keeping sugar levels balanced and warding off botrytis during wet weather or through days when the damp is slow to dry under a sluggish sun. Birds are a sudden and terrifying menace, not only to the grapes, but to the Vinifera themselves. Small, rapidly moving bodies can be snatched up by a passing bird without so much as a by your leave.

The very young, out of school for the summer and without gainful employment, are most at risk from the feathered fiends. Games like cane hopping and leaf skiing bring our young vine fairies dangerously close to the top of the canopy, exposing them to swooping prey. Thankfully, by autumn time, these small charges are safely back in their schoolrooms and far away from the inherent risks that harvesting brings.

Harvest time brings some interesting challenges for the Vinifera as they too undertake their own harvest. Careful to avoid being obvious but clever enough to recognize the best of the crop, these ingenious people have developed a way of siphoning the juice right out of the grape without the need for detachment. Their own highly secret method of wine making can scarcely be revealed here. Suffice to say that the end product makes man's nectar of the gods look like a chemical-rich fake fruit punch.

The harvest must be timed to perfection. The shortening days give the first clue to the grape's readiness, with the mellow sun casting weaker rays on the earth. The sugar levels in the fruit rise markedly while the acid levels ebb away. The leaves begin to yellow in patches and vine canes strain under the weight of full fruit. Then, not long after the Vinifera have completed their harvest, the rows of vines fill with a mass of human bodies and machinery as the culling of the fruit takes places. This necessitates the evacuation of the Vinifera population whose frail bodies are far from equal to sharp secateurs, or worse, mechanical monsters whose beater roads vibrate to such an extent that permanent damage can occur.

This evacuation is the precursor for the biggest change our small fairies undergo. At this time, as man retreats from the vines to start his process of tinkering, only a small contingent return home to stand guard in a vigil that lasts from autumn through to late winter. These stalwarts tend the vine through leaf fall and hunker down in their dwellings while bare vines slumber against post and wire while awaiting the first hint of spring. Man returns for a brief time to prune and mulch and fertilize but their presence is scarce. They, for once, content themselves with letting nature take its course.

As for the main population of Vinifera, these small fairies make a most surprising migration. Rather than flocking to a nearby forest as of old, these little people in the modern age choose instead to stay with the fruit of the vine. They watch carefully as man crushes, ferments, macerates, presses, blends and bottles his wine. Then, at an opportune moment, small groups of Vinifera fly unnoticed into the boxes in which the wine is sealed and stored, and hence begins a migration to wherever the wine ends up.

For some Vinifera this means a trip to the local supermarket or wine merchant, where they spend their days lurking at the back of shelves until some unsuspecting customer lifts both wine and fairy up bound for home. Some find themselves unexpectedly overseas which can bring a world of opportunities and travel. Such Viniferi can spend years making their way home or may even choose to settle permanently on foreign soil. Still others find themselves encased for years, trapped with the wine and set aside for investment or special occasion. These Viniferi will slowly eat the provisions they have brought with them then take a leaf out of the vine's book and simply hibernate. Many a fine tale has been told of wakening experiences, sometimes after periods as long as fifty years.

The majority of the Vinifera find themselves wintering in the homes of man, brought back by those who select random bottles now and then. It's fair to say that the Vinifera love our homes. It provides them with opportunities to expand their knowledge and winter in the coziest of fashions. They love comfortable lounge chairs, roaring fires and the smell of a good meal. They love exploring the pantry or reading over the homeowner's shoulder or watching television. In books they are especially fond of J.R.R Tolkien, a man once clearly attuned to the world most humans miss. They also love the works of Jane Austen. On television they have developed a love of game shows, although sadly one or two Viniferi have to be treated every spring on their return to the vines for an addiction to *Who Wants to be a Millionaire?*

In exchange for a winter's worth of board and lodging the Vinifera bring with them a certain joie de vivre. Their wholesome, happy, curious natures fill winter homes with a feeling only found there during this season. Their presence imbues the homes of wine drinkers with an extra spark of comfort and solace that overcomes the darkest of winters. And that, dear friend, is why there is nothing better in the whole world than a glass of wine and a copy of *Pride and Prejudice* in front of a roaring fire in the middle of a frosty winter.

Want to find out more about The Journey?
Sign up for Keitha's newsletter and receive exclusive
Behind the Scenes bonus content

www.keithasmith.co.nz

And, if you have enjoyed this book,
please consider leaving a review at Amazon.com
It would be most appreciated.

Acknowledgement

With thanks to Sefton Revell for his assistance in understanding
the finer points of the law and of court rulings.